The Apocalypse Executioner
The Undead World Novel 8
A Zombie Tale by Peter Meredith

Fictional works by Peter Meredith:

A Perfect America
Infinite Reality: Daggerland Online Novel 1
Infinite Assassins: Daggerland Online Novel 2
Generation Z
Generation Z: The Queen of the Dead
Generation Z: The Queen of War
Generation Z: The Queen Unthroned
Generation Z: The Queen Enslaved
The Sacrificial Daughter
The Apocalypse Crusade War of the Undead: Day One
The Apocalypse Crusade War of the Undead: Day Two
The Apocalypse Crusade War of the Undead Day Three
The Apocalypse Crusade War of the Undead Day Four
The Horror of the Shade: Trilogy of the Void 1
An Illusion of Hell: Trilogy of the Void 2
Hell Blade: Trilogy of the Void 3
The Punished
Sprite
The Blood Lure The Hidden Land Novel 1
The King's Trap The Hidden Land Novel 2
To Ensnare a Queen The Hidden Land Novel 3
The Apocalypse: The Undead World Novel 1
The Apocalypse Survivors: The Undead World Novel 2
The Apocalypse Outcasts: The Undead World Novel 3
The Apocalypse Fugitives: The Undead World Novel 4
The Apocalypse Renegades: The Undead World Novel 5
The Apocalypse Exile: The Undead World Novel 6
The Apocalypse War: The Undead World Novel 7
The Apocalypse Executioner: The Undead World Novel 8
The Apocalypse Revenge: The Undead World Novel 9
The Apocalypse Sacrifice: The Undead World 10
The Edge of Hell: Gods of the Undead Book One
The Edge of Temptation: Gods of the Undead Book Two
The Witch: Jillybean in the Undead World
Jillybean's First Adventure: An Undead World Expansion
Tales from the Butcher's Block

* Stop! If you haven't read **Tales from the Butcher's Block** You will be a little lost about what happened to Jillybean between Book seven and book eight. I strongly suggest you read that before proceeding!

*

*

* Chapter 1

Jillybean

Within a second of opening her eyes, Jillybean could tell that something was, not exactly wrong, but different. Without moving a muscle, she gazed all around, seeing nothing but a green haze and smelling nothing but musty wool.

An old army blanket covered her completely, turning the air stale, making it taste used up in her mouth. Past the blanket, the usual morning noises came to her muffled but, beyond a few waking birds, a soft sighing wind that would blow itself out by midday, and the creaking of a nearby birch, there was nothing to hear.

Still, she didn't budge. Ever cautious, she lay there for a full minute before she decided that, different or not, she was safe. Gradually she slid the blanket down, stopping just as the trail edge hit the small bump of her nose.

"What happened?" she whispered, confusion twisting her little girl features. She sat up, staring in astonishment, her breath forming clouds in front of her face. "Ipes? Ipes what happened?"

She looked all around and saw that the leaves of the trees had turned to oranges and reds—all while she slept—but that couldn't be! Even the long grasses in which she was nestled had turned into brown spears edged with frost.

When she had gone to sleep, the forest had been green and the mosquitos huge and fat as humming birds. It had been late summer and now it most definitely wasn't. This realization made her insides feel queer.

Time flies when you're having fun, Ipes said, as if the idea of fun was a bad thing. *You've been acting the part of a cricket for way too long.*

This odd statement only added to her confusion. What she knew of crickets were that they could jump real high and, when they rubbed their legs together, they made a sound like a bad violinist, and she also knew they tasted like earwax…like crunchy earwax.

The thought of earwax brought back a memory of summer. She and Ipes in a mass of ferns, bugs buzzing and sweat dripping down her chin with the sun straight up overhead. The rays felt as though they were smashing down on her and she could barely keep her eyes open.

Yet she couldn't sleep. There were monsters nearby, eating the heads off of flowers like the world's most gruesome rabbits. She had huddled lower into the massed ferns that crept up from the river. Like a living shag, the ferns carpeted the earth in green, three feet in height. Everything was green on green, including Jillybean, who wore layers of camouflage that had been a week in perfecting. The blend was so exact that one of the monsters that was all of five feet away couldn't see through the illusion.

The diseased hunk of grey meat stood so close its shadow fell across her and for a long moment neither moved. She didn't dare and the monster didn't have the wit to.

A bird cawed, an unnecessary intrusion that was more than an annoyance as the monster swiveled its head, the pull of exposed tendons making a creaking noise, sounding like ropes on a decaying sailing ship.

It snuffled air through the half-healed remains of its nose. Jillybean kept perfectly still, knowing that the monster couldn't smell fear or sweat or even an Olympic pool filled with ammonia. None of *them* could smell worth a darn, but it could catch the slightest motion.

For a long time, maybe an hour, maybe two. Jillybean squatted in the ferns growing ever more sleepy and ever more hungry. Hungry enough to eat a cricket. One just happened to flit through the air to land right next to her hand. Her stomach made a gurglily noise as she looked upon it.

Don't, it looks gross, Ipes had said.

To Jillybean it looked no more gross than a skinned rabbit or a plucked pheasant or the hairy legged spider she had swallowed on a dare from Ipes. She cupped the cricket where it made desperate squiggly motions against her palm.

When the monster finally turned away, she had popped it in her mouth and crunched it into a gazillion pieces as she made a face. It tasted horrible, but worse was that the pieces of cricket had the consistency of popcorn husks. They stuck in her teeth so that the bitter taste lasted.

Ipes put his hooves on his bulging, cookie-bloated hips. *That's not what I meant and you know it. Remember the fable of the cricket who whiles away the summer day in fun while the ant labors preparing for winter?*

It was vaguely familiar. "But what happened to the summer?" Jillybean asked, a note of fear in her voice. The last thing she remembered before waking up with frost all around her was damning up a river to catch catfish, and it had been hot as blazes that day. She stood up and gazed around at the forest, not recognizing a thing. "Are we still in Missouri?"

Oh sure, and don't worry about the date thing, Ipes said, giving his head a sympathetic tilt. *It's happened before. Time gets away from you. I think it's normal.*

The forest was so foreign to her that she could have been in Siberia for all she knew. "How is this in any way normal? What happened to those kids? Remember the ones I rescued from the witch?"

They left a long time ago, Ipes told her. *Months ago, but that's okay. These things take time.* She was about to ask him: what things? When he answered: *Healing. You needed time to heal, mentally, that is.*

"And…and am I healed? Is that why I can think now?"

Oh, you've always been able to think. Thinking is not your problem. Coping is your problem. Understanding the unfortunate nature of humanity is your problem. Dealing with grief is your problem.

"Grief?" she asked, as a spasm of fear ran up her back. Had someone else died? The list of people she knew who had died… or whom she had killed, was long. When she pictured them in her mind, they lined up in a velvety blackness as if waiting to get into a movie in hell. Another spasm struck her.

No one else has died as far as I know. We've been out here hiding so there's no way to know, but I would bet not.

"Hiding?"

I don't know what else to call it. You abandoned those children and you keep us away from every settlement. We haven't spoken to anyone in months.

Jillybean's mouth hung open and, for a long while, as the sun gradually rose through a murky haze of clouds, she could only blink, her lids flapping closed over her huge blues eyes in a slow rhythm.

Finally, she asked: "And do I ask these same questions every morning?"

No. Normally, you hop up and start playing. Since you didn't, I figured it was a good time to mention the cricket and the ant fable. You have got to start preparing for winter or there will be trouble.

She had a vision of gathering nuts in the hollow of a tree. A shake of her head cleared that picture. "I was sick in the head, but now I'm better. Huh? But how would I know if that's true? How does a crazy person know they're not crazy?"

The circular nature of the question was too much and she could only shrug it away. "Well, since I'm no longer crazy what should I do?"

Find a hotel? Ipes suggested. *I hate roughing it. You know we haven't seen the inside of a package of Oreos in...I can't remember the last time. And you should really think about finding a bathtub.*

Self-consciously, she put a hand to her fly-away hair and was shocked to feel the knots in it...and the twigs. Her hair felt like some sort of failed wicker experiment.

"Wow," she whispered, glancing down at herself. Caked dirt under her fingernails, filthy hands, clothes that reeked of old sweat and stained with what she hoped was bog mud. Next to her was an oddly familiar backpack that she was sure she had never seen before. It was as foul as she was.

It was jam-packed with stuff and not the usual Jillybean survival gear, either. For the most part, it was packed with toys: a pair of matching Barbie dolls, a white and pink tea set made of molded plastic, a magic wand that flashed lights when she touched a button, a tutu and fairy wings in gold, sized for a little girl.

"Where's my knife? And my multi-tool? Where are my books?" She could remember she had been halfway through an eighth grade algebra book and was nearly finished with a text on the physical sciences.

Ipes shrugged his sloping shoulders. *You took the summer off, I guess.*

She was about to admonish Ipes for being silly, because no one took summers off anymore; survival was a full-time occupation, even for a seven-year-old, but as she opened her

7

mouth her mind was flooded with images and memories. They came to her disjointed and out of sequence: Ipes sitting on a chair in a clearing, her hugging him and crying; the two of them sitting in a strange house chatting over freshly brewed tea; the two of them at a playground, squealing with laughter, as she spun on a tire swing.

She saw them roasting marshmallows, playing tag, and hide and go seek. They put on a play about King Arthur and rode bikes. These wonderful memories played through her mind like a movie she had starred in and it was fantastic right up until the last memory: her and Ipes having a "who can make the biggest splash" contest in a clear blue pool. The pleasant memories ended with a strange flash of light. It was an explosion, a massive one and she saw herself lolling listlessly in a river of black water that was filled with dead bodies.

"The River King's barge," she said in a whisper as a cold tingle ran up her spine, and her skin tented with a million goosebumps. "How did that get mixed in with those other memories?"

Ipes remained silent, sitting on the green blanket. She shook off the unanswered question, and glanced around, trying to get her bearings. With the sun just rising, she knew the direction of the cardinal points of the compass, but that was about it. She had no idea where she was and no real idea where to go.

Neil Martin's face came to mind—he was young with clear blue eyes, a sweet smile and a baby face. For the briefest of moments, she smiled, only then the image of Neil changed. His face became scarred and scabbed and his eyes grew dark and his always pleasant air was now shaded by the burdens of worry and regret.

This was the real Neil Martin. This is what he had become. "Because of me," Jillybean said.

Suddenly the other memories of the past summer faded as well. She saw herself sitting quietly in an empty playground where everything squeaked with rust. She saw herself sitting in a dark house with a tea set in front of her knobby knees; the cups were empty of tea and the marshmallows were old and stale. She saw herself in a garage, staring at a pair of bikes which sat on deflated tires.

"What is this?" she asked Ipes. "What's…what's real?" He shrugged again and she grew angry. "I thought you said I was healed."

I said you were healing, not healed. These things take time. You have to be patient.

The image of Neil came to her once more, his scars standing out in ugly pink lines. "What if this is as far as I heal? People don't grow hands back if they get chopped off. Maybe this is it."

Maybe you would heal more if you were around people who love you, Ipes suggested.

An image sprang to mind: Jillybean crushing pills into powder and putting it into a baby's bottle.

"But…" she started to say as tears filled her eyes. There were no "buts." She had killed her little sister. She had poisoned Eve's bottle and had stuck it right between her pink lips. The memory was faded and grainy as if it was an old-time movie, but those had been her hands dealing in death. "Who could love someone who did that?"

Sadie and Mister Neil, Ipes said without hesitation. *They know it wasn't your fault. Sadie said so. They'll take you back.*

"What about the others? What about Mister Trigg and Mister Captain Grey? And Mister Michael, and all of them?"

You have to try, Jilly. You'll die out here all alone. Can't you see that? Can't you feel it?

Jillybean hadn't thought about it before that moment. Now, she took stock of herself: the dirt and the smell struck her right off the bat. She reeked like one of the bums she had seen in Philadelphia years before. Looking closer at herself she saw that her arms appeared oddly thin. Lifting her shirt, she noted that her ribs stuck out as though her skeleton was growing out of her skin.

When was the last time she had eaten a proper meal? She couldn't remember. This was perhaps why she had woken feeling so abysmally tired.

"Yeah, I guess I better do something." Her eyes fell on the jumble of toys that spilled from the backpack and a part of her wanted to dig through them once more, to lose herself again in the fantasy world she had built. Fake or not, it had been at least fun. This real world wasn't fun at all.

It can be, Ipes said. *You have me, after all and everyone knows I am the funnest of persons.*

Jillybean rolled her eyes as she picked up the zebra. "You're not even a person. You're not even…" In mid-sentence, her face froze in place. The next thing she knew she found herself

9

walking quietly through a forest, her near disaster conveniently forgotten.

She couldn't heal all at once and that meant she couldn't admit what Ipes really was. He was a Band-Aid holding her psyche together and if she lost him again, her mind would break and there'd be no coming back.

Chapter 2

Jillybean

Before she could consider a trek halfway across the country, the little girl had to do something about her stink.

Ipes couldn't tell her how long it had been since her last bath. He claimed to have lost track of the days and she supposed that was very possible as she didn't know what month it was, let alone the date.

On a near empty road, she found a house whose front door had been cracked square in half, the lock and hinges proving sturdier than the wood.

Inside, magnetized on the side of a refrigerator was a calendar. The picture on top was of a cartoon haunted house with the words: *Happy Halloween* written in ghostly lettering. The month was for October and that didn't help Jillybean at all.

"Is this for now or for last year?" It was nippy enough out to be October. The year stamped on the calendar wasn't any help, either. She'd been six when all of this had started and at that age years didn't mean much.

I say we act as if this is October until we find out different, Ipes said. *In fact, we can pretend that today is Halloween and you can go as a little girl.*

Jillybean made a face of disgust. "That's hardly a costume. Now, I wish I kept that tutu. A tutu is what means you're a ballerina and that is a costume."

I think if you saw a mirror you might change your mind about what is and what isn't a costume. He led her through the house in search of a mirror and found one in the master bedroom. Her reflection wasn't the first thing that caught her eye, however.

An odd pile of moldering bones, partially wrapped up in a sheet, lay on the carpet of the room. A long-decayed arm stuck out as if it was reaching for something. "Ugh. It looks like someone was getting ready to bury it and it came back to life."

I think animals got at it. There's teeth marks on the ulna that aren't from a human.

"Oh." Jillybean had a soft spot for animals and didn't like to think that they would eat people when they got hungry enough. She turned from the corpse and then stepped back in fright, ready to run. At first, she thought that a monster had somehow managed to sneak up on her, but then she saw that it was just her reflection.

"Ho-lee mo-lee," she breathed, turning her head this way and that, seeing herself as Ipes saw her. She looked like a beast, part monster, part yeti. She addressed the mirror, "Maybe you're right. I think I should go to Halloween as a little girl."

Bathing in a house with a corpse usually wasn't a problem, however she kept imagining the thing upstairs crawling across the floor towards the door. After poking around for food and coming up empty, she decided to bathe at the next house she found.

After a ten minute walk down the empty road, Jillybean came across a home that was partially destroyed. A fire had eaten the garage and part of the main house. The remaining two-thirds leaned on its foundation looking as though a stiff wind would send it crashing down.

Jillybean went for it, eagerly, her stomach growling. Chances were that the owners of the house had set it alight in a last ditch effort to stop rampaging monsters. If so, it was a good bet that there was a cache of hoarded food inside.

She wasn't disappointed. A locked trunk sat in the middle of the living room begging to be broken into. Without a pause, Jillybean knelt down in front of it and dug in the back of her wild hair for the simple tools she kept there.

Three broken paperclips and an hour later, the lock finally clicked. With excited fingers, she lifted the lid to discover a treasure: seven cans of soup, a bag of flour, a half bag of rice and two cups of sugar in a tin. The owners of the house likely thought the stash was meager. In contrast, Jillybean's heart raced at the find and she put off the idea of bathing until she had collected some wood and stacked it on a cookie sheet. She started a fire right there on the kitchen floor.

Using a screw driver, she poked two holes in the lid of a can of tomato soup, set it directly into the flames and then stared at it, mesmerized. She saw in the licking flames images: her picking every strawberry from a wild patch she had stumbled upon, her stuffing her cheeks with crab apples and later getting a bad case of the runs, her chasing crows from a carcass of a fawn, and finally, her coming across an opened and very stale bag of marshmallows. They were so hard they couldn't be chewed. She let them dissolve in her mouth and after finishing the bag, she had a case of the shakes as the sugar raced through her system.

This was the fare she had been living on over the last few months. She was wretchedly malnourished.

The smell of the soup had her stomach hurting, while drool pooled in her mouth. It was a struggle for her to wait until the red juices started to boil up out of the can, and, sitting at the kitchen table, her left leg shimmied, pumping up and down as if it was running a race. When the juices finally started to bubble, she fished the can out of the fire with a heavy pair of barbecue tongs.

With Ipes unhelpfully pointing out her eroding manners, she slurped down the entire can of soup. *How barbaric*, he muttered when she sat back, her tummy comfortably full. To spite him, she let out a burp and then stuck her paw in the empty can, bear-like and scraped up any juice she might have overlooked.

Are you done being disgusting?

"Almost." She licked each finger and then tried to force out a burp like the boys at school used to do, however she was unskilled in that area and only managed to look as if she were about to vomit.

Instead of a burp, a sigh escaped her as she sat back and gazed up at the smoke-blackened ceiling. A moment after the sigh, as the kitchen had become pleasantly warm, she yawned, suddenly overcome with a desperate need to sleep.

Forgetting the smoldering fire, she took Ipes upstairs and found a girl's bedroom. As tired as she was, she couldn't sleep right away.

"What if I wake up crazy again," she asked Ipes.

You would never know, so try not to worry too much. You need sleep. Proper sleep. She didn't know what he meant by that, exactly. Before she could ask, he said, *you had nightmares all the time and yes you would kick me in your sleep.*

"Oh, sorry. Though I'm sure you…" Another yawn stretched her little mouth and caused her eyes to spring tears. She fell asleep soon after without finishing her sentence.

She didn't dream as far as she knew and was utterly confused when she woke up with a sound ringing in her head. "Was that a gunshot?"

Ipes swiveled an ear. *I don't know. Maybe it was an…* A second gunshot rang out. It was distant, a mile off at least, but sounded closer in the still air. *Okay, it was a gunshot.*

The pair waited to see if there would be another and as they did, Jillybean looked around, frowning. The shadows were wrong and the noises were way off. The birds were doing their wake-up songs and the sun was coming in through the wrong window and the air had that just warming up quality it had as it got over its night shivers.

"It's morning," she said. "How strange. Did I sleep the entire night…" She stopped as fear gripped her. "Was I crazy again?" she asked her stuffed zebra.

Crazy? No, you were just sleepy. Remember what Mister Neil always said about how you needed rest to get better. Well, I guess you did that. So, now that you're all better, what do you say to a bath?

She was sure she wasn't all better. Her head felt, well haunted, actually. It was as if she was still hearing an echo of that gunshot in her mind. It was mixed with others. And there were near silent screams running beneath that and the sound of fire crackling, and not the kind of fire that kept you warm, either. It was the kind of fire that ate boats and buildings and people.

Speaking of fires, maybe we should get that one downstairs going again. We can heat stones and water and use soap, lots and lots of soap.

"What about that gunshot? Maybe there are people." Along with her new-found sanity she discovered a great sense of loneliness. It seemed like forever ago that she had been around real, living people.

You have me. What more do you want? And besides they could be bad people. They could be slavers or bounty hunters or they could be just plain mean.

"Or they could be nice," she countered. "Or they could be in trouble and need my help."

Ipes grumbled over the idea of her helping people. He pointed out how small she was and how weak, and how they were big people for sure and big people could make do on their own and that they probably… "Oh, hush," she said, cutting him off in mid-rant. "I think I'll be less crazy if I find nice people to be around."

So far, the only really nice people she knew lived in Colorado and, as much as she loved Mister Neil and Sadie, she felt a nervous, guilty sickness in her belly at the idea of seeing them again.

Without any further argument, she slipped out of the house on cat's feet and angled straight through the forest in the direction she had heard the gunshots. The woods were close and at times were difficult to traverse, especially as she tried to move quietly.

A ghostly wail off to her right told her that at least one monster had also heard the sound of the gun and was moving ever closer. She angled to her left for ten minutes until she could no longer hear the creature and then she struck diagonally to her right.

After another ten minutes, she slowed her pace even more and began searching for any sign of a human presence. It wasn't long before she found something: blood. Along the forest floor were drops of blood stretching across her path, forcing her to choose right or left. In both directions, the forest seemed to go on forever and so, on a whim, she went right.

Traveling in a hunched stoop, her eyes locked on to the trail of red drops, she crept along for a few hundred yards until she came upon what looked like a crime scene. At the base of a sycamore, she found a pool of blood that was still warm. A few feet further on she discovered what looked like a mass of intestine and other entrails.

She shrank back, her face twisted in a mask of fear. Ipes was all for running. *What did I tell you, Jillybean? There's a killer in the woods!*

"That's not what you said," she corrected. "You said slavers or bounty hunters. Most bounties are only paid for living people." She edged forward, her senses on full alert, her body primed to dart in any direction at the least sound.

So far, she and Ipes were the only ones making any noise, and in truth, Jillybean was moving so quietly she probably couldn't have been heard from twenty feet away. First, she inspected the pool of blood and then she crept to the pile of innards, shooing away a fly and poking at them with a stick.

What are you doing, Jilly? Ipes hissed from the crook of her arm. What happens if they come back?

"Why would they? They got whatever they were after and carried it out of here. I'm starting to think it was a deer. Look, there's a tuft of fur and right there is a hoof print." The tension in the air bled away.

Oh, well it's still gross. You shouldn't touch it. You might get rabies or scabies or whatever it is these things carry. They're not all like Bambi, all cute and pr…

He trailed away as a new sound came to the forest: that of a truck rumbling to life—it wasn't close and soon it rumbled away out of earshot. "Drat," Jillybean whispered, alone once more, alone and hungry. The soup had been the day before and now her tummy made its own rumbly sound.

She dropped into a squat, hunched over the deer guts considering them. *Jillybean?* Ipes asked. *We have food back at that burned-up house.*

"There's not enough to last and there's no guarantee we'll find nice people or our way back to Colorado before winter." The zebra nearly lost it when she shoved him into her shirt and commenced to dig in the guts. "Stop pretending to be sick. It's distracting and that's what means it's annoying. Hmmm. Which part do you think is the liver? Ipes? Is this it? Ipes?"

Don't talk to me. I've fainted. I'm unconscious.

"Hmph!" she snorted. "No wonder you're a herd animal. You would starve to death as a lion."

I'm still unconscious. Can a person throw up when they're unconscious?

She didn't bother pointing out that he wasn't a person. Ignoring him as best as she could, she pulled at something flat, ugly, and maroon, guessing correctly it was the liver. Next, she coiled the intestines and was momentarily taken back when a greenish mass poured from the bottom of it.

"I didn't want that anyways," she said, swallowing loudly. In her time with the fugitives, she had seen a number of deer butchered and had never been grossed out. It was different now that she had her red hands wrist deep in the steaming pile. After taking a breath, she went on, going so far as to sling the coiled rope over one shoulder.

Because Captain Grey used to say that the heart was where "all the good stuff" was, she tried to yank it out only it wouldn't come unstuck from the hose-like arteries that ran out the top of it. Although she could have taken the kidneys as well, she thought they were too gross and settled on taking just the intestines and liver.

Weighted down with her mucky mess of offal, she grew tired on the way back to the house, and after twenty minutes, her attention wandered to such a degree that she practically walked into a monster standing silently in the shade of the forest before she realized it was even there.

It had to have seen her. It had to know she was just a little girl. She wasn't in her monster costume, after all. But it was right on top of her and she couldn't do anything except drop her chin to her chest and let out a low moan.

That's not going to work, Ipes hissed in her ear. Run! Drop that stuff and run!

She couldn't. The monster, a tall, lean thing, dressed in rags and smelling like death and poop came to leer over her. Its moaning breath was worse than an overflowing latrine and Jillybean nearly heaved up the remnants of yesterday's soup. If she had, or even if she retched or just coughed, she would be killed right there.

Without a weapon, she could only rely on her big brain, except she could think of nothing except to keep moaning and start praying.

Her prayers went unanswered. The monster grabbed her, its diseased claws digging into the soft flesh covering her.

Chapter 3

Jillybean

The claw on her shoulder dug deep, sending something warm dripping down the front of her shirt. Her moan went higher, nearly turning into a frightened whimper, but she held back the tears by the barest of margins.

Even Ipes refrained from making a single sound. The monster had her in its grip, but it was still uncertain. It bent down and sniffed Jillybean, it's hot, horrid breath blowing her brown hair this way and that. And then, with a shove, it turned away from the little girl, looked up at the hot sun and went back into the shade.

What the heck? Ipes asked. Why did it do that?

Remembering the barely human image she had seen in the mirror, Jillybean knew the answer. She had fallen to such a disgusting state that even when she wasn't trying, a monster thought she was one of them. This made her so sad that she wanted to cry, but just then she couldn't even frown. *It* was still too close.

Gradually, she moaned and teetered her way through the forest until she was far enough away, then she fell to her knees, shaking all over and feeling too weak to even stand. Right away she clutched her shoulder where the monster's claws had dug in...and she felt the coiled intestine. It had saved her from being clawed and had "bled" pinkish juices all down the front of her shirt.

An unsteady laugh escaped her. "Do you think it's ruined?"

What? Your shirt or the intestine? As if it matters which! Your shirt needs to be burned anyway, and the intestine is intestine, for crying out loud. It was ruined the second it was pulled out of that deer.

She glanced at it and frowned. "I don't think I can eat it now, even if I cooked it. But, it still might come in handy."

How? Do you plan on jumping rope with it? Are you going to use it as streamers for your next birthday party?

"You're being gross. I can use it to trap other animals or maybe to bait fish. Do you think there is such thing as an underwater trap? I mean for fish. I know they have them for lobster and stuff like that."

In the old world, back before the monsters, she had never been one for fish except for the kind that made "fish sticks." In the new, monster-filled world, she was far more open-minded. The only problem was in catching them. Sitting on the edge of a pond, lazing in the sun with a fishing pole in her hands, seemed fine for one of those July days where it felt as though summer would last forever, however she found herself in October and the days were getting shorter.

And if we get going to Colorado, then we'd be fine. I'm sure Captain Grey's got them all set for winter by now.

Jillybean sighed, "Getting there's the problem. I don't think I should try to drive through the lands of the Azael. If they see a lone car, I bet they'd come after it for sure and I'm not all that good of a driver."

Oh, really? I would never have known.

"Hush! You should try driving with sticks tied to your legs. It isn't easy, you know." She stooped and picked up her bundle of intestine and the liver she had set aside, nearly dropping Ipes out of her shirt and into the sticky pile.

"Sorry," she said, absently, no longer thinking about fish traps. "If I can't drive, I'll have to walk. Say, ten miles a day, divided by seven hundred miles puts my ETA in Colorado sometime in February."

A vision struck her of a blinding snowstorm sweeping across the prairies that made up long stretches of eastern Colorado and practically all of Kansas. The cold would be intense and if the snow got any deeper than four inches, she'd have to cut her projected ten-miles a day in half.

"That would put me well into March, if I even stay alive that long." Freezing to death was a distinct possibility, but so too, was starving to death. Every house along every major highway had to have been picked over a hundred times.

So…what are you saying? Are you not going to make the attempt until spring? Oh, Jillybean that would mean an entire winter alone. That can't be good for you. Remember the crazy?

As she still had one foot in the land of crazy, it wasn't something she was going to forget anytime soon, unless of course she went back to being super crazy and then she'd never know, and then she'd die. Her mom had died from a case of the crazies so Jillybean knew it could happen.

"I'll have you with me, Ipes." She said this without enthusiasm as if she knew in her heart that the toy zebra wouldn't be enough to keep her mind from slipping down the rabbit's hole once more. Unfortunately, she could see no other way except waiting out the winter.

Maybe you shouldn't rule out driving, Ipes suggested. *For one, we can swing way south where it's always warm. And we can take backroads. There's no law saying that we have to take a highway, right? Think about it. We can take a road trip, just the two of us. We can explore America. Hey! We could go see the Grand Canyon...just as long as we don't get too close to the edge. That has to be written down as an untouchable rule. And I bet there's an Oreo factory out there somewhere, just waiting to be explored and looted. So, what do you think?*

In truth, Jillybean thought it sounded lonely, but it was better than spending an entire winter cooped up in...she still didn't know where she was. Finding that out would be her first order of business.

"There's no sense planning to go somewhere when you don't know where you are to begin with. That's logic. Really, this could be Colorado, after all." Colorado wasn't all green mountains and icy peaks. There were deserty plains and forests of pine and pretty towns tucked up in lush vales. Who knows? Maybe they had this sort of deep forest as well.

She went back to the half-burned up house and quickly found its address on a letter. The state initials were M.O. Ipes thought it meant Montana, to which Jillybean had asked: "As in Hannah Montana? That's a person, not a place." He explained that Montana was a state, but he had no idea where it was in relation to Colorado.

They began a new search, this time for an atlas. They found a globe, but there weren't any words on it that marked states. In frustration, Jillybean slapped it so it spun around on its axis. When it slowed, she spun it again and found herself mesmerized by it. The globe went round and round until she felt herself beginning to float in a strange way as if the floor had fallen away and...

Jillybean! Ipes cried, suddenly, bringing her around. Hey, you don't want to do that. Come on, let's find a new place. One with a map and an intact roof.

She noticed that the room had cooled off and that the sun was slanted in the sky. "Was I dreaming or..." She broke off, realizing that she hadn't been dreaming or even asleep. She'd been sitting in the same place, staring for hours. She'd been crazy again.

A wave of fear swept her and she quickly jumped up. "This house is no good," she declared, rushing about, gathering odds and ends: The food, the liver and intestine, a knife, a lighter, a partial box of candles and some string.

Everything went into a green garbage bag which she slung over one shoulder. Out the front door she went, heading further down the road. It didn't matter where it led; what lay behind her was too frightening to think about.

A cold sun was setting by the time she found the next house on the lonely road. It wasn't special: a three bedroom ranch with a weed-fouled yard and crooked shutters. Just like the last house, it didn't have a fireplace and so she had to construct one, complete with a chimney which she made out of flat baking pans glued to two ladders which she wired in place against the wall. It was an ugly affair, though it did its job of directing the smoke up and out of a carefully broken window.

Next, she busied herself, forming her nest for sleep and then she prepared the house for an attack from monsters or bad people. Below windows and before doors, she set noose traps and trip wires and all around the outside she threw crunching glass so no one could sneak up on her.

Just in case, however, she worked out two escape routes and three perfect hiding spots.

Dinner came next in the form of barbecued liver—it didn't taste good even with the few seasonings she found in the house thrown on haphazardly.

After that, it should have been bedtime, only she was afraid of going to sleep. What would happen if she didn't wake up? What would happen if the crazy came back? Monsters that could tear her apart were something she could deal with. People with their evil and their greed were harder but still manageable when she could turn the conditions to suit her.

But crazy wasn't something she could fight against, except by staying busy, busy, busy and putting her mind to work. She stayed up past midnight searching the new house, not just for an atlas, but also for all those useful items she used to carry around. Going systematically room by room, she discovered: screwdrivers, tape, bandages, copper wires, C-batteries, LED flashlights, camping gear, fishing supplies, a 24-pack of bottled water and a small stash of cans in a box labeled: *For Church!*

21

"Church food, huh. Do you think God will be mad if I eat it?"

Ipes crawled up onto the box and looked at the cans. *Ooh, pineapple! No, I don't think God'll be mad at all. In fact, you know what? He wants you to eat it. This box is like a miracle coming in our time of need!*

She had to admit she was in all sorts of need, and so she hauled the box, with much grunting and straining on her part and much lip-smacking on Ipes' part, back to the kitchen where it was comfortably warm.

To stave off sleep, she arranged the cans from least desirable to most. It didn't help. Her eyes grew heavy and she finally nuzzled into her blanket nest and fell asleep.

When she woke, with light creeping from beneath the kitchen door she asked: "Is this tomorrow morning or this some other morning?"

Who cares, Ipes answered. *It's morning, let's break out those pineapples!* Neither of them could remember eating anything sweet in the last few months, save for the stale marshmallows and those had been disgusting…but not as disgusting as the leftover strips of barbecued liver she had bagged up; they were in their own class of disgusting. With a sigh, she took a dusty plate from a cupboard and laid out the cold liver.

You're not serious, Ipes said, making a gagging noise in the back of his throat

"I'm saving the pineapple for Sadie and Mister Neil. It's gonna sorta be like a present on account I killed Eve. I have to get a present for Mister Captain Grey, too cuz I killed General Johnston. I bet he's still mad about that."

Probably, but he blames that mean ol' King Augustus for that, and since you killed him and won the war I bet you're going to be forgiven by everyone. You might even get a parade. She doubted that. Crazy people never got parades. Oh, stop talking like that. Let's discuss presents. You can't go wrong with cookies. Everyone loves them.

"And you would eat them before we got halfway to Colorado. No cookies would be too much of a temptation. I think we should get him a gun. A big one, like a machine gun or a fifty cal. Hmm, but where do you get those in Montana?"

She went to the atlas she had found the night before and flipped through the glossy pages until she found Montana. Most states had only one page, however Montana was so big that it took up two. "Let's see. Where in all of this is Viburnum?" It was the strange name of the town in which the little house was supposedly located.

According to the index, there wasn't a Viburnum in Montana. "That's weird," she whispered, looking again at the mail. The name Viburnum, MO was on every piece, so that meant it was a real place. She opened the envelopes one after another hoping to discover answers, but instead found bills and advertisements for credit cards.

It was only after she had tossed aside the mail, grimaced her way through her breakfast of liver and decided a change of clothes was in order that she discovered where she was.

The only clothing that came close to fitting her was found in a boy's closet where half the shirts were red and emblazoned with a most unmanly red bird. "A cardinal? Ah, the St. Louis Cardinals," she said, not realizing that she had left Ipes in the kitchen and was now talking to herself. "I get it, he likes baseball. So, that means the MO stands for Missouri? Why wouldn't they use MI? Wouldn't that make more sense…oh right, there's Mississippi and Minnesota."

Relieved to know where she was, Jillybean went to the atlas and began plotting a route to Colorado. On paper, the safest way was to head directly southwest and quickly. It was a bit shocking how close she was to Cape Girardeau and the River King. He would love to get his hands on her and do…things.

A knot in her throat caused her to swallow hard and a strange "being watched" feeling crept up on her from behind. Abruptly, she spun trying to catch whoever it was in the act.

What? Ipes asked, looking, perhaps for the first time in his life, actually innocent. *I didn't do it. Whatever happened, it wasn't me.*

"No, it's me," she said. "Sorry." She turned back to the map and the first word she saw was "Fort," as in Fort Leonard Wood, Missouri seventy miles west. A brief flare of excitement was followed by a sudden let-down.

There was no way that a military base so close to the River King had gone unplundered for so long. "But…" she said, her mind working, seeing things, not as she wished and not as others saw them, but as they were.

According to the atlas, the land in and around the base was hilly and deeply forested. There would be monsters there, drawn to the people coming to search. They would be hard to spot and very dangerous, even for grown-ups. They would make extensive searches difficult and perhaps not worth the risk.

Jillybean could imagine little homes hidden from sight, tucked up in the little vales and down dirt roads leading to weed-choked hollers. Many of these homes would belong to soldiers or ex-soldiers and likely, there would be guns and bullets in them. She needed both and not just as gifts to Captain Grey. If she was going to venture out among people, she would need a gun of her own.

"Then that's the plan. We go to this army-man base and we find some guns and some food and stuff."

Smelling like that? Ipes asked, with one hoof covering his face. She glanced down at herself and her nose wrinkled. On the spot, she stripped down and saw that not only was she too skinny, her flesh was scabbed and bruised and utterly filthy.

Naked, she started the fire going before padding down to the bathroom. For the second time in two days, her reflection startled her. Her head looked huge on her skinny body and her fly-away hair was no longer so flighty. It stuck up, here and there, stiff with dried mud.

The image in the mirror bothered her and she turned quickly away to start the water running. "Come on water," she whispered, hoping that the town water tower still had something in reserve. Sometimes they did and this was one of those times.

"Ew," she said, leaning back from the faucet. The water chugging out was the color of mud and there were flecks of rust spitting out with it. Gradually, it began to clear until after a few minutes, it looked like normal tap water from "before." Although it looked good, she didn't trust it enough to drink it. It would have to be boiled first.

The next hour was spent heating the water to the perfect temperature, finding the little girl she used to be beneath the grime, and hunting for Ipes, who needed a bath as much as she did. Another hour was spent gathering her supplies and preparing clothes.

She ignored all the Cardinals jerseys in the boy's closet and went for the more neutral greys and browns. As she was so small, nothing actually fit her. A pair of kitchen shears and a cinched belt fixed the problem though she was sure she looked ridiculous. The shears also transformed a winter coat into a monster costume that hung from her in tatters.

A red and blue Spiderman backpack, filled with what she considered essential knickknacks and two day's worth of food went under the coat. The remaining food and water went back into the church box, which she pushed beneath the front porch and covered with damp leaves.

Once Ipes, still slightly damp in his round bottom, was set in the front pocket of the coat with just his bulbous nose and two beady eyes sticking out, Jillybean was ready to go. There was no hesitation on her part or looking back. Behind her was a past filled with sadness, in front of her were her friends and all around her was death, destruction and danger.

Chapter 4

Sadie Walcott

Eight hundred miles west of where a lonely girl walked along a lonely road, Sadie Walcott eased her M16A4 to her shoulder and sighted down the P4Xi 4x24 scope at the lead battlewagon. At three hundred yards, she had a perfect shot, her crosshairs on a long-bearded man in a knee length coat standing in front of the lead vehicle. She could see his lips move as he spoke into the radio.

She recognized the man. He had been one of the Azael—all of the men clambering around the machine had been as well. *But that was before*, they all said. And: *We didn't want to be a part of the war. They made us.*

Supposedly, the people of the plains had changed their ways. The empire of the Azael had fractured and now there were seven warlords ruling the wide-open lands which cut the country in half. They claimed to be peaceful traders.

These particular traders called themselves Rangers. They came from a wide belt of grassland that took up most of Oklahoma and northern Texas. Sadie didn't trust them or their fake smiles. Like the rest of the former Azael, they still bought and sold slaves, and they still forced people to pay "protection" fees to cross their lands and yet, in spite of this, people still disappeared in the long crossing.

Sadie swept her scope across the battlewagons that were parked just down the hill from the new and improved Red Gate 1. There were four of these immense and ugly machines. Essentially, they were 18-wheelers that had been modified to such an extent that only with a scope such as Sadie's could someone guess at what they had started out as.

Teams of expert welders had turned the trucks and their trailers into fortified warehouses on wheels. The trailers had been widened, so they took up most of the two-lane road. Rising up from this sturdy base were metal walls, thick enough to withstand small arms fire. They rose straight up twenty feet, and atop this structure was an armored turret from which a fifty-caliber machine gun jutted.

Along with the machine gun, each of the walls had firing ports from which people inside could shoot their weapons without exposing themselves. The cab was as fortified as the rest of the machine, including a retractable armored slag of metal to protect the driver. To protect the tires, two overlapping curtains of chain hung like a metal skirt from the bed.

Although the Rangers claimed that the battlewagons were designed with zombies in mind, the amount of armor and firepower suggested otherwise—not that Sadie was worried. The wall of Red Gate 1 stood sixty feet above the road. It was a tremendous structure of cement and rebar that could take direct hits from the largest of howitzers.

"I count twenty-eight," Grey said after glassing the vehicles with heavy binoculars. He was pale and still sweating from the climb to the top of the Red Gate 1. His recovery had been slow and extremely painful, and he was just a shadow of his former rugged self.

Next to him, resting her elbows on the wall and letting her small belly sway, was Deanna Russell in her seventh month of pregnancy, though to look at her, one would have thought she was not even four months along. Her belly was only slightly larger than a volleyball and instead of being a griping, sweaty mess, she had the proverbial glow.

"Twenty-eight's not a lot," she said.

"You're not going," Grey growled at her. Sadie's eyebrows went up, but other than that, she made sure to keep her face as neutral as possible, not wanting to get involved in their little feud. The larger her belly got, the more over-protective Grey became. Just climbing the ladder had instigated a near-silent fight as the two glared. He ended up climbing up behind her with the ludicrous idea that he would catch her if she fell.

"Sorry, Grey, but she's coming," Neil said, ending the argument. "You know me, I'm too pessimistic. I need a counterbalance, someone who will keep her head."

That wouldn't be Sadie as everyone knew. For some reason, she got excited whenever the traders came by. For the most part their stock consisted of the basics: guns, bullets and fuel, each of the five ton trucks towed a 3000-gallon fuel tank. These were also armored and looked strangely boxy.

It was the more "exotic" items that had made her eagerly hurry to the wall…her stomach rumbling. The traders frequently carried hard to get items: cookies, strawberries, brown sugar, Hostess Twinkies—all of these were now so rare that they commanded ridiculous prices.

There was a third reason that she rushed to the wall. Although slavery was illegal in Estes, everyone eventually made their way to the slave truck, looking for loved ones. There was only one person beyond the gates that Sadie cared for: Jillybean.

If the little girl was ever captured and her identity found out, her price would be outrageous, perhaps more than Neil would be able to pay. Estes, the land where honor meant as much as life was a poor land, mired in poverty.

The east coast city-states had their fisheries. The midwest had their horses and their cattle, plus the crops that flourished without the hand of man helping. The Texas states had their oil, and the "Over the Mountain" lands had stockpiles of goods from the hundreds of cargo ships that had been left to rot at the docks in places like Long Beach and Seattle.

The River King had his pontoon bridge and the tolls from it generated a fortune. Much wealthier was Yuri Petrovich, who had his much-needed vaccine which he sold without bias to anyone with cash.

Even the Colonel was doing well. Taking a cue from the River King, he had moved his base of operations to Davenport, Iowa. It sat astride a northern stretch of the Mississippi on a large island that lay smack dab in the middle of the river. As all the bridges had been demolished, he sent parties north into Canada to find ferry boats. He had three operating at very competitive rates, allowing him to control the trade across the upper part of the country.

Estes, on the other hand, had no natural resources. It sat on a direct route across the mountain passes, however there were other mountain passes that could be used, and so nothing was gained from their position. It had been discussed that perhaps these other roads could be destroyed at key points forcing trade through the valley, but the honor-bound Neil Martin wouldn't hear of it.

Most of the population farmed the rich soil along the Big Thompson River, but there were some who hunted almost exclusively, and others who scoured the high plains for cattle and already there were two-hundred head grazing in valley pastures. Because of the cattle, there was a growing population who made forages out onto the plains to gather the wheat that grew abundantly. Flour was ground for bread and the leftover stalks were stored for the cattle.

The people of the Estes Valley were undoubtedly some of the hardest working people in the world. Despite this, they had little left over to trade and what they did have wasn't in great demand, at least compared to bullets and fuel. And they were in desperate need of both. The war with the Azael had left them with dangerously low reserves.

Their fuel situation was so bad that no one drove any more. Everyone rode bikes or walked, pulling handcarts. The lack of ammo was even worse. It was so bad that Neil kept the truth hidden from everyone except for the six members of the commission and Sadie. Neil feared what would happen if word got out.

If his enemies found out that they were down to four thousand rounds and that the munitions bunker was mostly filled with empty boxes, it was a good bet that they would attack immediately. If his people found out, they would leave in droves, tar and feathering Neil on their way out of town.

"Well, let's see what they have for us this month," he said with a sigh, heading for the ladder.

"Don't be so glum," Captain Grey chided. He was technically, either General Grey or Commissioner Grey, but since he refused to use his power as Commissioner of Defense to give himself a promotion, he still wore the black bars of a captain.

"Food is important and we're well stocked. You never know what the current demand is," Grey added as he went down the ladder wincing and slow. Neil went down even slower, his hands white-knuckled and sweaty. Above them, Sadie groaned at the delay.

Deanna heard her and raised an eyebrow. "You're always too eager. If you want good prices, you have to act like you don't care. You have to be all: *Is this it? Is this all you have? Meh.*"

"I know, I know, but it's hard." She was tired of being poor and she was tired of doing without.

Finally, the men were down. Sadie slipped ahead of Deanna and, nimble as a monkey, the girl in black zipped down the ladder receiving glares from both Neil and Grey. "I'm cool," she insisted. "Don't worry about me."

When Deanna made it down—awkwardly with her butt pushed out to keep from hitting her protruding belly on the rungs, Neil led them to the gate where they set aside their weapons and emptied their pockets. Unfounded accusations of stealing had occurred in the past and this was the simplest way to keep that from happening.

As representatives of Estes, the four looked extremely underwhelming. Neil stood just an inch taller than Sadie and had maybe twenty pounds more muscle on him. He was disfigured, scarred and ugly. His left hand was missing two fingers, both bitten off by zombies.

Captain Grey's scars were mostly hidden beneath his BDUs which hung off him, giving him a gaunt appearance. Deanna was tall and regal, however her belly ruined her graceful lines and the protective hand she kept over it gave her a nervous air when she was anything but.

Then there was Sadie. Few, even in Estes had her bravery and determination and yet, she wore mascara that was as black as her head to tail clothing. She was a "goth-girl" and looked it, with an emphasis on girl. She seemed younger than her eighteen years. The four Estes leaders would be easily discounted, if it wasn't for their reputation.

Neil stopped twenty feet shy of the first truck where a number of burly, bearded fellows stood, most of them giving Sadie a lecherous eye, something she secretly enjoyed. Normally, she disappeared into Deanna's shadow whenever the two were around men.

"Before we bother with all of this," Neil began, "please tell me your exchange rates concerning beef and game. I don't want to waste your time."

"Well, that depends," the largest of the men said. "How much beef are we talking? Is it butchered? Is it dried and salted?"

"I have six full-on mature cows, aging nicely in an ice house. They're skinned, but not butchered. All told, almost five-thousand pound. We also have seven hundred pounds of bear which is tastier than you could imagine, and another two thousand pounds of elk and venison."

This was all he had to make deals with. After the war with the Azael, many people were on the verge of leaving, forcing Neil to make concessions. Taxes on all goods produced or brought in to the valley were reduced from sixty percent down to fifteen percent.

This meant he couldn't afford the military that had sacrificed so much to save the valley. In a move that did not initially go over well, Neil had ordered the soldiers to become "self-sufficient." Instead of constantly training or standing guard, part of their time had to go towards tending fields or hunting.

This worked so well that the army could now feed itself and, for the first time, was actually paid. It was good for them, however the valley government didn't dare try to tax these earnings for fear of a revolt and that left the treasury depleted.

"Seventy-seven hundred pounds?" the leader of the Rangers asked. He had introduced himself simply as Maris. The others weren't introduced at all and now looked at Maris as if he were the only one of them who had the ability to think. He blew out a long breath, sounding disappointed. "Only seventy-seven hundred…well, I suppose we could do twenty-five hundred gallons of unleaded for that."

"And if we choose bullets? How many rounds?"

"Two thousand. You know how it is. With so many new oil tanks being discovered, the exchange rate is getting to be pretty screwed. Hell, I can remember when it would cost you…"

Neil held up his disfigured hand. "Two-thousand is ridiculous. Thirty-eight hundred is the lowest I'll go."

"Then I guess we're done here," Maris said, his arms crossed. Almost like a group of back-up dancers in a choreographed move, his men crossed their arms as well.

"Seems rather short-sighted on your part," Neil answered, "but I suppose you know your business better than I do. Have a good day." Neil turned on his heel and marched straight away, Sadie and the others following behind.

"I do know my business," Maris said, raising his voice. "I know I'll get my price from your people if you won't deal."

Neil paused. Without turning, he spoke over his shoulder: "That's not going to happen. The gate will remain closed as long as you remain out here. I will not have my people swindled."

Maris' backup dancers started whispering, looking shocked that Neil would close his doors in their faces. Maris waved them into silence before addressing Neil. "Hold on! Who's swindling who in this deal? Thirty-eight is too much and you know it. I could do twenty-eight hundred…maybe."

Neil tipped Sadie a wink before turning back to Maris. "I said thirty-eight and I meant it. Here's what I know: this will be your last trip up here before winter really sets in. You used up a ton of gas hauling these great big trucks up here and you'll use a ton more going back again. And once you're down in the plain what are you going to do?"

"There are plenty of people who are looking for what I got, Mister High-and-Mighty," Maris growled.

"Really? The next closest settlement is that tiny one down south of the Springs and they get regular traders all the time. You'll be losing money just going there. And after that, where will you go? New Mexico? It's a long way and a big risk. If it pays off, you might come away with what you could get here. If not, well, you probably don't want to think about it."

The back-up dancers began to whisper to each other again. Maris glared them into silence. "It'll pay off. Trust me, anything is better than getting swindled here by a cheat."

Neil shrugged, seeming unconcerned at Maris' rudeness. "Like I said, you know your business. Have a pleasant trip."

Once more, the little group turned away and had made it halfway back to the wall before Maris called out: "I'll get to have free trade with the rest of your people?"

"Bingo," Neil whispered, sharing a quick smile with Captain Grey. Louder, he called out: "Of course. I will not interfere with free and open capitalism. Deanna here will work out the particulars of our deal. One rule: no smoking around her."

As Deanna left to arrange the transfer of their meat for the trader's bullets, Grey clapped Neil on the back. He was weak compared to what he had been, but he was still stronger than most men and Neil began coughing from the blow.

"That was something else, Neil. I would have caved and got maybe twenty-five hundred. Too bad you can't bargain for everyone. I always hate when our people get rooked."

Still trying to catch his breath, Neil said, "I have bargained for everyone. I have set the exchange rate. Tell everyone who comes through that gate what the bullets to beef rate is. I'm sure they will get a little short-changed here and there, but it won't be that bad."

Grey squeezed his shoulder in a friendly pinch and then hurried up the slope to get everyone up to speed. When he was gone, Neil began massaging his shoulder. "It's good to see his strength is finally returning."

"Yeah," Sadie agreed. "So, what sort of allowance can I get?" Neil was feeling magnanimous and told her a hundred. She left grinning her way to the trucks. The first three were filled with bombs and bullets and guns, items she didn't really need or want.

The next truck had the *goods*. Cookies and cakes and chips, and much more. Men were busy pulling the boxes out and setting them up to be displayed better. Sadie watched with her eyes simply jumping out of her head—they even had ice-cream.

"How much for a scoop of chocolate?" she asked.

One of the men quoted her a price that was twice what it should have been based on the exchange rate Neil had set. She shot back a much smaller amount to which the man only glared.

"I don't care what they dickered for," he said, "this ice-cream will sell for what I say. When was the last time you saw ice-cream?"

It had been a year, at least. He wanted thirty for a scoop, which was way too much. Thirty could feed a family for a week. Depressed, she walked away, heading for the last truck—the slave truck. The slaves were always in the last truck, as if the sellers themselves were embarrassed to be dealing in human flesh.

The man standing at the metal door didn't look the least bit embarrassed, however. He gazed down at Sadie's trim form as he munched on the back end of a wet stogie. "Looking for you mommy?"

Sadie hesitated before mounting the crude ramp up to the door, but only for a moment. She had nothing to fear. If this man tried anything, Neil would personally cut his balls off and stuff them down his throat—after Captain Grey had incapacitated him, of course.

"My mother is dead," she answered coolly. "Thanks for the reminder."

"Then maybe you're looking for a daddy. I could be your daddy. I could take care of you real nice."

"I have a dad. Two of them, actually. My adopted father is Neil Martin, the man who runs this place, the man who personally kicked the Azael's ass. And my real father is the River King. We're not so close, but if you try anything, I will gut you right here." She paused to show him the eight-inch bowie knife she always carried. "I will slice you right up the middle and I think dear old dad loves me enough that he would come all the way out here to piss into your open guts."

The man tried to smile only he looked as though he had eaten something slimy that kept trying to crawl back up his throat. "Yeah, right," was all the retort he could muster.

"Just stand aside. My father is looking for a reason to drop the exchange rate even further and you might be it." This, more than the bluster had the desired effect and the man stood aside.

The lighting inside the eighteen by forty-foot room was purposely dim to hide the pallor and the bruises. The shadowy nature also hid the fear in the women's eyes. People do not thrive living in chains with the threat of rape constantly hanging over their heads. They tended towards lassitude and depression. Still, the women did what they could to look either beautiful or sexy or, if they couldn't do either, they tried to appear at least pleasant.

With the cloying incense coating her flesh, Sadie went down the main aisle where the women stood outside their curtained-off rooms. At the back was a short ladder leading to the second floor. She had just put one foot on it when "sexy" music started up, thrumming the walls with an endless dance beat.

She went up, growing nervous. If there was a child, she would be up here and it would be heart-breaking. A dozen women eyed her sullenly as she went down the aisle. The last stall didn't have a woman in front of it.

With a look of nervous disgust, Sadie inched the curtain back with two delicate fingers holding just the very hem of the curtain. As expected, there was a mattress on the floor. The sheet had a horrible crust that made Sadie's throat tighten-up. Quickly, she turned away. "Excuse me?" she asked over the beat of the music. "I'm looking for someone. A little girl. Her name's Jillybean. She's kinda quirky, but very smart. She's got brown hair and blue eyes and is about this tall." She held her hand just beneath the curve of her ribs.

"I met a girl like that" one of the women said. "Was she seven?"

Hope exploded in Sadie's chest. The other women all seemed to draw back, so Sadie had a good look at the one who had spoken. She was neither sexy nor beautiful, and now she wasn't exactly pleasant either. She was gaunt and pale with a feverish, haunted look to her eyes.

"Yes, she is," Sadie said. "Where did you see her? Is she okay? Is she still alive?"

"I'll tell, but you have to do something for me first," the woman replied urgently, her words bubbling over each other. She advanced towards Sadie until she was brought up by the chain at her neck. "I'll tell you, but you have to help me."

"What? Anything?"

The woman waved Sadie closer and then glared the other women back. When Sadie got close, the woman grabbed her and hugged her in a foul-smelling embrace. She whispered, tickling Sadie's ear: "You have to get me out of here. Buy me off of them and I'll tell you where she is I promise."

"Sure, yeah, sure. Wait here." The other women having heard this crowded close, grabbing at Sadie and begging: *Buy me, please. Over here! I know Jellybean, too.*

Sadie pushed through them until she was out in the clean Colorado air where the man who ran the slave truck sat, picking his teeth. "Find something you want?" He had an evil, knowing look about him that stopped her short. Had he heard their conversation? If he had, there'd be trouble.

"I'm interested in one of the women. Black hair…wears a print dress. Kinda skinny. Kinda ugly. Actually, she's really ugly, but she reminds me of my mom, so…how much? Fifty?"

"Maybe for the hour. If you want to buy her outright, it'll be three thousand." The number left her speechless.

Chapter 5

Neil Martin

Neil knew better than to go down to the traveling market and gaze on and touch and linger over all the things his body longed for. He'd be lying if he said that all these were food-oriented. Sarah had been dead for five months and lately the days and nights seemed to stretch out, especially the lonely nights.

But there was no way he could go down to the slave truck. In his heart, he was a foolish romantic who would end up falling for each of the women. He wouldn't fall in love with them or even in lust, he would feel for them, he would empathize with their pain and sadness and he'd want to save each of them.

It hurt him inside that he couldn't help them. To try to free them through violence or trickery would mean that the traders would never come their way again and the Valley's needs had to come first. The traders, though frequently evil people, were necessary for their survival.

Because of this, he stayed behind the wall and coached the groups going through on how to deal with the hagglers and the pricing strategies that were being employed. When his people came back, he took down notes of what was paid for each item and who had sold it.

There were a number of weak links among the Rangers, men who weren't natural salesmen. These tended to sell at lower prices and were easily pushed around by a headstrong buyer. Neil made sure to send his people to these weaker ones first. It gave them a psychological boost which helped when going up against a hard-charging salesman.

He had just finished talking with Fred Trigg and his little crew of "Trigglydites" as Captain Grey referred to the sycophants who hovered around Trigg due to his position on the commission when Sadie came bustling through the gate.

"Neil! I might have found her," she said, racing up the ladder. Neil didn't even have time to ask who might have been found when she blurted out: "It's Jillybean. One of the, uh, ladies in the last truck…the you-know-what truck, said she saw her. She described her perfectly."

Fred grimaced. "Jillybean? Really? Do we want to go down that path again?"

"Yes, we do," Sadie shot back. "She has her issues, but she is also a genius and I don't know how many times she risked her life to save ours, and that includes your life as well, Fred."

"Of course, and she has my undying gratitude, but…" He paused to let out a long, tired, theatrical sigh. "The time of rescues and bombs and blowing things up is over. Now is the time to bring about a sense of normalcy to the Valley. We need to get on with living our lives."

"This *is* life, Fred," Sadie shot back. "Life isn't about sitting behind our walls while the world goes on. Life isn't about… what's the word, Neil?"

"Complacency," Neil said, filling in the blank and taking over the conversation. "We don't know what the future holds. It could be all about puppies and apple pies and barn dances, or it could be dangerous and deadly."

As Neil took a breath, Fred jumped in to answer. "And that's why we don't want Jillybean around. She is the very danger you speak of. A swirling vortex of chaos surrounds her that strikes friend and foe alike."

Neil shared a quick look with Sadie. The little girl was a double-edged sword, there was no arguing that point. Though in Neil's mind, there was no arguing any point. He wasn't just the governor, he was virtually a dictator.

To overrule him on any little thing, the six-person commission would have to vote unanimously and Neil was personal friends with three of the commissioners: Deanna, Grey, and Veronica Hennessy, a stout-hearted ex-whore who blossomed more every day.

Fred Trigg controlled what he called the *Opposition Party*, although the *Opposite Party* would have been a better name. No matter what Neil said or did, Fred took the opposite view. It was annoying, however Neil felt it wasn't necessarily a bad thing. It was a check to the governor's power. In truth, if he wasn't the governor, he would have suggested even more checks, but as a self-described benevolent dictator, he didn't feel he needed them.

"I think you fear the unknown too much, Fred. You can't control Jillybean and that makes you nervous. Sometimes it makes me nervous as well, but it doesn't stop me from seeing the tremendous potential there is in Jillybean. Have you considered what improvements she could make in our lives? If she were here right now, I would immediately put her in charge of energy production and I would bet good money that she would have the lights on in a month."

Their current electrical supply came from four commercial diesel generators each of which could put out 2,000 kilowatts per hour. This was more than what they currently needed, the only problem was that they sucked up diesel at a prodigious rate, a rate that could not be sustained day in and day out.

"Oh, I'm sure she could get the electricity back on," Fred agreed. "Knowing her, she'd set up a nuclear reactor down at the *Denny's* and then accidentally blow us up."

"Stop being melodramatic," Neil chided. "The girl needs a loving home *and* supervision. She won't be constructing anything more dangerous than a kite. Sadie, where did this lady say she saw Jillybean?"

Sadie cleared her throat and avoided looking in Fred's direction as she said: "She wanted to talk to you, Neil."

His daughter wasn't a good liar and Neil caught the air of deception in her voice. It made him nervous, but he didn't let it show. "Right to the top? I suppose I understand. I'll go talk to her…alone." He could tell Fred was about to propose coming along and the way Sadie's eyes widened, he knew it wasn't a good idea. "Why don't you show me which one she is, Sadie?"

They left Fred and his little band of followers whispering behind their hands and scooted down from the wall. When they were through the gate, Neil only had to raise his one remaining eyebrow to get Sadie talking. "She says she knows where Jillybean is, but she won't talk until she's been bought free and clear."

"Oh Jeez. How much?" When her smile grew tight, Neil stopped her. "How much?"

Valley people were walking by and so Sadie smiled and waved and refused to answer the question while they were within earshot. "Three thousand," she whispered when they were alone on the highway.

"Oh, jeez," he said again as he turned away. He stood staring at one of the most beautiful mountain scenes on the planet. The aspens had turned to gold and the valley shimmered in the cool light of day. He didn't even notice. His mind was elsewhere, trying to balance his responsibilities. On one hand, he had the entire valley to think of and on the other he had a little girl who he had helped to warp into something sad and horrific.

Undoubtedly, the girl could be a wonderful asset to the community…but three thousand, just for some possibly dated and useless information, seemed nuts. "Maybe I can talk them down," he said to Sadie.

"Or maybe you can convince the lady to tell us," Sadie replied. "I mean, I'd love to buy her and all of them, I just know we don't have the money for it."

"We don't have money for anything," Neil grunted. They made their way to the last truck and were both taken back to find the leader of the traders, Maris standing at the bottom of the ramp. He was practically giddy. Neil thought the wet stump of a stogey stuck between his yellowed teeth was the perfect complement to his shit-eating grin.

"So, Mister High and Mighty is looking to make a substantial purchase. A woman doesn't come cheap, no not at all, right Lou?"

Another of the traders leaned against the side of the truck, his hand on the butt of a pistol holstered at his hip. He wore the same sort of ugly grin as Maris, only his was for Sadie. She glared right back.

Neil stepped between them. "Actually, I was hoping just to talk to one of your ladies."

"Talk?" Maris laughed. Lou's grin widened as his boss went on through his chuckles, "My women aren't for talking to, they're for screwing. The standard rental is ten for half hour, but the results are guaranteed."

"I just have a question for her."

"And it will cost you ten in order to ask it. This isn't a difficult concept. You have to pay to play."

Much to his embarrassment, Neil was forced to count out ten brass 9 mm rounds and drop them in Maris' open palm. "Have fun in there," Maris chortled. "Don't forget protection."

Lou brayed over the top laughter at this. Neil ignored them and went up the ramp with Sadie following. Maris grabbed her hand. "If you wanna go in, you gotta pay. Remember, threesomes are extra."

Although Neil didn't see it as all that funny, Lou had tears in his eyes as he laughed. "No thanks," Sadie said, glaring and wiping her hand on her black jeans. She went to stand by the side of the truck where her very presence kept some of the Valley men from heading down.

The soldiers of the Valley were some of the most honorable men left in the country, but there was a ten to one ratio of men to women in Estes and so it was somewhat understandable that the slave truck was already rocking as Neil went in.

The interior was so dim that he stopped just inside the door, blinking, trying to peer around. "Don't be shy, sweetie," a voice cooed in his right ear as someone took his deformed left hand— the hand was dropped a second later with a little gasp.

The cooing voice spoke again: "She's got a problem with you, but I like a man with scars."

"I do too," the woman on his left said, quickly. Finally, Neil's eyes adjusted to the sad display of humanity. Curtains were drawn on four of the stalls leaving six very desperate women standing just inside the aisle wearing very revealing lingerie. Neil wasn't turned on in the least.

The desperation in their eyes was too great. This desperation plus the partially healed bruises made him think that the women were on some sort of quota system and that there would be beatings if they didn't hit their number of screws.

It broke his heart to disentangle himself from the women. "Sorry, sorry," he said, over and over again, until he reached the ladder in back. Its rungs were as grimy as everything else and his sadness was offset by a quick undulating wave of nausea.

He bit back on it and went up to the second level where the ceiling was even lower. The second floor was even more disheartening than the first. The women were older, more exhausted, and uglier. The makeup they wore looked to have been painted on with a roller and the fear in their eyes was deep.

Probably for these reasons, the light could only be described as scant. "Excuse me?" Neil said to the eight women doing their level best to appear sexy—and failing. "Which one of you knows Jillybean?"

"That's me!" one said, excitedly, raising a hand. Instead of grousing at their ill luck, the other women drew closer as Neil pushed down the aisle. To them this was a very interesting change of pace to their miserable days.

The woman who had raised her hand was thirty-something with long brown hair that she streamed down the sides of her face, detracting rather than enhancing her looks. Her eyes were very brown, like the dark muck at the bottom of a slow-moving river. The tears in them stood out like glimmering wet crystals.

Just as obvious to Neil was the fresh, cherry-red handprint on her left cheek and the duller purplish bruises on her arm. Despite all of this, she was eager. "I know the little girl. Her name was Jillybean and she was this tall." The woman put her hand next to her ribcage. "And she had all this brown hair…like she never brushed it or anything. And she's skinny. Her face is very skinny. It makes her eyes almost bulge out."

"What color are her eyes?" Neil asked.

Without hesitation, she answered: "Blue! A very pretty blue." The woman waited for the next question, her hands quivering in front of her.

"And where did you see her?" This doused her excitement. She leaned back away from Neil, folding her arms in front of her chest.

"I'll tell you that only once I'm out of here. You see, I know who she is. I know that she might be valuable to the people here in Colorado and that means what I know is valuable. And I think it's valuable information to other people as well. Maris tried to beat it out of me a few minutes ago, but I wouldn't talk. Nothing is free anymore. That's what I've learned since all this started. Everything has its price and freedom is my price."

Her face was like stone. Her lips defiantly tight as if no force on earth could pry the needed words from them. Neil tried on his warmest, most endearing, pleading smile. He even clasped his hands in front of her as he begged: "Please. I just want to save a little girl's life. I owe it to her."

The woman shook her head. "The price is nonnegotiable. Take it or leave it."

Neil tried once more, but she remained obstinate and refused to budge. This left him with the terrible choice of either forking over basically six months' worth of tax revenue or possibly letting a little girl perish in the coming winter or be scooped up by one of the roving bands of slavers that were terrorizing the empty parts of the country.

"She won't talk," Neil whispered to Sadie, keeping his mouth covered and his back to Maris and Lou. "And I don't know what to do. It's so much money and we're struggling already. If something happened, like an attack or something, we'd be screwed."

"And if something happens to Jillybean?" Sadie countered. "Personally, I think the answer is easy. What would Jillybean do if your positions were reversed?"

41

A sad grin bent Neil's mouth. "Knowing her, she'd probably blow something up. Why am I saying probably? She definitely would. But I can't do that. I have other responsibilities."

"I know she's worth it and so do you. I say we do it. I say you figure out how you're going to haggle Maris down. Three thousand is crazy. You saw that woman. She can't be worth three thousand."

Three minutes later Maris agreed. "Lou here, misspoke. Gayle's price is actually four thousand." He let Neil and Sadie gag on that for a few seconds before he added: "Situations change. As we all know, information can be very valuable, especially information concerning Jillybean. Don't pretend the name isn't infamous in certain circles. I know some of the old members of the Azael would pay a thousand for her head."

"I could do a thousand," Neil said, speaking rapidly. "I mean, she may not have up to date info. She looks like she's been with you for a while. I may be buying nothing but a wild goose chase."

"There is that," Maris allowed. "I'll knock off three hundred. You forget, she still has value as a whore and as a final sale to some lonely farmer or hard-up soldier who'll take what he can get."

The idea of buying another human being was repulsive to Neil and it got him fired up. "Oh, please. We both know you're not making much off of her and who is going to pay top dollar for a woman who could be swimming in disease?"

"Another fine point. I'll knock off two hundred more. So that's thirty-five hundred. Would you like her as is or washed and waxed?"

Neil held up what used to be a prissy hand, now it was mangled and eye-catching. "I don't think so. If you ask me, a thousand looks like a poor investment. And tell me, which of these former lords of the Azael would be willing to pony up thirty-five hundred for a rumor? Not one, I bet."

"Maybe you're right," Maris said. "But if they'll pay a thousand for her head, I might get five hundred on a sighting. And sure, Gayle was able to withstand a few measly slaps, but she'll cave when I start breaking her toes. Broken toes won't stop her from sucking a dick, right?"

Next to Neil, Sadie was a mountain of rage. Her hand slid behind her back for the Bowie, but this time Lou was armed and pulled his pistol halfway from its holster, stopping her.

"And here's another thing. You had me by the short and curlies earlier, Neil. I'll admit that was hard bargaining on your part, but now our roles are reversed. You want this girl, badly. All this talk of yours cements that in my mind. You'll pay what I'm asking, I'm sure of it." He turned and began walking back to the truck. Over his shoulder, he added: "Come back when you have my money—thirty-five hundred, not a bullet less."

Lou slid the pistol back in place. "Ta-ta, love," he said to Sadie. "I wouldn't come back here after hours, snooping around or you'll end up in that truck for good." With a grin firmly fixed on his face, he flipped Sadie off and then marched after Maris.

Sadie gave him both barrels right back. "What are you going to do?" she asked when Lou was out of sight.

"I don't know. I should talk to the commission and see what they have to say."

"What?" Sadie said, spinning Neil around to face her. "You know precisely what Fred Trigg will say. He may not have the votes to overrule you, but he'll definitely spread it around that you wasted all that money on just one woman. Here's what I think: if you go to the commission, it's your way of getting yourself off the hook and not having to make a tough decision."

She was right, of course. If he went to them, he'd be lucky to get two votes. Deanna knew and cared for Jillybean, however she was very pregnant and very worried about the future. Even Captain Grey could go either way. His men were the ones who'd have to do any fighting in the future and a day didn't go by without him grumbling about the lack of weapons training.

That left only Veronica Hennessy on his side. She would vote to release anyone stuck in Gayle's place. As well, she had always liked Jillybean.

Having one vote on his side would make it so much easier to say no, so much easier to avoid the hard choice. "Alright. We'll buy her."

Chapter 6

Neil Martin

"We'll buy her, but I have to say something to the council. I'm not king. I will tell them what I'm going to do, demand a count and unless it's six to zero, I'm going to buy her and hope to God she knows something more than just Jillybean's name and her description."

The way Gayle had answered the questions, he knew in his heart that she had been in Jillybean's presence. The only question was how long ago had it been? Was Jillybean still deep in Missouri, looking for Ipes? Or had she moved on, perhaps somewhere even further away and if so what would he do? Would he mount an expedition? Would he send Sadie alone as he had before?

The moment Sadie had left on her last trek across the country in search of Jillybean, he wished he hadn't given the order. As strong and capable as Sadie was, she was still just a kid. Still so vulnerable and still too stubborn for her own good. And nothing had changed. Wherever Jillybean was, Sadie would insist on going to get her, even if it meant going alone. There wouldn't even be a discussion—there would only be an argument that Neil would lose.

Neil sent her after Deanna, who was preparing to move the meat they had traded to the Rangers. Fred and Grey were still on the wall, joined by a few dozen others waiting their turn to go down to the traders. They all chatted freely and happily, sounding like children on a field trip to the zoo.

Since he didn't like ladders or heights, or really even fences or walls, he waved the members of the council down.

"Meeting back at the hotel in twenty minutes…it's a voting meeting and I won't delay a vote on account of tardiness." Before Fred could begin to whine, Neil held up his mangled hand—he felt it carried more weight when he used the left rather than the right. People generally couldn't take their eyes off it, causing them to falter.

Fred was no exception and before he could recover, Neil stalked off to where he had leaned his bike against a tree further up the road. As governor, he could have driven a Humvee and not have anyone say a thing, but he chose the garish, red Schwinn in order to set an example. Just then, it was a particular regret. It was six long miles back to the Stanley Hotel, and at least half of those miles were a grueling uphill slog. At eight thousand feet above sea level, the air was thin and it wasn't long before Neil was gasping.

Within minutes he was passed by Fred and, embarrassingly enough, by Captain Grey *and* Deanna, who had to be careful not to knock her baby bump against the handle bars. He ended up being the last one to arrive at his own meeting. Perhaps worse, he came in out of breath and sweating like it was a summer's day.

Since he wasn't going to put up with a long discussion, he kept his helmet firmly fixed to his head as he explained how he wanted to drain the treasury and, in effect, hamstring the military. He expected an uproar, but instead got silence.

The silence was strange. Like poker players, the members of the commission looked back and forth at each other out of the corner of their eyes. They had been voted into their positions and, yes each had been voted into office by some group: farmers, hunters, soldiers, women, etc, but it was still unnerving to Neil that they were already playing politics after only four months.

The silence spun out for so long that Neil began to blather on, taking both sides as if he were trying to convince himself instead of them. Finally, Fred stood as was customary when making an official vote and said: "I think this is an easy no. What you're taking from the tax payers is equivalent to months of work, and for what?"

"For saving at least one life," Veronica answered, jumping up, her eyes boring straight into Fred. "And maybe two if we can find Jillybean in time."

That shut Fred up. Deanna began to stand, next, but Captain Grey stopped her. Without looking in Neil's direction, he said: "He has his one vote. The rest of us don't have to commit one way or another."

Grey's move was calculated with his constituency in mind. Although the votes of the commission were never supposed to go public, Fred or one of his sycophants had a bad habit of leaking the details to the Valley's biggest gossips, where the news was guaranteed to spread.

"You're abstaining?" Fred asked. "Is that even allowed? I mean, he should have to vote so the people can know whose side he's…" He stopped, realizing that his words implied that he was quite ready to rush out and blab to everyone how the vote went down. "I mean, he should have to vote so the people can know whether or not you have the full confidence of the commission."

Neil stood and planted his knuckles on the table. "I don't need the full confidence of the commission. What I need is one vote and I got it. I think we can be done now." He yanked open the door and was ready to stride out of the room, but almost fell over Sadie who was listening at the keyhole.

"Let Maris know." She left in a sprint, blazing out of the hotel and leaping on her bike almost as if were a stallion. Neil had to restrain himself from following after. He went to his room and looked out over the valley and waited, second-guessing himself endlessly, wondering what sort of repercussions he had unleashed.

When Jillybean was involved, there were always repercussions and they were usually tragic. He began to pace the small room, but only tracked back and forth three times before he caught sight of Sadie walking her bike next to the now freed slave.

"Please be good news," he whispered to himself as he headed down the plush carpeted stairs to his office, where he was surprised to find the entire commission waiting. "I'd prefer this was a private conversation."

"Of course you would," Fred said, "because when we find out that this lady doesn't know diddly, you're going to want to lie to us, or should I say massage the message?"

This was precisely correct, but it wasn't something he cared to admit to. "Actually, I am worried for her sake. She's just been released from captivity, and there's a lot riding on what she tells us. It has to be a bit scary for her."

"You could have Deanna talk to her," Fred suggested. "Or maybe one of the *other* women in the valley." By that he meant one of the ex-whores. Deanna glared and muttered something under her breath. "What was that?" Fred asked, as if unaware of how he constantly treated these women as if they were second-class citizens.

Before she could spit out either a caustic answer or actual spit, Neil spoke. "I will talk to her, alone and that's final."

This time it was Fred who muttered under his breath. Neil didn't bother to question him; he was too antsy to care what Fred Trigg thought about anything.

Sadie and Gayle, whose last name Neil would later find out was Houghton, were on the wide, sweeping front stairs, moving slowly up when Neil found them. Gayle wasn't used to the thin atmosphere and her breath came quick. Although she seemed a little dizzy, she wore a tremendous smile and her words of gratitude flowed out until she was gasping for breath.

"Just tell me where Jillybean is, please. That's all I want to know."

Right away she said: "She's in Missouri. The last time I saw her was about two months ago, but I'm not exactly sure since the days just sort of flow together. We were in this town…I don't know the name, I just know it was south of St. Louis by Highway 44. She saved me and my daughter and these friends of ours from this horror of a woman who was making zombies on purpose. She had us chained up in the basement of this house…it was terrifying. Even being a sex slave was better than that."

Gayle went into some detail concerning the rescue and the days that followed, in which Jillybean grew even weirder than she had been, and then took off out of the blue. But Neil wasn't listening.

Although he had been expecting something along those lines, the words: *two months* hit him like a punch in the gut. He grew queasy and had to clutch the railing. He could hear Fred's annoying voice in his head: *You wasted thirty-five hundred to find out Jillybean was in Missouri two months ago? We already knew that. And you know she could be anywhere by now. She could be across the ocean for all you know.*

The worst part of the story wasn't the two months, it was the fact that Jillybean had found Ipes. If she'd had him for two months, that meant she really could be anywhere. She could've walked all the way to Colorado from Missouri in that time. Hell, she could have crawled.

Which could only mean one thing: she wasn't coming back.

"Ok, Gayle. Here's what I want you to do: I need you to tell this story again to a group of people, only this time do not mention the zebra. Just forget it, like it's not a part of the story at all. You got it? I put my ass on the line for you and I'm only asking this one favor in return."

"Sure, sure, anything."

Neil brought her into the council room, what used to be the hotel manager's office. Here she told her tale and dutifully left out the zebra. Almost immediately, Fred made a stink over the lengthy time lapse.

Snapping his finger as if he were an embarrassed mom trying to quiet her children in church, Neil said: "This is not the time, Fred. Save the arguments for the commission meeting."

As she wasn't a member of the commission, Sadie had waited outside the door as she had before—with her ear pressed to it, or so Neil guessed. Now, he asked her to show Gayle to the admin building, where housing would be assigned to her.

The minute the door was closed behind them, Fred started right in. Neil let him go on, not contradicting a thing or making a single rebuttal. Grey made them for him. "You heard the lady. Jillybean hasn't found Ipes yet. She'll still be looking down that river. I think we should go after her."

"We?" Deanna asked, raising an eyebrow. "You're not going anywhere. Not until you're healthy again."

"I'm getting stronger every day, and I owe it to Jillybean."

"And I want him to go," Neil said before Deanna could mount a verbal comeback. "I need someone reliable, someone who can take care of Sadie. We all know she's going to want to go again."

Suddenly Fred quieted and even tried to make suggestions about where they should start looking and what they should pack. Neil saw right through this. "While Grey is gone, I'll choose his temporary replacement. There won't be a need for elections."

"Maybe not now, but what happens in a month or two?" Fred asked. "What happens if they don't come back? There has to be a cutoff period. I'm sorry, Deanna that we're discussing this but it has to be done beforehand so we all know what's what."

"I can do two months," Neil said. "Although I'm sure it won't be needed, Deanna." She thought otherwise and railed until Fred and his friends left. Only when it was just Grey, Veronica and Deanna left in the room did Neil tell the truth: "He won't be going after Jillybean. I, uh, have a confession. Gayle lied about Ipes. Jillybean actually found him two months ago."

"What? So, where is she?" Deanna asked, puzzled. "Why didn't she come back? Oh, I guess she's still crazy, isn't she? That poor girl, she really could be anywhere. Wait, so if Grey is not going after Jillybean, where are you sending him?"

"We need supplies, badly. Munitions, fuel, everything, especially since I, uh, ha-ha after I just gave so much of it away.

If it gets out how low we are on everything, it'll invite an attack by every two-bit dictator out there."

Grey nodded. "It definitely will and we can't risk it. Alright, if I go I'll need to pick my own team."

"Just make sure they can keep their lips sealed," Neil advised. "Speaking of which, I can't expect Fred to keep his mouth shut about how much I paid for Gayle's release, so I'm going to pre-empt him. I'll get ahead of the scandal by releasing that information myself. It'll help that we can add the fact that we are rescuing not just Jillybean but Gayle as well. Thirty-five hundred is a lot, but for two people, maybe we'll be able to squeak by."

In the days that followed, Fred did everything in his power to turn the population against Neil, and there was a lot of talk about electing a new governor, however his bacon was saved by an unlikely person: Gayle Houghton.

Tirelessly, she sang not just Neil's praises, but also Jillybean's. She built the little girl up into something almost mythical and when people mentioned her insanity, Gayle said: "Someone with that level of genius might look insane to normal people, simply because we can't understand it."

That usually did the trick right up until someone mentioned Ipes or Jillybean's murder of General Johnston or the baby, Eve. Gayle always changed the subject to Neil when the conversation went against her.

He had no greater cheerleader than Gayle and when he tried to tell her it wasn't needed, she answered: "I owe you my life. I owe you everything." She gave his arm a warm squeeze and her fingers lingered, touching him in a way that made Neil's heart run a little faster.

"Oh…okay," he stammered. "I have work to do. So, I guess, I'll, uh, see you later then." When he left her, she wore a smile, but it wasn't a real one. There was hurt in her eyes and he had to ask himself why he had snubbed her so obviously. It wasn't the fact that she had been a sex slave—she'd been dragged into it involuntarily and no one, especially the women in the Valley looked down their noses at her for that. Many of them had done some very questionable things to survive.

"We all have," Neil said as he walked away. Neil's list of wrongful acts was as long as anyone's and some of the choices he had made could only be called evil. A large part of Jillybean's insanity rested squarely on his shoulders. No, he wouldn't pass judgment on Gayle.

Suddenly the obvious answer came to him in the form of an image. A very beautiful image. Sarah's face came to mind, only for the first time he realized that her face wasn't as tight and crisp as it once had been. The picture was a little blurry. How long was her hair, exactly? And her ears… they were small, but how small.

He was beginning to forget what she looked like.

Chapter 7

Captain Grey

Grey's seven-person team left the day after Gayle gave her testimony to the commission. There wasn't much need to wait longer. An expedition of this nature didn't need months or even weeks of planning. There was too much unknown outside the bounds of the valley to make plans beyond the obvious: what to bring, where to go and how to get there.

The regular groups that went down into Denver to scavenge never strayed too far beyond the suburbs. It was too dangerous. Sometimes the plains teemed with the undead in the thousands and sometimes they were eerily empty and silent, and always there were slavers lurking in the ruins of the outlying towns, ready to snatch the unwary traveler.

Grey's plan was to strike north through the mountains until he got to the Wyoming border, where he would head east to Cheyenne. Not a lot of people knew there was an Air Force base just west of the city. The main reason for this was that there wasn't a single runway on the base and no planes or helicopters, either.

Warren AFB was home to the 90th Missile Wing, meaning they were all about inter-continental ballistic missiles—nukes, in other words. Every one of which was pretty much useless now. The people who operated the computers were all dead taking their passwords and encryption codes with them to the grave.

It would take more than a Jillybean caliber genius to hack into the secure computers and get them up and running.

But that didn't mean there weren't valuable items to be found there. There had to have been military security protecting the base, at least a company's worth, and that meant guns and ammo. The only question: was any of it still there?

Had the base been overrun by one huge wave of stiffs? Or had the men taken what they could carry and run away? Or were they still there, hiding in some deep bunker?

He aimed to find out. Other than Sadie, his crew was all military, men he had fought alongside for the last year. He trusted them to keep their mouths shut, when and if they returned, that is. No one said a word or complained about the sudden change in mission, in fact, Grey was sure they were all secretly relieved. Though it was true that Jillybean had saved the valley, they weren't going to forget the murder of General Johnston who had been a father figure to all of them.

To save fuel, they took only one truck: a big black Dodge with an extended bed and a winch in front. Even with an over-sized cab two of them had to ride in the back at all times where it wasn't just uncomfortable and cold, it was also dangerous.

Mountain roads were treacherous with steep drops on one side and looming cliffs on the other—the cliffs were the more terrifying of the two. The undead did not care about heights and had no fear of falling. When they saw humans, they attacked regardless of any other factor.

The team found this out the hard way at noon the day they left the valley, as they were winding up the face of some unknown twelve thousand foot mountain. The constant switchbacks and the deadly hairpin turns were bad enough but the mountain road was also strewn with boulders. It looked as if giants had been using them to play a game of marbles.

Since he knew that it would take only one to break an axle or ruin a tire. Grey was tooling along at an easy twenty-miles an hour, dodging the rocks. With his concentration squarely in front of him and the sun near vertical, he hadn't glanced up in a few minutes and didn't see the dozens of zombies crowding the road above them.

His first inclination that they were in trouble was when the beasts started "raining" down, splatting across the hood or thunking loudly on the cab. Immediately, everyone began screaming all at once, some telling him to stop and others pounding on the dash for him to go faster. Right then, he could do neither.

Grey dodged the truck as far to the right as he dared. When the edge of the road disappeared from his view, he used Lieutenant Wilson's reaction to gauge how close he was to the sixty-foot drop. Wilson, who had happily taken the window seat after their first stop, was now leaning back, his face elongating as if he were preparing to let loose a titanic scream once they went off the edge. Grey could understand. Wilson's view wasn't of a forest but of a thousand spears pointing straight at him.

The terror warping his face was the signal Grey was looking for. With gritted teeth, he eased the Dodge a few inches back to the left as the truck swished along the gravel, feeling as though the passenger side tires were half on air and half rolling on just a few blades of grass.

Meanwhile the screams of his men had died away, leaving only the grisly wet thuds of the undead falling to splat onto the road. When they hit, regardless of the bones jutting up out of their grey flesh, the zombies began crawling after the truck.

Although it felt as though they had been riding along the edge of the drop-off for a mile, it was really only a minute before they were clear of the immediate danger, however ahead of them was another hairpin turn that would send them straight up to where the remaining zombies were stumbling down the pavement to greet them.

Grey stopped the truck. "We're going to have to make some room, so everyone get cozy. Sadie, get on Wilson's lap. Same for you Hendricks. Cuddle up with Raoul and try not to like it too much." He leaned out the window where the two men in the back were white-faced and clutching their guns to their chests.

"I ain't never seen nuthin' like that," a sharp-shooting PFC named Keene said. He had a thick "porn star" mustache that quivered as he spoke. "They was just raining down on us. I mean…I ain't seen that before."

"Well, now you have," Grey remarked. "We've made some room in here, so come on get in." They piled in, still shaking from the experience. Once everyone had bitched their way into as comfortable a position as they could, Grey put the truck in four-wheel drive and drove uphill, trying to gain enough momentum so that when he plowed into the beasts he wouldn't lose headway.

He hammered into them, the truck shaking and rumbling as the bodies became fleshy speed bumps. Perhaps worse than the bouncing was the sound their nails made as they screeched against the metal. It went on and on.

"Now I'm wishing I had a cow-catcher on the front of this thing," Wilson yelled over the noise of the engine and the wailing moans of the zombies. Having found it at a burned-out dealership in Boulder, the month before, it was technically his truck. "I was going to put one on, only we had that war and I just plain forgot."

"Would've been helpful," Grey said and then was forced to down shift as the bodies began to pile up in front of them. The truck responded with an extra spurt and they lunged ahead only to be brought up short with a crash that almost sent Sadie through the windshield.

Her eyes went crossed for a moment. "What the hell was that?" she asked, rubbing the welt on her forehead. "Did you hit a fire hydrant?"

At first, he was as confused as she was. It was impossible to see the road ahead as it swarmed with the undead and all around them hands slapped the windows, leaving smears of pus. Then he remembered the boulders.

"Oh, balls," he hissed, yanking the truck into reverse and throwing an arm over the seat. Downhill was infinitely easier. Compared to the rough corpse-paved road of seconds before, it felt as though they were gliding on clouds. He went back down to the hairpin turn. Slowing just enough not to kill them all, he turned the car around and then took the remainder of the road to the next turn at an easy pace, dodging the crawling zombies, but not at the expense of hitting one of the boulders.

"I need another little cliff for them to lemming off of," he said in response to the raised eyebrows. He found one a few hundred yards further on and turned the truck around to point back uphill, keeping as far from the cliff face as possible.

Then came a wait of several minutes in which everyone stared up at the cliff, like tourists waiting on a Bigfoot sighting. With the windows up and so many sweating men piled in on top of each other, the air in the truck was becoming a little stagnant.

"I don't mean to be rude, but one of you is not using deodorant," Sadie mentioned, breaking the tension. "And by the way, it's probably a good idea to start now that you're all adults."

Everyone glanced around until Wilson proclaimed, in pure innocence: "It's not me, I promise." This set the men to laughing so hard that the truck began to rock on its springs. They were still chuckling when the first zombie toppled off the cliff to land eight feet from the truck.

The sound it made when it hit the pavement killed the mood. Grey began to tap lightly on the horn, coaxing more and more of them off the cliff's edge. A few went the long way, lurching down the road, perhaps drawn on by the pull of gravity, however an ungodly number fell to land in a growing mound near the truck.

Grey edged forward so that the creatures would have solid pavement to land on where massive injury was likely and death from head trauma possible.

The steep drop mangled the zombies horribly, though they didn't seem to mind. Dragging shattered limbs, they crawled to the truck and began scratching or hammering on the doors. At first it was a nuisance, but then as the numbers grew and the threat escalated, Grey climbed the truck over the squirming bodies in front of them and, once again, took on the sharp hill with its hurdles of boulders and zombies.

This time it was a far easier assent and in twenty minutes they crested a ridge where the land fell away on all sides, giving them a fantastic view of the world.

"Let's get some air," Grey suggested, climbing out of the vehicle. It had been only half a day in the truck and already his muscles and limbs were stiff. Although the air was biting, turning his breath to plumes of white, walking around the summit helped to work out the kinks.

The men either smoked or bull-shitted about this girl or that back in the Valley, until Lieutenant Wilson saw Sadie's discomfort. "You boys sure do like to run your mouths. Let's put out those cigs and get the truck cleaned up."

In the long bed, among the rifles, crates of ammo, packs, boxes of food and all the rest of the items needed to keep a squad in the field, were three gallons of bleach and two rolls of paper towels. Wilson set the men to wiping down the now dented and scratched up truck.

Sadie pulled her M4 rifle from the pile and started heading back the way they came. "Doing a little guard duty?" Grey asked as she walked by.

"No, I gotta pee. Don't leave without me, k?"

"That depends. How long do you plan on peeing?" She grinned and flipped him off, which caused him to chuckle…and wince. The cold air was hard on his lungs, which of his many injuries, had been the slowest part of him to heal.

Every breath came with a wheeze and a pain deep inside and a little cough that he tried to hide.

"You okay, sir?" Lieutenant Wilson asked after Grey coughed one time too many.

Grey pulled his shirt up and breathed into it to cut the sharpness of the cold air. "I'm fine. Just a tickle in my throat is all. Hey, good job putting those boys to work. We don't need that sort of talk around Sadie."

"Speaking of Sadie," Wilson said, his voice suddenly an octave higher. "Does she have a, uh, a steady man back in the valley?" Grey glared, the only answer he was willing to give. "What?" Wilson asked. "I'm trying to be respectful here, sir. I'm just looking for your blessing to speak before I even ask her out. I'm not asking you as my commanding officer. Everyone sees you and Neil as sort of father figures to her."

The word "father" brought to mind, not Sadie, but Jillybean. Sadie had always been able to take care of herself, while Jillybean had been practically begging for someone to love her. Grey had failed her, unable to see past her peculiarities.

"Sadie turned eighteen last month," he told Wilson. "She's her own woman now, she can make her own decisions. You can ask her out if you wish…having said that, if you mistreat her I'll beat your ass into the dirt." A cough followed the threat, which only made Grey glare all the harder—he hated the very idea of weakness.

Wilson hadn't seemed to have heard the cough, he was totally focused on Grey's ferocious stare. "Of course, sir. I understand completely and, uh, you can trust me."

"Good, now get those men in the truck. Why don't you and Hendricks take a turn in the bed? Don't worry, I'll keep a sharper eye out for falling zombies."

They had to wait five minutes for Sadie to come back from her pee break and then they were off again. As Grey promised, he drove with an eye out for overhead zombies whenever they drove through a series of switchbacks. Now that they were higher up, it was rare.

The real danger they faced were the very sizable hordes that were funneled by the mountains into the narrow roads. Even as few as a hundred zombies could be very difficult and disgusting to plow through. The big tires on the Dodge turned the creatures to sludge. When they ran into larger hordes, they simply couldn't attempt to go through, it was just too dangerous and with the steepness of the surrounding mountains, there was no way to try to slip around them.

What they needed was a way to draw them away from the choke points. Sadie didn't hesitate to step up when they came to the third such horde of the day. She slid out of the cab while Grey was still weighing his poor options.

"What the hell are you doing?"

Her answer came as part innocent shrug and part question: "What do you mean? You brought me for a reason, hopefully because I can contribute."

She started warming up, lunging so deeply that the other soldiers dragged their eyes from a thousand zombies as if they were no more dangerous than a like number of trees. Sadie acted like she didn't notice—and yet, she lunged deeper and arched her back, making one of the men whisper: "Oh my."

Just like their stares, this was ignored as well. "You know our only option is to drive back two hours to that last main road," she said to Grey. "And there's no guarantee it'll be free of zombies, in fact, you know it won't be. Hey, trust me, I got this. I'll run up the hill and get them all crazy for me. When they take the bait, you drive on through. I'll meet you down the road a bit on the other side of the hill."

"But…"

"But nothing. I'll be perfectly safe. It'll take them, like twenty minutes to get to the top of that ridge, and by then, I'll be long gone. I'll be sitting right here in this truck. You'll see."

It seemed as if he had no choice but to trust her. Without waiting for his permission or any more of an argument, she jogged off down the road, straight at the horde. Grey swore under his breath and then turned off the truck, ordering the men not to move if they could help it.

They were happy to comply, and stared at Sadie as she loped easily down the road. She had such a fluid running style, like a beautiful thoroughbred, that even Grey found himself watching. He pulled his eyes away and glanced down at the dashboard and for the first time saw that the needle of the fuel gauge had fallen over to the left and now leaned toward the "E."

He decided he would fill up once they met Sadie on the other side of the hill. "How far is she going to go?" he asked. "She doesn't need to get that close." She ran another hundred yards until she was toy-sized with the distance and then she began jumping up and down and waving her arms.

Then without warning, she darted to her left and went at the steep slope on the left-hand side of the road. It was sparsely wooded, but there were enough anemic pines for her to monkey upward. Below her a brigade's worth of undead charged up after her, swarming over the hill until not a blade of grass could be seen beneath their thousands of feet.

"Shit," Lieutenant Wilson whispered as Sadie stumbled. Her feet went out from beneath her and in a blink she had lost, not just momentum, but also fifteen feet of height. She caught a heavy stone that stopped her, however when she used it to pull herself up, it broached the earth and went tumbling down into the mass of undead.

With a deep breath, she faced the mountain and pushed on. She was young and in good shape and still the zombies gained on her. The ten-thousand foot elevation was nothing to them. They didn't tire and they didn't waste energy on fear. If they fell, they tumbled down into more of their fellows.

Sadie couldn't afford to slip again, some of the zombies were within ten feet and yet she stopped fifty feet from the top of the hill.

"Give me my rifle!" Grey demanded, jumping out of the truck. His M4 was handed down to him. He threw it up to his shoulder and scoped the hill, searching for the girl in black and finding her against one of the thin pine trunks. With perfect vision, he could see her chest heaving. She was winded, close to exhaustion, but she was also determined.

Sadie wasn't done yet.

"Are you going to fire, or what?" Wilson asked. He had a rifle of his own in his hands and was ready to start shooting at Grey's order.

"No," Grey answered, watching as Sadie went at the hill again, keeping just ahead of the monstrous horde. "She'll be fine. Once she's on the other side there's not much on this planet that would be able to catch her."

Grey handed back his rifle and went to the driver's side, only before he could get in, Wilson stopped him. "How do we know what's on the other side of that hill? It could be a cliff for all we know."

"Yeah," Grey agreed. He knew the risks just as Sadie did. "Mount up. Everyone inside. Let's go!" There were still a number of zombies near the side of the road. They were the very lame and he didn't expect them to be much trouble. His precautions were for the ones he couldn't see, the ones that were possibly just around the corner. There could be none or there could be a thousand.

He figured there weren't going to be many. Zombies were herd animals. If one went running off, the rest would likely stampede after it without a thought.

For good or for ill, Sadie was over the far side of the hill. Grey gave the gas pedal a little goose, setting them rolling along the road. He kept the truck rumbling gently along. There was no need to race through the now open section of roadway. They would just end up waiting on Sadie.

The road ahead of them curved sharply. It followed the river which bent at a ninety-degree angle as it ran up against a formation of granite that couldn't be worn down. When Grey got to the bend, he had to crane his head upwards and press his ear to the glass to see the top of the walls of rock that rose up around them. The steep hills on either side had transformed into vertical cliffs that loomed, throwing them into what felt like sudden evening.

Shadows grew so thick that at first the tremendous boulder sitting square in the middle of the road seemed as if it were part of the background rock. The closer they got to it, the more they realized they were screwed. The boulder was too big to push aside, even if they used the truck's three hundred horses.

To get around meant possibly going in the river, which was shallow but very fast. The rocks making up the bottom were undoubtedly slick. Within the truck, the men either groaned or cursed their luck.

"Stop your bitching," Grey said, slipping down out of the cab. "We adapt and overcome. Hendricks and Raoul, go back a ways and take care of any stiffs that might have been trailing. Keep it quiet. Use rocks. The rest of you come with me."

Unarmed, they piled out of the truck. Hendricks, a pale Irishman, was just reaching down for a rock when movement out of the corner of his eye stopped him. "Captain!" he hissed, taking a step back.

On the dry side of the road was a run of scrubby bushes and tall grass. Hiding within it were two men, both in camouflage and both carrying M16s. They had been crouching, but now they stood.

Grey spun around and as he did, he caught more movement on both sides of the boulder. Two more men crept around it, aiming guns, and there was a third higher up in the rocks. The last had a deer rifle that Grey could swear was aimed right at his forehead.

"Well, this is a special day," said one of the men who had come from behind the boulder. All the strangers were rather nondescript: loose and raggedy camo, straggly beards that went high up on their cheeks and hung well below their chins, filthy, long hair that blended with the beards. They were a dirty lot of bandits...or so Grey hoped.

"Special indeed," the man who had spoken continued. "First our little zombie problem takes care of itself and now our little web has managed to snag an entire squad of Estes-testes."

"If you know we're from Estes, then you should know to turn around and head on out of here," Grey said. "We have two companies scouring the area, probably looking for you. We had rumors of bandits working the area and we were sent out to capture and kill them."

The leader of the group wasn't fazed by the lie. "Am I supposed to be scared? Why should I be when I have six hostages? Or should I say I have six new fighters for the arena? We were hoping to snag us some women, but you'll also do."

In a very quick minute, Grey's squad was trussed hand and foot with stiff plastic zipties, and herded into a waiting van that had been parked around the bend in the road. Grey's threat must have carried some weight, the Dodge truck was stripped of their belongings and then driven into the river at a spot where the walls cast the deepest shadow.

"One of your helicopters would have to fly right into this canyon to see that truck," the leader of the slavers said. "Ain't nobody going to find you now." He started to turn away, but a thought struck him. "Hey...how much do you think they'd give for you guys? You know, like a ransom."

"Nothing," Grey said, the truth coming out of him in a whisper. Neil had nearly emptied the treasury—there was simply not enough to pay one ransom, let alone six.

Chapter 8

Jillybean

Though it was only seventy miles distant, it took the little zombie two days to travel to Fort Leonard Wood. The first day was spent endlessly searching for fuel in the desolate scrap of Missouri, where houses decayed, hidden from the world in an ever-thickening forest. It was a tiring and trying experience for Jillybean.

As she was alone and exposed, breaking out of her monster character could mean her death and so she monstered her way slowly along, checking every house she passed, collecting dribs and drabs of fuel from lawnmowers and gas-powered weed-whackers, and, every once in a while, from the little red jugs that every garage seemed to have. The jugs were, for the most part, bone dry, but a few still had a trickle.

Eventually, she collected four gallons. It was impossible for her to carry all of it at once and so she left a little here and a little there, hidden under porches mostly.

It was night by the time she felt she had enough and so she nested in some old granny's house. Even after a year, the house smelled of "grandma" in a sad, generic sort of way. There were also frilly lace doilies on each end tables, and yellowing family photographs in the hallway, and the bed in the master was neatly made, covered with a hand-made patchwork quilt. It only had one pillow at the head, which made Jillybean feel even sadder.

Had the granny died alone somewhere on the road outside her house, running for her life, her dentures clicking up and down? Were her children dead and her grandchildren as well? "Probably," Jillybean whispered, picturing a mangled and half-eaten toddler in footsie pajamas lying discarded and forever forgotten deep in the forest.

Let's not go down that road, Ipes said, steering her away from the pictures on the nightstand. *There's only unhappy thoughts where it leads. Instead, let's see this house for what it is —it's perfect.*

"How so? There's no food or nothing." The front door had been kicked in ages before and the kitchen and pantry ransacked. Nothing else had been touched because it was a granny house, after all.

I bet there's candy and maybe more. You saw the pictures. The lady who lived here had to be at least two hundred years old. She's got stashes. It's what your daddy used to call 'depression era' thinking, whatever that means. Remember what he used to say about his own grandma? Remember the hidden Tootsie Roll story?

"Yeah," she replied looking around the place, eyeing the little cubby of a house more closely. The living room was central and she went there first, spinning one long, slow circle. Scratches on the arm of the couch, little white hairs sprinkled about. "She had a cat."

Her tummy rumbled as she went back into the kitchen, the one room in the house that had any sort of mess. There was a spray of dried spaghetti noodles that crunched under foot. Quickly, she dropped to her knees and began to scrape them together in a dusty pile.

There weren't many, not even enough to fill half a ziplock sandwich bag. Regardless, the bag went into her pocket. Nothing else was obvious. The door to the pantry stood open, showing the world barren shelves. The refrigerator was closed and it was a mistake to open it. The only thing in it was a mural of green mold that covered the walls, and a stench that leapt out at Jillybean.

Ipes threw a hoof over his bulbous nose. *What? Did you think that everyone who checked this house before you forgot to look in there?*

"Just trying to be thorough. It's not like I enjoy cat food any more than you do."

You don't know if they even have any…and really the seafood medley isn't bad. Anything has to be better than the liver you've been eating.

"You got that right," she answered, heading across the kitchen where the cat bowl sat right under a row of cupboards. She could guess that someone who was two hundred years old probably wouldn't want to travel far just to feed a cat. Jillybean pictured the cat as being a frail thing as old as the old lady.

Sure enough, there was a blue bin in the cupboard, so filled with cat food in the shape of salmon that she could barely lift it.

We have won the lottery, Ipes said, his beady eyes entranced at the sight and his big nose working overtime at the smell. *What are you waiting for?* he demanded when she didn't immediately dig right in. *Are you thinking you wanna mix the cat food with*

the spaghetti? Cuz that would be weird. Spaghetti and cat balls?
Sounds gross.

"I'm checking for mold, dorko." There wasn't any she could
see and so she tried a piece, finding it, as expected to be both
stale and flavorful. She grabbed a handful and went through the
home, her little feet leaving little tracks in the plush carpet. As
she poked about, she popped the cat food into her mouth like
they were peanuts and she was belly-up to a bar with a beer in
front of her and the Phillies on the tube.

They found the expected stash of sweets in the old woman's
bedroom. On a shelf in her closet were a number of bowls. One
held loose change, one held pens and paperclips, and one held
eight pieces of hard candy.

"Her going-out candy," Jillybean whispered, picturing the
old lady placing precisely two pieces in her purse before she left
to run her errands. Always two pieces and that meant there
would be more close by. Her eyes slid over the room. Everything
had its place. Everything was neat and organized. A crinkly bag
of hard candy would never be left out for someone to see. No,
the old lady couldn't have that—even if it meant having to bend
all the way down under the bathroom sink eight shuffly steps
away.

Under there was where the messy things went. Jillybean
pictured it all: the open bag of cotton balls she had bought back
in 2008 was down there, the comet with dusty green powder all
over the lid sat nestled with the other cleaners, while tossed on
top was a blue sponge as hard and warped as an old shingle.

In front and somewhat separate from the other odds and
ends was the bag of multicolored candy. Its open top, neatly
folded because, of course she never knew who would look under
there and for what reason.

The old lady would never have believed a seven-year-old
girl could have guessed each item and their placement without
ever opening the cupboard doors.

She was wrong about two things: the sponge was green
instead of blue and the top of the candy bag wasn't neatly
folded…well it was actually, however, Jillybean hadn't guessed
that two clothespins had been used to clamp it shut.

Despite Ipes' begging and her own demanding urge,
Jillybean refrained from popping one of the hard candies into her
mouth. Only after the cat food became too cloying for her to

take even one more bite did she unravel a single piece of candy and savor it until it was nothing but a sliver.

The remaining candy went into her backpack, causing Ipes to exclaim: *You are mental!* She didn't argue, though she felt saner than ever. Ipes went to the corner for saying under his breath: *Yeah, you're a regular forty-eight card deck.*

She spent the night in the old woman's home, though not in her bed. It felt haunted to Jillybean, and so, she camped it in the kitchen. Beds really weren't her thing and she liked to be near the back door just in case a quick getaway was called for.

The next morning, she declared herself ready to make the trip to Fort Lenard Wood. She had food, gas, water, candy and two sticks that she could tie to her lower legs to help in the driving process, something she would later change to children's wooden blocks, which she glued one on top of the other and then glued to each pedal so that she could reach the gas and the brake.

Her one problem just then was the fact she didn't actually have a car. Another search was required, but she couldn't find one with enough of a charge left in the battery to crank the engine over. She wasted four hours searching for a vehicle, but after a lunch of cat food sitting in some dark garage next to a dead Camaro with four flats, she had to accept the fact that she was searching in vain.

She went back to the newest of the cars she had found: a red one with the word KIA emblazoned in a number of places. She popped the hood and gazed down on the battery with it twin poles: positive and negative.

As she stared, her mind centered, becoming so focused that Ipes fell from her hand, plopping on the floor of the garage with a small thump, the exact sound one would expect to hear when a toy zebra was dropped. The stare went on for three and a half minutes and in all that time Ipes simply lay inert and, for once, silent.

She blinked out of her fugue state, thinking that not even a second had passed. "Oh, sorry, Ipes, but you can't play on this floor it's all dirty and stuff. And there could be rats, you never know."

You're the one who dropped me, sheesh. So, you're gonna need magnets?

She didn't seem to notice that he had read her mind. "And some copper wire and at least two bikes...tools, like those grabber things and the ones that go back forth with criick, criick sound."

Socket wrench?

"Yeah, that's what I said. And I'm going to need a hammer to smash things with." The house that was attached to the garage had everything she needed, including the magnets. Jillybean knew all about magnets and where to find them. The average home had more than she would ever need. The problem was getting at them.

Everything with an electric motor had batteries, but they were always encased in hard plastic and surrounded by electronics and gizmos.

She started with the Dyson 320 Upright vacuum cleaner found in the hall closet. The hammer made short work of the plastic housing of the motor. Once exposed, she used a paperclip from her hair to find the magnet. Next a screw driver was used to pry it out—it seemed awful small, not even the size of her thumb.

I don't think that's big enough, Ipes said.

"Yeah." She knew the basics of creating electricity, having read all about the subject in one of her big people books. The process was simple: spin a magnet within a field of copper wiring and, good morning mama, you had electricity.

But this was book knowledge, purely theoretical in her mind. She had never actually made electricity before and didn't know how much wiring was needed or how big the magnets had to be to charge a car.

Ipes wrinkled his nose at the one magnet. *I'd get more.* She had to agree. Tucking the magnet into a pocket, she went into the living room, happy to see the old-fashioned turntable and the row of records. She had never actually seen or heard one play and thought it looked clunky, which she hoped would equate into a larger magnet.

It turned out to be smaller than the one from the vacuum, however the magnets in the speakers were each the size of her palm. She clacked them all together and still didn't think the odd blob of magnets was big enough. Only after she tore apart two televisions and the refrigerator did she feel she had enough.

The clump was the size of a man's fist. Now she just had to get it to spin and this was where the bike came in. Using the socket wrench, she popped off the back tire, whereupon the bike fell right on top of her. Ipes snorted and then noticed he had an extra stripe of grease on him.

Ah, man, he whined.

"Serves you right for laughing!" Jillybean griped as she crawled out from beneath the bike. She gave the mishmash of metal a good long look before she decided she had it all wrong. Grumbling, she reattached the tire and then hoisted it with a spun set of sheets so that the rear tire was off the ground.

Now she needed a clamp to super-glue the magnets to the sprocket, and a coat hanger to form a stiff structure to hold the copper wire snugged in a loop around the magnets. It was very tricky with all the moving parts since none could touch the other.

The easiest part of the entire operation was the copper wiring. A fifty foot extension cord gave her all she needed. Everything else, from the hoisting to the coat hangers was a pain, literally.

She was scratched, bruised and covered in grease and what felt like reptile skin from the super-glue that had somehow got out of control and seemed to be everywhere. Ipes made sure to keep a straight face as she mounted the bike, acting as though it were a skittish bronco that was apt to boot her off if she sneezed.

"Here goes," she whispered and started to pump her legs, going faster and faster, her eyes on the spinning magnets, afraid that something would break and she would either fall or something would jump into the chain and take down the entire contraption—in her mind, when this happened there would be zapping sparks and possibly an explosion.

The magnets didn't spark at all. They just went round and round. Jillybean followed the wire with her eyes as it hooked to the jumper cables...there was smoke at the connection.

"Oh...um, Ipes? Is that normal?"

None of this is normal! Maybe walking isn't such a bad idea. Think of all the fresh air and the exercise you'll get.

As she was already sweating with the work, she didn't think she needed too much more exercise, though the fresh air sounded good just then. The smoke trickled up grey and stinky and the wires had begun to glow from the heat, still, she kept on pumping for all she was worth. The interior engine light had begun to blink on and off!

Ipes cried out: *It's working! Keep going.* Though she wanted to say: *No duh!* she was too winded. She was too tired to even hold her head up. It hung, lolling back and forth, her chin on her chest and the arches of her shoulder blades poking up like the flesh colored stumps of what had once been angel wings.

When she couldn't take it any longer, she leapt off the bike, jumped into the KIA and began pushing down on the wood blocks on the right—five pumps and then she turned the key.

On the first attempt, the engine only said: *row-row-row*. Ipes screamed in excitement. *More gas! Keep going!*

Grimacing, as if turning the key and pushing down with one foot was harder than it looked, she kept going until the engine caught, flooding the garage with a haze of blue smoke.

She had been prepared to zip out of there and so now it was only a matter of disconnecting the cables and raising the garage door before she choked to death on the smoke. For a moment, she glanced down at the mini-generator she had created and considered taking it along with her.

In the end, she took only the magnets and the wire. It had been an amateurish attempt and she was a little embarrassed by it.

Don't be, Ipes told her. As he would get car sick if he couldn't see out, his battle station was sitting on the dash. Briefly, he turned from keeping an eye out for monsters and smiled at Jilly. *Not very many adults could have done that. You should be proud.*

"I just wanted it to be better." In fact, she wanted it to be perfect. Did that make her like the old grandma? Would she die like the old grandma as well? Running with wide eyes and her dentures clacking up and down, her...

Watch the road, Jillybean, and don't think about any grannies. You're going to be fine. Now where is the nearest of your stashes?

The nearest was the grandma house; she didn't go in. The stash was under the porch. She got it and left without looking in any of the windows, suddenly afraid to see a ghostly image of the dead grandma staring out at her with blue eyes...with Jillybean eyes.

Shaking, she left, hurrying with the box of cat food to the still running KIA. She climbed onto her seat, the three couch cushions barely allowing her to see over the steering wheel. The view wasn't good. A few monsters had heard her drive past and were now on the road in front of her, shambling and lurching on rotted limbs. Foolishly, she stared into their faces, looking for the granny.

67

Ipes warned her again to watch the road as her driving "skills" were put to the test. "Sorry, sorry. Look out, please. Get out of the way...ugh!" The KIA a stubby four-door without much in the way of power, swung back and forth all over the road as Jillybean fought to correct her over-steering by using more over-steering, culminating in a shriek of metal as she hopped a curb and broadsided a post office.

Try the middle of the road, Ipes suggested. *If you hit them, you hit them. At least you're not going so fast that they'll explode. It'll be more like bowling for monsters.*

She was afraid to go fast and barely pressed the top block, goosing it every once in a while to keep the KIA moving at just under twenty. She left the monsters behind, at least the ones who lived near the old granny's place. It made her wonder if they were her neighbors and if so, did that make it worse that they probably ate her?

Ipes corrected her once more and she went back to focusing all her attention on driving. By the time she had picked up the last of her stashes, she had gained enough skill to usually keep the KIA in the middle of the road, and most of the time she could dodge a single zombie here and there.

Still the KIA was a gruesome red/black sticky mess with a hunk of scalp stuck under the lip of the hood. The scalp flapped in the wind like a leaf from a maple tree and it was all Jillybean could do not to stare at it and think morbid thoughts.

Was the zombie that went with the waving flap stuck under the car? Or worse, had it somehow crawled up from underneath and was now in the engine compartment, waiting to leap out at her like some sort of horrid jack-in-the-box.

Again Ipes snapped but this time the images hung up in her head and lasted until the sun was half hidden by the endless trees and she finally saw a sign for Fort Leonard Wood.

Six more miles, Ipes said with worry in his voice. *Are you okay? You're not your usual self.*

Did she even know what her usual self really was anymore? How do you lose two months or three months or however long it was and not wonder that your usual self might be crazy? Only she didn't feel crazy, she felt afraid, and for good reason.

There were real monsters outside her window. They had killed the old grandma and a billion others just like her and they would kill Jillybean too. She could see it happening so easily in her mind's eye: Jillybean running, her fly-away brown hair, flaring and streaming behind like a lion's mane that had gone to seed. She could see Jillybean's old Keds and hear them slapping on the pavement, strangely like a palm coming down on a pile of poker chips, and she could hear her breathing get harsher and more ragged and more desperate.

It was the sound of a person who couldn't go on. It sounded like a person about to be eaten, because beneath the ragged breath and the slapping feet was the sound of the monsters moaning. At first it had been a low sound, a background rumble, only gradually it had grown so loud it took over her mind…

Jillybean! Ipes shouted.

She jumped, accidentally spurting the KIA faster as her foot jolted outward in alarm. "What? What is it?" she asked, her breath coming fast and sweat dripping from beneath her hair.

I just wanted to point out that we're here. You made it.

Chapter 9

Jillybean

As Fort Leonard Wood was primarily a training facility for combat engineers, its layout was confusing to the little girl. It seemed as if hundreds of building projects had been begun all at once and not one finished. There were countless open areas where bulldozers and cranes and graders and other monstrous green hunks of machinery just sat lined up in front of fields of sun-blasted dirt.

But there was no other equipment to actually make anything. And there weren't any materials, either. There were no brick or stone or rebar, no bags of cement. Just open fields one after another each lined very neatly with machines to move dirt.

"Weird," she commented as she drove by the last. "I'll never understand the army."

You understand that, don't you? Ipes asked, pointing with a hoof.

Where the forest opened up next was a shooting range. "Of course. Army mens have to practice. That's what means they'll miss if they don't shoot a lot."

And where there's shooting ranges, there's got to be bullets, Ipes said. *Do you see any bunkers?* The afternoon had slipped into a quiet dusk making it especially hard to see the dirt covered mounds that marked where ammo bunkers would be.

"No…maybe we should look in the morning. It's a little freaky out here." She couldn't put her finger on why she was so nervous, but the absolute quiet had her driving faster than was smart. Ipes asked if she would have preferred the moans of a thousand zombies.

"That's a silly question. Of course not. And speaking of which, we're probably making a racket. We should find a place to hide for the night." Ipes raised a fuzzy, black brow at her use of the word "hide" instead of sleep, but he didn't say anything.

She pulled onto a side road where she could see the rusting corrugated roof of a two story warehouse rising just over the trees. To the left, the road opened up on another range where the firing lanes were being overgrown with weeds and shrubs. Jillybean guessed that in another year all of the ranges would be swallowed by the forest, hidden forever. There was already a quiet timelessness to the place as she stopped the car and climbed down from the pillows.

A row of derelict sheds sat lined in front of the crumbling warehouse. Their doors were flung, their walls bent and many had strange holes in them that made it look as though nature had taken her fury out on them. Had all of this destruction happened in the last year? Was that possible?

It almost seemed to Jillybean as if she had stepped out into some distant future and was staring at the relics of a primitive culture.

"Spooky," she said with a little laugh. Ipes only shrugged his droopy shoulders. "Well, it's spooky to me."

I don't see why. I can't hear any zombies and I don't think anyone would live in there. I bet there aren't even any rats in there.

She didn't have much of a choice of accommodations and so she tip-toed towards the front doors of the warehouse, angling slightly to her right so that she didn't come on them from straight on where she could be seen.

No, it was best to move in the shadows. It was best to be Jilly-mouse and scamper and flit from cover to cover. She edged to the building, and slid along it, ready to bolt at the first sound. Only there was no sound from anywhere around her, except a hidden metallic creak that came whenever the light wind managed to slip down between the trees.

When it did, she froze, clutching Ipes in a death grip. *Hey, chill, Jill. You're bending my mane. Jeez, you've given me a comb-over.*

She didn't apologize. That would make too much noise. Trying to "chill" she took a breath before easing to the door and poking just enough of her head around the corner so that she could spy inside with one blue eye.

What she saw didn't ease her fear. The inside of the warehouse was gloomy: shadows casting shadows. It was so dark that it was hard to tell what was what. Slowly her eyes adjusted and she saw gouged and pitted workbenches, and dusty green machines with knobs and chains and cutting blades. There were big bins that had been knocked on their sides. They looked like faceless mouths that had just retched up spews of metal.

The floor had a fine litter of metal across it. Mostly nuts and bolts of all sizes, but there were also hundreds of odd scraps that looked terribly sharp.

"I'll think I'll sleep in the car," she said.

Wait, Ipes said as she started tip-toeing back towards the KIA. *Hold on now. Won't it be cold? And...and it won't be all that safe. Those KIA people didn't spend a lot on the windows. They're pretty thin. Any ol' monster could come by and punch them in.*

"Lucky for us there ain't any monsters around here."

Ipes corrected her grammar, but she wasn't listening. There weren't many monsters and for some reason, that bothered her as well. Everything seemed to bother her. Her nerves were on edge and she didn't know why.

That night, after a dismal meal of cat food and beans, she slept in the car. The wind picked up just before two and she huddled in a shivering ball as it howled. The storm brought with it an early snow that was mostly cold mush that made driving the next day annoying.

The KIA refused to stay to the center of the road, though it didn't help that she over steered a few times and spun in big out of control circles. It wasn't until Ipes said, in her daddy's voice: *Steer into the skid*, that things became manageable.

The first part of the day she spent heading south, which was pretty much the opposite direction of the rest of the base. And yet, the trip bore unexpected fruits. Because it just seemed to meander through the forest, uselessly, almost no one had gone south on that road and there were a number of unplundered properties with overgrown driveways that could only be seen by an alert person going slowly along.

Jillybean was barely making steerage in the KIA. A fine dusting of snow sifted down from clouds that seemed so close she thought she could reach out and stir them with a rake. The snow and the heavy clouds made her nervous again and so she putt-putted along and was moving slow enough that she noticed a gap in the trees that could only have been man made.

By then, the gas gauge was far into the red and so she went down the drive to the house, praying for a miracle consisting of cookies and gas, with Ipes fervently praying for the former. He was so loud in her head that she had to hush him—although the noise in her head was loud, all around her the world hung in an eerie snow-muffled silence.

Again, she found herself sneaking up on what looked to be an ordinary two-story red brick home.

Jillybean rattled the knob on the front door and found it locked. "Strange," she whispered, moving around to the backyard where a snow covered swing set sat across from an above ground pool which was empty, save for a collection of moldy leaves.

She found the sliding kitchen door locked as well, *and* the side garage door. Stepping back, she looked up at the house and really didn't know what to make of the home. She couldn't remember the last time she had found a house that hadn't been touched by zombies or man.

A sudden thought came to her: *Maybe the people who used to live here still do!* Quick as any cat, she slunk down below the level of the windows, her heart going like crazy and her mind going even crazier: *What if the people who lived here were weirdos? But, what if they were normal? What if they were nice? What if they liked her and what if she liked them?*

"I don't know," she said in a shaky whisper. *What would she do if they invited her to live with them? Would she actually stay and forget Sadie and Captain Grey and Neil?* "Maybe...they don't know about all the stuff I did...and I wouldn't have to tell, neither. They could like me if they didn't know. And don't people who have kids like kids?"

She waited on an answer from Ipes, but he was just sitting in the crook of her arm staring at the brick as snowflakes came to land on it for just a half second before disappearing, leaving behind tiny wet marks as though, when they left, they forgot their shadows.

Would the people in the house understand about Ipes?

"No," she said, her excitement draining away. No one understood about Ipes. "Well, Sadie does. She knew I had to find you and she didn't even try to stop me. *She* knew you're important."

I always liked her, Ipes said, coming awake. *You know, there isn't anyone home in there, right? You would have felt it or sensed it. The pool would've been cleaned out and the grass hasn't been cut all summer.*

"I guess I was thinkfully wishing. It would be pretty cool to find kids, you know? I wish I hadn't let those other ones go." She shivered, not from the cold but at the memory of where she had found the kids and how she had rescued them from what was, in essence, the torture chamber of a witch. The shiver went deep into her core.

It was a moment before the little girl got over it. "That's…
that's all in the past. They're probably in Estes by now. Like I
should be."

She knew she had to break into the house, but a part of her
wanted to leave it alone. In a way, it was perfect in that it hadn't
been desecrated. If the family was still out there, what would
they think when they came back to find the doors smashed in?

"They wouldn't be happy," she said, feeling unhappy for
them, because in her heart she knew they were dead. Most
everyone was.

Stepping around some prickly bushes below a deep bay
window, she stood on the tips of her Keds and stared inside.

The house was perfect or as close as any house came
anymore. She could see part of the kitchen where a few
cupboards were flung open as if the owners had left in a hurry.
Other than that, there wasn't anything out of place, but not in the
stringently neat way the old grandma's home had been.

This house had proper messes: a school bag sat on the
kitchen table, some papers, crooked and uneven, spilled half out
of it. Next to it was a text book, which for some reason got her
excited. In the sink was a small pile of dishes and in the doorway
of the kitchen was a sock. It was a clean sock, Jillybean could
tell by how flat it was.

"Probably fell out of a laundry basket."

Or a suitcase.

"Yeah." Had it fallen out of a suitcase that had been
hurriedly packed by a frightened child? Likely. Jillybean
remembered how it had been back at the beginning of the
apocalypse when no one knew what was happening: the over-
riding and constant fear, the suitcases packed and repacked, the
complete uncertainty that made every minute of every day
nerve-wracking.

"We should go in, shouldn't we?" She didn't need the
zebra's answer, she knew the truth—she was in a desperate
position and the people who had lived there were dead. "They
would understand, if they were alive," she told herself.

A minute later, she broke a basement window, kicking it in
as gently as she could, trying not to disturb the beauty of the
house. Inside it was agreeably warm and, yes, just as homey as
she thought it would be. She came slowly out of the basement
but didn't rush for the kitchen cabinets where she had spied a

few cans and nor did she hurry to the garage where there was possibly a second car filled with gas.

Instead, she walked all around the home and, with the snow falling, the place was well lit with ambient light, probably looking as it had back in the Before. It was fantastic, but not perfect.

Year-old fear sat heavy on the air. Little touches, such as the sock spoiled it. Not knowing why, but only knowing that she needed to, she fixed the house. She shut the cabinet doors and picked up the sock. In the master bedroom, she shut the empty drawers of a dresser and in the bathroom she put away the few remaining pieces of makeup that had been scattered about.

Gradually, as she tidied up, the fear in the air dissipated, being replaced with a feeling of anticipation. Once again it was a home waiting for its people to come back from wherever they had gone: the movies or church or a long camping trip.

Grinning now, Jillybean went back to the kitchen, equally excited about what lay in the cupboards as she was about the text book. There had been a piece of paper sitting squarely on top of it and she hadn't seen what it was.

Pulling the piece of paper away, Jillybean's face drooped, unhappily. It was a language arts book. Back in the Before, it had been her favorite subject—now it seemed superfluous. People could speak and write and read enough to get by, but no one cared anymore where commas were supposed to go or what a gerund was.

Jillybean certainly didn't. What interested her now was how a water pump worked and how to make a homemade bomb using fertilizer, racing fuel and a blasting cap, or how to weld.

With a sigh, she put the piece of paper back exactly where she had found it. As she lined up the edges, she saw the handwriting; it wasn't a child's as she had expected. It was from a woman…the "mom" no doubt.

Dear Jack,

We're going to my mom's place. I'm sorry, but we waited as long as we could, but the girls are getting scared, and so am I. The army isn't telling us where you are or what's happening at all. This is the third time I've written this letter. I don't want to leave, but we can hear the guns now and I don't want to wait until the last minute. That'll be worse.

If the army lets you go, get up to Scottsbluff as fast as you can.

75

I love you, Jack, always,
Lauren

"Jack and Lauren. They sound nice." Jillybean flipped open the language arts book and found a real piece of homework with the name Tristyn written across the top. "I know where Scottsbluff is. It's in Nebraska. Remember the sign? It's practically on our way to Colorado. We could go see if Jack just went straight there. Maybe we can play with Tristyn. Do you think that's a boy or a girl? I bet it's a girl, cuz of the letter. Well, I hope it's a girl, like me."

Only there weren't any girls like her and Jillybean knew it. She was a seven-year-old mass-murderer…a one of a kind.

"We can still go," she mumbled.

Ipes swiveled his head up to stare hard into Jillybean's face. *Why? You already have a family who loves you.*

"Never mind," she answered, putting the homework back where she had found it. Ipes tried to question her some more, but she ignored him, busying herself with climbing the kitchen counters and emptying the shelves of what remained.

Lauren had only done an adequate job of packing for her trip to Scottsbluff. All of the "real" food was gone, but there was plenty left over that fell into the edible category that wasn't quite food: apple vinegar, a gallon of vegetable oil, a two-pound bag of sugar and a five-pound bag of flour, a tin of cocoa powder, tea, coffee, salt, etc.

It was all quite valuable. *And tasty*, Ipes said squirming, eagerly in her arms. *If I'm not mistaken, flour, sugar and cocoa can be ginned together to make some sort of cookie conglomeration.*

"Not yet. We can't just start baking. We got to load up the car and finish exploring. Besides there aren't any chocolate chips. What good are cookies without chocolate chips?"

This quieted him enough for her to finish emptying the shelves. Next, she went to the garage and was disappointed not to find a car there. There was a riding mower and a red jug that netted her three gallons of gas.

It wasn't quite a miracle, but it was a relief. Three gallons would get her ninety miles further west. The garage also had a number of items, very few of which Jillybean really needed: hand tools and camping supplies, bikes and bottles of alcohol.

Turning her nose up at it all, she went back inside looking for Tristyn's room. She was a girl and a girly girl at that. Everything was pink and wonderful. Tristyn was a year younger than Jillybean and yet they wore the same sized clothes. It was a relief to get out of the "boy" clothes she had been wearing.

Jillybean first tried on a green and white dress, just for fun. *We have time for dresses but not for cookies?* Ipes asked, outrage making his voice squeak.

"This is different," Jillybean said, without explaining how. Any argument went right out of her head when she saw the shoes in Tristyn's closet. One pair especially jumped out at her. They were made of a clear rubber and, sitting there in the closet, they didn't seem like much. Once they were on her feet, however, they came alive.

Whenever she stepped, the shoes lit up in a variety of colors, each flashing for a brief moment, almost as if there were a circus attached to her feet.

Jillybean stared down at her feet as she paced around the room, mesmerized by the lights. She went around the bed for a few minutes until Ipes rolled his beady eyes and sighed: *You know you can't ever wear those outside this room.*

This deflated her and she went back to the closet one more time to look at herself as she was possibly supposed to be. It was a perfect picture, except for her hair. It had grown past fly-away and was now long and full of waves that coursed down her back almost to her non-existent hips.

The dress came off and was hung back up in the closet. The shoes were harder to part with. Jillybean was only seven. Those shoes would have been perfect for her budding expression of individualism.

In the end, she let them go and put back on her Keds that fit her little feet perfectly. A pair of girl blue jeans went over these and then a warm sweater with a big-eyed anime character decorating the front went on her skinny torso. Above all of this she tugged back on her monster-wear so she could blend in an instant.

Reluctantly, she loaded the car and said goodbye to the house, secretly vowing to go to Scottsbluff if she ever had the chance. She would go as the bearer of bad news: Jack had never come back—Lauren's husband and Tristyn's daddy was likely dead.

Jillybean followed the road south, still heading the wrong way and still not realizing it. She also failed to realize that the KIA was leaving tracks in the light snow that any idiot could follow.

She passed a number of homes that could be seen from the road and after stopping at the first three and finding them disappointingly torn apart, she ignored the next few. It wasn't until she saw another break in the trees that couldn't be explained in any natural way that she stopped.

Down a forty-yard drive she found another pristine house. This time she didn't pause for emotion or wishful thinking. Those things only hurt. Once more, she went in through a basement window, but only because they were easier to reach.

This house had the car in the garage that she was looking for and it, too, had cupboards that hadn't been picked over properly. The Kia was, for the first time in a year, topped off, while it's cramped interior practically overflowed and that was okay. In fact, it was more than okay.

If she could find another few houses like this one, she would have enough in the way of supplies to see her all the way through to Colorado.

The idea so contented her that she gave in to Ipes' pleading and made cookies, adding ingredient after ingredient to the batter in the vain hope of striking on something close to her mother's recipe. The cookies were desperately missing eggs, and more importantly, a properly functioning oven.

She only had cord wood and a jury-rigged stove. She pulled out the lower drawer and used the ten-inch space for her heating element, shoving the smaller pieces of wood in. Smoke billowed up the sides of the oven and it wasn't long before the kitchen became blistering hot. She opened every window to keep from passing out and, red-faced, she tended the cookies, flipping them over and over again so they wouldn't char.

As they baked, she saw many errors in this first attempt and knew that the next time they would turn out far better. Still, the cookies weren't bad, especially compared to another meal of cat food or liver. The chocolate-sugar cookies were smoky and a little stiff, like cool taffy, and yet they were the tastiest things she had eaten in months.

Her and Ipes scarfed down an entire plate. Before she knew it, there were only crumbs left which she caught up with her tongue. Groaning with a bursting tummy, she sat back in her nest, staring at the hazy ceiling.

As the fire slowly ate itself into nothing, she worked her tongue around the inside of her mouth, capturing the very last of the flavor, and yawning every thirty seconds or so.

Eventually, she fell asleep, her mouth hanging open, Ipes tumbled away, dangerously close to the oven and the sparks that snapped every few seconds. For an hour she lay there, sweat building across her brow dreaming in short bursts about a big man named Ram, a white dress and a doll house that gradually grew bigger than the world, and during that time the fragrant smoke puffing up from beneath the oven grew thin and grey.

And yet it still hung over the house, and the neighborhood and half the countryside around it. The nearby monsters, as always, grew confused at the sweet, and now nearly alien aroma of cookies. The humans nearby were not. They were drawn to it.

The sound of trucks in the driveway woke Jillybean. She sat up, just as confused as any of the brain-dead monsters wandering around in the snow. As her eyes blinked at the last of the smoke, and she stretched in a long and back-cracking yawn, her heat-dulled mind tried to work out where she was and why she was suddenly filled with dread.

It was then that she heard the sound of footsteps crunching in the snow. They were slow steps, stealthy steps…evil steps. The sound came to her from both the front of the house and the side, and she knew right away that people were coming for her. They were coming to get her and do who knew what with her.

Chapter 10

Sadie Walcott

She hit the peak of the hill, expecting to see a down slope similar to the one she had just climbed. Instead, she found herself looking nearly straight down at the river, three hundred feet below.

"Holy shit," she whispered. It wasn't a straight shot down the side of a smooth-faced cliff, but it was close, at least it looked that way to Sadie, who had no choice but to take this frightful route. Behind her, the moans of the zombies drew closer.

Down she went, moving like an inverted spider: head back, butt scraping against the rocks, hands and feet out, grasping at every tenuous hold as gravity pulled her on. She wasn't exactly "climbing" down.

What she was doing was delaying the moment that she would fall, bouncing off of one outcropping of rock after another, tumbling and spinning out of control until she either hit the road with a bone-crushing thud, or the river with its two feet of icy water covering a stone bed.

She felt hitting the road would be a cleaner death…or rather, a quicker death. "Not that I want either. Come on, Sadie, you can do this." She needed the pep talk. The "gentle" slope of rock had given way to a vertical plunge and now she had to flip over and climb for real.

What gave her hope was that the cliff was made from stratified rock. Over millions of years, one layer of sediment built on another and with each layer there were minor ledges and dusty handholds. "It's just a ladder," she told herself. She wished she could tell herself not to look down, but that was the only way she could plan where to put her foot or hand next.

Looking down was dizzying and terrifying, and necessary, but so was looking up.

Sadie had just taken her eighth step down when pebbles started cascading around her. She looked up, just in time to see a huge grey figure sliding down the rocks right at her. There was no time for curses or screams, there was only time to lunge to her left, grasping desperately for a new hold as the beast came so close that it thudded heavily against her shoulder.

The blow sent her just a hair too far and the ledge she was aiming for slipped past her fingers. She made a wild grab at a second one, only the shelf of rock was strewn with fine sand and she lost her grip. Now, a scream built up as, along with a rain of pebbles, she slid down the front of the cliff face.

The scream became a heavy grunt as her feet hit a ledge and her right hand found a nodule of granite, a stout knob that could hold ten times her weight. She breathed a sigh of relief just as a second zombie tumbled past not two feet away.

She snapped her head up as three more came flying down the cliff. Two passed safely to her left, but the third came right at her. Trusting the granite nub, she swung out, holding on with just the one hand. The zombie passed so close she could see her reflection in its greasy black eye.

Then she swung back, her feet finding the ledge. For the next few minutes, it rained zombies and sometimes parts of zombies: teeth, fingers, scalps and a few times, even heads. She did what she could to dodge them, but even with the little knob giving her some room to maneuver, she knew she wouldn't be able to last. It would be just a matter of time before two came down close enough together and knocked her off her perch.

Her one chance at even temporary safety was to get beneath one of the larger ledges and hope that it would be enough of an umbrella. The closest one sat twenty-three feet to her left and eight feet down. With no time to plan, she began shuffling along the rock layer, the heels of her Converse hanging far off the edge, her calves beginning to sing with pain.

As she went, zombies continued to come up to the edge of the ridge and either fall off on their own or get pushed from behind. There were so many now that they fell continuously and Sadie was forced to climb faster and faster, her feet breaking off parts of the ledge as she went.

Halfway to the overhang, the ledge gave way completely. Somehow she kept her wits about her and refused to panic. She slid down the jagged cliff, her feet pointed in opposite directions, her hands held out like claws. She slid seventeen feet before she hit another little ledge that stopped her.

More than anything she wanted to hug the wall and catch her breath, but there was no time. The zombies were still falling all around her. She made the mistake of looking up just as one toppled directly overhead. It bounced off rock after rock, hitting one just above her and cartwheeling right over her.

It was so close she could have kissed it. The near miss caused her heart to race and her muscles to spasm. Panic was close to setting in. Whimpering and dripping tears on the rock, she was somehow able to get her feet moving.

Only when she was "safe" beneath the overhang did she let herself cry. Safe really wasn't a word that could describe her predicament; she was two hundred feet from safety, clinging to the side of a cliff and the rest of the climb wasn't going to be exactly easy.

"At least the zombies can't get me," she said, gingerly taking one hand from the wall and wiping away her tears. That bit of knowledge buoyed her and after a thirty second rest, she began to climb down again.

After so many near misses, going the rest of the way down seemed anticlimactic. Rocks continued to break under her weight and she slipped plenty of times as her hands grew tired and numb from the constant pressure, but she always managed to catch herself, and as long as she kept beneath the overhang, the falling zombies weren't a problem.

By the time she finally reached the road, there were grotesque piles of corpses ranging along the bottom of the cliff. The piles undulated and squiggled in a manner that had Sadie turning away. Sucking her aching fingers, she walked to the middle of the road, looking as far down it as she could see.

The Dodge truck was nowhere in sight. "What the hell?" She spun, looking back the other way, but all she saw was the bend in the river two hundred yards away—no truck anywhere.

"If they are messing with me, I'll…" Sadie didn't know what she would do, mainly because she was suddenly too afraid to think straight. Captain Grey wasn't one to play pranks while on a dangerous mission.

Her fear took charge and she ran the two hundred yards in twenty-three seconds. Not her best time, but not her worst, either. Gusting loudly, she pulled up to the mega-boulder that sat across the road and felt relief—they hadn't been able to get by, of course.

"All that was for nothing then? I nearly died and we…" She stopped abruptly. They weren't on the other side of the boulder, either. "Captain Grey?" she called as loud as she dared, going completely around the giant boulder. On the far side, she spotted the Dodge in the river and reached maximum confusion.

No one was in the truck. No one was up on the rocks on the other side of the river. No one was lurking in the bushes near the bend. She was alone except for a huge pile of zombies, most of which were actually dead. Still she slunk back into the shadows of the boulder waiting for something, anything to happen.

Nothing did. "What the hell?" she repeated, after ten minutes went by and Grey and his team hadn't returned. Their disappearance had a UFO quality about it that made hiding seem like the only smart thing to do. But she couldn't hide all day.

Her one obvious clue sat in the river, its upgraded tires not quite covered by the rushing water. With one last look around, Sadie eased into the icy water. "Jeez! Oh, God! Shit, shit, shiiiit." She cursed between teeth clenched so hard she thought she might crack a tooth.

The mountain rivers were always cold, but it was now November and the edge of the river had its first planes of ice beginning to extend outward. The cold stung, but didn't turn her numb as fast as she wished. Her legs were still in agony by the time she reached the truck.

What she saw inside the bed caused her to forget about the pain. Almost all of their gear was missing. Gone was the food and the extra ammo and the jerrycans full of diesel. The only thing left were their backpacks and these had been rifled through and were scattered about in a most unmilitary fashion.

Slogging to the cab, she climbed up where it was warm and again messy…Sadie suddenly saw what else was missing: "My gun, oh, damn it!" All the guns were gone.

"Slavers," she whispered. Glancing over at the boulder, she saw how the ambush must have played out: the slavers hiding, the soldiers probably more worried about her than keeping an eye on things. One or two get out to check to see if they can get past the boulder and then, out come the bad guys, shouting orders, guns aimed with dreadful accuracy.

Sadie sat back in the driver's seat, her raw and aching fingers drumming on the steering wheel as she thought over her options. They were very few. Run back to Estes and tell Neil, which would give the slavers an eight to ten-hour head start. Or go after them herself.

How long was their lead? An hour? Could she make up an hour before sundown?

"Do I have to?" She leaned far over and opened the glove compartment. A map jumped out at her as if it was spring loaded. She began tracing the road system finding the scraggily little one they had been traveling on. She saw that it intersected Route 14 only a few miles ahead, where there was a tiny hamlet of a town labeled Poudre Park.

If the slavers rushed it, they could make it to Poudre Park by sunset and they likely wouldn't press on from there, not at night. It was too dangerous to travel at night.

"Just not too dangerous for me," Sadie whispered as she reached under the wheel, hoping, but not expecting to find the keys jingling in the ignition. Her fingers found them. "Interesting. You leave a perfectly good truck just sitting here with a quarter tank of gas in it? I don't get it."

She didn't pause to try to figure out what that meant. She put the truck in 4-wheel low and coaxed it back to the road. And then she was off, speeding to catch the slavers before the night came. Driving at night frightened her. Not only would the zombies key right in on her lights and the sound of the engine, the slavers would too.

"It is what it is." The only chance she had was to drive like a mad woman. "Or a professional." Only she wasn't a professional and the truck wasn't a performance vehicle. Twice, she nearly careened back into the river and three times she scraped up against the side of a mountain, making an enormous screech that sent shivers down her back.

Still she barreled along, the diesel engine so loud that it rattled the last golden leaves off a stand of aspen. As she drove, she wondered what she would do when she found the slavers. She didn't have a weapon or Jillybean's smarts, or her penchant for destruction. "But I am pretty slick. It'll be dark and they won't know I'm coming."

Her plan was founded on the hope that the slavers were the usual lazy sorts and that they would hole up in a house or business and trust that the lock on the front door would be enough to keep them safe. In her mind, they wouldn't post guards and they wouldn't bother unloading their trucks.

There would be plenty of guns and ammo sitting out, ripe for the taking. "And if I can get the drop on one of them, that'll be all she wrote."

Sadie liked to focus on the positive even when it flew in the face of reality, mainly, because in her view, reality "sucks."

Her reality was that the zombie menace kicked up the closer she got to Poudre Park. And worse, she lost her race with the sun. The mountain canyons went from a dim dusk to a full-on dark in what felt like no time. And even worse than that, the Dodge ran out of diesel a mile and a half away from the town.

If she couldn't find and overcome the slavers, there was a good chance that she would be walking back to Estes Park. It would be three days of starving, running endlessly from zombies, and praying fervently that a snow storm wouldn't sweep down on her. Without shelter from the storm, she would freeze to death without question.

"But that's not going to happen," she whispered as she climbed out of the now silent truck, listening to the last echoes of the engine fading away. When the echoes had rolled down the canyon, never to return, Sadie was left with only the sound of the river, the rush of wind among the peaks above, and the moan of the zombies coming closer.

In the dark, zombies weren't much of a threat to Sadie. There wasn't a need for zombie make-up or clothes. She just had to act like a zombie to blend in.

"Uuuuhhh," she moaned and began limping diagonally away from the truck. As usual, Sadie over-played her role as a zombie, which caused a few of the beasts to stray closer. Her heartbeat revved, and her feet wanted to kick it out of there, but she forced herself to ignore them and keep going.

A mile and a half wasn't a long way, unless one was moving at the languid pace of the undead. Sadie had time to kill, however she wanted to get to Poudre Park as quickly as possible, and not just to find the slavers. With the sun set, the temperature dropped alarmingly.

Her toes were little frozen carrots in her canvas Converse sneakers, her chest rattled and shivered, protected only by a thin, black jacket, and her fingers were icicles—zombies did not put their hands in their pockets. Zombies rarely had pockets. More and more they wore rags or nothing.

There was nothing worse than the naked dead.

Slowly, without even knowing it, Sadie picked up the pace, while behind her, the dozens of zombies she had passed, trailed after her, drawn on for reasons that were as inexplicable as they were unfortunate. Sadie would have enough trouble dealing with the slavers without the zombies hanging around.

Deciding that she would have to chance breaking character, she waited until she got to the next bend in the road, and when she was out of sight of the zombies, she took off in a sprint. In the eleven seconds it took for the first of the zombies to reach the bend, Sadie was a hundred yards away and invisible in the gloom.

It felt good to run. It felt good to build up enough heat to cause a trickle of sweat to slip down the back of her shirt. But it would not be good to show up in Poudre Park winded and tired. She cut back to a slow jog, letting her senses speak to her.

The smell of smoke grew as she moved down the two-lane strip of black top. Undoubtedly it was the slavers thinking they were safe and sound. Sadie followed her nose, moving quieter now, keeping to the darker shadows.

She looked nothing like a zombie. She looked exactly like what she was: a teenage girl sneaking up on a slaver camp. The smell of smoke brought her to the edge of town and led down a road that was little more than a long scratch of dirt that sat nestled in a gulch. With the walls of the gulch so sharp, there was little cover besides the sparse trees and the few ragged-out cars parked along the side of the road.

The smell grew stronger as she progressed until she finally saw the grey smoke puffing up out of a run-down little ranch. There were two black trucks parked out front, both with trailers hitched behind. One of the trailers was completely full with a bulging tarp strapped over it, while the other still had a little room, but not much.

So far, it had been a successful trip for the slavers, "But not anymore," Sadie said under her breath as she eased forward. She went to the less full truck, guessing that the supplies that had been stolen last would be in it.

It was so dark beneath the tarp that nothing could be seen and she was forced to dig out her trusty lighter, though she paused before clicking it on. *What if the light from it was seen?* She eased up, looking over the trailer towards the ranch house. It was quiet and the curtains were drawn. Whoever was in there had gone to great effort to remain hidden.

And if I can't see them, it follows that they can't see me, Sadie thought, using standard but faulty kid logic. She ducked back down and clicked on her lighter. It was bright, startlingly bright it turned out.

Though she was expecting the little flame, the man sitting quietly in the bed of the second truck did not. To Sadie, it looked as though a bag of laundry burst into life as the man leapt up.

He was tall, made even taller by the height of the truck. He had on camouflage, but what Sadie had mistaken for laundry was a heavy green blanket. In his hand was an M4.

"We been expecting you, but boy-howdy you snuck up quiet."

Sadie was caught and could do nothing except raise her hands.

Chapter 11

Jillybean

The slyness of the steps in the snow immediately shocked Jillybean into full consciousness. Ice cold logic suggested if the people outside were friendly, they would've knocked on the front door. That meant they were evil and, by the sounds of it, they were coming for her, looking to trap her.

There was still time to get away. If she hurried, she could run out the back door, but…but then where would she go? To the last house? To one of the pillaged houses she had passed on the way?

The snow was still falling as was the temperature. If she ran, she wouldn't be able to take anything except her backpack, which held only a day's worth of food and a single water bottle. If she ran, she would be back to where she started from: empty-handed and lost in the middle of Missouri.

And that's if she could get away. A sprint outside wouldn't guarantee freedom since she would leave prints in the snow that anyone could follow. Then again, she couldn't *not* leave, either. If she jumped into the open cupboard and closed it behind her, the people who were after her, and she could picture their dirty, hairy faces perfectly in her mind's eye, would know she hadn't left and all it would take was a thorough search in order to find her.

So, you have to leave and not leave? Ipes asked. How?

"Easy." There was no time to explain. Sliding across the floor, she stuffed her pack and Ipes into the cupboard closest to the oven—it was always the "frying pan" cupboard and the last one searched—and then shut the door almost all the way. Then she rushed down the hall to the garage and waited with her ears cocked and her breath blowing out of her in plumes.

When the front door was smashed in, she made her move, stepping out into the snow, her old Keds leaving size 10 prints in the snow. Thirty feet to her left was the sliding glass kitchen door—a man was already slipping through the heavy curtain of blankets that she had hung over it to keep in the light from her fire.

Jillybean charged across the backyard towards him, slowing only when she came parallel to the sliding door. She had to pass by making as little noise as possible while stepping in fresh snow. Her feet crunched with every step as she made her way around the side of the house. Only then did she step into the footprints that were already there.

They had been made by a booted man with feet that were longer than her forearm. Purposely, she let her feet make marks in the first few prints—and then she turned around and made her way back the way she had come, careful only to step in the man's footprints. She followed them to the kitchen where she paused just inside the blankets, listening to the sound of boots scuffing and thudding through the house.

"Little girl?" a man's voice called out. The cold was suddenly forgotten and yet, she was frozen in place. How had he known she was a girl? Her pack was hidden and even if it hadn't been, there wasn't anything in it that suggested she was a girl. She didn't even carry a hair brush.

"Where are you, little girl?" The steps moved away and the voice was slightly muffled. "Come out, come out wherever you are," he sang. "Olly, Olly in come fr…"

A new voice hissed: "She went out through the garage!"

She couldn't stay where she was even if it meant running into one of the men who were suddenly racing through the house. Jillybean dodged inside while at that instant one of the men stepped out into the snow from the garage. In one hand he carried a heavy, black pistol and in the other a flashlight. For the moment, the light was down on her tracks.

He didn't see her or the flick of the blankets as she stepped through into the kitchen. The dark house seemed filled with noise: more boots stomping, a crash of furniture, a curse, and someone yelling: "You go out through the front, I'll go through the kitchen."

Jillybean didn't have time to get into her cupboard. She ran on tip toes to the edge of the refrigerator and pressed up against it just as a great beast of a man stormed in from the dining room. In the dim light, she saw a quick flash of his eyes as he gave the room a glance.

Then he was through the blankets, tearing them down in his haste. From the side of the house she heard a man call out: "She went to the front! She went to the front!"

That was Jillybean's cue to get out of sight. She ducked into the cupboard and shut the door completely. There was nothing she could do now except to hug Ipes to her and hope. The men ran around for a few minutes and then came back into the house, cursing.

"She didn't disappear, Dave. Stop being a dick. Her tracks went right to the front. I saw them plain as day."

"Maybe they were old tracks, like from earlier," another suggested.

"No, they were fresh. You saw that one. It had those little waffle prints in it. No, she's around here somewhere. I say we wait. She'll have to come back or she'll freeze."

This was agreed to, and as the men waited, they poked around the house, paying particular attention to the kitchen. The fridge was opened, eliciting a volley of curses from all three. Next, the cupboards were opened one after another.

Jillybean could see the light from the flashlights through the door's cracks. They were right on top of her and she was so afraid that she was close to peeing herself.

If they catch you, let them do whatever they want, Ipes said. *Just close your eyes and don't say a word. You saw how it was on that bus with the Azael. The more the women fought, the longer it went on.*

She remembered everything.

A shudder ran through her entire body, it coursed through her and all she could do to keep from making any noise was to hug herself and grit her teeth to keep from whimpering as the door to the cupboard she was hiding in opened.

It opened four inches when a voice from right above her said: "You know what you should do, Perry? You should go out to the road and look for prints up there. It's the only thing that makes sense. That's probably where I would go if I was her."

The door creaked open an inch wider and Jillybean could see Perry's dirty fingers and hairy knuckles. She could see the lower part of a man's pants; they were wet with melting snow. For a moment, a beam of light swept right across her and then it shot upwards.

"If it's such a good idea, why don't you go out to the road yourself, Dave? You're always making these suggestions but you never…"

"I think you both should go," a third voice said. "Check the tire tracks. If she's smart, she'll have walked in them." This third person was clearly in charge and clearly angry at having not caught Jillybean right away. His frustration was so apparent that the other two didn't dare backtalk him. They left, grumbling at each other.

This left Jillybean alone with the most villainous of the three and she waited in trembling fear for the door of the cupboard to finish opening and for her to be found. Would he be mad? Would he beat her before doing those horrible things to her?

Just close your eyes and don't think about it, Ipes suggested. *Try to relax.*

She closed her eyes and a bloody, violent picture assaulted her: there were bodies around her, dead men without faces. There was blood up to her ankles and a heavy axe in her hands —it was red and slippery. She was covered in the blood, right up to her eyeballs.

She clicked her eyes open, on the verge of screaming, only her breath was caught up in her throat. Where had the image come from? She never thought like that so that meant it had to have come from...

I think you're safe, Ipes said, and somehow his voice was easy and relaxed.

This was even more confusing to Jillybean until she realized the man was walking away from the partially open cupboard door. He went to the kitchen table, pulled out a chair and groaned his weight down on it.

See? They'll give up soon and leave and you'll be okay. Only, she wouldn't be. She would be stuck without supplies and without gas or a working car. She'd be stuck and yet she wouldn't be able to stay in the snug house. If the bad guys came back, her luck would run out and she would be caught.

No, she couldn't stay in the house, or any of the houses nearby and so she'd have to move...she'd have to walk in the snow, which was exhausting. How far could she honestly get before sunrise? Two miles? Maybe three? And how far could she get if the snow came down any harder?

Not nearly far enough, she thought. *So, what do I do?* The bloody image came to her a second time, just a flash, but enough for her to catch her breath. Had she been alone, she would have cried out: *Who's doing that?* and, horribly enough, probably would have received an answer.

Now, there was only silence in her head. Not even Ipes spoke. It was just her, alone with a slaver...or worse. There were scarier people in the world than run of the mill slavers.

As the two of them waited, he played with a revolver, spinning the cylinder round and round with a constant clicking sound. It was the sound of death, and yet she found it soothing—anything was better than the nothing going on in her head. She was more afraid to explore that "nothing" than she was of the man with a gun.

Eventually Dave and Perry came back, stamping their feet, leaving splotches of wet mush everywhere. "She's not out there," Dave said, going to sit down at the table. Jillybean could see his legs stretching out as if he was relaxing at his own table.

"Trust me, she's out there," the leader said. "She's out there freezing her ass off, but she won't come back in as long as we're here."

"So, we leave and slip back?" Perry asked.

The leader grunted: "Maybe…or two of us leave and the third hides inside. With the snow coming down so hard, I doubt she's close enough to see who's in what car."

"So, who'll stay?" Dave asked, trying to sound as if it was an innocent question.

"Not you," the leader snapped. "I'll stay. Perry take the KIA. Dave take the truck. Drop the car back off at the camp and then come and get me in two hours."

"Two hours?" Dave asked. "I doubt you need two hours. She'll be back in fifteen minutes at the longest. We should…" The sound of the hammer on a pistol being drawn back stopped him in mid-sentence.

"You're going to do what I tell you to do. You don't know when she'll be back. She could be hiding in one of the other houses on the road, nice and warm. Hell, she might be there all night for all we know. I know I wouldn't come back any time soon."

Dave grumbled something Jillybean couldn't hear and the leader laughed: "What I do with her is my business. I'll radio when I'm ready to be picked up, but I wouldn't expect it to be before ten."

Jillybean listened with a sinking heart as her KIA was driven off. It had been the key to her future. Without it she was dead, or the next worst thing. Without it she would have to slog through the snow to the next town, which was a place called Lebanon. There were twenty-two miles of forest and iced-over scrub between her and the town. If she didn't get lost, or killed out in the wilderness by monsters, or abducted by roving bands of slavers, she could look forward to three long days of walking during which she could freeze or starve.

Her toes would get frostbitten and maybe her face as well. And, once she got to Lebanon, she would have to search the ruins of the town, dodging monsters and hiding from slavers to scrape together anything close to the treasure trove that was being driven away.

It was annoying to think about and irritating and... maddening. For the first time since she could remember, Jillybean was angry right down to her wet Keds. In fact, she was furious.

But what can you do? Ipes asked. *They are grown-ups and they have guns. You...you don't have anything and you're small and tiny and weak.*

He was right. She was all of that, and worse, she was just a girl. She pictured what she would do if she were a boy with muscles. The images were unpleasant.

"No," she whispered. "I'd rather be a girl. I'd rather do things my way." Now, she imagined what that would look like. It would start with patience. It would start with her settling in and outlasting the grown-up. He would break first. He would either fall asleep or have to use the bathroom, or just grow agitated and pace. When he did, she would pounce. She would slip out of the cupboard, grab the revolver and then she would be in charge.

Oh, how things would change. Strangely, the very idea of making someone afraid was comforting to her. If they were afraid, it only made sense that she wouldn't be.

"I'm tired of being afraid," she said under her breath. She had lived most of the past summer in a pleasant haze where fear was forgotten—and she missed it. She closed her eyes, thinking about those warm days and at some point must have fallen asleep, because when she blinked it was light out, brilliantly white.

It was too white, shockingly so.

There was no way such brightness should have penetrated the cupboard walls. Sharp fear and confusion swept her, and without moving a muscle she spun her eyes around and found herself in a bedroom...a girl's room...a messy girl's room. There was a pile of maybe clean clothes just off the side of the bed, and the pillow had drool stains and the quarter of a desk in sight was piled with books and make-up and loose change.

It was all very normal and in a way, pleasant. The panic in her receded as she discovered that she was actually quite comfortable in a nest of blankets. She wasn't in pain or even hungry.

Where am I? Jillybean wondered. This was followed up by a second quick question: *When am I?* Had she blacked out and missed months like she had before or just hours? Or something in between? She waited for Ipes to answer, but he remained mute.

Slowly, she sat up and saw the girl's room completely. The cluttered desk and the pile of clothes and the strewn shoes didn't stir a single memory. The house was utterly silent and the air was still; she was sure that she was the only one in it. In fact, Ipes wasn't even in the house. She knew that even though she didn't know how she knew it.

Out the window she saw snow-covered trees. That it was still winter didn't answer any of her "when" questions, and as the trees were pine, it didn't help the "where" question, either.

On the desk, pushed to the back by the mess, was a picture of a preteen girl standing with a soldier. This helped. Likely she was still near Fort Leonard Wood. "I guess that's something," Jillybean murmured, feeling a little disappointed. In her mind, she thought that if she were going to have a blackout it would've been better to get the entire winter out of the way and wake up fresh in spring.

Going to the window, she saw it wasn't anywhere near spring. The blood in the snow was too red for spring.

Chapter 12

Jillybean

A trail of blood led away from the house to disappear from view among the trees that lined the property. The blood reminded her of acid. It had eaten its way through the snow and in a couple of places she could see down to the maroon stained grass.

There was a lot of blood and it had to have been hot and fresh to cut through the snow. The thought was disquieting, and the very fact there was blood at all was unnerving, and yet, she felt nothing but an inner calm.

She stared at it for a long time trying to come to grips with it in an emotional way, but the blood didn't seem to have any hold on her whatsoever. It was just blood and the world seemed full of it these days.

With a lift of a single shoulder, she moved to the door, as always creeping quietly along, just in case. The door led to an upstairs hall that sprouted three other doors. They were all open: two bedrooms and a bathroom. None were special in anyway. The people who had lived here in the Before had been messy. Other than that, they were just rooms.

Jillybean made her way down a central set of stairs to the main floor where, despite the open front door, the house smelled cloyingly of fried food as if something had been burnt. She walked toward the open door in something of a daze. Nothing looked familiar. It was as if she had been "beamed" into the upstairs bed through some sort of science fiction gizmo.

"Are those real?" she asked aloud. She didn't think so. Nothing in any of the old sci-fi movies was ever real: there weren't any light sabers or flying cars in the world. There was only blood. She could see it just fine from the front stoop. The blood could only end in pain and yet she felt she had to follow it to where it led. Right in front of the stoop were footprints in the snow.

One set was tiny, so small they could just fit Jillybean's Keds. The other were man-sized, but they weren't boot prints. Someone wearing only socks had run out the front door. "They must've been ascared to do that," she said.

After a deep breath, she put one of her Keds in the closest of the grown-up prints and as she did, a ghost of an image came to her: she saw herself stepping into a print very similar to it, but in the memory it had been dark and her body was quivering in fear.

Now she only had a bit of a quiver going as she stepped into the dead man's print. Trying to match a man's stride, she took three giant steps before she came to the first splotch of blood. It sat, shaped somewhat like an uneven maple leaf, where the snow had been smushed down by a falling body.

The blood and the two sets of prints went on and so did Jillybean until she saw a man's leg sticking out from beneath a bush. Although she was thirty feet away and she could only see the leg from the knee down, she recognized it immediately. "That's Dave. Ipes, that's the guy from…" She paused as she realized she was talking to herself. Ipes wasn't anywhere near her. "He has to be around here someplace. If only I could remember."

She tried to picture where she had last seen Ipes, only instead, she saw herself standing in a darkened kitchen, standing next to the cupboard she'd been hiding in. She had one hand on the counter and the other over her mouth. Her breath was hot and coming quick with excitement, now that she had made her decision.

"Huh? What decision?" Jillybean asked, looking around at the trees. She actually expected an answer to come to her, perhaps from the trees or maybe from her own head. No answer came and the only sound was that of snow, falling in clumps from over-weighted tree branches.

Nervous now, she moved on through the brush, stepping in Dave's big people footprints. She wasn't exactly nervous about what she would see when she got closer. After all, she had seen plenty of dead bodies in her day, quite a number of her own making. And she had the sinking feeling she had killed Dave—who else would have? Who else could have made the tiny set of prints?

What scared her was what she might have done to Dave. It was one thing to kill a slaver to protect yourself, it was another to do evil things to him first. She didn't want to be evil, but sometimes it happened, which made her sad.

Dave had died unpleasantly, Jillybean saw as she followed the smaller second set of prints around the bush. Dave had died in agony, sitting with his legs splayed and both hands clutching his belly, which was stained a dark maroon. More of the maroon had poured out from beneath his shirt and was now a congealed black pool between his legs. Jillybean guessed he had been shot at least once through the stomach.

His face, contorted in misery, was hoary with frost and looked waxen from the frigid temperatures which had frozen it in a mask of pain. His eyes were still open—that bothered Jillybean. They looked like painted grapes and they bothered her, but at least they weren't staring at her. They stared at something just to her left, but what Jillybean didn't know.

She glanced around and saw nothing except the tiny prints in the snow. With morbid curiosity, she placed one foot after another in the prints and found them an exact match. When she looked up, she saw the painted grapes staring at her and, in silence she stared right back.

"Why don't you say sumptin?" Dave asked, his voice came out slurry as if he were drunk.

"Ah, jeepers!" Jillybean cried, so startled that she fell down, snow sliding up the back of her shirt. She was all set to race out of there, only Dave was still again, or rather, he was still frozen like the world's most horrible statue.

Unnerved, Jillybean got to her feet, her eyes never leaving Dave's face, noting that the hoary ice crystals hadn't cracked or fallen away. "That's what means he didn't really talk." She was slightly disappointed that the corpse hadn't begun talking out of the blue. "It's what means I'm crazy," she whispered, her chin hanging down, her long brown hair falling in front of her face.

She didn't want to look up. She didn't want to be crazy anymore, but Dave had something to say and if she didn't hear it now, he would haunt her, maybe in her dreams, maybe when she was walking along, minding her own business.

If Ipes were there, he would have told her to face her fears and get it over with. She sighed and asked: "What do you want?"

He wouldn't answer until she looked up again—as expected, Dave was staring right at her. "Why don't you say sumptin?" Dave asked, again.

Confused, Jillybean replied: "Like what?"

"You're going to shoot me and then just watch me die and not say a fuckin' word? Well, fuck you."

Jillybean had no idea what to say to this and so stood there in silence waiting for something to happen or for the strange vision to end. Dave wasn't finished and a moment later he went on: "You could at least kill me, you dumb bitch, instead of just watching me die. Come on, do it! You got the…" A spasm of pain crossed his face as he released one of his hands from his belly long enough to point at something at Jillybean's side.

She looked down and saw she had a gun in her hand. It was a warm and heavy and very familiar gun. She had seen it through the crack of the cupboard door as the leader of the slavers spun the cylinder round and round with a hypnotic zzziihh noise. And later when the house had been quiet for an hour, she had seen him spinning the gun itself. He had been sitting at the kitchen table, twirling the gun on the table as though he were a middle-schooler at his first boy-girl party playing spin the bottle.

And she had seen the gun an hour later when he finally got up. The leader of the slavers only took three steps away, but the gun was right there, lying on the table. Although now there was a blueish tint to the metal, in the dark it had looked like a twisted hunk of black shadow.

She was little more than a shadow herself when she slid out of the cupboard, her decision made. She would kill them. They were evil and deserved to die. That was justice and it would be a mercy to the world. She would shoot them in the…

"Oh," Jillybean said stepping back and looking down at her right hand, where a moment before a .357 Magnum had sat in her sweaty grip. Now her hand was empty, though it still vibrated as though she had recently fired the gun—and she had. The memories were coming back to her like pieces of a puzzle.

"Maybe I shouldn't try to put them together," she mumbled, glancing a last time towards Dave's frozen corpse. It didn't move and it hadn't moved. It had all been in her head and that was okay with her. "Maybe I should just be happy that they're dead and I'm alive. Really, ha-ha, what's the use of being mental if you throw away the only good thing about it?"

If her brain thought it was best to forget what had happened the night before, then she would forget. Yes, it was crazy and she was crazy, but Mister Neil had always said that her craziness was an adaptation that helped her cope with scary stuff.

With that thought guiding her, she ignored the footprints and the blood and headed back to the house, only to pause as she made it to the snow-covered drive. There were more tracks in the snow on the other side of the drive. They were small, which meant they had to be hers.

Where they led: to the back of the house was obvious. Where they came from wasn't so obvious, they went up to the road and then disappeared behind the trees.

"Did I walk here?" she asked aloud. As she didn't know where "here" was, she thought that it was entirely possible. On a whim, she followed her tracks back to the road and saw that she hadn't walked, at least not far.

Sitting about a hundred yards up the road was a Ford Focus in midnight blue, the very same car she had siphoned gas from the day before. It had been sitting in the garage of the house that the three bad guys had been broken into. How on earth did it get here?

As this seemed the sort of puzzle that she should understand, she trudged to the Ford, her little face sprouting lines of worry the closer she got. The Ford was banged up in a way it hadn't been the day before…if it had only been a day since she saw it that is.

The front bumper was stove in, the passenger side mirror had been torn off and there were huge gouges on both sides. It suggested strongly that she had driven, but had she been chased? The idea stopped her in her tracks and she shrunk down, listening to the forest and the world beyond.

There were no human sounds, only natural earthly ones, birds and squirrels scampering around after the first snow, sounding foolishly excited, but not afraid.

Jillybean continued to the Ford and looked inside, hoping to see Ipes. He wasn't there and, really, nothing else of importance was either…except the bottle of gin sitting on the passenger seat. That hadn't been there before. She went to reach for it and the hidden memory came to her:

She had decided to kill the leader and had sat in her cupboard next to the oven waiting with endless patience. She waited almost in a transcendental state. Time meant nothing to her. The cold meant nothing. Next to her, Ipes was only a bit of cotton and some fluff. She waited with part of her mind attuned to the leader's movement and the rest utterly unfocused.

An hour passed in this strange conscious state before the leader finally got up from the table. "Gotta take a leak," he mumbled. The chair scraped back and his boots were loud on the kitchen tile. Jillybean was fully aware by then and perplexed. The man had not crossed either towards the hall bathroom and nor did he go to out the sliding door.

Strangely, he went to the basement door but did not go down it. He stood on the top step and started peeing down into the dark. It was an odd sound and triggered the same urge within Jillybean.

The urge to pee was easily ignored. She was too focused and the danger so great that, had Ipes been sentient, he would have been screaming his head off for her to run away as fast as she could. Instead she moved softly toward danger. The gun was six feet away and the man only three feet beyond that.

He stood on the top step with one hand on the dusty edge of the doorjamb above his head, while his other hand held his penis and pissed in an arc. He seemed to enjoy the fact that his urine reached almost to the floor of the basement. With his attention on his childish antics, he didn't see her slither from the cupboard and nor did he see her step slowly across the floor, making sure to place each foot just so.

Despite how careful she was, the floor creaked beneath her. Quick as a wink, his head spun to the side. She had no idea what she looked like in the dark; he was just a hulking form with glints for eyes. She had to appear as nothing more substantial than a shadow.

To his credit, he didn't jump in fright. However, he did jump for the gun. She was closer and faster and her focus was on it completely. She didn't think about Ipes or snow storms or her next meal. She didn't think about Sadie or Mister Neil or poor dead baby Eve or the evil Eve who had lived in Jillybean.

Her mind was on the gun and she snatched it up. The thing was heavy and clumsy—exactly how she expected it to be. She knew the trigger would be too difficult for her tiny hands to pull back without spoiling her aim and so she stuck the hammer against the kitchen table and shoved with both hands, just as the man lunged still with his penis sticking out of his zipper and dribbling pee.

His hands flailed for her, but she danced to the side the heavy pistol up and pointed at his chest. The moment of action ended as abruptly as it began.

The leader stood somewhat bent over, ready to spring at her, one hand on the back of a kitchen chair, the other on the counter. However, he didn't spring. "That gun is on safe," he said.

Jillybean guessed that this was a lie. "If that were true, you would have taken it from me by now."

"You're a pretty smart little girl."

"And you're not as smart as you think you are," she shot back. "If you were really smart, you wouldn't be a slaver and a thief. I want my stuff back."

He finally straightened, lifting his hands in front of his chest, his palms out towards Jillybean. "Sure thing, of course but first, why don't you point that just a little bit away. We wouldn't want it to go off accidentally."

The gun did not waver. "That's true. I want it to go off on purpose. That's why I'm pointing it at you, and I will keep pointing it at you until I get my stuff back."

"Pointing a gun at me won't get your stuff back. You see, I'm not afraid of you and I'm not afraid of getting shot. That being said, I don't want to get shot. It's unpleasant. So, this puts us at an impasse. Do you know what an impasse is?"

"That's what means we're stuck, right?" When he nodded, she went on: "But we're not stuck. I can make you call your friends. There are six bullets in this gun. I can shoot you five times just to hurt you and still have one left over. I don't wanna do that, but I will."

The man stared at her for a long time, his face dark and shadowed except for the glints of his eyes, his face was like a devil's face to Jillybean. "That's pretty cold," he told her and then moved to sit down. Through reflex alone, she almost shot him. "I'm just going to sit. Hands will be on the table. Good. See? You have nothing to fear from me."

"I know."

The calm way in which she said this made him lean back and whistle. "You really are something, aren't you?"

"Yes, I am something." It was true that just then she didn't feel like a "someone." She didn't feel like herself or like evil Eve or Ipes or anyone. Since she didn't understand the term "cold," she would have used the term "empty" to describe herself. Her emotions were switched off. She wasn't afraid or angry or sad. She was determined. She had made her decision to get her stuff back and she was going to, no matter what.

"I think we are at an impasse," the man said. "You won't shoot me. You're a little girl who's afraid and all alone."

"Yes, and I need my stuff."

"But I can't get it for you like this. If I go back there with a gun to my head, those other guys will let you shoot me."

Jillybean actually believed this. "Because you're a mean person."

He shrugged. "Yes, I suppose, but nowadays everyone is a little mean. It's the only way to survive."

She knew that this was definitely a lie. Mister Neil and Sadie weren't mean at all and Deanna was always nice and so too was Captain Grey, though he was also a bit growly. Really, the only person who had been mean in the valley had been Jillybean.

"Not everyone has to be mean, but I guess it's true for some people. Some people and some kids have to do bad things sometimes. I think shooting you would be bad, so please call your friends and tell them to bring back my stuff."

He shook his head and simply said: "No."

"Please!" she insisted. "I don't want to be bad."

The man didn't seem to understand how much danger he was in and Jillybean didn't know what to say to get him to realize it. Probably there wasn't anything she could say and so with her little lips cast down at the corners, she aimed the .357 with one eye closed.

She had hoped to hit the man in the shoulder, thinking that it wouldn't be so bad, only he must have guessed her intentions and tried to leap up. The bullet struck him in the crook of his right arm and blasted out the back of his elbow. He sat back, his glinting eyes now wide and for a moment there was only stunned silence as their ears rang with the crash of the pistol.

Then he screamed so loudly that Jillybean took a nervous step back. He screamed and screamed until Jillybean began apologizing. The apologies went unheard and he kept on screaming until she cocked the gun a second time and advanced on him.

"You need to hush, mister. You're gonna bring the monsters and they'll eat you."

"Fuck you!" he yelled. "Look what you did for fuck's sake." His right arm sat in his lap, bleeding like a fountain of ink. In the dark it was hard to see what sort of damage she had done. "I can't move it. Damn it! You hear me? It doesn't work and there ain't any surgeons running around anymore to fix it. You...you bitch...you turned me into a cripple!"

Jillybean really was very sorry, but was shocked when the man actually started to cry. "Don't cry. It'll be okay. We can wrap that up and..." She had put the gun down and took a step towards him when he lunged at her, left-handed.

He caught hold of her shredded-up monster coat and when she pulled away, a length tore off and he fell to the kitchen floor, moaning in pain.

"You are mean," Jillybean hissed. "You're just like that bounty hunter and he was evil and nasty and he deserved to die." She shied around him and went to the gun on the table and this time she aimed for the head. "You will call your friends or I will kill you."

"Fuck y…"

She pulled the trigger.

Chapter 13

Jillybean

The thunderous blast shocked her and when she blinked, she found herself standing outside in the snow, the sun blinding her. Tears ran down her face, but she didn't sob or cry out in misery. She had too much self-control for that. Putting her hand out to the Ford, she steadied herself and waited for the tears to pass.

"I killed him, just like I killed Dave and probably Perry. But I'm hiding the memories from myself. Is that a good thing? Is that healthy? Or will I explode later and go super-duper crazy? Mister Neil said that was a possibility. He said I could be a super-nova. Though that doesn't sound that bad, if you ask me, right Ipes?"

Again, she had forgotten that Ipes wasn't with her. He was more important than any bad memory. She had a bazillion of those and there was only one of him.

"Do I check the house for him?" she asked herself, afraid that checking the house would lead to finding Perry's dead body. Her only other option was to check the car she was standing next to or go search for the KIA, which was likely parked in back.

Since the Focus was closer, she opened the passenger side door, pushed aside the bottle of gin and sat down, almost stepping on a little homemade gizmo. It looked like a poorly constructed school science project with coat hangers bent in a crude circle holding copper wiring that had been braided into a thin rope.

As crude as it was, the wiring was tighter than the last one and the circle of bent hangers was smaller. "That couldn't have been easy. I probably…" She glanced down at her thumb which had suddenly throbbed. She had cut herself making the gizmo and reflexively she stuck her finger in her mouth—just as she had the night before…

The echo of the gun still thrummed through her body as Jillybean sucked her thumb. The taste of blood was copper and clean and the pain, disappointingly minor. It was nothing compared to what she had done to the dead man in the kitchen. His screams, just like the gun, still seemed to hang around her like a black cloud.

Don't think about it, Jillybean, Ipes advised. *Concentrate before you hurt yourself again. Remember, tetanus is a real thing*. The zebra had climbed out of the cupboard on his own and had tottered past the dead body and out into the garage where Jillybean, with a handful of wire and three coat hangers had been gazing down on the Ford Focus considering how she was going to get it moving.

"What's ethanol? Is that like alcohol?"

I think so.

"So, this thing runs on alcohol? Do you think if I stuck some of those grode-up drinks in the gas tank, it would go?" Ipes had only shrugged his shoulders. "You're not much help," she groused. "And you weren't all that much help with that man, neither."

What can I say? I'm just a tiny zebra. I was scared. So... what are you going to do with this car? A fast getaway? Very smart. I'll go check out the alcohol and see if any says ethanol.

"We're not doing a getaway," she answered, beginning to work on her electricity making gizmo. "We're getting our stuff back and before you say anything, we'll find them the same way they found us. They had to have left tracks in the snow, too."

Ipes must have guessed that she wasn't in the mood for joking around and so he left to look over the different bottles of booze in the house. Eventually, he came back with 151 rum. *It's seventy-five percent alcohol. Maybe it'll work.*

Jillybean knew all about percentages and fractions, what she didn't know about were blended gasolines. Earlier, she had siphoned all the gas she could from the Ford, but from experience, she knew that there would be some at the very bottom that couldn't be sucked out. On average, it was about ten ounces. She poured in the rum and could only hope the mixture would be close enough.

After exhaustively charging the car's battery with her bike/magnet/wire gizmo, she cranked over the engine and it sounded terrible. *Bllatt! Bllatt, brrrugh, brrugh bllatt.*

"We better hurry," she said, grabbing her backpack, the pistol and the extra rounds that the dead man in the kitchen had been carrying in his pocket.

Ipes took one look at the stuttering engine and whispered: *Oh, boy. We're going to get stuck in the snow for certain.*

"If we *don't* go, we'll be stuck in the snow for weeks if not months, so hush," Jillybean said. "I need positive thinkings."

I'm positive we're going to freeze to death, he mumbled.

She ignored him, her mind too focused on what she needed to live. The people who owned the home had been childless and so there weren't blocks or toys available to glue to the gas and brake pedals, which really didn't matter as she had no time to wait for glue to dry.

She guessed that she had a quarter of a gallon of "gas," and had no idea how far it would get her, so she grabbed the only implement in the house that was the right size for her needs: the fireplace poker.

The trip started off with a bang and a crash as she backed into the side of the garage on her first try. Rakes and shovels came crashing down, as did a wall-shelf filled with tools and cans filled with long-congealed paint. It rained down with an ear-shattering sound, causing her to panic and shove down harder on the gas with her poker.

She hadn't corrected her steerage and so she hit the corner of the house: the sound of the metal tearing against brick, coupled with the hideous noise of the engine had her nerves on edge, making her shoulders squinch upward and her face cave into a cringe.

The ghastly noise had one plus: it drove out the sound of the gunshot and the man's awful screams that had been replaying in Jillybean's head over and over.

She felt almost free as she spun the Ford in a wide reversed turn that culminated in two crushed trashcans. Leaving a trail of blue smoke and an obscene *blatt*, she bounced onto the road only to sideswipe a tree, which knocked her straight.

Her perfect alignment with the road didn't last. She swept down a hill and for some reason, her back tires decided, completely on their own, to careen wide, so that she was pointed at the side of the road, but driving forward. This seemed to defy the laws of physics as she knew them and, properly freaked out, she shifted the poker from the gas to the brakes, which immediately sent her into a spin.

Ipes went flying, screaming for her to stop, only she couldn't stop. The car went round and round until it slammed into a tree on the side of the road. As was proper, Jillybean had on her seatbelt, so the crash was more or less only jarring to her and she was clear-headed enough to keep the engine from stalling out like it wanted to.

"Maybe we drive slower," she said, as she tried to maneuver the poker back onto the gas with shaking hands.

From the footwell, Ipes asked: *You call what you were doing driving? I don't think anyone else in their right mind would. But it was kind of fun...just don't do it again.*

She didn't. The collision with the tree had bounced her back onto the road and, once more, she began following the tracks laid out by Dave and Perry. It wasn't a long trip, maybe only eight miles, but the last half mile was scary. The Ford's engine began to hitch and sputter worse than ever as it slowly ran out of the "gas" she had fed it.

Eventually it died on a gentle slope and she let it coast along until she saw smoke rising up from behind the trees on her right. "Wait here," she told Ipes. He said nothing and didn't even twitch as she got out of the car with the heavy gun in her hand.

Slowly she made her way around to the back of the house, creeping along near the tree-line that abutted the property. She didn't actually need to sneak. All of the windows were covered and the two men had a huge fire going; she could hear it from outside. It covered the sound her small feet made in the snow.

The rest of the memory came quickly to her: silent as a wraith, she slipped in from an unlocked back door, tiptoed to the living room and surprised the two men who were relaxing, Dave on a couch and Perry in a recliner in front of the fireplace.

"I want my stuff," she said. They jumped in fear and then stared at her in bafflement, so she repeated: "I want my stuff. That's my KIA out back. You guys stoled it and that's what means you're bad. But I won't hurt you if..."

Perry reached for a rifle that had been lying on the floor next to the recliner. Jillybean screamed for him to stop, only he didn't. She even waved the gun at him just in case he missed it, but he still, almost casually, picked up his gun.

Jillybean fired the .357 from ten and a half feet away, and missed. She even missed the recliner. The sound of the gun had the opposite effect on Perry and Dave. Perry froze with his hand on the gun while Dave went nuts. He'd been under a blanket and now he kicked like mad trying to get up, only he got entangled in the blanket and his spastic efforts were wasted.

The distraction he caused lasted only a second and then Perry picked up the gun as Jillybean advanced on him straining with both hands to squeeze the heavy trigger and keep it aimed at the same time.

When it went off again, it seemed to surprise all three of them. Perry's eyes were wide circles and his mouth was a perfect "O," pretty much the same shape as the hole in his chest.

"Fuck!" Dave cried, finally untangling himself from the blanket. He turned to run away.

"Stop!" Jillybean shouted. She didn't trust that he would run far enough. It was cold and snowy out, and she was sure that he would only run around the house to the truck that had been parked next to the KIA. What if there were guns in there? What if he came back with one looking for revenge?

Dave didn't stop. He rushed for the front door with Jillybean chasing him. "I said stop," she said in a calmer voice, but he wouldn't. He was furiously scrabbling at the locks when she pulled the trigger of the .357. Again, she missed. The strength needed for her to pull the trigger caused the barrel to lift up and she hit the door a foot over his head.

Jillybean corrected her aim, pointing the gun at the back of his right knee and firing again just as Dave opened the front door. She didn't know if she hit him until he fell into the snow a few seconds later and she saw the blood. There was a shocking amount.

"I said, stop," she whispered. "You should have stopped."

She supposed that he didn't hear her. He staggered off to the side of the house and fell into some bushes. She followed him there to make sure he would die, to make sure that he was no longer any threat to her. He asked to be put out of his misery, but she wouldn't do it. There were monsters to worry about and the gun only had so many bullets…and he was a bad guy who deserved his pain.

In silence, she watched him die. It took seventeen minutes and she was a shivering mess by the time she walked back into the house.

You did what you had to do, Ipes said from beneath her. She blinked and in the course of that blink, suddenly night became day and the living room with its roaring fire became the Ford Focus with iced-over windows. She fished around beneath the seat and brought Ipes out. Wearing a droopy-eyed look, he patted her hand. *They were bad men.*

"Yes, but I liked it better not remembering nothing…"
Anything.

"Okay, yeah sure, 'anything.' I liked it better when I didn't remember anything. Maybe next time I'll go find a different place to stay and then it'll be like it never happened. Wait, maybe I can do that now."

I don't think memory works like that. I think once you remember something, you remember it for always.

"Maybe, but I'm also crazy so I can make my memory do what I want. I'll show you." She tramped back the way she had come, purposefully not looking at the blood leading from the front door or the body on the couch or the bullet holes here and there.

"Do-ta-do, bah-ba-bah," she half-sang as she went first into the kitchen to see what sort of food was available. There were a couple dozen cans of beans and soup, but nothing really good. She took a can of soup, opened it and went back into the living room where the fire was only a pile of ash.

It was hot enough to heat the soup and so, carefully, she stuck the can in the ash and then sat back on her heels and waited, again purposefully keeping her eyes straight ahead.

Have you forgotten yet? Ipes asked.

"Not yet. You know these things take time. How long has it been? Five minutes? No one can forget stuff in five minutes."

They waited a while longer and eventually he said: *It might help if that guy stopped staring at you. It's creepy. Could you close his eyes?*

Perry had been staring at her this entire time and it was skeeving her out. So far, pretending that he wasn't there hadn't helped at all, in fact it had made trying to forget practically impossible.

Jillybean wasn't about to touch him. She settled on throwing Dave's blanket over him, which still didn't help. She could feel his eyes bore through the blanket and lock onto her.

Eventually, she got up and explored the house, finding all sorts of interesting things. Each of the men had claimed a portion of the living room and each had a little cache of what they considered their personal property. All of them had naked-lady magazines, which Jillybean pushed aside without looking closer.

She was after the guns and the bombs. The men had been scavenging around the base for long enough to acquire all sorts of stuff. The neatest of which were the claymore mines, the hand grenades and the M79, what she called a "bomb shooter" that seemed to have been made with a child in mind. With an overall length of just over two feet, it looked like a miniature shotgun and was exceedingly simple in its construction and use.

Jillybean pressed a single latch on the side and it fell open, showing her where one of the stubby "bomblets" would go. Wearing an impish smile, she slid one in.

What are you doing, Jillybean? Ipes' voice held both early onset panic and a warning tone.

"Just making sure I know how to work it. It's not like it comes with instructions…oh wait, it does!" Along with nearly two dozen little bombs, there was a box for the bomb shooter and in it were actual instructions.

Excitedly she read them, memorizing each detail. When she was done, she held the weapon up and sighted down its length, a grin on her face. "I like it. This is even better than my old guns."

Well, it doesn't make you a soldier and you should be careful with it. I wouldn't keep it loaded, especially in the house.

"Jeeze, you sound like my…" The word *mom* got hung up on her tongue. She hadn't thought about her mom in ages and now she could barely remember her face. Here she was hoping to forget ol' dead Perry with his staring eyes, but it was her mom she couldn't picture with the same clarity that she used to.

"Do I lose all my memory when I try to forget stuff? Cuz, if so I don't want to do it. I'm sorry about Dave and Perry, but they kinda got what they deserved…except for maybe Dave, but I don't know."

I don't know how memories are made and unmade. I think they're like pictures like you see in some of the older homes. Remember that old grandma's house? Some of her pictures were faded and I bet that one day there won't be anything left but empty frames sitting on the walls.

"That's kind of sad. Well, I wanna keep my memories, so I'll just have to find a different coping mechanism. You hear that brain?" she asked, cocking her eyes at an upward angle as if she could see into her own head. "Find another way."

After a moment of waiting, Ipes asked: *Did it say anything?*

"Naw, it's probably still thinking." She let her brain think, and as it did, she went around the house collecting all the stuff she thought would be useful. A very small .38 caliber police special that almost fit her tiny hand, bullets, food, more guns and gas were the obvious things and they had first priority. Next, she grabbed pillows and blankets, and her charging gizmo from the other car.

She wanted to take the batteries out of the truck, but they were too heavy and she didn't want to waste time setting up a pulley and winch system to remove them.

Finally, with the last bit of room left in the KIA, she added firewood. A blizzard on the prairie could very well kill her if she wasn't prepared.

As the sun began to set, she took a hammer from the garage and smashed in the KIA's tail lights and the blinkers and the dome light inside. It would be an eight hundred mile journey and every one of those miles would be driven in the dark and she couldn't have the least thing give her away.

Chapter 14

Sadie Walcott

She was caught dead to rights. The man was twelve feet away with a gun pointed at her. That should have been enough for her to admit defeat, but she was awful pig-headed when it came to losing, and this was the ultimate loss.

Her hands went up, and at the same time she bent slightly forward, her legs becoming tense springs beneath her. She knew she couldn't outrun bullets, but she hoped that a slaver wouldn't just shoot an unarmed person. *Of course they may not know I'm unarmed,* Sadie thought.

"Hey, I don't have a gun on me or anything," she said. "I was gonna steal one, only you scared me half to death. Ha-ha."

"You're a girl," he said, in surprise. "I wasn't expecting a girl."

"How were you expecting me at all?" Sadie said, doing her best to keep her tone neutral, almost to the point of being conversational in the hope of lulling the man into a sense of security. It seemed to be working as his gun came down *slightly*. It was no longer aimed right at her face, but only in her general direction.

"You got a loud truck. You can hear that sucker for miles in these mountains. But I never expected a girl. You shoulda turned around and went back to the valley. That's what I woulda…"

The springs in Sadie's legs sprung. She had gotten all she needed from the brief conversation. He knew she was "just a girl" and an unarmed girl at that. He wouldn't shoot and that meant she had a big advantage.

Her legs powered her from standing still to twenty miles per hour in three seconds, while behind her the slaver let out a cry: "She's here! It's a girl. Doug, she's headed for you!"

Not anymore, I'm not, Sadie thought as she darted to her right and began to climb the wall of the gulch. It was a much easier climb than the two she had already been forced to make that day, and she was halfway up the forty foot wall before the man she had run from came puffing up.

"Get down or I'll shoot!" he yelled.

"I doubt it," Sadie answered. "If you miss, you'll have wasted bullets and if you hit me then you won't be able to sell me, right?"

His quiet reply of: "Fuck," was pure frustration. Sadie grinned as she heard the sound of the man slinging his rifle before he started up the gulch after her.

"Brian! I don't see her," Doug called from the throat of the gulch. "She might be climbing up the walls. Brian?"

Behind Sadie, Brian was huffing badly, the altitude getting to him. "Of course…she's climbing…the walls. She's heading east. Get Pecos and Mike. We'll block her in."

Sadie doubted they'd be able to, especially if she killed Brian. She didn't know Kung Fu or have ninja skills, so a fair fight was out of the question, but she could drop a rock like nobody's business. Twelve feet from the top of the hill she found a rock the size of a soccer ball, half buried in the dirt. A couple of good tugs and it came loose to bound down at Brian.

It wasn't as smooth as a soccer ball and the hill wasn't nearly as even as a pitch. The rock tumbled right at Brian, but at the last second it clipped something and bounded up, just nicking his head.

"Mother fucker! What the fuck? What the fuck! If you try that again, I will shoot you. I promise you that." To be on the safe side, he angled behind one of the scrubby little pines that grew up out of the side of the hill. Because of the hard angle and the rockiness of the slope, none of them would ever grow into much more than what they were now.

Since the chance of braining him with another rock was now slim, Sadie put her efforts into escaping. She crested the hill and found herself on a small plateau overlooking the town of Poudre Park. There really wasn't much more to it than being a relatively open area along the Poudre River.

Altogether, there were sixty homes, one church, a few sad businesses that had somehow held on right up until the apocalypse, and a gas station that appeared to have been partially burnt to the ground.

There were also a few dozen zombies wandering around. Sadie headed right for them, slipping and sliding down the hill. As she jogged, she pulled her jacket partially off so that one sleeve dangled off to the side. In the dark it somewhat resembled a third arm which wasn't exactly normal, but that was the whole idea. She also threw in a limp and a low moan.

The zombies accepted her as one of their own without hesitation as did Doug and Brian who stayed high on the hills, afraid to come down among the undead. They yelled back and forth to each other: "Do you see her?"

She wanted to limp and fake her way to safety, but two trucks rumbled into life and spun through town, trying to cut off any escape. In order to blend in, she charged the trucks along with the other zombies. It was twenty-five minutes of going back and forth as the slavers searched for her, never realizing that she was chasing them.

The two trucks kept out of reach of the zombies and eventually they split up, each racing to either end of town, guarding the one road that passed through it. They disappeared from view and the moment they did, they cut their engines and switched off their lights. She could picture them propped up under blankets watching the road with gimlet eyes.

This was what Sadie was looking for. She was sure they wouldn't expect an unarmed girl to go back to the house where the Valley soldiers were being held prisoner. They would expect her to run away, which was silly because where would she go?

With no truck, no gas, and no weapons, going on the offensive was probably her safest course of action. Just then it seemed better than the alternatives: either dying of hyperthermia or exposure, or becoming a snack for the thousands of zombies between here and the Valley.

Leaving the pack as half went one way and the other half went the other, she headed back to the gulch, moving in the shadows. Her plan was to sneak up on the house, slip in and use her speed as well as the element of surprise to disarm whoever had been left to guard the prisoners.

It was a sound plan and in her black attire she melded so perfectly with the night that no one saw her and she made it to the little house without anyone raising the alarm—even the man who had expected her to do just this didn't see her.

He was practically invisible himself hiding in the brush on the side of the road. Invisible, but not silent. He had a case of the sniffles and every thirty seconds or so he would snort back a run of snot that threatened to slip out of his nose.

Sadie cursed under her breath. Her plan was ruined; there was no way she could take on two armed men with any expectation of winning. Using even more care to remain silent, she eased back the way she had come, only to almost run into a man on foot hurrying back to the house.

Fortunately, she heard his huffing breath before she saw him and she stole beneath a pine tree where the needles on the ground muffled her footfalls. Hoping that his appearance would signal a change in the dynamics, Sadie crept after.

"Smitty? Smitty? Where are you?"

"Shut the hell up, I'm right here. Why aren't you out looking for the girl?"

"I was just wonnerin' if you saw her, is all."

There was silence for a few moments and then Smitty said: "Yeah, she's right here sucking my dick. Don't be an idiot, Doug. If I saw her, I think I might have said something."

"Well, there's just a lot of stiffs out tonight and we only have the two trucks and me and Brian are on foot you know and what if somethin' happens?"

"Then scream. Now, get your ass back out there and find her. You know a girl is worth all these guys put together."

Sadie hid again as Doug literally tiptoed past. He had a military rifle of some sort that he pointed here and there, looking ready to kill the first squirrel to show its head. Sadie considered trying to sneak up on him, but figured that he was too wired, which would make her chances slim to dead.

And yet, all of her chances seemed to run along those lines. She had to get lucky or somehow make her own luck. The latter was likely her only option...unless she could use some sort of Jillybean type plan, only that would mean using her head.

"Hmmm," she said, turning the noise into a grumble. She wasn't good at using her head. She was good at sudden violent action in which her gift of speed would give her the edge. "I'm also pretty sneaky, but sneaking up on some of these guys is too dangerous...at least the ones on foot."

But not the ones in the cars—the thought brought with it a little bit of a Jillybean-esque plan. She could use the zombies to get close to the trucks and then...what?

"I'll figure that out when the time comes."

As creeping in the shadows wasn't the fastest method of travel, she adopted a moan and a limp and went straight down the road, seeing Doug freeze in fear on the side of the gulch's steep wall. She could hear the rattle of the sling of the gun against the stock as steady as a clock.

It was strange to find someone so afraid of a lone "zombie" after a full year of being around them and yet, there were some among the Valley soldiers who had quit the soldiering life rather unexpectedly in the last few months. No one ever said anything when this sort of thing happened. The soldiers simply became farmers or tradesmen and that's who they were.

Everyone has their breaking point, Sadie mused, hoping she would die before she ever reached hers. She didn't have much in the way of skills outside of her speed and her bravery. Yes, she could do menial labor, but for some reason she found it degrading, which was really silly, and yet, wasn't she the daughter of both a king and a governor? Shouldn't her destiny be correspondingly greater?

When Neil had tasked her to hunt down Jillybean, she had jumped at the chance. Alone in the wild with just her and her wits had been a freeing experience for her. No one had judged her. No one had looked down on her spiked hair with a raised eyebrow, or commented that she could now choose her "own" clothes if she wanted.

And she had succeeded where no one else could have, not even Captain Grey...if he had been healthy, that is. Sadie had hunted down a desperate little girl alone in the wilds. And not just any girl. She had hunted down Jillybean, whom everyone, including their enemies considered to be a genius.

It made everything else seem simplistic and that included outsmarting a band of slavers. "I hope," she whispered when she had left Doug forty yards behind. She left the neck of the gulch and struck east on the highway, heading to where the larger of the two trucks had disappeared behind a bend in the road.

Just up the road from the truck, zombies milled about looking like tourists in hell, staring at all sorts of nothing. Sadie joined them, mingled with them and then began a loud moaning as she headed for the truck which sat as silent as the hills around them. She could see the lump of navy blue blanket sitting behind the steering wheel, letting out a light plume of grey with every breath.

There was a man hiding there ignoring the zombies and watching the shadows at the edges of the road, looking for a girl trying to sneak past, not realizing that Sadie was now almost within arm's reach.

For the most part, the zombies loitered around the truck, because why would they come closer or attack it? There were millions of derelict trucks and cars just sitting along the thousands of roads criss-crossing the country, why was this any different? Sure, they had chased it minutes before, but now it was dead and cold, and any sign of humanity was long gone—or hidden beneath a blanket.

Sadie broke character just long enough to take a step up on the running boards to peer in at either Mike or Pecos huddled beneath the blanket. Only his eyes were visible, looking out past the zombies and towards the river. Sadie stared a second too long and his eyes shifted her way.

In a flash, she was down against the side of the truck. Its metal was cold against her ear as she listened to him shifting in the cab, probably trying to see if the movement in his periphery had been real or imagined. Going to her belly, she moaned and scraped at the pavement with her thin fingers as if she had just fallen, something zombies did a dozen times a day.

There were four or five undead beasts nearby who had seen her step up on the running board and were now more curious about her than they were of the truck.

They came closer. Sadie refused to panic. She clawed listlessly at the quarter panel, letting out an even longer moan. If they attacked, she was all set to roll under the truck and escape, however they were fooled by her act. They stood around her for a few minutes, smelling of rotted meat.

Eventually, they turned away as a single gunshot cut through the quiet night. With the echoes bouncing along the walls of the mountains, it was hard to tell which way it had come from and so the zombies went in circles.

With their attention directed away from her and the truck, Sadie had a moment to assess her situation: There were too many zombies around for her to try to sneak into the back of the truck or into the trailer without being seen, and she hadn't noticed a gun sitting in the cab where she could snatch it up and stick it in Mike's or Pecos' face.

Which leaves me where? she wondered. She realized that she wasn't going to get lucky, so that left her with the option of trying to come up with a plan. Cold minutes ticked by and her mind remained an utter blank. When she began shivering, she realized she had to do something before she either froze to death or the guy in the truck drove back to town. Both were bad things.

She liked them spread out. It made it easier for her to slip past them, and if she could catch a break, they would be easier to deal with one at a time.

So, the question was: *How do I make sure this truck stays here?*

One answer popped right into her head; it made her grin. With a quick look around to make sure that no one or no thing was watching, she slipped a hand into her pocket and fished out her pocket knife.

Slashing the tires would be too loud and too violent and so she went with the next best thing. Letting her incessant moaning cover what she was doing, she pressed the tip of the knife to the tire's valve stem. An immediate hiss of air turned the grin on her face into a mischievous smile. It took some time, but gradually, the first of the dual tires began to settle.

She only paused from her work whenever one of the zombies wandered too close. With no other acting choice available, she pretended that she had been run over by the truck. It didn't take much besides a flailing arm and a dismal moan— just as long as she didn't act human she was fine.

When the air ceased to hiss, she snaked an arm past the first deflated tire to the next one in line.

The valve stem was harder to reach and thus the tire took what felt like ages to deflate. It sank so slowly that the driver didn't seem to realize that his truck was now listing down and to the right, like a boat that had sprung a leak and was gradually sinking.

Once both tires were flat, Sadie shoved the point deep into the rubber of both, forever ruining the tires. Forgetting her zombie character, she crawled beneath the truck to get at the second set of rear tires, working on the inner one, first.

Deflating it from beneath was a lot easier and in three minutes, she stabbed the now flat tire. She crawled out from under the truck to finish off the outer tire. In spite of her painfully cold hands, she emptied the air out of it very slowly and once again the driver didn't notice the slight change in angle.

One down, one to go, thought Sadie, as she stumbled her way back towards town. She worried that it looked strange for a lone zombie to be walking around and so she took a page from Jillybean's playbook. Taking her lighter out, she put it behind her back and flicked it a few times until she had a good-sized group following her.

She led them the half a mile that separated the two trucks. This one sat pointing straight downhill square in the middle of the road, and for some reason warning bells went off in her head. Only the dark hid the fact that she wasn't a zombie. If the driver, Mike or Pecos, flicked on his lights, she'd be discovered for exactly what she was.

Unfortunately, there was no time for her to change her appearance. She was just too cold to stop. Her feet felt wooden, her insides were jittering and her lower lip wouldn't stop bouncing up and down. She had to disable this truck and then find somewhere to hole up where she could wrap herself in three or four blankets until her body heat stabilized.

With the temperature dropping, she looked like the stiffest zombie in the world. In fact, she thought she looked more like Frankenstein's monster than a zombie. Regardless, the driver seemed to take no notice of her. Likely because a girl walking straight down the road with a gaggle of zombies coming behind her was the last thing he would have expected.

Still, he was a much more observant blanketed lump than the other driver. He sat up higher and had a better view. And with the truck in the middle of the road, she could not exactly sneak up from the side as she had with the last. A quick look in a side view mirror would doom her.

She passed the towed trailer and then stopped just behind it. This seemed to be the cue for the other zombies to stop as well, which wasn't a good thing for Sadie. She couldn't exactly pull out her knife with fifteen zombies within reach of her.

What she needed was patience, only she didn't have time for patience. The cold had turned her lips blue and her fingers ached. Her options were to take a chance right there or leave.

As a gambler, she went with her instinct for chance. Turning away from the zombies, she clicked open the knife and leaned against the tarp covered trailer, just above the wheel. The knife slid right in. She feared there would be a popping sound like a balloon pricked with a pin, instead there was quick rush of air that seemed tremendously loud to Sadie.

Moaning with even greater enthusiasm than before, she took a step away and then slowly turned around to stare at the tire as it sank to the ground. All the zombies stared—not one of them able to connect the sound to Sadie. The air rushing out just *was* in their limited view.

Now for the next one, Sadie thought as she slouched around the back of the trailer, only before she could get to the other side, the driver started his truck. It was so startling that Sadie was the only one of the zombies not to immediately charge the cab.

The driver put the truck in gear and roared out of there. He went about fifty yards before he slammed on his brakes and rolled down his window. A second later, a black gun was thrust out and fire leapt from its muzzle as the man began firing at her.

She was already in a full sprint for the river and the bullets swished the air in her wake. The zombies did not see her. Their focus was squarely on the truck and before the driver could get a proper bead on her dark figure, they were tearing at the doors and pounding the windows.

He was forced to speed off and by the time he got to the bottom of the hill, the one tire was in shreds and threatening to come off completely. At the edge of town, he had no choice but to keep going, leaving Sadie all alone.

Even alone, she couldn't break character. Who knew if any slavers were up on one of the steep hills with some sort of hi-tech night vision goggles. She was forced to slowly lumber into town, and whether the bad guys fixed their tires and left was beyond her now. She had to save herself before she could save anyone else.

On the east end of town, there were a few homes across the river, each with its own little bridge. She resisted the urge to rush into one of these—they were too secluded. They seemed to scream: *Hide here!*

That's not what Jillybean would do. She would be slicker than that. In fact, knowing her, Sadie guessed that the little girl would hide as close to her enemies as possible. She would get in close where they wouldn't expect, where she could react to any mistake, where she could listen in on their conversations and count their numbers and assess their weaknesses.

It would be dangerous, but it was a gamble that could pay off in a big way. Sadie rolled the dice and headed right for the little scratch of dirt that the ranch house was on.

Chapter 15

Jillybean

Traveling at night had never been much of an issue for the little girl and her stuffed animal companion. They were smart, self-contained and careful. *Driving* at night was an altogether different thing and it held a special kind of terror. They both learned to fear the sunset.

The little KIA was not a tank. In fact, it seemed particularly delicate—its metal was thin, its glass brittle and its engine prone to mishap.

A side window was the first casualty, not an hour into the journey. Jillybean was easing down the center of Vienna, Missouri, a nothing little town with a living population of two, if Ipes were counted. Its undead population seemed out of synch with the local-yokel environs. There were more undead than there were houses, cars, mailboxes and telephone poles put together.

They were also oddly congregated in the center of town as if waiting on the one-KIA parade. "Oh jeeze," Jillybean said, taking the first left she could onto Mill Street. She was usually good at left-hand turns and rarely hit anything at all; right-hand turns were another story. She could never tell exactly where the front of her car ended and the edge of the sidewalk began.

There didn't seem to be a mill on Mill Street, there were only more houses and the road was cluttered the way many in-town roads seemed to be. There were bikes keeled over on their sides, and suitcases flapped open with people's undies and sweaters showing, and papers everywhere like a book tree had lost all of its white leaves. And of course, there were dead cars which were rarely parked in an orderly manner. Perhaps strangest of all to Jillybean were the number of microwave ovens sitting in the gutters.

Had people forgotten that microwaves ran on electricity and only just remembered after lugging them out to the curb?

It was mystifying as well as aggravating to Jillybean. She almost hit one. As she was carefully porting around it in the dark, she didn't see the monster until it was right on her. There was a thump on the other side of the car that jerked her around in her seat.

At first, she thought she had hit something, but a second heavy thump came and she realized that the opposite had occurred: something had hit her! Before she could properly react, it hit the KIA a third time and in went the window. Cold air and glass splashed inside.

Ipes screamed and so did Jillybean—these were not the proper reactions, but her body knew screaming better than it did the controls to the car which were still so foreign to her that she had to consciously direct her feet to the gas or the brake.

Only once the monster was half-inside did she find the gas and squirt ahead through the debris. She fully expected the monster, a scabby disgusting thing, to just fall away, however it had too good of a grip and it didn't just hold on, it began to climb inside! She found herself swinging her head back and forth from the monster to the road.

If it gets in, how do you propose to get it out again? Ipes asked. In the last year, they had both seen a number of monsters trapped inside cars. How they got either in or out never crossed her mind.

"I don't know." She usually relied on her old standby: *I'll think of something*, but just then she was having all sorts of trouble of thinking about anything, including driving.

Just to keep the KIA in a straight line usually took all of her concentration, only now her concentration was divided between a monster invasion and not killing them by running into something sturdy, like a building or a tree.

"Shoo! Shoo!" she yelled in a ridiculous attempt to get the monster to leave.

Shoo? That's your plan?

"I don't have a plan!" She was getting crazy nervous as the KIA sped faster and faster! In her panic, she didn't realize that she had her foot mashed down on the glued stack of blocks that represented the gas pedal. In the dark, things just seemed to materialize in front of her: a parked car on the side of the road, a monster in the middle of it, a deer bounding across it, and a tree growing up out of someone's lawn.

Car! Ipes cried, making a jabbing motion with one hoof. A second later, he jabbed again and again. *Monster! Deer! Tree!*

Jillybean broke out into one long scream as she dodged the speeding KIA all over the road, and the sidewalk and a front lawn. The tree took off the side view mirror that had already been dangling by a few wires and at same time, it made the monster disappear.

There was a bang and a metallic scream and some sparks and a lot of tree bark flying around, and when she glanced over, the monster was just gone.

Brake! We're safe now. The brake is on the left…no, that's the gas again. Are you trying to kill us, or what?

"Don't blame me, I can't see which is which. It's too dark. And really, we're fine and I'm sure the tree is fine and we didn't hit that deer, so that's good."

When they made it the rest of the way through the little town unscathed, Jillybean pulled over and went around to inspect the damage, hoping there wouldn't be much beyond a few dents and scratches.

"Not bad," she remarked after making a short tally: a headlight was smashed into shards, the front passenger side door was crumpled in and wouldn't open, the mirror was gone and, of course, the window where the monster had been was now in a thousand little pieces. She also noted the remnants of a forearm with attached long-nailed, grey hand lying on the seat. She coolly picked the arm up and hurled it off to the side of the road

I think you're going to have to take a class on what constitutes good and bad. We've barely gone thirty miles and already you've turned this car into a heap.

"It still runs, but if you're too ascared, you can…" A flash of light dried up her words. It had been just a blink, as if someone had pulled back a blackout curtain for a peek out into the night.

Or they pulled back the curtain long enough to slip outside, Ipes suggested.

"Ah, jeeze," Jillybean whispered as she rushed back around the car and climbed up onto the pillows she kept stacked on the driver's seat. As much as she wanted to rush out of there, she kept her foot off the gas and crept along, hoping to slip past without being seen, or heard and that meant she couldn't hit anything.

Not hitting anything wasn't easy as the road was still littered with all sorts of trash that had to be dodged. Even going only five miles an hour wasn't easy since Jillybean couldn't stop staring off to her right, looking for more flashes of light.

Concentrate, Jillybean. Don't look over there. If there was a bad guy coming, we would have heard his car. So, we're safe just

as long as you concentrate. He talked for five straight minutes, and only sat back with a sigh of relief when they had left the light a mile behind them. *Maybe it had only been someone going out to go pee or something?*

It was possible, but to be on the safe side, she detoured onto a little blacktop road that wound through the forest and hills in a generally southwest direction. The name of the road kept changing from names to numbers until, even with a map, they were lost.

She pulled over at the first gas station she came across. *Please let them have cookies*, Ipes prayed as Jillybean climbed down from her pillow-seat and came to stand next to the pumps. *Or Cheetos. I love Cheetos. Remember when we used to beg your daddy for Cheetos every time we went to get gas?*

"Shush." Although they were miles from where they had seen the light, it didn't mean they hadn't stumbled into new danger. Nowadays, everywhere and everything could be dangerous. She paused, listening, straining her ears to hear any sound that could be human or monster in origin.

I think we're clear, Ipes said after a minute of silence. *Now, about those Cheetos…*

"Trust me, I'll get some if they have any, but you know they won't. Though they might have some gas. The smell is pretty strong and that's what means there might be gas in one of these pumps."

But what about that sign?

Taped across the front of the pump was a piece of paper. She leaned in closed, squinting at the faded lettering: *Empty!* it read.

"It doesn't smell empty. Maybe the guy who owned this place was holding some back, just in case, you know?"

Maybe he was holding some Cheetos back, too.

At Ipes' urging, she went to the station first and found a terrible mess. She risked beaming her flashlight around for a minute. The risk paid off and she came back to the KIA with a map of the area, seven lighters, two Slim Jims she found beneath an empty candy rack, and two cans of *fix-a-flat,* which always came in handy since one can could mostly inflate a flat tire.

Ipes only cared about the food. *Slim Jims? I guess they're better than nothing.*

"Don't eat them, then. There'll be more for me. Now, wait here. I don't want you getting all gas-smelly. It is kinda gross."

She left the zebra sitting on the dashboard as she walked in parallel lines up and down the parking lot, searching for the fuel intake ports. There were usually four of the little disks, one for each type of gas and usually they were situated all in a row so the gas trucks could get at them easily.

But this was an older station and she found the seven inch circular covers scattered here and there, each one clasped and locked with little Yale padlocks.

"Here we go," she said when she saw the first. She dropped down, cupping a hand around her little mag light and shone it down at the lock: there was rust eating up the keyhole. She almost squealed in delight—no one had gotten to the underground tanks yet!

This was found treasure! It was just a matter of discovering how much gas she had found. She began working on ideas to break the locks off using levers and fulcrums and heavy chains, when Ipes yelled: *Why don't you look for the keys inside?*

She found them behind the counter on a little hook beneath the cash register. Next to it was the delivery schedule for all the items the station sold. The last time the tanks had been filled was three weeks after the first monster sighting occurred in New York. The country had fallen apart soon after.

"Which means there could be…" She scanned the delivery slips attached to the clipboard and her eyes widened. "Seventeen thousand gallons." She tried to whistle, but as she had never mastered the proper lip position, it came out in a breathy hoot.

"Let's not put the cart on top of the horse just yet," she said, taking the keys out to the first locked cover. It came open after a tussle and a struggle, but when it did, the chemical smell of gasoline wafted up making her pert nose wrinkle. "P and U!"

She shone her light down into the tube, but saw nothing but more tube. "I wonder how deep this is?" A weighted rope gave her the answer and it also showed that there was four feet of fuel sitting in the tank. It seemed like a lot though without the actual dimensions of the holding tank there was no way to know how many actual gallons sat waiting to be brought up.

"I bet it's a lot, but it's gonna have to wait. I would need a gas truck and those trucks have the gear system with the shift-stick thing and I can't use that. But there's also pull-able ones."

By that she meant the smaller tanks that could be towed behind a smaller truck. She considered everything she would need: a generator, a drivable truck, a tank, and a fuel/water pump. It would be manageable, and she loved the idea of showing up in the Valley with five thousand gallons of gas.

"They'd forgive me for certain and they'd probably even like me, too. What do you think, Ipes?"

They should like you even if you don't bring anything. And you do have those guns and the bomb shooter. Besides there is also a time element that is prohibitive. What happens if it snows again?

He was right. It could take her a week to get everything she needed and with winter coming, days were more precious than fuel.

"And I guess it's not going anywhere, right? If it hasn't been discovered yet, it might not be discovered for years and I have time." She set the cover back where it belonged, marked the position of the station in her memory and then drove away, gnawing on a Slim Jim.

It was old and tough as leather. She set a piece in her mouth and drooled around it as she drove. The night passed with slow miles drifting beneath her tires. She had a scare right around midnight as she saw a string of headlights coming straight at her.

Were they friendly people traveling at night so they could slip by the bandits and the slavers, just like she was? Or were they slavers cutting through someone's territory?

A small, lonely part of her wanted to find out which it was. Could she sneak up close and see? And if they were bad, could she help to free any slaves. "I am good at that after all."

No, I forbid it, Jillybean. They're going the wrong way and they're going too fast. You would never be able to keep up and it would be dangerous, way too dangerous.

She sighed, knowing that he was right. It wouldn't be smart. She found a little dirt, side road and went up it for a spell and waited for the cars to pass. To make sure she wasn't surprised by any passing monster, she turned the heater off and opened the three windows that could still go up and down. She made a face at the broken one, realizing that she couldn't leave it like that. If she ever found herself surrounded by monsters, which she was sure she would, she couldn't have such a weak spot in her defenses.

"Maybe I can finally weld." The idea of joining two pieces of metal in any way she chose was strangely enticing to her, perhaps because shaping metal was somewhat like shaping the world. In a significant way, it reduced her limitations. Making the KIA safer was only one minor example of this.

Doesn't welding use flames? Ipes asked, his paws nervously touching each other.

"It'll be fine. Don't be such a worry-wart. Wait, here they come." They both paused to listen as the cars she had seen coming her way swept past with a great deal of rumbling. To her, they sounded like train thrumming down the tracks on its way home and she loved the idea of getting on that train and finding a real mom and dad and big brother. People who would take care of her and baby her, and let her grow up in a land without monsters and guilt and constant…

Since you don't know how to weld, you'll need a library, Ipes declared, cutting in on her fantasy. It was like a balloon being popped. What she wanted didn't exist anymore. "Yeah, yeah, a library or one of those big man stores with all the wood and tools and stuff. They have books in 'em, too. I saw them before and they'll have the things we'll need, probably." With so many necessities just lying around, free to the first person to come by and take them, the concept of "fixing" things was rarely put into practice anymore and hardware stores were still relatively full.

Jillybean knew that the mindset couldn't last forever, because "things" didn't last forever. After only a single year, America showed a significant decline. As she drove, she saw that the polish had faded and rust was beginning to set in everywhere.

The roads she drove along sported potholes and long cracks, out of which grass grew. In places, trees had fallen against power lines and fences leaned at crazy angles, keeping nothing in or out. Many houses and businesses looked, not just empty, but abandoned. Every town was a ghost town and every state was empty and sad.

She drove into Oklahoma with the sky behind her turning from black to indigo and even with all the pillows beneath her, she was stiff and her bottom was sore from sitting in the car for twelve hours. Still, she drove on, risking driving in the early morning grey haze, trying to make it to a town called Vinita where she hoped to find a big tool store.

After slipping through so many one stop-sign towns, Vinita was bigger than she had reckoned it would be. It wasn't an actual city, but it was built up and densely packed with homes and businesses. This meant danger. The population before the apocalypse had been north of five thousand people but for some reason there seemed to be double that many monsters lurking in among the cul-de-sacs, the elementary schools, the Jiffy-lubes and all the rest that made up the town.

The undead watched the car go by with greedy hunger in their otherwise blank eyes. Jillybean must have looked like a rolling snack to them and they came rushing to feed. The broken window was now more of an issue than ever.

With a touch more light to see by, Jillybean was able to hurry the KIA through the neighborhoods just south of the main thoroughfare that jutted up into the town. The monsters lurched along in her wake, looking like they were marching in a fantastically disgusting and haphazard parade.

Ipes stared back the way they had come. *You know that if you find a store, they'll just follow you in. You're going to have to lose them.*

She didn't have the luxury of worrying about the ones behind her. There were dozens in her path that had to be dodged. "What kind of town is this with so many monsters?" Ipes didn't have an answer to the rhetorical question. Despite his natural wisdom, the migratory and settlement pattern of monsters was beyond him. It was just a fact that they lived by: sometimes there were very few of them, sometimes there were bazillions.

Fearing that the KIA was too fragile a vehicle to plow down more than one or two monsters at a time, she took her first left, where she once again ran into more monsters. "Oh, boy, look at them all."

Next time go right, he suggested. She took to the sidewalk to escape and did as Ipes suggested, taking a right and then another right. After that she pretty much went in circles so that, very quickly, Vinita looked as though it had been struck by a tornado of monsters. They were going every which way.

This made driving even more perilous and when she eventually found a *Home Depot*, she was only too happy to get out of the KIA. She parked just down the block from the hardware store and hurried into her monster gear. Her makeup would take more time, so she grabbed her kit and slipped out of the car with an entire battalion of monsters bearing down on her.

Sprinting for all she was worth, she raced down an alley between a strip-mall and the back end of a Holiday Inn. The hotel suited her purposes. She lost the following horde and ducked into a room with a door that hung on one hinge. It was dark, empty, silent. Still she kept her hand on the butt of the .38 in her pocket for close to a minute.

Only when she was sure she was alone did she go to the curtains and open them, very slowly to give herself some light. The scene outside her window was unnerving. There were hundreds of monsters just on the street in front of her.

Do the monsters in this town have some sort of homing sense that isn't normal? Ipes asked. He was afraid and rightly so, however she wasn't. She had her tricks and her make-up that would turn her into a proper appearing monster. They would never know there was a little girl in their midst.

When she was a wild thing, her face grease painted in splotches of grey, and her hair teased into a rat's nest, she headed outside. Other than her size, she looked like all the rest of them. There were very few child monsters her height or smaller. Generally, when children were attacked they were ripped apart so horrifically that there was rarely anything left over to reanimate.

She stumbled out into the early morning sun and made her way slowly up the block until she was just across the street from the immense stretch of empty parking lot in front of the big box store. She was wary of moving too quickly.

Even as brave as she was, every time she had been in one of those hardware stores she had been spooked out. They were always such great big places and the shadows so deep. Even in the day time, it was very dark in the corners and pitch black in the far side of the stores. It gave her the willies thinking that anything or anyone could be hiding there.

To make sure there wouldn't be any "human" surprises waiting for her inside, she spent a chilly forty minutes walking around the entire building, weaving in and out of the monsters that had flocked after the red KIA, which was just within eyesight.

Jillybean just happened to look back at it and was so shocked by what she saw that she broke character and stood straight, with her mouth hanging open. The KIA's driver side door sat wide open and there was someone or something with their butt hanging out of it.

Her first impulse was to shuffle out of sight and hide. Her second impulse was to grab the .38 caliber "police special" and march down there and shoot whoever it was in the back.

Chapter 16

Jillybean

Neither option was possible. She couldn't hide because that was her stuff! She had killed for it and she would again if she had to. And yet, she couldn't just march down there and shoot the person in the back, either.

It wasn't ethical, and besides, what if there were more of them. What if they were a three person team, two watching at either end of the block and one ransacking her car? She was going to protect her stuff, but she was also going to be smart about it.

The little girl zombie crossed to the opposite side of the street, taking an agonizingly slow time. She paused frequently, as most zombies did, however, she used these pauses productively to look for the person's friends, whom she was sure had to be in one of the little 50's style tract homes.

She carefully eyed each monster on the street but found them to be the usual undead, gruesome creatures. Next, she checked the parked cars to see if anyone was hiding in them; there were only four and she quickly ruled them out. That left the rinky-dink houses on the block. They were the only cover that was angled well enough to see the car and close enough to provide immediate support.

But they were all empty. All this added up to one of two things: either the person in her car was all alone or his friends were ten times more sophisticated than Jillybean and that suggested military, and why would any military person want to scrounge in someone else's car?

Then the person is all alone, Jillybean concluded as she tottered across the street. *He's probably dressed up like a monster and he's probably armed and dangerous. But he's not the only one.*

The person was small and oddly dressed. Jillybean would have guessed that since he was acting like a monster, he would have worn ripped up monster clothes, but the person wore what looked like a spider web of shawls, one over the other.

He had moved on from the front seat and was now in the back, busily unloading Jillybean's gas and bombs and guns and what not—the what not being mostly food which was stacked next to a little handcart that Jillybean had just noticed.

In the handcart were odds and ends, the exact sort of things that Jillybean usually carried on her person: string, knives, wire, lighters, etc. Every once in a while, the person would hold up a can of food, or the bag of flour and make happy, chuckling noises and set it down next to, but not in the cart.

Jillybean monster-walked right up behind the person and whispered: "I have a gun." He didn't react, but only went on rummaging. Jillybean had to poke him in the small of the back with the gun. "I said, I have a gun."

"Huh? What's that?" Startled, he straightened and turned around, only it wasn't a *he* at all, it was a *her*. It was an ancient *her*. Jillybean couldn't ever remember seeing someone so old. She had an explosion of grey hair on her head that went everywhere as if she hadn't seen a mirror in years. Her face wasn't just wrinkled, it was *cragged*. There were valleys older than Jillybean running across her forehead and down her cheeks. Her glasses were huge on her face and amazingly thick and yet she still squinted down at Jillybean as though she were trying to see an ant standing next to her foot.

Not that she had far to look downward. Jillybean had grown all of an inch in the last year and barely cleared three and a half feet. This woman only topped her by a head, likely because she had a stooped and hunched back.

"A zombie with a gun? How strange." The woman had a croaky, thin voice. There wasn't the least bit of fear in it, either for Jillybean, her gun, or the monsters that were staring as they passed by.

Since the gun seemed useless as a tool to frighten the woman into compliance, Jillybean stuck it back in her pocket, saying, "I'm not a zombie or a monster. I'm a girl and all that is my stuff, thank you very much, and I'd like for you to put it back in the car, please."

At Jillybean's non-monster pronouncement, the woman leaned in even closer until they were almost eye to eye. "I see. You're in disguise. That's very clever."

"Thank you. And, uh, my stuff? Are you going to put it back?"

"I wasn't going to steal it, dear. I was going to make trades. Everyone needs something that they haven't got. That's the rule. So, I was going to trade some of my extras for some of your extras."

Without permission? Ipes asked from beneath Jillybean's monster coat.

"Maybe she's afraid of people?" she whispered back. "People can be mean; you know that." The old woman had turned slightly away and missed the quick conversation. Jillybean liked that. With her poor hearing and her bad eyes, Ipes became a non-issue. Jillybean wouldn't have to explain or make excuses.

Yes, the old woman was dismally unobservant, however the monsters were getting curious to a dangerous degree. "Do you have a home around here where we can talk?" Jillybean asked... twice. The first question went unheard and she had to raise her distinctly human voice the second time.

"Oh, yes, dear. Follow me." The woman took her cart, which doubled as a walker, and proceeded to plod away, hunched over it. In spite of the fact that she wasn't wearing a disguise, she didn't look very human. Her shawls hung, hiding her frame and her hunch protruded upwards in an unsettling manner and the cart let out a high-pitched metallic squeal that she seemed oblivious to.

Jillybean started to follow but stopped when Ipes asked: *What about the car and all your stuff? She's going to want to trade, you know.*

"Did she have anything I wanted?" Jillybean hadn't been able to see into the cart very well since it was all a jumble.

Probably not. We should take off, Jillybean. Remember the hardware store and the broken window and all that? And I'm getting tired. We were up all night.

She was tired as well, but she was irresistibly drawn to the woman, especially her big eyes and her feeble voice. They were human eyes and it was a human voice, two things that Jillybean missed very much.

Following the old woman in the car was not easy and Jillybean, who was relying on the brake and not the gas, began to get a new appreciation for the story: *The Tortoise and the Hare*. The woman moved at such a painfully slow pace that Jillybean found herself yawning over and over again, her eyes watering, as the woman took ten minutes just to walk the remainder of the block.

Then it was on to a new block; this one a full seventy yards long. Fifteen minutes later she crossed the street, looking very tiny. In the passenger seat, Ipes was snoring loud and pointedly.

After seven more minutes and five more yawns, Jillybean put the car in gear and coasted up the block. It was a waste of gas, she knew, but it was either that or fall into her own coma. She slid up next to the woman and with the monsters coming to attack the KIA, Jillybean yelled: "Is it much further?"

"Oh no, not at all. Just two more blocks. You can go ahead if you wish. It's number eight, one, three."

"Thanks, I'll see you there!" With the monsters only steps from the rear bumper, Jillybean had to yell the last part as she hit the gas and spurted away.

813 Moline Way was the oddest of places to Jillybean. Amazingly, the old woman had not done a thing to fortify her home. Her door had the strength of two-ply balsa wood and the only nod to the current apocalypse was that her blinds were drawn.

Really, any old monster could smash its way right in with very little effort. Perhaps the most redeeming "safety" feature was the immense run of bushes that surrounded her property. They looked to Jillybean as if they hadn't been trimmed in years.

She scooted the KIA up the drive and although it was a small car, the bushes were so overgrown that the branches on both sides scraped her car. They also hid it, for the most part, from the monsters. But to be on the safe side, she darted around to the side of the old woman's house and watched from the corner to see what the trailing monsters would do.

They mulled around the car for a while and then stood in the brown lawn. Though it was cold in Oklahoma, the snow had fallen far to the east, leaving the ground bare. Every once in a while, one of the monsters would stoop and pull a handful of grass up by the roots and munch away.

"What are they going to do when winter really hits?" Jillybean wondered, aloud.

Probably the same thing they did last winter, Ipes answered. *They'll get really skinny and come spring they'll eat all the flowers until they've fattened up a bit.*

"I kinda meant, what are they going to do here. Oklahoma is all barren and dry. You'd think they'd starve to death."

Starve? I doubt it. Remember that one that ate all the bark off your daddy's cherry tree? I think they'd eat rocks if they had to.

Sadly, Jillybean thought that he was likely right. She watched the monsters feed or just stand around doing nothing.

Eventually the old woman came through the small break in the hedges, the annoying squeal of her cart preceding her by five minutes.

As if they were no more dangerous than a pack of garden gnomes, she walked right between the monsters. She went on up to her garage, bent all the way down as far as she could reach and hauled the door upwards. The garage was empty except for a single monster, a disgusting woman zombie with one eye hanging out on her cheek. She was clutching the remains of a long, pale blue coat, now stained with blood and urine, to cover herself.

"What are you doing in here, Jenny?" the old woman demanded. She wheeled her cart around behind the monster and banged it into the back of her legs saying: "Git. Git going now, ya hear?"

The monster allowed this, something that fascinated Jillybean, reminding her of how compliant the monsters had been with the Azael. The other monsters continued to ignore the woman as she pushed the monster named Jenny, and they ignored Jillybean as she came out of hiding.

Of course, she moaned and lurched about like a proper monster. Once more she fooled the old woman, who came at her with the cart. "No, it's me," Jillybean hissed.

"Why didn't you say so. Put your car in the garage. I'll keep the zombies back. They're pretty stupid you know."

Jillybean was actually more worried about parking the KIA in the garage than she was about the monsters. Her ability to go from gas to brake, and to steer in tight corners was admittedly weak. Still, she only had to keep the car aimed straight and stop before she rammed out the back.

As expected, the monsters immediately bustled after the car when she turned it on. In her fright at being trapped in a small car that would be trapped in a small garage, Jillybean gave the KIA too much gas and it practically leapt into the garage, careening into a lawnmower and snapping a rake square in two.

Still, she didn't hit the back of the garage and that was somewhat of a victory. The moment the KIA stopped, she jumped out and through the back door. The backyard was as unkempt as the front. The surrounding bushes were even wilder and there were countless "baby" bushes sprouting all over the place. Jillybean guessed that it wouldn't be long before the term *yard* wouldn't be applicable.

As expected, the old woman's kitchen door was unlocked and Jillybean found herself in a surprisingly clean little bungalow. There were three neat little bedrooms with cozy quilts layered on each mattress, a dining room set for six, a warm den with a fireplace that had hot ash banked in the corner, and a bathroom that needed airing out.

It was a perfect little place—and that's what had Jillybean on edge. If there was something Disney had instilled in her, it was that witches were old, ugly, and lived by themselves out in the wilderness. And they seemed to have an appetite for helpless little girls. Jillybean pulled out the police special and waited for the woman to bustle inside.

"What's that for," the old woman asked after squinting down at Jillybean. Up close, she had a smile that displayed alarmingly over-sized dentures. She had a stale smell to her, too. It wasn't a yucky smell, just an old one as if her and her clothes hadn't had a thorough washing in a while.

"I just need to be careful," Jillybean answered, feeling self-conscious about the gun. "And that's what means there are a lot of bad people in the world. Are you a bad person?"

The old woman said: "I don't think so, but that's up to God to decide. I don't steal if that's what you're worried about, and I couldn't hurt a fly even iff'n I wanted it to, and I wanted to this last summer let me tell you. I chased them all over but I couldn't get them at all, no ma'am."

"I don't like flies either," Jillybean admitted. She looked down at the gun and decided she would keep it close, but not out in the open. It seemed rude to have it out. "So, what do you want to trade?"

Everything it seemed. The old lady started offering everything, including her house, and all she wanted in return was Jillybean's flour and sugar.

Jillybean made a face that suggested pain. "That's the stuff I want the most. When I get to Colorado I'm going to make bread and sugar cookies for my family."

"You still have family?" The idea at first shocked the woman and then made her sad. "I don't know where my family is. Dead, probably. I only had two boys left and they were old. They wouldn't have lived. My grandkids maybe, but they were in Florida, where a lot of all this started. I like to think they would have come to get me if they were still alive, but maybe that's wishful thinking."

"Maybe not. My sister came to get me a few months ago. Maybe your grandkids just got held up by things. It's not easy crossing the planet anymore. There's lots of bad guys out there."

The old woman eased herself down on a couch that someone had, oddly in Jillybean's view, covered in plastic. She sat still as stone for a few moments and then began to cry. She wasn't loud about it, the tears just leaked out of her eyes, disappeared among the crags of her face, only to reappear on her surprisingly hairy chin.

After sometime, in which Jillybean fought off a succession of yawns that wanted to stretch her face, the woman spoke: "That's why I don't hold out hope of ever seeing them. Chances are they're dead and if not, they have to think I'm dead. But… but why am I going on like this? We should be talking deals."

"I'm afraid there isn't anything I want of yours," Jillybean said, frowning a little. "And all the stuff I have, I kinda need."

"I guess that's the way it is then. No hard feelings, little miss." Jillybean started to get up and the woman's face bent in sudden misery once again. "Wouldn't you like to stay and chat awhile? I haven't seen anyone in an age. Well, no one I care to talk to. You say you have a family? In Colorado? How did you get way down here?"

Jillybean told an abbreviated version of her story. She left out entire sections such as everything that had happened before they got to the River King and half of what happened after. When she had to tell longer parts, she made sure not to use words like murder and execution and insanity, saying instead that she had done: "bad things" and was "not right in the head."

"Oh you poor dear, you should stay here with Granny Annie. That's what my grandkids used to call me when they were little tots. Why, we could have just the best time. I could show you how to make bread and cookies. I'm a whiz in the kitchen, you know. My late husband got so fat he couldn't even tie his shoes!"

Jillybean got momentarily caught up with the words "late husband" thinking that Granny Annie might be a little crazy herself since it was obvious that she lived alone and that her husband wasn't late, but dead. But as it was a harmless sort of crazy, it didn't bother Jillybean so much.

Either way, she couldn't stay. "I wish I could, but I have to get back to my family."

Granny Annie humphed: "They don't sound like much of a family to me, letting you go off on your own like that, and not hauling you back when they found you. I'm sorry, Jillybean, that's not the way a true family behaves. I could be your family. Will you please think it over?"

The little girl yawned so wide that she showed all her teeth and her tonsils as well. "I guess I could but I have to sleep first. Maybe I can swing by this afternoon to chat before I go."

"What? You're leaving? But I have a spare bedroom. It's very comfy. Come look."

Jillybean was shown to Granny Annie's guest bedroom, though to her it didn't look like any guests had stayed there in a very long time. The dust was thick and the air strangely heavy as if it were getting tired of waiting around to be breathed.

She didn't want to stay in the room, mainly because a part of her didn't trust the hunched-over witchy looking old woman, and yet Jillybean didn't want to be rude. She agreed to stay, but as a precaution, she pushed the dresser in front of the door and slept with her .38 under her pillow.

Chapter 17

Sadie Walcott

At just about the time Jillybean closed her eyes for a seven-hour slumber, Sadie awoke, stiff and cold, and hungry and scared…and she had to pee.

It was too cold to pee. Going to the bathroom would mean getting out of the three comforters she had wrapped herself in. It would mean exposing herself and sitting down on a freezing toilet seat. That sounded like torture.

Of course, holding it was a torture in itself and eventually she got up, hurried to the bathroom and relieved herself in a stiff squat, hovering inches over the seat. It wasn't pretty, but it kept her flesh from touching. The bathroom had been looted of toilet paper long before and so she used a washcloth and for some reason, felt the need to apologize to some long-dead homeowner.

"Sorry," she whispered, tossing the cloth in a half-filled hamper. "Now what do I do?" she asked herself as she took one of the comforters she had used the night before and wrapped it around her shoulders. She had escaped the slavers and lived through the night. Both were fine accomplishments, but in the clear light of the cold morning she realized that what lay ahead would be infinitely more difficult.

She had no food or water. She had no weapons and no transportation. It was true that she could escape the little canyon town and make her way back to Estes—if she wasn't killed by zombies, captured by the slavers or die of the cold—but what would happen to Captain Grey and the others?

"Maybe ransomed, maybe sold to the River King. Maybe they would die in some two-bit Azael arena fighting like gladiators? Or maybe I help them escape." She said this last bit without much enthusiasm. It didn't seem likely, especially as her enemies were all armed with guns and the most she could scrounge was a long, kitchen knife and a rock the size of a baseball.

She crept to the front window, her "weapons" in hand. She had heard a clang of metal and a muffled curse. Two of the slavers were out in the cold, changing the slashed tires on one of the trucks. Next to the truck were the two tarp-covered trailers parked side by side. One of them was sitting on a blackened rim and nothing else.

The taller of the men yawned, spat and farted all in a row, making Sadie's lip curl. With the clean cold air, she heard it even from across the road.

"That bitch isn't worth this," the farter said, sitting back and letting the tire-iron clang to the ground. He started unscrewing the now loosened lug-nuts with a grease-stained hand. The hair on his head was a shaggy brown mop, hanging five inches below his collar. His beard matched it in color and style.

"Watch what you're doing," the other snipped after giving a glance over his shoulder. This man was lanky with a hooked nose and protruding, watery eyes. "You know there's stiffs around. They can hear good, you know."

"I dropped a tire-iron, so sue me, Doug. You shouldn't even be blaming me. It's Pecos who sat there and let his tires get popped. How could he not hear it? Too close to the river? What a load of bull."

Doug shrugged as he glanced once more over his shoulder. "I don't know. The river can be loud and there were a bunch of stiffs out last night all around him and they aren't quiet." He grunted over his own tire-iron, his face going red with the strain. Finally, it budged and he began to spin the tire-iron in quick circles. "You may be right about the girl. She is a nut-bag."

"Yeah, she is. I wouldn't have gone running around with all them stiffs out there. Not without a gun. Fucking crazy, but as long as she looks good. That's what counts."

The two were quiet for a time working on the tires, lifting off the outer ones and going to work on the inner ones. Doug glanced over his shoulder down the road every few minutes and licked his lips continually until he finally whispered: "Hey, Brian, do you think we'll get a shot at her?"

Brian stopped working at the tire and just sat there for a minute before saying: "I hope so, especially if we get her before Smitty gets back. Hey, you know what? If you finish here, I'll go back up to the plateau and scout for her and if I see her, we'll share her."

"Okay, sure, sure, but why don't I go instead. You had a chance at her last night and couldn't catch her. You're too slow."

"We'll go together," Brian said, "so hurry up with your side." Doug actually finished first by a good margin and left Brian, heading straight up the side of the gulch. Brian cursed under his breath and rushed the next tire into place, barely tightening the lug-nuts. Then he too was tromping up the side of the gulch.

Sadie watched him go and then glanced back at the unattended vehicles. They were ripe for the taking except they were within feet of the house which the slavers were occupying. Smitty, Doug and Brian were gone and that left how many men? She knew of Mike and Pecos, but were there others? And if so, how many others were there? And how many would be keeping watch?

She went to the door and peeked out. There was thirty feet of open road that had to be crossed. "I can make it…if I'm quick. And there's nobody quicker." She hoped. If she were caught, her speed was all she had.

Out she slipped, keeping low. Anyone looking down from the plateau would spot her in an instant, but why would Doug or Brian be looking back the way they had come? No, they'd be looking out at the town. And the men inside the house? It had been a long night, probably even longer for them than for her.

They'd be sleeping, all except whoever was watching the prisoners—that guy would be bored. He would pace or read or alternate between staring out the window and watching the prisoners. The thought froze Sadie halfway across the street.

With her nerve shattered, she couldn't move a muscle except to whisper: "Shit." She was still standing there when a man walked out of the house with his hands working at his zipper. He turned immediately to his right and began peeing against the side of the building in a long stream.

Sadie slunk down and judged that it would be safer to slink forward, using the truck as cover, rather than to try to run across the open road. She started creeping forward when the man made a noise. At first, she thought it was some weird hissing growl, but she realized he had sighed only in the middle of it, he'd been struck by a yawn. He made no pretense at being quiet and nor did he bother with aim. His urine arced higher and higher onto the side of the house.

A new look of disgust twisted Sadie's features as she made it to the back of the truck and watched the man's lower legs and the spray of yellow as it banked off the siding. It seemed to go on forever.

Eventually the spray turned to drips and there came the sound of a zipper going up. Her expectation that the booted feet would head back inside were dashed as he turned and started walking straight for the truck!

Quickly, she crawled, spider-like, beneath it, desperately trying to keep her black coat from scraping against the dirt drive. The coat was some sort of nylon weave and any scrape no matter how slight would have been heard. As she crawled on, one foot at a time, she watched the boots approach the front of the truck.

Please just look in the front seat. Please just look in the front seat, she pleaded, silently. He bypassed the front seat and kept going around to the back and stopped at the dual set of back tires.

"What the hell?" he growled, squatting down. With the twin tires in the way, she could only see part of his knee, but that didn't mean he couldn't see her. She froze as he reached out to touch the tire. "Those stupid fucks." He straightened, his feet first pointing one way and then the other.

It was now fifty-fifty for Sadie. Her black Converse sneakers were sticking well out from beneath the back of the truck, but she couldn't move any further without alerting the man. If he went to the back, she would try to crawl the extra few feet, only she didn't like her chances.

To her great relief, he went to the front. "Smitty is gonna kill them both," he whispered and then went inside. Sadie slumped in relief, her cheek resting uncaringly in the dirt.

"That was friggin' close." Her limbs were jumpy and weak, and she wanted just to lie there for a minute to collect herself, but there was no telling who would come out of the house next. She slithered backwards until her head cleared the rear bumper.

Very gradually, she lifted herself up so that she could peer over the bed of the truck. The windows of the house were hung with festive blankets of pink and white. No one peeked out.

"Finally, a good sign," she said to herself as she squatted down again, going on her hands and knees to the first trailer. It was out in the open, and so she made sure to keep as much of it between her and the house as possible.

She scrambled a hand up under the tarp and felt around. There was no mistaking the edge of a cardboard box and so she moved further up the trailer. More boxes.

Thankfully, they weren't sealed, only folded down. She stuck her hand in one, hoping for guns, but finding food instead. Like the boxes, canned food always felt just like canned food and nothing else, except for maybe very old motor oil.

She pulled out a can and made a face. "Beets? Hmmm. Let's try that again." She reached in once more and took the first can on top. More beets. A third try and a third can of beets. She put them back.

In her opinion, beets tasted like dirt and eating the brown leaves from the forest floor would have been more palatable to her.

It was a big trailer; there had to be more than just beets. The next box yielded sauerkraut. She groaned, shoved the can back and moved on to the next. "Finally," she whispered as she gazed down on a can of beef ravioli. Her next reach into the grab bag revealed a second can of ravioli, but the third gave her pinto beans and the next was pickled jalapeños, something she had never heard of before.

She was in the middle of another grab when she heard the gravelly crunch of a coming vehicle. "Smitty," she whispered. She had an odd fear of the man. She imagined it had been him lying in wait for her the night before.

None of the others she had run into had struck her as all that smart, but the leader would be different. He would be smart enough to outguess his opponents.

Stuffing cans into her coat, she backed away from the trailer, her eyes flicking from the house to the road with every other step. "Sound carries, Sadie," she said to herself, realizing she had misjudged where the danger to her was really coming from.

The truck was far off but Doug and Brian had to have heard it. They'd be hurrying back from their "Sadie-hunt."

Sadie turned and sprinted for the house she had spent the night in, foolishly thinking that its relative warmth was some sort of refuge. Gently, she clicked the front door closed behind her and then went to the window and stared out through a slight gap in the curtain.

A minute later, Doug came hurrying down the road, trying to appear as if he had been gone only a minute. Brian acted the same way, going straight to the truck and squatting down next to the rear tire. He went to work tightening the lug-nuts and likely would have even if they had been as tight as they could go. He wanted to appear busy.

Hunkered down, Sadie watched as a truck came barreling down the road, kicking dust into the air. By the way they were acting, Sadie was altogether sure this was Smitty. He pulled up, kicked the truck's door open and then gazed down at Doug and Brian with a distinct lack of fondness on his face. He was a big, beefy man who filled the doorway of the truck and then some. "Still at it? What the fuck? I gotta wonder, how long does it take you bitches to change a fucking light bulb?"

"The nuts were frozen on there," Brian answered. "You know how it is."

"I know you two morons have about three minutes to get those tires on before the stiffs show up."

Brian popped up, wiping his hands. "I'm already done. I was just keeping Doug company. He gets scared out here by himself."

Doug looked like he was about to argue when Smitty cut him off. "If you're done, you can get this tire on the trailer. Let's see if you two can work together for a change." He reached back across the seat of the truck and pulled out a sturdy little tire. "I pulled it off one of those dinky Airstreams down at the RV park. It's good as freaking new."

"Great," Brian said, forcing some fake excitement into his voice. "If that stupid bitch thinks she can mess with us, she's got another thing coming, right Smitty?"

Smitty's eyes flicked up at the walls of the gulch for a moment before he answered: "I don't know about that. I bet she's just getting started. We know she's got guts. She could've run but she didn't. She could've stayed hidden, but she took a risk and went on the offensive. No, she ain't done. She's out there planning and scheming."

This was news to Sadie. "A plan? I don't have a stinking plan, unless not dying and not getting caught by these bozos is a plan. Which it isn't."

Seconds later, Smitty went inside, leaving his two flunkies to rush around. Brian jacked up the trailer, while Doug went to work on the lug-nuts. They were halfway through when the first zombie could be seen making its way slowly down the road.

The two men fled into the house. Sadie hoped that a hundred more zombies would join the first. They would provide excellent cover. She'd be able to sneak out, do some more mischief and maybe steal some more food.

Only three more zombies showed up. "Great. Four zombies aren't enough. So what do I do?" Nothing came to her and she ended up sitting next to the window for the entire morning, half

143

of which was spent snoring with her head lolled over on her shoulder.

When the sun was as vertical as it would get at that time of the year, the slavers ventured outside, armed with shovels and axes, and, in one case, a strange spear. They attacked the four zombies, killing them rather easily.

"Okay, I want three teams," Smitty said, tossing aside a bloodied shovel. "No Doug, don't go stand next to Brian. You two are worse than an old married couple. Doug and Bill. Brian and Mike, Pecos and Juan. You're going to search each house quickly but thoroughly. Bill you take the houses on the north side of the street, Mike you and Brian got the south. Juan and Pecos will take the little offshoot roads. If you see something, give a yell."

"But not too loudly," Mike added. "You don't want to stir up the stiffs. But if you happen to, pull the old 'in through the front door out through the back.' Try not to shoot your guns if you can help it."

Sadie was still trying to rub sleep out of her eyes when the three groups broke up. Though she should have been ready, her mouth fell open as Juan and Pecos headed straight for "her" house. She had all of twelve seconds to hide and ten of those seconds were wasted as she stared around in shock.

It was an average little cottage. Other than the living room she stood in, there were two bedrooms, a single bathroom, a kitchen and a dining room. And there wasn't much to any of the rooms other than just the usual stuff. The living room held a single sofa pushed up under the front window, two high-backed chairs, a coffee table and a knickknack shelf.

That was it.

The only places to hide were places a two-year-old would think was smart. Of course, she could run out the back door in broad daylight, making who knows how much racket and have all seven slavers, with their perfectly working trucks, after her in no time. They would hound her into exhaustion.

Sadie had no choice but to go with a pathetic hiding spot: behind the couch. There was a gap of about eight inches so the curtains could hang straight. She wiggled into it sideways, just as the door opened. She stopped in mid-wiggle, not knowing if her feet were sticking out or not.

She closed her eyes, her teeth gritted, figuring that any moment one of them would grab her by the ankles and haul her out of her idiotic hiding place. She was still in her state of rigid uselessness when she heard a click and suddenly, there was light playing through her lids.

For a foolish moment, she wondered if they had flicked on the overhead light, but then she remembered the power was out and she nearly blew out in exasperation at her own stupidity. It was a flashlight that had been clicked on and it gave her some hope.

The house was lit in two shades: dim and darker than dim. As always, she was dressed in black and hiding in a naturally dark spot. *Maybe they won't get me*, she thought. *Yay me.*

It wasn't that she was apathetic to her fate, she only wished there was more to it than crawling around in the shadows. Yes, Jillybean always advocated "getting close" to her enemies, but she also *did things*. So far, the only thing Sadie had managed to do was temporarily disable two trucks and steal four cans of...

"Uh-oh," she said, under her breath. The four cans of food she had stolen from the trailer were sitting on the couch just next to the armrest. If one of the men looked down and to their right they would see the cans plain as day.

"I'll get the kitchen and the backyard, you check the back rooms," one of the men said.

They moved through the house, creaking floorboards and knocking into the various items that had been strewn about by previous searchers. At the first opportunity, Sadie unsquiggled and crouched next to the couch, watching as light beams went this way and that in two different parts of the house.

With four deft movements, she snatched up the cans and hid them beneath the couch and then she re-squiggled just as the sound of footsteps approached.

"Nothing," one stated.

"She's not going to be this close," the other stated.

"You never know. If she was smart, she would be cuz we'd never..." The two men left, their voices trailing to nothing as they shut the door behind them.

Sadie wilted in relief and laid in her uncomfortable hiding spot for a few more minutes before she squiggled out again. She eased up to the window, but there wasn't much to see. The three teams were off searching homes, and the house across the road was quiet and seemingly dead.

What was going on in there? Were the soldiers being abused? Were they handcuffed together? Were they being fed or given water?

"I gotta do something besides hiding and stealing a few cans of food." She sat there for a few moments as her mind spun—as it spun in useless circles. No plan came to her. No crazy idea of an explosive device made of pickled jalapeños, bleach, and year-old dish soap sprang to mind.

Time passed and Sadie's nails were bitten down to ragged edges and still she hadn't come up with a plan. "I could rush Smitty. He's in there by himself. He won't expect it. It would be a total surprise. I could use a, uh...I could use...son of a bitch! It's a stupid idea, damn it!"

She beat herself up for her stupidity for the next three hours and then the teams came back empty-handed and cranky. In that time, she decided that if she couldn't think of a way to free her friends she would do everything in her power to keep them stuck in the crappy little town of Poudre Park.

"Maybe if I keep messing with the slavers, they'll give up and just leave," she said. It would be dangerous, but she planned to use the dark to disable the trucks on a more permanent basis. She might not be able to make a bomb, but she had a lighter and there was gas in the trucks and gas would burn, big time.

At about four in the afternoon, she ate half a can of ravioli, thinking she should begin rationing her food. "I'll be here a long time harassing their sorry assess." Or so she thought.

Night time was supposedly her time, but as the sun set there was a lot of activity outside the house across the road. The slavers went back and forth from the house to the trucks carrying bags and boxes. It wasn't long before the soldiers from the Valley were dragged out, one after another, their hands cuffed behind their backs and their heads hanging low in defeat.

"They're leaving," Sadie whispered, feeling a shiver of insanity come over her. A part of her wanted to rush out there wielding her stupid knife and her even stupider baseball-sized rock.

"But that would be giving up," she said. It wouldn't be suicide. They wouldn't kill her. They would take her and use her and when they had their fun, they'd sell her.

In defeat, she watched as Captain Grey was pushed into the back of the second truck. He was the last. "Mount up!" Smitty said to his men as he climbed into the lead vehicle.

The evening was on the verge of becoming night and the sound of their diesel engines was a roar. It almost seemed to be a challenge to Sadie's courage. She gripped her knife until her knuckles turned white, and then she let it clatter to the floor as Smitty turned onto the road and drove out of there with the second truck following.

A minute later all that was left of them were the echoes bouncing around the walls of the gulch. "Fuck," Sadie said, going to the door and creaking it open. She stood on the porch, not knowing what to do with herself. Without gas—and where would she find gas in the middle of the mountains—she couldn't follow after the slavers.

"It's going to be a long walk home," she said to herself as she visualized her new plan: go back to the valley, gather the entire army and march on whatever city the slavers sold Captain Grey to. It was as sound a plan as she had ever made. She planned to leave that night, that very instant in fact.

"A long walk, but at least I won't starve." She could make three and a half cans of food stretch a long way, especially if one of those cans was pickled jalapeños. All by itself, that could last a week.

She stood in the road as the echoes gradually faded. When they were gone altogether, she turned to go back into the cottage she had commandeered to get her few belongings, only she stopped as she saw a glint of something metallic on the ground.

"That's a can," she said to herself, with a touch of excitement. The can was an omen, she felt it in her bones. It was food and it would give her the strength to run part of the way back home. "Spaghetti and meatballs!" she said, forcing her voice from a scream to whisper. "What if there's more," she asked the night as she hurried to the house across the road.

Cautious as always, she paused at the door, leaning in towards it, listening for any movement. Even when silence greeted her, she didn't rush in. Slowly, she eased the door back. The house was dark as could be and stunk of sweat and other unpleasant manly odors.

But smells didn't bother her. What sat in one of the chairs did, however.

"That was easier than I thought." One of the slavers shone a light into her eyes and blinding her.

Chapter 18

Jillybean

Normally, for Jillybean, waking up in the new undead world was a slow, cautious affair. Normally, she tested the air with trepidation. Normally, her mind cycled from sleep to consciousness without missing a beat.

On that late afternoon, Jillybean seemingly woke in a whole new world. She was snuggled under soft blankets, the air was warm and bright, and the room clean without the least hint of danger. Stranger still, when she awoke, it felt as if she were still in a dream.

She'd been dreaming of her house back in Philadelphia. Her daddy had been reading the paper at the kitchen table as her mommy bustled around making dinner. In the dream, Jillybean had been starving and she asked over and over: *How long until it's done?*

Soon, her mommy said. *You are almost done, but you have to have patience.*

I don't mean me. I mean the cookies.

That's when Jillybean woke up, warm and safe, and with the scent of baking cookies in the air. It was wonderful, and caution went out the window as she hopped down from the bed, padded over to the dresser, and heaved it back from the door.

The smell was stronger in the hall, almost overpowering. She was close to running headlong into the kitchen with tears in her eyes, expecting not to see the old hag, but her mommy, miraculously alive and well.

But it was only Granny Annie in the kitchen, an apron decorated with reindeer and mistletoe tied about her midsection and white powder on one cheek. There was a tea set put out with light tendrils of steam lifting from delicate cups. Jillybean wanted to obsess on the intricate floral pattern, but the old lady spoke in her creaky old lady voice: "Oh, hello dear. I hope I didn't wake you. I was just trying to prepare a surprise."

Jillybean went up to the counter, standing on tiptoes to see what was being made. "What is it? It smells wonderful. It smells like cookies." If such a thing were possible nowadays. Fresh baked cookies were not a part of this world of zombies and blood.

"Of course, they are cookies. Cinnamon, syrup cookies with a sugar glaze. Those specs? It's sage, can you believe it? It's all I had, but it works. Not that it was easy, baking, using a wood fire is devilishly tricky but I think I did pretty well with this batch. Here, try one."

Carefully, Granny Annie picked up a delicate cookie in her blue-veined and liver-spotted hands, and gave it to Jillybean.

Her first bite was just over a nibble in size and yet, the flavor exploded in her mouth. Her next bite was bigger and the third finished it off. For a long time—a minute is a long time to a seven-year-old—she savored the remains of the cookie as the mushed remains disintegrated in her mouth.

With her eyes closed, she announced: "That was yummy. I mean it was really, really good." This was her highest compliment. "Ipes would have…" She stopped, her eyes losing their focus as she tried to recall the last time she had seen her zebra. Amazingly, she had left him in the car!

"I'll be right back," she said and headed for the garage.

The old woman mistook what she was after and said: "That's not necessary, dear. I admit, I used some of your flour, but I also used my Crisco and syrup and a lot of other ingredients. And I didn't use very much at all, just a few cups. I thought it would be a nice surprise."

Jillybean turned back to the old woman, her mind quite spun around by the cookie and the confession and the wonderful smell of the house. "You…you used my flour? You took it, you mean. That's stealing."

Granny Annie shook her head. "I don't know if I'd call it stealing since I used it for you. The cookies are for you, dear. Remember, you said that you wanted to use the flour for cookies? I saved you the trouble and look how good they turned out. I don't mean to disparage you, however, baking takes practice and you might have wasted that whole bag of flour trying to make cookies half as good as this."

"You're right, I think," Jillybean admitted, calming quickly. "I just wish you had waited and showed me how to make them." She was sure she could learn the basics of baking from a cookbook, but she was also sure she could learn a great deal more from a lady who had taken a hodgepodge of odd ingredients and turned out such wonderful cookies.

"Don't you worry your shaggy little head about that, I'll show you with the next batch, dear."

149

Jillybean forgot all about Ipes as she stepped forward eagerly. Granny Annie frowned at her. "We aren't going to make them now, dear. A baker's dozen should last you a week, if not longer. You know it's almost winter. We should be thinking about conserving what we have because Oklahoma can get brutally cold on occasion."

"Conserving?" Jillybean asked. She knew the word, of course, however she was thrown off by the pronoun "we" which had been used just before it.

"Oh yes. We have to be careful with our supplies. But don't worry, we have a good start between us. I have an entire pantry of preserves. Have you ever canned anything, dear?"

"I caught a bumble bee in a jar once," Jillybean answered, "but my mom made me put it back in the garden."

Granny Annie laughed at this, her overly large dentures nearly falling out of her mouth in the process. "No, dear. I'm talking about canning fruits and vegetables. It's a way of keeping them from spoiling for a long time. I can teach you how."

"I don't think I have time for that. I have to teach myself how to weld before sunset. Is canning a long process?"

"It is," the old woman said, as she made her way to her kitchen table and eased into a chair. "It's a long process and one that can't be taught in a few hours. You're going to have to stay with me, dear. I'm afraid I'm going to have to insist on it. I can't in good conscience let a five-year-old wander around the country without adult supervision. There's just too much bad stuff out there."

Jillybean's hand slipped into her pocket and found the grip of the .38. "I'm seven," she declared. "I'm a May flower…and I'm sorry, Miss Granny Annie ma'am, but I can't stay here. I have to go find my family and I have to go today. You can't stop me."

An image bloomed in her mind…an awful image of blood and flashes of light leaping from the .38 and an old lady lying on the floor, staring up at the ceiling with odd, cloudy eyes. Jillybean squeezed her eyes shut as hard as she could and when she opened them again the kitchen was as it was supposed to be, or nearly so. There was silence in the room; a tense silence on Jillybean's part and a sad one on Granny Annie's.

After a few moments, Granny Annie asked in a voice that was close to begging: "Will you come back to visit me when you find your family? I'd like to meet them and…and maybe we could spend some more time together, then. I can show you how to bake and to can preserves and you can tell me about your adventures."

Now it was Jillybean's turn to grow sad. Her adventures weren't the type you shared with someone whose first name was "Granny."

"I'll visit if I can…but hey, why don't you come with me to Colorado? There are a whole lots of good people there. You could be a baker or a canner-person. I don't know if they have any grannies in the Valley and they probably need some."

She shook her head, her loose jowls swinging gently. "No, I couldn't. Thanks, though. It's just I couldn't make the trip. It's too dangerous. And my back has issues. I can't sit in a car for very long. And what happens if my boys come for me? If they showed up while I was gone, I'd never forgive myself."

Jillybean knew her boys would never come for her. They were dead. Another silence settled over the room. Jillybean could tell that Granny Annie was preparing to make another attempt at persuasion and so she cut the old lady off.

"I have to go." It wasn't a lie. The sun blared directly in through a west window, telling Jillybean that it would set in the next two hours. She had to get to the hardware store before it did. Jillybean started heading for the garage.

"Wait!" Granny Annie cried. "Your cookies. I'll wrap them up for your trip and I have some extra cinnamon for you. For some reason everyone forgets to take cinnamon, don't ask me why."

Granny Annie bustled about, packaging the cookies and the extra cinnamon and some salt and two jars of blackberry preserves. "They give me the trots," she declared.

In Jillybean's mind, that didn't seem like a bad thing since she knew, as everyone did, that trotting was the same thing as running. "Thanks so much…would you take a gift from me? I have some extra flour, I guess, and some sugar. You wanted that before."

A momentary longing swept over Granny Annie's face, but it lasted just a blink before it turned to one of reluctant pain. "No, I couldn't. It wouldn't be right."

With gratitude, Jillybean took the pendulous plastic bag filled with preserves and cinnamon and all sorts of what not. She dangled it from the crook of one elbow as she accepted the plate of cookies that were wrapped like a mummy in cellophane.

"I'm glad you were nice," Jillybean told Granny Annie. By this she meant: I'm glad I didn't have to kill you for being evil and taking my stuff.

"I'm glad you were a good little girl," Annie countered. "I miss that in people, goodness."

They hugged, awkwardly, each wanting what they couldn't have. After, Jillybean went to the KIA and Granny Annie went to the garage door, making a production out of stooping and pulling it up.

Don't be mean, Ipes scolded. He had been sitting in the front seat of the KIA all day and yet didn't seem the least bit upset about it. *That's not a 'production.' She's getting tired. Do you think she bakes cookies every day? Getting all that wood and preparing everything probably took a lot out of her. She is really, really old.*

"I didn't mean it like that," Jillybean whispered out of the corner of her mouth. With Granny Annie standing right there, smiling, showing her overly large dentures, the little girl didn't want to appear too crazy.

I know what you meant. You think she wouldn't stoop to a little showmanship to have a little company? She has to be lonely, just like you.

"But I'm lonely by choice," Jillybean countered as she gave a last wave before sticking the KIA in reverse. When she reversed, whether in a garage or an open field, she did so with her full trust in God, not in any skill that she possessed. She put the KIA in reverse, gritted her teeth, hit the gas, and closed her eyes, *hoping* that the car would go straight back.

Something banged as she tore yet another groove into the side of the KIA, and yet, she made it out into the sunshine. With the help of two monsters whom she plowed over, she was able to stop before she rammed the bushes that marked Granny Annie's property line.

With more care, since she could see where she was going, she turned the little car as if it were an ocean liner. Even with power-steering, she had to go hand over hand and just barely made it out onto the street. She looked back for Granny Annie, one last time, however the bushes blocked the view completely.

You should get going before you change your mind, Ipes suggested. The car was silent during the short trip to the hardware store. Ipes didn't even mention the cookies, though he eyed them on the sly, or so he thought.

"You can have some," Jillybean told him. Despite how delicious they were, she was somewhat apathetic to them. Just then, she was somewhat apathetic to everything. "Did I make a mistake by not staying?"

She expected Ipes to be all over the idea of staying with a lady who could bake as well as Granny Annie, however, Ipes shook his head. *She's right about winter out here. And supplies will be hard to come by. And she can't live forever. It'll be lonely when she dies.*

"Yeah," Jillybean answered as they pulled into the wide expanse of parking lot. The town was devoid of humans and so the little girl dressed as a minimalist monster, doing just enough to fool any she might come across.

There were none in the tremendous warehouse-sized store. She stood just inside the entrance listening for their tell-tale moans until she decided it was safe to flick on her flashlight and hurry to an overturned kiosk. The glossy covers of the books gleamed under the light as she pawed through them, glancing quickly at their titles and setting them in two proper piles: keep and don't keep.

Although she was there to learn the art of welding, she was also interested in a variety of subjects and she kept books on carpentry, plumbing, and electricity. There were two books on metal working and she took the one with the prettiest pictures back to the doorway, sat in a stream of warm sunlight with the book across her knees and began reading.

It didn't take her long to figure out that arc-welding wasn't the way to go. It required electricity to generate enough heat to melt the metal rods which basically acted as glue.

The store had gas-powered generators, which of course used gas, which she didn't have in great supply, *perhaps* just enough to make it to Colorado.

Another welding method was through the use of an acetylene torch, however the store was out of acetylene.

There's soldering, Ipes suggested, pointing at one of the pictures from the table of contents. *It looks pretty simple.*

"Oh, yes, it uses fire. I like fire. Electricity is a little scary. You never know when it's gonna jump out and zap you. 'Member back in the old days? Mommy used to always tell us to keep away from the plugs and to never never put a toaster in the bathtub, though I never wanted to anyways. Who would want to eat toast while taking a bath? It could get all soggy."

Ipes, whom Jillybean had accused of being part zebra and part chicken on more than one occasion, heartily agreed with her about all of it, including the toast. *I don't care for fire, myself*, he added, *but a little flame is better than a lot of monsters.*

Gathering the propane torch and the soldering supplies was easy, however finding the right piece of metal was not. It had to be the right size to fit over the car window and still allow the door to open. Her choices were too big: four foot by four foot, or too small: one foot by one foot.

She needed a size in the middle, which meant a trip to another hardware store or… "I can solder four of the small ones together so that they overlap making a two-by-two piece."

The little girl was quite the sight, squatting over the pieces of metal like a frog with her knees jutting and her soft face made stern by concentration. After a few mistakes where she used too much heat and boiled away the soft soldering metal, she got the hang of it and quicker than she would have guessed, she had the covering ready for her window.

Getting that attached was a little more difficult since the window frame on the car door wasn't exactly flat. It had been through at least three crashes and now it was bumpy and crooked and she couldn't get the metal cover to sit on it evenly. And she couldn't get it to stay in position; it kept wanting to fall down, and when it did it clanged loud enough to draw a crowd of walking dead.

Jillybean ran and hid among the giant shelves that stretched to the ceiling. In the gloom of the building, she could see the beasts walking around, staring off into space.

Maybe we should run out the back, Ipes suggested.

"Maybe *they* should run out the back," Jillybean countered. The hardware store had all sorts of items that she could use to attract the attention of monsters.

Moving like a ghost, she went to the painting section and gathered materials: paint thinner, clean tarps, long-handled roller brushes. Weighed down, she made her way to one of the back doors and opened it with her back.

The monsters saw the sudden influx of light and came charging, leaving Jillybean very little time to douse the tarps with the paint thinner and hang them on the roller brushes. She had hoped to be able to make a scarecrow of sorts, but all she had time for was to lean them against a dumpster and run a line of thinner to her hiding spot behind the door.

When four of the monsters were out back, she lit the line of paint thinner and jumped back. It flared so quickly that it almost caught her hair on fire.

The flames sped along the ground to the paint brushes and then *foomp!* the white tarps went right up. The flames were bright as flares and crackled so loudly that soon all the monsters were outside doing what they did whenever they saw fire: they stared with slack jaws. Jillybean used the distraction to slip inside and shut the door behind her.

She was alone now and had to come up with a way to hold the metal cover while she soldered it in place. Walking along the rows of shelves, beaming her light all around, she had a hundred ideas burst in her mind like popcorn, none of which had anything to do with the car—a tree house with running water, homemade cranes for lifting heavy objects, perhaps into the tree house, watermills to generate electricity and move water to distant fields, fish farms made from inch-thick poly...

Hey, concentrate! Ipes cried. *What about securing the metal to the door? Wasn't that what you're supposed to be doing?*

"Oh that's easy. We can use some *Liquid Nails* and a caulk gun. We'll just glue it into position, no problem. Boy, I might have to rethink the whole tree house idea. I could live in a hardware store. There's just so much stuff!"

Her excitement dimmed a moment later when a yawn struck her. She'd only had six hours of sleep and now she faced another long night of driving. Using the caulk gun, she slapped the metal in place over the broken window and, although the glue set quickly and the metal plate seemed exceptionally sturdy, she soldered it in place as well, though this was mostly for the practice.

After gathering a few battery-operated tools and a 9-volt charger that she could plug into the KIA she set out once more, hoping to knock off another two hundred miles from her trip. By sunrise, she hoped to be most of the way across the northern strip of Oklahoma.

It was endless hours driving through endless country. At three in the morning, she crossed the Arkansas River after detouring far north in order to make the crossing where there was nothing but brown scrub shooting up from a frozen brown land. Then she detoured south again to skirt around the minor town of Newkirk that had a pre-apocalypse population of twenty-three hundred.

Even that felt like too many people to chance. She stuck to the loneliest roads on the map. They were so empty that she was able to "race" along at twenty-one miles an hour with just the moonlight guiding her.

One road in particular was so empty that there weren't even monsters on it. She saw a herd of deer, two raccoons, a skunk, and what might have been an opossum, only she didn't know what one looked like. The road was so empty and the trip so easy that when headlights suddenly flicked on behind her, she just about had a heart attack.

Instinctively, she hit the gas and spurted ahead. Just as instinctively, she knew that it was no use. Even if the KIA had been a sports car, she wasn't much of a driver and the car behind her was flying to catch up. She was going to be caught.

"Maybe they're friendly," Jillybean said, grasping at straws. "Maybe they're more ascared of me than I am of them."

I don't think there is anyone that is that scared, Ipes replied. If they were that afraid, they would have stayed hidden and needed a change of underpants.

"That's not funny," Jillybean snapped. It was true, it just wasn't funny. "They're getting closer. Do you think they can see me?" The lights seemed very far away, maybe a half a mile, it was hard to tell in the night.

Perhaps. Go faster.

She looked down and saw that the KIA was doing forty-four. She had never gone that fast before. Still, she nudged the gas pedal further down. When she looked up from her feet, her eyes went to the rear-view mirror instead of the road and she ran over something with a tremendous thump that caused her to jerk and scream.

The KIA slewed to the right, its tires running over the rumble strip on the edge of the road with a thrumming that made it seem as if the car was coming apart. Jillybean's scream reach new decibels until she fought the car back to the center of the road.

Her foot came completely off the blocks glued to the gas pedal, and gradually, her speed bled away until she was doing a manageable thirty-eight. The car behind her was now less than a hundred yards off. "Ipes," Jillybean asked in a frightened whisper, "what do I do? They're going to get me."

Like you said, they could be friendly.

"And if they're not?" They both knew that friendly people weren't likely to chase a car for no reason in the dead of night.

Then close your eyes if they do anything bad to you. Close your eyes and think only good thoughts. Close your eyes and go somewhere else.

Jillybean couldn't believe what she was hearing. She glanced over at the zebra, but he refused to look up. "You want me to go crazy in the brain, again, don't you? What if I'm gone for years? What if they do things to me while…" She couldn't bring herself to finish her sentence.

Then you won't know and that'll be good.

The car was close now, its high-beams blinding Jillybean every time she looked back. It had begun to blare its horn; they wanted her to pull over. "It won't be good," she said in a whisper. She knew the bad things they would do to her. They wouldn't care if she were a little girl or not—evil people never did.

"I won't do that," she said. "I'm not going to go crazy and I'm not going to give in." She had decided.

Her hands gripped the wheel, her downy brows came down and her jaw clenched as she found the gas pedal by memory…

…And the next thing she knew, she was standing in the night, staring at the KIA that sat some ways off down the road. Above her the stars were bright, diamonds. They were cold as ice.

"How did I…?" she didn't finish the question. A second before she had been barreling down the road and now she was standing in the middle of it. Behind her came a crackling sound.

It was a fire. And now she smelled a reeking chemical smoke. And now she felt a strange pain in her throat, as if she had been strangled. And now she realized there was something in her hand, something heavy and hard. It was a gun.

She wanted to look back at the fire, but something deep inside pleaded: *don't look back, just keep walking. Let this memory die.*

Chapter 19

Captain Grey

With his arms trussed behind his back, the pain in his chest was a constant nag that made every move, including breathing, a misery. The only halfway decent position that allowed him to take even half a breath without groaning aloud was lying on his side.

Sleep was impossible until Lieutenant Wilson insisted that Captain Grey use his lap as a pillow. "I won't tell Deanna if you won't," Wilson joked. It had been a whispered joke. Everything spoken between the men had been whispered.

When they had first been captured, Grey ordered the men only to reveal their first names and nothing more. They all knew the score. Their enemies were many and their friends, few. If their captors realized who Captain Grey was, the entire lot of them would be sold off to the Azael or to the River King or to the remnants of the people of New Eden, who had looked for and found a new messiah.

This was likely to happen, either way, but there was no reason to make it a sure thing.

As Grey knew they would, his men had obeyed his orders. They spoke to their captors only when spoken to and only after getting permission. Not much had been asked, not until Sadie had come to rescue them.

The night before, when Grey had heard the distant rumble of the truck coming in and out as it made its way along the mountain roads, he had cursed and tried to will her away. But she kept coming.

"Who is that?" Smitty had demanded.

"No one say a word," Grey ordered. If Grey was valuable to their enemies, Sadie was three or four times as valuable. Everyone wanted a piece of her, including Yuri Petrovich far off in New York City.

Smitty had threatened them with a knife that was so long and sharp it was practically a short sword. Two of the men were cut, but they were minor wounds and both men had only gritted their teeth, harder.

As much as Grey liked and admired Sadie and her spunkiness, he fully expected her to be caught within minutes.

She flummoxed them all night long and through most of the next day. Finally, Smitty broke down the problems she faced: "She doesn't have a weapon and she doesn't have a vehicle. If we leave, what will she do?"

"She'll begin searching for both," Mike answered.

"Exactly. More importantly, she'll come out of hiding to do both." When evening came, Mike hid while the others made a show of getting ready to leave.

"Who drives at night if they can help it, Sadie?" Grey asked under his breath. "See the trap, Sadie! The signs are right there in front of your face."

Sadie was no Jillybean and was caught much faster than anyone could have guessed. Smitty turned the two laden-down trucks around and chugged back. "Everyone inside, hurry!" he hissed as they pulled up to the little house they had departed from not a half hour before.

Before the zombies could follow them all the way down the gulch, the prisoners were bustled out of the back of the truck and into the house. Sadie stood next to a burly man who had her by the upper arm in a tight grip—her signature black clothes were disheveled and her eyes burned with hate. Both Grey and Smitty glared.

"What's been going on?" Smitty asked, his voice now cold.

"Nothing," Mike answered. "I had to make sure she wasn't armed. I didn't fuck her if that's what you're asking."

Smitty remained silent for a moment, his eyes assessing Sadie and her clothes and then Mike and his clothing which looked just as it had before they left. "Alright, good. I'll take her from here. The rest of you feed and water the prisoners and get ready to turn in. I want to leave at first light."

Grey and the others were shoved back to their spot in the corner of the dining room while Smitty leered at Sadie. "What's your name, darling?" he asked in a gentler voice.

"First name only, Alice," Grey barked. He caught Sadie's eye, hoping to warn her of her danger.

"Bill, shut that man up!" Smitty ordered. Grey was punched in the stomach, but barely felt it. Even recovering as he was, Grey was a tough one. Though he had lost weight, he was still gristle and grit, and still had the reflexes to turn quick enough so that the blow didn't land square. He was also smart enough to ham up the playacting so he wouldn't be hit again.

He was still coughing when Smitty shoved Sadie into a back bedroom with one hand. The other was already working his zipper.

"I wouldn't do that if I were you," Grey warned. Sadie was about to be raped, the first of many rapes that night. He had to take a chance to stop it. "You don't know who she is." The casual way he said this stopped Smitty. He turned hard eyes on Grey.

"And who is she?"

Grey shrugged as nonchalantly as he could, trying to buy every second that he could to think of something to save Sadie. "It's not, uh, who she is that matters so much as, uh, uh, who she used to be with." Before Smitty could ask "who" Grey followed up with: "Let's just say, he's got an evil reputation as a jealous man and the power to back up that reputation."

"Someone from the Valley?" Smitty spat. "Like I'm afraid of any of you pussies."

"I said he has an evil reputation. Who in the Valley has an evil reputation? You should try listening."

Smitty's lip curled and his fists balled as he advanced on Grey. "And you should be careful who you piss off."

Grey was still grasping at straws when he said: "That's what I've been trying to warn you about."

"Wait, it's not the Colonel, is it?" Smitty asked. His anger seemed to disappear in a blink. He glanced back at Sadie, an eyebrow raised. "It is the Colonel. There was a rumor that he lost a bunch of girls last year. You one of them?"

Sadie had her eyes down, but she lifted them slightly at Grey before answering. He barely moved his head in a nod. The list of Sadie's enemies was long, but the Colonel was not among them. Perhaps, in a diplomatic move, the Colonel could be persuaded to buy and release the group. Grey's and his men were soldiers, after all.

"Yes, I was the Colonel's," Sadie lied, "but he was too jealous. He had a man beaten for looking at me. It's why I ran away with the rest. I was afraid he would go too far."

Smitty was quiet for well over a minute and in all that time, no one said a word. This was theater to them. Finally, Smitty ordered Sadie to describe the colonel: "In detail."

"Tall, slim, about forty-seven or so. Short, sandy brown hair, grey eyes, a sharp nose. He always wore a gold ring with a ruby in it." She rattled off these facts so quickly that even Grey was surprised until he remembered that she had met the colonel on two different occasions.

"And his scar?" Smitty asked.

For a moment, Sadie looked confused, but then the corner of her lip jerked up in a smirk. "He didn't have one that you ever saw, I can guarantee that."

This brought out a laugh from Smitty, but the smile was covered over by a look of cold calculation. "Hmmm, the Colonel. Maybe you're worth a little more than I thought. You good in bed, is that what he saw in you?"

Sadie's haughty glare returned. "I'm not going to answer that. But one thing is for certain, you'll never find out. You put your dick anywhere near me I'll bite it right off."

Juan said something in Spanish that had Pecos chuckling. "He said he give a thousand to break in that filly."

"No one's breaking in any one," Smitty snapped, his beetle black eyes glaring around the room with such malevolence that the other slavers didn't dare look him in the face. "We won't get top dollar from the Colonel for used goods. The girl stays out here with the rest of the prisoners and if I catch any of you pawing her, I'll break your face. Juan, take the first watch."

They spent their second miserable night, just like the first, sitting, leaning against each other or lying in uncomfortable positions. In the morning, they were so stiff they could hardly stand.

Since none of the slavers were interested in undoing the zippers of six men, their hands were cuffed in front of them. It was such a relief that Grey moaned aloud. He moaned again as he urinated onto a tree that sprouted up from the slope that ran down to the Poudre River.

The water was frothing white and running fast. Had it been late July with the river swollen with the winter run off, he would have charged down the slope and jumped in. He *probably* would have been shot in the back, but it was a risk he would have taken for freedom.

His life expectancy wasn't great one way or the other. It was pretty much a foregone conclusion that he would be back in the fighting pits in a week's time, if he wasn't simply strung up by the neck first. The old Azael princes would kill him out of hand if they could get their hands on him—and there was seven hundred miles of what used to be Azael land to cross before they got to the Colonel's island.

One of his men caught his eye and raised a brow at the river. Grey shook his head. "Not yet," he murmured.

The load of goods in the truck and the trailers were shifted around so that Grey and his men were put into the bed of the lead truck. A tarp was tied down over them that kept out most of the icy wind, but not all. At first they shivered, huddled in on themselves.

Eventually, Grey ordered them to, "Get cuddly." Though jokes were made, no one complained, it was just too cold.

Sadie rode in front with Smitty and two of his men. She was warm and definitely safer than the men in the back were. A number of times they were thrown from side to side as Smitty dodged the truck all over the road to keep from hitting the zombies.

Once they were surrounded by the beasts. The truck shuddered as it rolled into a crowd of undead. The stench was horrific and the moans were so loud that Grey could imagine they were pushing through a sea of walking dead.

Scarred and scabbed hands reached up into the bed, causing the men to pull into the middle. Their training and discipline kept them alive. Not one of them made so much as a whimper the entire time they were in the horde. Afterwards was another story. Everyone one of them sighed with relief and then joked about what a close call it had been.

The relief was short-lived. Five minutes later, the trucks stopped and there was a good deal of cursing coming from the front. Grey crawled on his forearms and knees to the front and lifted the tarp high enough to see that part of the mountain had fallen across the road.

Curses from the soldiers matched those of the slavers. None of the captives wanted to get to The Island any faster than they had to, but at the same time the mountain roads were painfully cold and a new snow didn't help matters.

Just as they turned around, heavy clouds pushed across the sky and a sifting of white powder filled the air. It wasn't one of the mega-storms that struck the mountains at least three times every winter, it was just a dusting, but with the swirling wind that couldn't make up its mind which way it was coming from, it made for white-out conditions.

Lieutenant Wilson poked up the tarp and whistled. "I got zero visibility out here and everything is slick as shi...I mean, it's very icy. If I were driving, I'd pull over at the first opportunity."

Smitty must have seen the danger differently. Even though their speed dropped away, he kept them moving, detouring steadily north, hoping to come across a road that would lead them east, out of the mountains. Twice they struck roads heading east and twice they dead ended—once at a private ski slope and a second time at a pretty little lake surrounded by rustic cabins.

They stopped at both, hoping to pick up more supplies, however everything of value had already been taken.

During the second stop, Grey asked for and received blankets for his men. They also ate a late lunch of barely heated beans in one of the cabins.

When they were forced back out into the snow, one of the soldiers, PFC Keene, nudged Grey and showed him something he had palmed: a gleaming silver paperclip. His thick "porn star" mustache twitched upwards in excitement.

"Hide that," Grey said, speaking low and glancing around to see if the young man's foolishness had cost them a chance at escape. No one had noticed. All the slavers were bent forward, their chins tucked to their chests to avoid the stinging wind.

One by one, the prisoners were shoved up under the tarp in the back of the lead truck. It was like sitting on a block of ice and the men began calling for the blankets. "Hold your stinking horses," Smitty snapped, "or I'll let you freeze for an hour, first."

The six soldiers quieted and it was only a few minutes before the blankets were brought over. As Grey struggled to wrap himself in a blanket with his hands cuffed, he gave Keene a warning look.

"Not yet," he muttered. Only when the trucks rumbled into life and began to slush forward through the snow did Grey nod.

"Look what I found," Keene said holding up the paperclip as if it were some sort of exotic treasure. "It was just sitting on floor of the cabin." The soldiers leaned in, and comically, at least to Grey, oohed and aahed over it.

"Does anyone know how to pick a lock?" Grey asked. Every one of the soldiers shrugged as they looked around hoping that someone else would have a different answer. "Well, it can't be that tough. Jillybean did it on at least one occasion and she's just a little girl. So who wants to try?"

With their fate resting on the thin metal, none of the soldiers were eager to volunteer and so Grey volunteered one of them: "Hendricks, you're good with electronics, that's kind of close."

Hendricks, who had been a signalman in the army and who had small, nimble hands, scrunched over, moving like an inch-worm in the cramped, low-ceilinged bed to get close to Grey. He put out both of his manacled hands and accepted the paperclip from PFC Keene in just the same way he would accept a communion wafer in church.

"Hold your hands closer, will you, sir?" he asked Grey. He studied the lock on the handcuffs, squinting at the tiny keyhole. "The keys to these things are usually pretty simple. If I can remember right, I just have to bend the clip a little at the end."

The clip disappeared from Grey's view as Hendricks tried to shape it properly. "Oh, crap, it broke. Here, Keene, hold this part. It's a little more brittle than I thought it would be. Maybe it's old."

"Straighten it all the way out," Lieutenant Wilson suggested, "and then you can work the end into the shape that... hey, did you...it broke again, didn't it?"

"It's not my fault. I think the cold is turning the metal brittle. Maybe if we warm up the pieces." For five minutes, the pieces were held tightly to warm them up and then, once more they tried to make little keys only to break the clip even further.

Everyone groaned in defeat. After more attempts, Hendricks held up one of the pieces. "This one should still work. Do you guys see? This one piece has a lip to it, just like a key."

But it didn't work. No matter how much Hendricks jiggled and twisted the metal, the cuffs remained stubbornly closed.

Chapter 20

Jillybean

The fire behind her crackled. In front of her was a wavering shadow of a little girl with a gun in her hand. Jillybean wanted to turn and look back and not just for curiosity's sake.

"What if there are supplies back there?" she asked the empty night. The answer was obvious: if there was gas to be had, it was now on fire. If there were guns, they would be dangerously hot, even to the point of "cooking off" and sending bullets spraying in every direction. If there was food, it was being flambéed.

No, there wasn't anything worth saving. "Unless there's people trapped in the wreckage," Jillybean said. Then she remembered the gun; it was still warm.

She walked back to the KIA, her neck as stiff as if she'd had her vertebrae fused. When she got to the car, she saw that Ipes was trapped under the M79 "bomb shooter."

Once she pulled it off of him, he said: *We have to get out of here! You can see that fire for miles.* There was something she had to do first. Leaning between the seats with her bottom pointed at the windshield, she dug for the spare bombs and her extra .38 caliber ammo.

"If the fire can be seen, it's best to be prepared." As she reloaded, her eyes were drawn to the fire. The flames shot fifteen feet in the air and were in the process of consuming a pickup truck.

A ghostly scream echoed suddenly in her ear: *Pull over, bitch!* It made her jerk and she looked around to see if Ipes had heard, but he was just sitting in the passenger seat with his floppy arms hanging over the seatbelt that smooshed his belly in.

Does this KIA make me look skinny? he joked. He hadn't heard the scream and she couldn't tell if that was a good thing or a bad thing.

"I think it's okay."

What's wrong? he asked. *Are you worried about those guys? I wouldn't be. They got what they deserved. I'm sorry but attacking a little girl in the middle of the night ought to be a crime.*

"So, what I did was okay?" He told her: *Absolutely* and then begged for her to get her tail in gear before any more bandits came. With a final glance back at the burning truck, she stuck the car in drive and headed due west.

The KIA smelled of spent gunpowder and so she rolled down the window and that was fine for a few minutes until the wind whistling past turned into a haunting scream that was ugly…and familiar.

"It's not such a bad smell," she reasoned and rolled the window up. Not long after, the flames disappeared behind the curve of the earth and she felt immediate relief.

When the sun came up and the road began to exude steam as the frozen dew melted, Jillybean began to look for a place to turn off and hide for the day. She was tired right down to the bone and yet it was an hour of dangerous daylight driving before she found a turnoff that led to something greater than a lonely little homestead where the Kia would stand out.

The road was laid out straight and true, heading exactly northward and ended at a dilapidated little town that still bore the stench of cow, the chemical eye-irritating odor of tannins and the particular dusty scent of ground hooves.

Jillybean passed four different cattle processing factories without quite understanding what she was seeing. They didn't register as offensive in anyway until she reached a large penned off area that was simply carpeted in bones and moldering bits of cowhide.

She guessed at what had happened: the monsters came, the people ran off and the cows were left to starve to death. "That's awful sad," Jillybean said, not realizing that the cows had been doomed no matter what.

The actual town was just upwind of the processing plants and she had to steer the KIA through an area where a hundred evil eyes could be watching her from the shadows—she held tightly onto her "bomb shooter" as she drove. The grip had a memory that wanted to run up her hand and on into her body, but she shut it down.

"Find us a spot, Ipes," she said through gritted teeth. There was a reason why she wasn't letting herself think about the burning truck and she trusted that it would be a doozy. "I gotta protect my brain," she said. "Something bad happened… something bad always happens."

And why dwell on the bad? Ipes asked. *I say from now on we only concern ourselves with the good things in our lives. We have our health, we have most of a plate of cookies, and we have the open road.*

Just then, the road dead-ended at a trailer park. *Well, tonight we'll have an open road. Careful, there's a monster in that trailer.*

Even though the mobile home in question looked as though it had been torn in two, and had a gaping hole in one end, a monster stood at a bedroom window scraping at the glass as Jillybean passed.

As far as monsters went, it seemed like a very weak one. It was small and skinny and she guessed that it had been a sixth-grader before it had been turned into a monster. "That's awful sad, too," she said. "I wonder if it lived there."

Hey! We're supposed to be concentrating on the positive. When you see a monster in a house, then you say: look it's come home. How nice. And look at these trailers, they're so cozy that they'll be a snap to heat. Now you try it.

Jillybean looked down the rows of trailers, each one flimsy and weak, each one with their thin, aluminum doors hanging open and most with their single pane front windows smashed inwards and drapes hanging out. There was trash scattered everywhere: old toys, rags of clothes, televisions with their screens shattered, shoes, though never a full set.

And bones. There were plenty of bones.

"Uh," Jillybean stammered, gazing around at the mess. "The positive thing about this place is that, uh, there isn't a lot of monsters here?"

Yes, exactly! And there's no bad guys here, either. It's just a little out of the way spot that should be perfect to spend the day in. At that moment, they ran over a glass milk bottle which shattered, sending shards into the front right tire which popped with a sound that was part bang, part hiss. Jillybean groaned and glared at Ipes as if it were his fault. *And isn't it good that we only popped one tire?* he asked.

"Sure, I guess," the little girl said, as she got out to inspect the damage, which was basically absolute. The tire was ruined and the spare was under a trunk full of heavy supplies. She stared at the popped tire with heavily lidded eyes. "I'll fix it first thing when I get up," she said. "That's what means I can't keep my eyes open."

You'll do no such thing. You know the 'what ifs' same as I do. What if bad guys come or monsters or a flood or a flood of monsters? You will fix it now and the positive thing about that is…

He hesitated for so long to come up with something positive that the little girl balled her fists on her skinny hips and asked: "What? What could possibly be positive about changing a tire when I'm this exhausted?"

Easy. You'll be so tired that you'll fall right to sleep the second your head hits the pillow.

"That is good, I suppose," she said, without any enthusiasm. She knew she couldn't let the tire go unchanged, however it was such a big job for a little girl that she wanted to just find a different car, transfer her belongings, siphon the gas, jump start it, and let the KIA rust away with the rest of the trailer park.

That seems like a lot of work, as well, and where would you get this 'other' car? He waved a hoof around. There were only two cars in sight and both of them sat on sets of flat tires.

A long sigh escaped her as she went around to the back to begin unloading her belongings. She cleared enough space to unearth the tire iron and discovered that she was too weak to loosen the lug-nuts. It really wasn't a surprise.

She tried standing on one side of the four-pronged tire iron, but her fifty-three pounds were not enough to budge the lug-nut.

Yay, we get to use our minds to overcome a problem, Ipes declared with feigned enthusiasm. Jillybean only glared at him as she went to the trunk once more.

Even as tired and cranky as she was, the problem of frozen lug-nuts wasn't much of a problem for her. Grunting, she hauled out the car's jack and brought it to the tire, but didn't set it under the car as it was designed. Instead she put it under the right side of the tire iron and began cranking the handle, transferring her energy, little by little, into the jack.

Gradually, the jack's load bearing platform went up and as it did, one end of the tire iron did as well, turning and loosening the lug-nut. She performed the same action on the other nuts and, in no time, they were off the tire.

Next, since the spare tire was far too heavy for her scrawny arms to lift, she levered it out of its nook in the trunk, using two broom handles she had taped together side-by-side.

There were more of these sorts of simple mechanical problems to be overcome before she had the spare in place, but they didn't faze her in the least. She met each obstacle with a look of concentration and overcame each with a yawn. What would have stopped most children *and* many adults wasn't even child's play for her.

"Are you happy, now," she asked Ipes, once the tire was changed and the car hidden away behind the mobile home she was planning on staying in for the night. She had chosen it because it was stuck in the corner of the lot, backing up to a scrubby little ravine.

Between the mobile home she had chosen and the main street that ran through town, she had set up two different "alarms." Both were practically invisible: thin aluminum wire stretched across the road, holding anchoring stakes in place. The stakes were attached to saplings which Jillybean had bent far over, using rope attached to the KIA's bumper instead of her own puny strength. The branches of the trees were strung with pots and pans.

In the still air, the sound of the pans would be heard for miles. Even with these precautions, Jillybean slept as if on her own hair trigger, ready to dart away along one of two different preplanned escape routes from the trailer.

She was as prepared for danger as she could be, however danger stalked her even in her dreams. The day wore away with her tossing and turning, reliving a long-running dream over and over again.

In it, she was back in the KIA, her hands slick on the wheel, her eyes nervously darting to the rear-view mirror every other second as the headlights drew closer and closer.

"What do I do?" she asked Ipes, her voice strangely low and slow, her words elongated, each symbol stretched out like a record player turning at its slowest speed.

Close your eyes, he answered. *Don't watch what they do to you. Slip away, slip away, slip away to somewhere nice. Slip away to the picnic. Do you remember the picnic?*

Of course she remembered the picnic: her daddy throwing the frisbee that seemed to float in the air forever, just out of reach of her outstretched hands; the wicker basket filled with sandwiches of every description, bags of *Pringles*, and *Lays*, and *Doritos* and more and more and more; the Golden Retriever that ran about, barking and swatting Jillybean with a tail as hard as a tree branch.

And her mommy sitting on a blue blanket. *You're a May-flower, Jillian*, she said, *and there's nothing prettier than a May-flower*.

Jillybean remembered the picnic. Her eyes filled with tears as she remembered it—but it was the past. It was a glorious past, but it was a ghost to her, haunting and filled with sadness.

Angrily, she swiped her eyes with her sleeve. "No!" she hissed, savagely. "I am a May-flower!" It came out as a defiant scream, silencing the zebra, making him freeze, causing him to stare out at nothing with blank bead-eyes. "May-flowers bloom, Ipes, they don't close their eyes and pretend nothing is happening."

In the dream, Ipes sat so still it was as if he were part of the seat. He didn't budge when a harsh light transfixed the KIA. The truck racing up behind them had a spotlight that sent forty-thousand candles blasting into the night.

To look back was to be momentarily blinded. Jillybean tried it only once and when she looked forward again, all she saw were orange blobs dancing all over the road. She wanted to fixate on them and watch them as they wobbled and stretched in slow-motion like the goo inside a lava lamp. But she couldn't. She couldn't ignore the road rushing under her wheels.

There were things in the road: tumbleweeds and trash and monsters and odds and ends of people's lives. In the dream, she saw each in a way she hadn't in real life. In real life, the things in the road were there to be dodged, in the dream they were there to dawdle over so she could put off what really mattered.

Pull over, bitch!

The harsh spotlight poured over the KIA and there was no hiding the fact that she was alone. A lone girl whose hair waved and rippled in the screaming wind. They thought she was a woman. She sat high on her pillows and her hair was long and flowing and beautiful.

They thought she was a woman, an adult, but it didn't matter to them. She was alone, girl or not, woman or not, she was all alone. She was easy pickings. She was their prey.

The wind blew her hair back because she had decided.

The wind blew her hair back because she had purposely lowered the window, just as she had purposely picked up the M79 grenade-launcher. "The bomb-shooter," she mumbled in her sleep.

It seemed no bigger and no more dangerous than a toy, except that it was heavy. There was weight to it and heft. The heft made it serious. In the dream, it was *very* heavy and *very* important in her small hands. It was the tool of death.

A man screamed at her, his words swept away by the wind, but his tone came across all the same. He wanted her to stop. He wanted her to give up. He wanted her to close her eyes and think of a long-ago picnic so that he could do things to her. There were others in the truck with him and they wanted that as well.

They pulled alongside of the speeding KIA, guns aimed but mouths agape. They saw she was just a child—but did that matter? Yes. But only for all of a second. They saw she was a child and the last embers of civilization within them caused them to hesitate, but then they shrugged. They didn't care.

To them she was a thing to be used and a thing to be sold. She wasn't a person in their eyes.

They screamed at her to pull over and blustered with their weapons and their eyes grew huge as ping-pong balls when she answered by jutting the M79 out the window, like a child's version of a cannon.

Child's version or not, it was deadly when she gave them a broadside. In real life, she had expected the weapon to explode in a fury of fire and light as it shot its bomb, but it made only a muted *foomp* sound.

The effects, however, were out of proportion to the sound. The grill of the truck exploded, lighting up the night, and sending the vehicle spinning, at first, and then tumbling in the next second.

It rolled, glass flying, metal bouncing, flames spouting, men screaming. Mesmerized, the dream version of Jillybean slammed on the brakes of the KIA, her eyes huge in her face as she watched in the side view mirror as the truck tumbled over and over. When it finally stopped, it lay on its side burning furiously.

She stared for over a minute until Ipes said: *You know, there could be survivors.*

"Yeah," she said, her voice sounding even more like a little kid's than usual. She felt tiny as she slid out of the car and made her way with faltering steps to the wreckage. Someone was screaming. It had started as a moan and had progressed in volume.

There was a man in the truck, hitting a door with a weak fist as he screamed. He was pinned. The front seats were smushed in

171

on him, trapping him. "Help me!" he screamed to Jillybean when he saw her.

She saw that the KIA's jack, quickly applied, could have given him enough wiggle room to slip out—but then what? Why would she want to help this man? "Will he suddenly be like the lion with the thorn in his paw from Aesop's fables and become my friend?" she asked herself. "Or will he grab me the second he is free?"

"Help me!" he screamed again, reaching with one hand toward her. "The fire…please!"

As if it weren't there, she ignored the hand and watched as the fingers curled in, like claws. "He might become my friend, but he will still be a lion," she concluded, "and a lion can't change its spots." She realized that if she saved him, he might not be dangerous to her, but he would still be dangerous to everyone else.

"Sorry," she said and moved away. Behind her, his screams rose in fury and then went even higher as the fire crept towards him. She ignored him, knowing the fire would take care of him for her.

She walked on, more careful now. There was another lion and this one was free.

A man with a mangled arm and blood gushing down the side of his head was slowly moving through the brush on the side of the road. He couldn't crawl, he could only move by kicking out with one leg. His goal was an M16, seven feet away.

Jillybean walked over to the gun and stood on its sling. The man glared as he asked in a slurry voice: "What are you looking at?"

"A lion," she said, raising the .38 and peering down its stubby barrel. The questions of when she had picked up the gun and why she had picked it up, never crossed her mind. She killed the man with one pull of the trigger…and then she moved on to the next.

A third lion lay in the grass, this one moaning and just trying to sit up. "Lion," she said, pulling the trigger once more. In the dream, the echo of the gun went on and on, slowly turning into strange metallic crashes that jarred her awake.

The alarms! Ipes cried.

She sat straight up in the bed she had commandeered. "I hear them," Jillybean replied, as she focused her hearing beyond the frantic zebra and the sound of the pans banging against each other. Strangely, she didn't hear a car as she expected.

As silent as an adder on the hunt, she slid out of bed, going to the window. There wasn't anything to see or hear beyond the rustle of paper kicked up by a light wind. "Wait here," she whispered to Ipes before creeping outside into the late afternoon.

The wind was crisp on her cheeks. It was a silent wind. It did not carry on it the sound of cars or monsters or sneaking feet, not even Jillybean's. She made no noise whatsoever as she eased through the trailer park. The closer of her two alarms was still set. The further of the two had been triggered, but not by the hand of man. She came up close and saw there were deer tracks near it.

"And look, deer poop," she remarked. It was a moment before she remembered that Ipes was back in the mobile home. "Oh, right," she said, embarrassed.

She walked directly back to the mobile home and stood for a moment outside of it, staring at the trash, wondering if she should have picked up her own. The bodies she had left behind would have sat in the sun all day, they would have been picked over by vultures and ugly animals.

"They deserved it," she said, but she wasn't so certain. They *had* been bad, that was true, but did they deserve to die? And what about those bad men back at Fort Leonard Wood? She wanted to say yes, they deserved their punishment and yet her mind had blanked out the killings.

That suggested that they were wrong or she was wrong or something was wrong with her. "Probably something is wrong with me," she decided. There was always something wrong with her.

Chapter 21

Jillybean

She drove into an eye-watering, but beautiful sunset. It
wasn't smart to drive while it was still light out and yet the sun
drew her on.

It was the greatest of fires and she hoped that the light of it
would burn out the image of the truck and the man trapped
within it. Jillybean tried to shove the memories deep inside of
her, as if her mind were a trashcan and she was stomping down
on an overflowing milk jug that kept spilling out.

Enduring the pain of the sun was in vain. The memories
were still with her when the night extinguished the sun.

Ipes tried his best to get her to think about something else.
He laughed and joked and sang and kept offering her cookies she
didn't feel she deserved. Depression had her driving
mechanically, which, it turned out, wasn't really any worse than
her normal driving.

Two hours into the drive, they passed a truck-stop, sitting
out in the middle of nowhere. She slowed down as they passed
it, both of them staring out the window at the main building.

It had been looted down to the last drop of gasoline. Sitting
in the middle of the parking lot was a generator hooked up to an
electric pump. There was a hose snaking from it down into the
underground tanks.

We should stop and check that place out, Ipes suggested.

Jillybean gave him an odd look. "Why? There's nothing in
there, and we can't stop at every place 'just in case.' It would
take us months to get to Colorado if we did. We got lucky that
one time but…"

Trust me, Ipes assured.

She rolled her blue eyes and yet, she pulled the KIA over,
steering with a markedly better hand. Because of the glass and
the trash scattered around the front of the building, she parked
closer to the generator than to the front of the station.

Stepping out, the first thing she did was to pick up a rock
and drop it into the open intake port of the tanks. A clang ran up
the pipe. "See? Nothing."

No, duh, he answered. *I meant check inside.*

The dark hid a second eye-roll. "And what's going to be in
there? A buh-scetti dinner?" There was a diner attached to a

convenience store. She had seen it when they first pulled up and the sight of it made her tummy growl.

Probably not, but maybe we can find something that might help you stay awake tonight and take your mind off of things.

With her curiosity up, she ducked into the store, her Keds crunching on tiny crystals of glass that reflected the meager light filtering in from outside. She pulled a small Maglite from one of her pockets and shone it around at the mess.

The place had been ransacked by desperate people searching for food and supplies. "I'm not seeing any buh-scetti, Ipes."

Ipes looked around, nervous at first but then said: *Ah, right there. That's the rack I was looking for.*

Jillybean bent down and inspected what had fallen from the rack. "CDs? I doubt they have any kid music."

That's not music, silly. Those are stories that someone recorded. Look, that one is about a white whale. And that one is about army-men fighting the Nazis, and this one is about a girl who likes men without shirts—we probably don't want to listen to that one.

"Hmmm," she said, picking through the mess. "This is sort of like going to the library. I miss going to the library. I mean I miss it when daddy used to take us and we got to spend, like an hour there." She loved the library even more these days. Yes, they were always so dark and spooky, but at the same time, they were full of secrets, millions and thousands and tons of secrets that no one knew any more.

Jillybean felt that she could live in a library.

What about the hardware store? Ipes asked. *You said before that you could live in one of those and be marvelously happy.*

"I guess I did. Hey, maybe there's a combined library and hardware store out there somewhere. You know, like this is a diner attached to a convenience store."

I doubt it. Those two things don't mix very well. You don't generally see the same sorts of people in both. So, which one are you going to choose?

For a seven-year-old, the selection wasn't the best. She chose *Cat's Cradle* by Kurt Vonnegut, which, unfortunately had nothing to do with cats, at least the first thirty minutes of listening didn't. Yes, they mentioned something called a cat's cradle, but that had to do with string and the rest of the book had to do with atomic bombs and intricately bizarre forms of religion.

It distracted her as she drove, there was no denying that. But it wasn't an enjoyable listening experience and so she popped it out after dodging around a number of monsters and discovering she had completely lost the train of the story.

"Let's try the treasure one," she suggested. She had picked up *Treasure Island* because the main character was a kid and it was about pirate treasure—it was almost a guaranteed good book based on that alone.

For Jillybean, it was only an "okay" book for a number of reasons: the pace was unnecessarily slow, and many of the larger words used seemed to have been wedged into sentences to suggest the author had a big vocabulary rather than to advance the story, and lastly, the pirates were depicted as *really* bad people in a way that struck very close to home.

They reminded her of the land pirates she'd been forced to deal with since the beginning of the apocalypse.

Still, she listened all through the night as she slipped into the northeast corner of New Mexico and then on into the desert region of Colorado, which looked nothing like the beautifully green Estes Valley. This part of Colorado was vast and empty and if there were mountains, they were so far to the west that they were invisible.

The land was dusty, as well. When the sun came up, she saw that she had left a fantail of brown particles lingering in the air. Despite the lack of monsters, she immediately slowed and began looking for a place to hole up for the day. It was a long search before she found a sad little ranch-house sitting on two-hundred acres of dull scrub unfit for anything save for rattlesnakes and browsing cattle.

For a long time, she stared at the lonely little house with tired, dreamy eyes, picking out its good points and its bad. Seeing it in a way that no one else could.

Since the land was wide open, she wouldn't be able to run away if anyone happened to come by. She would have to fight or give herself up—or a combination of the two. In preparation for anything and everything, she hid the KIA in the detached garage and then walked around the house, seeing it as an attacking slaver might.

The emptiness of the land meant that it wouldn't be easy to attack. There wasn't a shred of cover whatsoever. The landscaping around the house consisted of a square of dead grass surrounded by sun-fried weeds. This meant that the slavers would have to come right at her with their intentions on full display. She didn't want to kill any good guys by accident.

A smoke grenade with a blue dot on it would suffice to warn her—it would be hidden in the weeds by the side of the road, its discharge lever held down by a filament of wire so thin that it would be practically invisible stretched across the road.

Standing there on the drive, she could picture what would happen in stunning detail: the bad guys would be surprised by the smoke. They would gibber and point and they would stop fifty yards from the lonely house. If they were smart bad guys they'd leave as fast as they could and perhaps they would set up an ambush somewhere down the road or come back under the cover of night.

But they wouldn't be smart.

They would pile out of their cars and aim their guns at the house, the sun glinting from their scopes. Maybe they'd yell threats up at the house or pretend to be nice, hoping to fool Jillybean into coming out for a "chat." She wouldn't be fooled. She would raise her voice, telling them to *Go away!* But it would be a waste of breath, she realized, because then they would hear the high, thin voice of a little girl and figure she was alone. They wouldn't leave such a choice morsel.

While some aimed their guns, others would make a break for the sides of the house. They would want to get in close where the weak little girl wouldn't be able to shoot at them with whatever gun she had managed to scrounge up.

We don't want to hurt you, they'd call out, when they were all up next to the house, leaning against the siding and grinning at each other, each picturing what they would find inside. Each fantasizing. *We just want to make sure you're alright. Why don't you open up before someone gets hurt?*

She knew that would be a lie. Someone who really cared, like an actual "good guy" would have left to begin with or they would've come up to the house unarmed and only one at a time. They would smile and hold up empty hands. They wouldn't skulk in the shadows and whisper plans.

No, these were liars and thieves and *pirates,* and they would get what they deserved as they tried to get at her.

Two would go around back as two others sidled up to the canted cellar door—these last two would go in first. Would they have flashlights? It wouldn't really matter if they did. They wouldn't be able to see the live grenade duct-taped to a support beam at the bottom of the stairs, not until it was too late, not until they had already sprung the trap.

Even with a flashlight, the filament of wire stretching across the entranceway to the cellar would be hidden in the trash that Jillybean placed with artistic hands. The grenade would go off with a shockingly loud explosion in the low-ceilinged cellar. It would blast out flame and smoke and killing fragments of metal.

In a split second, the basement would go from dusty and humdrum to something more like a slaughter house: there'd be blood splattered on the walls, and it would run down the coarse wood in trickling streams, and there would be pieces of meat and chunks of entrails flung across the ancient washer-dryer set.

And in that split second, the two men would become two shredded corpses, their eyeballs ruptured by the concentrated force of the explosion in such a cramped area.

The sound of the grenade would trigger everyone's next course of action. The pirates on the porch would freeze for all of three seconds.

What the fuck? one would ask, his once confident face suddenly shocked into a look of fright.

A moment later, the largest of them—she pictured a man with a mustache that seemed to fall off both ends of his lip—would yell: *Hey, Kevin! You okay?* Even if Kevin had been alive, the man with the drooping mustache wouldn't have heard his answer.

There would be four, maybe five men standing on the long front porch with their backs to the siding, clutching their guns with sweating hands. They feared getting shot through one of the windows. What they didn't suspect in the least was that they were all within the kill zone of one of the M18A1 claymore mines that Jillybean had found among Perry's possessions back at Fort Leonard Wood. It would be sitting in an overturned clay pot that Jillybean had positioned at one end of the porch.

Deep within the house, at the end of a long wire spool, she would be holding the "clacker" that was attached to the wire. She would be nervous, but determined—she would be *decided*. She wasn't going to die there and she wasn't going to be taken as a slave.

The clacker would sit in her hands at the ready, but she wouldn't be frozen in fear, she was only in pause mode, knowing that the slavers would have cringed and crouched because of the first explosion. Slowly, they would stand once more. She would count to ten and only then would she press the clacker three times, her face screwed up in anticipation of the explosion that would send seven hundred steel balls flying in a tremendous broadside across the porch.

She knew that every window on the front side of the house would explode adding to the deadly shrapnel of flying metal.

The men on the porch would be torn to shreds by the blast and hurtled through the air to land on the drive or the strip of dead grass next to it. They would look more like scrap from a charnel house than humans and gradually, over the course of the day, their blood would trickle out of them and soak into the dry earth.

In the back of the house, standing on either side of the kitchen door, would be two men, probably big and definitely ugly. They would be shaken by the back to back explosions, and afraid, both to go on and to stay where they were. They would wait with their heads cocked, hoping to hear something from the other men, but there wouldn't be any sound save the lonely wind rustling under the eaves of the lonely ranch house and the endless echo of the explosion.

Finally, one would work up his courage and try the doorknob. He would expect it to be locked but it would turn easily under his hand.

Maybe we shouldn't, the other said in a whisper, grabbing his friend's shoulder.

They might not know we're even here, the first reasoned. *Besides, we can't go back to the car. It's sitting out in the open. We won't get halfway to it. Trust me, we just have to be quick. We go in with guns blazing. Are you with me?*

The second fellow would nod, lick his lips and then nod again. *Now!* he would hiss and rush in.

Trip wires could be funny things. Jillybean would have to set it pretty low so as not to be seen, and as she didn't have a hundred bombs, she would have this one running to a pulley which ran to the trigger of a shotgun strapped to a chair. The chair would be on its back, anchored with a toaster-oven that hadn't seen toast in a year.

Maybe the first man would miss the tripwire altogether. Maybe it would be the second man who hit it just as he ran into his friend, who would have stopped in his tracks upon seeing the gun and the taut string.

Understanding would strike that first man just as the gun roared. He would fly back into the second man who would be completely unhurt by the blast, except for a tiny nick on the bottom of his left earlobe which he wouldn't notice until much later as he laid his head on a strange pillow that sat on a strange bed, later that night.

That second man, with his nicked ear, would run, now that his last friend was dead with his chest exploded by the shotgun. He would run straight away from the lonely little house with its dead yard and its dead bodies. He would run until his lungs burned and his feet stumbled. When he couldn't run any more, he would march with sweat in his eyes and his chin thrust back over one shoulder, staring back the way he had come, afraid that someone or something would be following him.

He couldn't imagine that the only thing in the house capable of following him was a little girl who was leaving little waffle tracks meandering through the blood of his dead friends as she went to each body, wearing a hard look on her face and thinking that they had gotten exactly what they deserved...

"Huh?" Jillybean suddenly said, her body giving a little shake and her eyes blinking rapidly. She was a little surprised to find herself sitting in her car, as the brightness of the day came more and more into focus around her. There was an echo of an image in her mind: the waffle tracks in the slowly congealing blood and the bodies...

The picture dissolved in her mind and reality sunk in. She was in the KIA, but it was facing the wrong way. Somehow it sat pointing away from the house. And that wasn't the only thing that was different: in the weeds by the side of the road there was a strange swatch of blue. It looked as if someone had spray-painted the sun-browned weeds.

She had stopped next to it and who knew how long she'd been idling there. Turning off the engine, she took her foot off the brake pedal and it came away with a touch of reluctance, as if someone had pranked her, putting a film of glue on the stack of blocks.

"What's on the pedal?" She bent in her seat and saw that there was something on the top block...something maroon and tacky that hadn't been there before.

A surge of fear went through her and she sat up and stared again at the blue weeds, noting there was a little canister in the midst of the blue. It had been staked to the ground by a steel tent peg and there was a line of wire hanging slack from it.

Her eyes darted to the rear-view mirror where the lonely little ranch house sat in the middle of a great emptiness. In its driveway were two cars: a black Camaro and a Shelby Mustang with twin white racing stripes running right over its hood, across its top and down the back.

She followed the driveway with her eyes until she saw the front of the house. The windows were shattered and the siding was streaked with lines of crimson and there was something bent and twisted hanging off the side of the porch. It had been a man.

"Did that really happen?" she asked Ipes. "Did I really kill all those men? Was that a memory or was that a dream…I can't tell."

Maybe you should just get going, he answered, his words muted by a ringing in her ears that she was just noticing.

Her little hand shook as she reached down and pulled back the transmission handle, sticking the car in drive. She began coasting, not knowing where to go and not really caring. She was numb.

For her, reality wasn't very real. She could only hope that the road, a strip of black cutting through a land of brown, was really there and not part of her imagination. "Maybe I'm dreaming this, too."

You're not dreaming, Jillybean, Ipes told her. *Your imagination is greater than this. Anyone could imagine an empty blue sky sitting over an empty brown land. If you were imagining things, I bet there'd be a unicorn or two thrown in to the mix.*

"I guess," she said, without much feeling.

Hey, how about you listen to more of that story. It'll keep you awake until you find a new place to sleep.

"A new place," she whispered, picturing the old one with all the blood.

She started the story again, noting that there was something more in view beyond the empty sky and the dead earth, something that caught her eye. Behind a distant hill, a far off trickle of smoke rose up, marring the perfection of the blue.

"The slaver's camp," she said, putting her bloody Ked back on the stack of blocks that was attached to the gas pedal. She should have pointed the KIA away from it. She should have gotten out of there as fast as she was able to drive, however Jillybean felt a burn of anger in her that thrummed along with the ringing in her head.

She'd been minding her own business, just driving through. She should've been left alone. If they hadn't bothered her, she would have slept the day away, and in the evening, she would've dismantled her traps and left. And no one would have had to die.

But they had come for her. They had seen the dust kicked up by her car and they had come to steal her and hurt her. So much was still such a vague blur in her head that she wasn't quite sure of every little thing that had happened. She just knew that now she was as riled as a beehive some little boy had taken a stick to.

Maybe the slavers camp was empty. Maybe all the slavers were dead—but maybe not, and a strange, but familiar part of her hoped not.

Chapter 22

Neil Martin

Another meeting. This one just as long and pointless as the last twenty had been, at least in Neil's eyes. He liked his meetings short and to the point, with no more than four people in attendance. His ideal meeting was thirty seconds long: *What's the problem? I see and what possible solutions are there? Okay, I like the sound of the third option, what are the pros and cons? Good. Make it happen.*

He knew that not all meeting could go like that, not when five thousand people counted on the outcome and yet the all-day snore-athons that Fred Trigg seemed to thrive on were often pointless and always wasteful.

Fred insisted that the reason so many people had to attend his meetings was that everything was connected. "We can't have a meeting about food production without people from human resources, because that's where we get the laborers from. And we need reps from the heavy equipment team, because, let's face it, we need to move beyond small plot farming. And if we have the heavy equipment guys here, we need people from the fuel depot to keep us up to date. And then there's salvage…"

Blah, blah, blah. Frequently, there'd be thirty people sitting around a table for hours. Fred also liked his meetings to run long. And he always suggested having lunch sent up or dinner or a late snack. He had put on quite a bit of weight in the last three months.

That morning's meeting was the worst yet. Forty-five people crowded the room, making the air stale and warm. The heat, combined with the usual torpid pace of the meeting, had Neil fighting, both to stay awake and to pay attention to what was being said. He found himself gazing up at the wall-sized map of Colorado, tracing a black line as it snaked its way north from Estes Park. It was the road that Grey had said he was going to take on his expedition to bail Neil out of the jam he had found himself in.

He still felt that the cost of freeing Gayle and finding out the whereabouts of Jillybean had been worth it. From a certain, abstract point of view, freeing any slave was worth it and he wished he'd had fifty thousand gallons of fuel to free the rest of them.

But he didn't live in the abstract world. He lived in the concrete world where each decision had repercussions—he had given up too much to free a woman who, it turned out, had no valuable information—to rectify that, he had sent his daughter and his most trusted advisor out into the wild in search of fuel and ammo—and now he had a weak-minded colonel running the army and Fred Trigg doing everything he could to undermine him.

Next to Neil sat Deanna Russell. For half the morning, she'd had a vacant look in her blue eyes as the meeting droned on and on, but now she was sitting up. She gave Neil a sharp elbow in the side.

"What do you think, Neil?" she asked, her smile pulled tight. "About winter fuel projections and winter training for the soldiers?"

"I think exactly what I thought yesterday, Fred. We'll wait until Captain Grey returns to make any decisions on winter training."

As if they had run suddenly amok, Fred patted down the few wisps of blonde hair on his head. He smiled one of his politician's smile, this one the: *this pains me to say this, but…*

"Yeah, about that. We may not be able to wait that long. With yesterday's…"

Neil interrupted him. "What do you mean, we can't wait that long? He's been gone for three days."

"Yeah, well, like I was saying, with yesterday's blizzard we now have to change our projections concerning plowing and fuel usage. It's something we haven't really considered."

"That's because there's not much to consider," Neil answered. He rubbed his eyes; they felt gritty and tired. "First off, that wasn't a blizzard. Four inches of snow is not a blizzard. Second, we haven't considered plowing because it's a waste of resources. To keep the road to Denver open all winter long would use up every drop of gas we have."

"And how many drops do we have, exactly?" Fred knew. Everyone on the commission knew their dire fuel situation. He feigned ignorance, placing a hand to his chest. "I only ask because we have so many needs that have to be met. The military has to be able to train. The salvage teams have to be able to get down into Denver. We're getting low on a number of different medicines as I've mentioned before on numerous occasions. And what about trade? If we don't plow the roads, we'll be cut off until spring. I don't think anyone really wants to be trapped in the mountains until then."

Neil glared at Fred until one of the people from Human resources asked: "Is there a fuel problem? Are we short of fuel?"

It was a planted question. The woman was a known confidant of Fred's, but that didn't mean Neil could simply ignore her. There were too many people in the room and there was no way Neil could order them all to keep the secret of their supply situation.

"Yes and no," Neil said, tempering his lie with a dash of truth. "We don't have the fuel it would take to plow out to Denver after every snowstorm. I doubt even the Texans have that much. And as for the military, *when* Captain Grey returns from his mission we'll discuss winter training."

"But how much fuel do we have?" the woman persisted. "You never answered the question."

"And what about ammo?" another of the Human Resource people asked. "I couldn't help but notice that the military hasn't been going out to practice with their guns like they used to before the war. Are we out of ammo, too?"

The room was whisper quiet now as everyone stared at Neil, waiting for an answer that he couldn't give. A true answer would mean his governorship would be over. And it could also mean a new war. If their enemies found out how weak they were, coalitions would form and a new conflict would certainly spring up.

"We have enough of both," he said. "Since there is a question of security, I'm not at liberty to give exact amounts. Suffice to say, the commission is aware of our supply situation."

He hoped that this would be the end of the discussion but the woman from Human Resources turned to Deanna and asked: "And do you agree with Governor Martin? Do we have enough fuel and ammo reserves to fight another war?"

"I believe the governor answered that already," Deanna replied, icily. "And it's hardly within the scope of the discussion before us."

"Actually, he dodged the question," the woman shot back.

Deanna stood, now. She was tall and beautiful with a great sweep of blonde hair. She was also hugely pregnant. "I did not realize that this meeting was going to get so far off point and my bladder is not prepared and neither is my patience. I don't know who you think you are, Miss, but I am under no obligation to answer to you. Maybe you think you're some sort of budding reporter, if so, I should warn you that the Valley does not have any right to a free press."

Neil watched, enviously as she left. It was true, there wasn't a freedom of the press clause in any government document, but so far there hadn't needed to be one. Either way, the woman was a citizen of the Valley and there were free speech rights. She could ask her questions and he would look as if he were hiding things if he didn't answer—but she didn't ask him a question, she asked Fred Trigg.

"Commissioner Trigg, do you agree with Governor Martin? Do we have enough fuel and ammo reserves to fight another war?"

I've been outmaneuvered, Neil realized. Fred had both a duty to the state and to the people of the state, and he would be well within his rights to answer the woman plainly.

Fred knew this as well, Neil could see it on his smug face as he stood, slowly, pompously, drawing out the moment so he could denounce Neil with a theatrical air and perhaps with a theatrical finger pointed in stern accusation.

He even cleared his throat as though what he was about to say was of such importance that it couldn't possibly be said with a scratchy voice. Just as he was about to speak, however, Deanna burst into the room.

"Neil, there's someone here to see you. Someone important." She held back the door and Neil fully expected Captain Grey to come striding through, his white teeth gleaming a confident smile, instead a tiny figure stepped into the doorway but didn't go any further.

It was Jillybean, looking wild and ragged. She was gaunt and pale, her hair was a thicket of tangles, her clothes were torn and stained with what could only be blood. In the nearly four months since he had seen her, she hadn't grown an inch and yet she took over the room with her presence and she was still only on the threshold.

She looked ready to bolt. "Hello Mister Neil, sir," she said.

"He's governor now," Deanna corrected. "You should call him by the proper title."

Jillybean's blue eyes widened. "I'm sorry, Mister Governor Neil, sir, I didn't know and that's because you don't look like a governor or nothing. I always thought governors put on blue suits and wore a sash or a ribbon or something."

Neil looked down at himself: green sweater vest over a white, button-up shirt and a pair of khakis. He supposed he looked more like a second-grade school teacher than a governor.

"No need for apologies. And you know you can call me, Neil. You and I go way back. I've known you longer than I've known anyone, except for Sadie."

She smiled at this. "Yeah that's true. So where is she? I have gifts for her and for you, too, Mister Neil and for Mister, Captain Grey. Though his are mostly just bombs and bullets and boring stuff like that. But that's what army-mens like, I guess."

Deanna and Neil shared a quick look. The hope he was feeling was matched by the look in her eyes. Before he could ask about the bombs and the bullets, Fred Trigg asked: "What is *she* doing here? Have you forgotten that *she* murdered General Johnston?"

"I haven't forgotten," Neil stated. "What's your point?"

Fred ignored the question and turned to Deanna. He gestured with both hands at her extremely round belly as if it were exhibit A. "And have you forgotten that *she* killed that baby, Eve?"

A touch of a shiver crossed Deanna's shoulders, but she squared them, resolutely. "She also saved us from the Azael, and the River King…twice! What have you ever done besides whine and point out people's mistakes?"

The two glared at each other until Jillybean said: "I did all of that, but I'm better now. I found Ipes and I killed a witch, only she wasn't a real witch because that's what means she didn't have spells or X-ray eyes or nothing. She was just mean and ugly like one. And I killed some pirates who had stolded some ladies and a kid. I brought them here and told them that people are good here. Is that still true?"

Jillybean's hard blue eyes were on Fred Trigg as she asked this. He stared right back and was likely going to mention murder a second time, however Neil spoke before he could: "How about we go see these ladies that you rescued. You say there's a kid? Is she your age?" He stood up ready to leave, but the little girl didn't move.

"We don't have to go nowheres, they're right here. And no, Aria is twelve, which is like a big kid, one that's almost a teenager. You know like thirteen except they don't have a twelveteen, which I think they should."

She stepped aside and waved in six women and a skinny girl. They were bedraggled and bruised, and as Jillybean introduced them they self-consciously tried to smooth out their clothing or they ran fingers through their hair, perhaps hoping to be seen as pleasing. The women had the haunted eyes of rape victims, while Aria had a dark fury in her eyes. There was so much hate in them that they made Neil uneasy.

"Welcome to Estes Valley," Neil said with a slight bow. "My name is Neil Martin. I'm the governor here. I think you will find that the valley is as safe as Jillybean told you it would be." He wrinkled his scarred face into the closest thing to a smile that he could and added: "We try to be the good guys. Deanna, can you show them around? And get them settled in?"

"Maybe we should have someone else do that," Fred suggested. "We still have votes to take. I for one wish to have a vote of *no confidence* in your leadership."

The bluntness of the statement turned Neil's gruesome smile into a worse frown. "You're going to have to play your games another day. I'd like to catch up with my friend, Jillybean." He was secretly eager to hear about the "gifts" she had spoken of. He was in desperate need of bullets and bombs.

"Yeah, about her," Fred said, lowering his voice. "I'm not sure she can stay in the Valley. She's simply too dangerous."

Though he had lowered his voice, the room was deathly quiet and everyone heard. The politician in Neil wanted to gauge the people around the table before answering. The guilt-ridden man who had failed Jillybean time and again was quick to answer: "I'll vouch for her."

"And what does that mean, exactly? Will you go to jail for her when she commits her next murder?" When Neil couldn't answer, Fred added: "And what about the stipulations concerning her release after her last trial. She wasn't supposed to come within five-hundred miles of the Valley."

Neil began to flounder, looking for an answer, however Jillybean spoke in her own defense: "That was for Eve. *She* wasn't supposed to come out within five hundred miles."

"You are Eve!" Fred cried. "She's one of your personalities."

"Eve is dead," Jillybean shot back. "Mister Neil...I mean, Mister Governor Neil killed her by throwing her in a fire."

This statement had the entire room buzzing with whispers. "That's not exactly what happened," Neil tried to explain. But then Jillybean took a step back, her eyes widening, perhaps thinking that Eve was still alive. "I mean, yes I killed Eve...she was in a doll that I had given to Jillybean to help her get rid of the, uh, Eve inside of her, uh, head."

"So, she's cured?" Fred asked, with disdain in his voice. "Does Ipes think so, as well?"

Jillybean glanced down at the stuffed zebra sitting in the crook of her arm. "He thinks I'm mostly cured."

Fred nodded with a smarmy look on his face. "I'm sure he does. He's a very smart zebra. Maybe the two of you should wait outside while the grown-ups talk."

She looked to Neil, who gave her a little nod. "It'll be for just a few minutes." When she left, Neil turned on Fred. "She's staying. That girl has done more to save this valley than anyone. And it's not her fault that she has issues."

"So, murder is only an 'issue' to you?" Fred asked, a sneer prominent on his thick lips. "Look, Neil, are you really going to hang your hat on this? First the supply debacle and now this?"

"I won't turn her away. I know what everyone thinks, but they're wrong about her." On top of all her actual crimes, Jillybean had been widely blamed for many things that had nothing to do with her: the attack of the Azael, the death of Marybeth Gates, and the death of an ex-prostitute from the Colonel's Island named Melanie.

What had been generally forgotten was her role in saving the valley. The people had congratulated themselves for their hard work and their amazing perseverance. The truth was, they would have all died if it hadn't been for Jillybean.

Fred shrugged and then smiled like a politician, all warmth except for the snake eyes that twinkled with malevolent glee. "Then I wish you luck."

Neil didn't bother saying thanks or even goodbye. He left the room, almost running straight into Jillybean. "I'm not wanted here, am I?" she asked.

Chapter 23

Jillybean

There had been pirates at the camp, which in truth hadn't been much of a camp. It was another drab, sun-faded little house sitting in the middle of the emptiness that was southern Colorado. To Jillybean it had likely been the house of a clerk or possibly the manager of some little shop in a distant town that sold knickknacks or bike tires or lawn services.

She drove up to the house, vowing to herself that she would remember everything that was about to happen, both the good and the bad. Not remembering stuff scared her, since it was a sure sign of craziness, and it made her wonder what else she had forgotten. Had she left a string of corpses…more corpses that is, running all the way back to Missouri?

Had she killed people there, too when she had been living in a fantasy world? All that summer when she was supposed to have been healing—had she been murdering people, left and right? Is that why it was all such a blur in her mind?

"But I only kill bad guys," she had said with a touch of hope in her voice. She had no idea if that was true. Had all those men she had blown up been bad?

Yes, of course they were, Ipes said. *There's no question of their badness. Just like there's no question you should be turning around.*

With the thrumming of the explosions still ringing in her ears, she could barely hear him. And besides, she didn't want to hear him. She knew all about pirates and slavers and bad men. She knew that they usually had captives and she knew what they did to them. She had seen first-hand how the Azael had treated their women and she had heard the stories of The Colonel and Gunner back in Alabama.

She guessed that there would be women in the house. "And what if they're all chained up and alone?" she asked herself. "They'll die of not drinkingness."

But that doesn't mean you have to rescue them. And what if the bad guys left guards? Ipes wanted to know. It was his way of getting her to chicken out.

Jillybean wasn't all that worried about any stupid guards. She was too angry for worry. She followed the smoke in the sky until she found the little house, and pulled up in a cloud of dust.

The fact that a curtain moved suggested that there were indeed guards, or at least one. "You better stay here," she told Ipes as she slid out of the KIA with her hands lifted. "Hello? Is there anyone here?"

A windowless van sat in the driveway but there were other tire-tracks in the lawn, tracks she recognized from the last house: the Camaro and the Mustang.

Jillybean glanced in the van and saw that it really wasn't a people van, unless the people riding in it were slaves. From this fact, she deduced that there weren't many guards in the house, if there were indeed more than one.

"Hello?" she called again, as she moved toward the house. Her voice was as small as she was and there was a warble of fear in it that was all acting on her part. She wasn't feeling fear. If there was fear in her, it was buried deep.

The front door came open and a man stood shadowed behind a screen door. She could see his silhouette turn from side to side as he looked from her to the KIA and back again. "You all alone?" he asked in a whispering voice. The smell of tequila carried through the screen and swept over her, making her blink and squinch her nose.

Although Ipes was still in the KIA, she decided to let him remain secret. "Yes, I guess so. What about you?"

"I have friends, but they're really nice. You'll like them. Wanna come in and meet them?"

She had smiled and said: "Sure," and went into the house as the man stood back, holding the door open for her. He was a skinny man with an Adam's apple that stuck out a good two inches, making it look as though he had swallowed a clamshell that was now stuck longways on in his throat.

The skinny man had a big revolver with a wooden handle and a silver barrel. It made Jillybean's .38 look like a toy and yet he didn't have it pointed at her. It just hung in his hand as if it were too heavy for him to lift and aim.

There was a second man in the living room. He was big and beefy and a bit of a slob. He wore a stained white t-shirt that had the sleeves cut off. His face was dark with stubble and there was something yellow at the corner of his mouth that might have been egg yolk.

"You all alone?" he asked. "You got no daddy around?"

She thought of Neil. Ever since Ram had been turned into a monster, she thought of Neil as the only thing she would consider a father figure. "He's in Colorado," she said, going to sit down on a high-backed chair upholstered in dusty mauve. "So, where's your other friends?"

"Some are downstairs," the skinny man said as he shut and locked the door. He looked past Jillybean and to the man on the couch. "I saw her first, you know," he said.

"Man, you're a moron, Jimmy," the bigger man said. "First, who cares if you saw her first. There is a certain pecking order to these things and you are dead last on that order. And second, if she's a virgin, she's worth a freaking mint and no one's gonna have her. Hey, honey, any guys get to you yet?"

"You mean in a prostitute sort of way?" Jillybean asked. When the man chuckled and nodded, she said, "No, sir. I'm too small for that stuff, don't you think?"

"I think so but there are some men who don't."

"And you two would sell me to one of those men?" she asked, holding out her left hand palm upwards. Their eyes tracked on the left hand as her right disappeared into the shredded coat she wore.

The skinny man with the poking-out neck tried to look as though the idea was preposterous while the heavy man on the couch only smiled a cat's smile and shrugged.

It was all the answer she needed. These were bad men. She turned to the skinny man; he was closer and he was armed. There was no need for her to pull the .38 out of her pocket to kill him. The bullet exploded out from the shreds of her monster coat and struck him at an upward angle just north of his belly button.

He appeared shocked at the sound of the gun and then he glanced down at his shirt, which was already showing blood. The big revolver fell from his hands and he toppled backwards. As he did, Jillybean calmly turned to the big man on the couch whose eyes were ping-ponging back and forth from Jimmy to Jillybean and back again.

"Anyone else here?" Jillybean asked, her coat shoved out in front of her, a small wisp of smoke drifting up from a black-ringed hole.

"Just some girls. I didn't touch them, I swear. You heard me before, right? I'm not like the others."

"Anyone else touch them?" Before he answered, he swallowed, the noise disgustingly loud to Jillybean. Although her ears rang from the gunshot, her hearing seemed to have become superhuman. She could hear Jimmy as he fought for breath with a blasted-out diaphragm, and she could hear the women in the basement whispering in fear. And she could almost hear this fat, evil man trying to come up with a way out of his situation.

"Some of the other guys, I guess, but I didn't. I swear."

"You stink of badness," she said, producing the .38. Hers was a sad life that she could smell the difference between a woman taken in fear and force and one who went happily to the bed. She fired three times. Two of the shots because he was a big male in the prime of his life, and the third, simply because of her anger.

If there was anything she would like to forget, it was the cold fury that had radiated out of her. She had pulled the trigger, feeling dead inside save for the anger which stayed with her like a hangover.

She left the top floor with the couch acting as a sponge for the big man's blood and with Jimmy dying slowly, taking tiny sips of air, his eyes rolling in his head. She went down to find the captives.

The women and the one girl were shackled in a row. They didn't know what to make of Jillybean and she didn't know what to make of them right back. She stared at them for a time, not understanding their looks or the locks that were still locked or why the one girl started talking: "I'm Aria Murphy, have you seen my mother?"

"No," Jillybean replied. Aria was a twig of a girl with a twig of a neck supporting a strangely large head. She was a pretty blonde thing, but with her big eyes and her big head and yellow hair, she looked to Jillybean like a sunflower and she hadn't seen a mom who looked like a sunflower.

"Her name is Kat. Kat Murphy but everyone calls her Kat."

Nor had Jillybean ever met a person that looked like a cat. Sadie with her black clothes and her black hair and her sleek, muscular body had been the closest.

"I said, no."

The women stared some more, their fear giving way to puzzlement as Jillybean stared right back—Why hadn't they fought back against the men? Why hadn't they picked their locks? Why couldn't they see their own power? What was wrong with them? The little girl tried and failed to comprehend such weakness.

193

They may not have your smarts, Ipes said, once she had fetched him from the KIA and, once he had gotten over his queasiness at the sight of the dead bodies in the living room; Jimmy was no longer taking those tiny sips of air. He was still, his eyes fallen back in his head. Ipes gave him a wide birth as he went on: *Bravery is easier when you're big or strong or well-armed. Or smart. You took on those two men because you knew what would happen, didn't you?*

She had known exactly what would happen. She knew that there would be only one or two of the pirates in the house. One to guard the captives and maybe one to guard the guard. As well, she knew they wouldn't be afraid of such a little girl as she was. They would let her walk right through the front door and they would never suspect her deadly nature.

"I guess you're right," she said, going to the dead man on the couch. He smelled of sausage and garlic and sweat…and bad sex and blood. Touching him was the last thing she wanted to do, but she had to find out if he had the keys to the shackles the women wore.

With a sigh, she pushed her tiny hand into his pocket and fished them out and then headed back down to where the women cowered. "It's okay," she told them. "The pirates are dead. Do you guys want to come to Colorado with me? Oh, wait, we're in Colorado. I guess I should ask: do you want to go to Estes Park with me? It's very nice and the people are good and not mean at all."

That had been two days before and now she was suddenly not so sure the people of Estes were nice. Fred wasn't the only one who had given her angry looks. Some of the men at the gate had recognized her. They had whispered and pointed. And a secretary in the front room of the Stanley had gasped when Jillybean had led the group of ex-slaves in.

"They don't want me here, do they?" she asked Neil right off the bat after he had emerged from his chat with Fred Trigg. It was to his credit that he didn't lie. The doors were old and the gaps wide, she had heard everything Fred had said.

He looked down at her, but in spite of the difference in height and in age and although he was the governor of five thousand people and she was only a seven-year-old girl, he looked at her as if she were an equal. She liked that.

"I want you here," he answered with that awful smile of his. She liked that, too.

Jillybean had hoped to find Sadie, who would have accepted her without any reservation, whatsoever. Instead she got Neil and his scarred face and his tired blue eyes—it was the next best thing and, in truth, wasn't bad at all.

He had always *wanted* to love her and to protect her, but in the past he had always been so busy trying to save everyone else that Jillybean had fallen by the wayside time and again.

But at least he had tried.

"I have presents for you and the others," she told him. She had scrounged quite a bit from the pirates: nearly a thousand rounds of ammo, a hundred gallons of fuel, and two hundred pounds of food. When it had been all piled together, she had looked the slave-women dead in the face and told them: "This is all mine by right of conquest."

They hadn't argued. They were a whipped lot, all save Aria, who had told Jillybean on the first night they'd been together: "I wish you had left Kevin alive. He was the fat one. I wanted to cut his dick off and stuff it down his mouth while he screamed."

"Oh…sorry, I guess." Jillybean found the idea strangely hateful. It was understandable, of course, only she didn't like the thought of revenge on such an unnatural level. That was how Eve had been and Jillybean was repulsed by the image Aria had produced. It was one thing to execute a man, to kill in cold blood out of necessity, it was quite another to give in to such hate.

Jillybean took Neil's hand and led him out to the KIA and the windowless van that were parked beside the hotel. She told him about her travels, leaving out the very worst bad parts and there seemed to be so many worst bad parts that the story was somewhat disjointed.

Neil didn't seem to care. He gazed in at the contents of the van and said: "It was awful nice of you to bring all this stuff, thanks Jillybean."

"I also got cookies from this other lady who was all alone and she had a hump, which was weird. Ipes ate some of the cookies and a few got smushed, but you can have some if you want. The rest are for Sadie. Where is she, anyways? Deanna wouldn't tell me and gave me a weird look when I asked."

"Well, you know Deanna, she can be, uh full of weird looks," Neil said, pulling Jillybean away from the van and walking her to the front of the hotel where the views were magnificent and where they could have a bit more privacy.

Neil gave the hotel a quick glance before saying: "About Sadie, she's on a scouting mission, or I guess I should say a scrounging mission. We're getting desperate around here for supplies but since that has to remain a secret, the official word is that she and Captain Grey and a few soldiers are out looking for you."

"But I'm right here," Jillybean said, pointing down at her feet. Neil laughed softly at this. There was little joy in the sound, and she gave him a keen look. "What's wrong?"

He cast a glance back at the old hotel and whispered: "Sorry, I'm just distracted. There's a lot going on, and, if I know Fred, he is going to be trouble. You know how I said we were getting desperate for supplies? It's partially my fault. I spent... wasted is more like it, half the supplies we had left in the valley trying to get information concerning you, Jillybean. And now people are starting to talk. If they find out how low our supplies are, it won't be long before I'm run out of town on a rail."

"Like a railroad kind of rail? I seen one on the way up here and it got me thinking about how to get it working again. Getting a train working, I mean. For, you know, like moving people and goods up and down the mountains. It'll be a little complicated but...oh you weren't talking about trains, were you?"

"No, I'm talking about the survival of the valley." He told her about the poor state in which the war with the Azael had left them and he told her about the traders and the sad woman he had purchased. Jillybean remembered Gayle's name and all the others she had rescued from the witch and she was more than a little disappointed that they had gone and got themselves captured again.

Neil went on: "And now I have Fred Trigg breathing down my neck about everything, you included, Jillybean. He's going to use you to try to undermine me and if that happens and he takes over as governor, I really do fear for the valley. We are in a precarious position."

Jillybean didn't know what to say to this because for once she hadn't done anything wrong or not a lot wrong—killing pirates and bad guys couldn't be all wrong. Ipes whispered in her ear: *I wouldn't worry about it. I bet they're always in a precarious position. The truth is, we all are in a precarious position and we probably always will be, at least until the monsters are all killed.*

That was probably true, she decided and she was about to agree with Ipes when a quartet of women came out of the Stanley just then. Jillybean recognized two of them as having been in the meeting in which Fred Trigg had made his onerous remarks. They stared hard at her monster rags and her wild hair and the M79 grenade launcher slung over her shoulder.

And it wasn't just the two she recognized. The other two, complete strangers to Jillybean, also stared with malice and hatred in their eyes.

"I think I made a mistake coming back here," Jillybean said out of the corner of her mouth to Neil.

Chapter 24

Captain Grey

The snow came down in a quiet manner like a rain of sifted flour easing at least one of Grey's many fears. Winter in the Rockies wasn't something to ever take lightly. At any moment, a blizzard could howl down on you cutting you off from the rest of the world, leaving you stranded for days, if not weeks.

For two days, Grey watched the clouds and listened to the wind as the white drifts built up outside the little cabin. Smitty had finally kept them from moving on. He was afraid the storm would suddenly pick up while they were trying to make it over some mountain pass or down in some sharp valley.

When his men complained, he told them the story of the infamous Donner Party who had been snowbound in the Sierra Nevadas back in the 1840s. Poor planning and rampant stupidity had left the party unprepared and trapped by a blizzard. Without food, they had resorted to cannibalism to survive.

Grey saw some of the same stupidity around him. The bandits, other than Smitty, were an ignorant bunch who ate too much, wasted too much wood and barely watched over their prisoners.

Escape seemed tantalizingly close, but unfortunately, the prisoners' ability to pick locks had been terribly haphazard. Sadie, brave and nimble fingered, had managed to snag a fancy pen from the desk in the main room and in the dead of night she had broken it down. She had hoped for a sturdier piece than the little clip that held the pen to a pocket, but there just wasn't much to the pen and she had to settle on that one inch piece of metal.

Grey held out his hands and she went right to work on his cuffs with the tip of her tongue sticking out of the corner of her mouth. It was slow going with a thousand failures before, finally, after two in the morning, they finally heard the muffled *click* of the lock turning.

"Oh, thank God," Sadie whispered, sitting back, shaking out her fingers beneath the blanket that was stretched over her, Grey and Wilson.

The seven prisoners huddled on the cold floor beneath three blankets which did little to keep out an icy draft coursing down from the two windows. They had been given a single bedroom to sleep in, one that had been emptied of all furniture.

They were watched every minute of the day by a single, rotating guard who sat on a folding chair in the doorway. Sometimes the guards would read, sometimes they did crossword puzzles. One man actually slept, but that was before Grey got his cuffs off.

With Grey's hands free, he went to work on Wilson's handcuffs. The more of them who were free, the better the chance they had at an escape. But try as he might, he couldn't unlock the cuffs. He blamed the hard angle and his over-sized hands that were perfect for crushing a man's windpipe but not as dexterous as he could have wished in this regard.

He was forced to wake Sadie to let her try, but her fingers were throbbing from her earlier work and she soon tired. She gave up the piece of metal to Lieutenant Wilson, who scooted down so that his legs stuck out of the blanket.

Before he could get the lock picked, the guard noticed his odd position and kicked him. "What are you doing?"

"Huh? What? I'm just trying to stay warm," Wilson answered, feigning grogginess as he deftly passed the sliver of metal to Sadie.

"Well you can get warm on one of the guys, but stay off the girl. Those are the orders, dip-shit."

"Oh, sorry, I didn't mean anything by it," he said as he moved back up. He stuck his shackled hands under his head, closed his eyes and pretended to fall asleep.

Grey watched the guard out of cracked lids, hoping that his attention would wander or that fatigue would cause him to nod off, but the man must have sniffed something wrong because he remained extra vigilant until the sun came up and the others started to wake.

They grumbled over the cold as they went to each window to stare out as if the view from one would be tropical.

"Stop your bitching," Smitty snapped. "Let's get the prisoners up. Bill and Pecos, take them out to piss."

If there was a chance for Grey to overpower the guards it would have to occur in the next few seconds while the bandits were still groggy and unsuspecting. They moved around the cabin, poking into packs or simply yawning. In spite of this, Grey knew he'd have to be fast, blazing fast, if he was to stand a chance. He'd go for Pecos first. Not only was he the closest to

Grey, he also held his M16 in a loose grip with one hand while the other was busy scratching his ass in such a determined manner that Sadie watched him with a curled lip.

Grey's muscles bunched, ready to fly at Pecos, only just then, the bandit noticed the look of disgust on Sadie's face. "What are you staring at, you dumb bitch?"

"A moron," she answered.

He bristled at this and now both of his hands were on his weapon. He looked ready to bash her in the face with the butt end of it.

"Pecos!" Smitty barked. "If you touch her, I'll put a hole your head. Take the men, I'll take the girl."

Grey's chance was gone and what was worse, Bill was checking the cuffs of the prisoners as they filed past, heading out into the cold. Grey faked a fall and as he rolled over, he re-locked the cuffs that had taken so long to unlock.

Wilson had been lurking near the doorway as if waiting his turn to leave. He cursed under his breath when he heard the distinct click of the lock.

"We have some bad luck on this one, Boss," Wilson whispered as they stood next to each other, emptying their bladders. As much as he wanted to, Grey wasn't about to agree. Displaying pessimism was no way to lead.

"We'll get our chance," he assured, but they didn't.

The snow had cleared up sometime during the night and the sun was brilliant and the sky a perfect blue. Smitty moved them out after they had scarfed down a quick and very light breakfast.

As usual, Sadie rode in the first truck, and as she had their one device to pick a lock, the soldiers remained trussed and impotent. The one speck of good news was that by noon, they crested the final peak and far below the land was flat and open.

It was also snow-free. The two trucks managed to pick up the speed and roared out onto the plain.

"We'll escape tonight," Grey told his men. "If we start early enough, we should be able to free at least three of us. Four or five would, of course, be better so everyone keep your eyes open for anything that might be able to pick a lock."

They had little chance to find anything that day. They sat in the open bed of the truck for fifteen hours, their asses turning numb. They stopped their eastward trek only twice for "piss-breaks" as Smitty called them, and both times the bathrooms were checked by the bandits before the soldiers were escorted in.

Eventually, as the sun started to go down behind the mountains, Grey was forced to realize that they would simply have to rely on the sliver of metal that Sadie carried—but then they came across a slaver caravan.

Immediately, Smitty pulled over down the street from the trucks—there were seven immense trucks, very similar to the ones that had visited Estes Valley the week before. They were basically armored buildings on wheels.

"Everyone out!" Smitty bawled, dragging Sadie from the truck. "Line up the prisoners. Let's have a quick look at 'em." They were lined up and for the most part, Smitty gazed at them with satisfaction in his eyes. Then he came to PFC Keene and he made a face.

"Let's see them with their shirts off. Uncuff 'em." While the other slavers kept their guns pointed at the prisoners, Bill went down the line of men and unlocked their cuffs. Smitty began to nod. "Okay, better. Now, drop and give me fifty."

"Are you joking," Grey demanded, growing angry. "It's bad enough that you have my men standing around, shirtless, in forty-five degree weather, but now you want to humiliate us?"

Smitty looked shocked that Grey had the temerity to say anything at all. "First off, dip-shit, these are not your men. You all belong to me. Get that through your stupid shaved heads right this second. If you don't believe me, keep standing there and see what happens. For every man still standing in the next ten seconds, I will give fifty lashes to that guy there."

He pointed to Raoul, whose eyes widened, but otherwise didn't move. "Test me," Smitty continued, "and you will lose. Ten, nine, eight…"

Grey believed that Smitty would do exactly what he threatened, and with escape perhaps hours away, there was no need to battle wills. "Squad! Drop and give me fifty."

"That's what I thought," Smitty said. He then turned to one of his men. "Mike, keep buffing them up until I get back. I want them to look like fucking Adonises. Oil them up if you have to."

As Grey and his men were doing pushups to "buff" themselves up, Smitty hurried Sadie into the nearest house. A minute later, they were out again and rushing to the next.

When they came out of the house, Sadie was no longer in her customary black garb. She had on a pink tank-top and it was altogether obvious that she was without a bra beneath. Worse, she had traded in her black jeans for an atrociously short skirt that barely covered the top of her thighs. It might have belonged to a sixth grader.

Red-cheeked, Sadie pulled at the hem as Smitty hauled her along by the hand. "Okay, let's see what we can get for you guys," he said, gleefully. They were pushed toward the waiting traders. "Don't speak to them," Smitty warned. "I don't care if all they ask is your name, you don't say a goddamned word. I'll answer for you and whatever my answer is will be the truth. If I say you're twenty-five and you can speak fucking Swahili, you just nod your head."

"We understand," Grey said, "But you're making a big mistake bringing the girl. She's not a common…"

"Stop!" Smitty said, clear as day. The formation stopped just shy of the traders. Regardless of the eyes on him, Smitty turned to Grey. "You just earned fifty lashes for your man. Do you want to make it a hundred? I've seen men bleed out with a hundred lashes. It ain't pretty and it's a waste of a good man, but I will fucking do it, if you open that sewer of a mouth of yours one more time."

Grey's jaw clenched and his eyes lit with an unholy fire of vengeance, but he kept his mouth shut.

"Good," Smitty said, smiling directly into Grey's fury. He then glanced at one of his men. "Go get the whip. If anyone else steps out of line, we're going to use it right here, right now." No one said a word.

Satisfied that he had cowed everyone into obedience, Smitty marched them the final fifty feet, stopped them in a line and went to greet the traders, alone.

"He found the pick," Sadie whispered to Grey, causing his shoulders to slump. "I'm sorry," she went on, "He wanted me to change clothes and I didn't think I'd get it back and so I stuck the pick in my mouth and…and I didn't know he was going to check my teeth, but he did, and…"

And now there was no way out of their predicament. "It's okay," he lied. "We'll think of something. Just, uh, buck up."

"Yeah." She smiled through her misery and fear as the traders came to inspect them.

It was the single most humiliating five minutes of Grey's life, though it had to be a hundred times worse for Sadie. The trader looked her over—all over. He lifted her shirt and her skirt, going so far as to sniff her nether regions. She bore it all with the fiercest look Grey had ever seen on her face and for a second, he felt bad for anyone who had the balls to buy her because he was pretty certain he wouldn't keep those balls for long.

The talk went back and forth for some time, but in the end, Smitty set the price too high for his prisoners. He didn't seem all that upset as he marched them back to the trucks.

"Just seeing what the market will bear," he said to his men. "Let's get everyone locked up…oh and let's do a complete search of the men. I want every pocket checked and their mouths too."

Pecos snorted, and said under his breath: "I'm not doing a rectal search. I'd rather just shoot these motherfuckers."

Thankfully, a rectal search was not done. The prisoners were thoroughly searched and then handcuffed once more before being loaded onto the trucks.

Because of the proximity to the traders, who were likely also bandits, Smitty had them drive deep into the night until they were well into Nebraska near a town called Ogallala. There seemed to be a veritable army of zombies milling around the town and as the two trucks approached, they swarmed in thick as the stunted, brown cornstalks that covered half the state.

Smitty calmly rolled down his window and shot a flare into the evening sky, creating a red sun that slowly fell to the earth. As the beasts turned to stare, he drove in and around them, without touching a single one.

A second flare was needed as a distraction before he found a clear area north of the town where a house sat in among a forest of bushes that had grown taller than the eaves. The prisoners were hustled in to spend a supperless night in a room stripped of everything but the floorboards and the dust. They had their blankets and nothing else.

That night was harder on them than the previous five. The snow had finally pushed out onto the plains bringing with it a biting cold that the thin blankets mitigated but did not hold back altogether. They shivered and shook and pressed in on each other, so that the people in the middle were warmish but unable to move and the people on the outside were half frozen.

What made matters worse was that what little sleep they did manage to get was disturbed every one and half hours. The oncoming guards woke them to check their cuffs to make sure that they were still secure. The only thing good about the night was that Smitty didn't follow through with his threat to lash Raoul.

Grey vowed not to give him a reason to. He would play the subservient slave boy right up until he got his cuffs off and he had the upper hand, then he'd crack some skulls—that was the plan at least, except there was never another opportunity to get free.

Another freezing day was spent in the back of the truck, shivering beneath their blankets as the blue tarp flapped over their heads. The snow petered out around noon when they crossed the Missouri River and moved on into Iowa.

Somewhere in the great flatness that was Iowa, they stopped to eat. Their dinner from the night before, their breakfast and their lunch was rolled into one meal that consisted of two cans of cold corn that the soldiers split between the six of them.

More zombies slowed their eastward progress and it was a very cranky Smitty who led them to another farmhouse for the night. They were only fifty miles from the Mississippi River and Rock Island, where the Colonel had set up his new base.

The soldiers went hungry again that night and even the bandits were on low rations. "Quit your bitching!" Smitty snarled at his men. "Everyone will get fed tomorrow."

He then stomped over to where the soldiers and Sadie were seated in a corner of the living room. The temperature had dropped into the teens and with the wind howling, Smitty had them all in one room. "One more day and then you'll be outa my hair. Unless of course you guys make trouble."

"What kind of trouble?" Sadie asked, sounding as if she were looking for ideas rather than things to avoid.

"Let's not focus on that. Instead, I want you to focus on what's going to happen to you if you do. If I can't sell you to the Colonel, then I'm going to need to dump you for the best price I can get. It's not cheap running back and forth across the country, so to cut my losses I'll sell you to one of the caravan traders. You know about them, don't you?"

Sadie was ghost-white as she nodded. Life as a whore in one of the caravans wouldn't be a life at all.

"And for you soldiers, well." He shrugged, a move that was half-apologetic. "You're all too old for one of them sadistic queers and too dangerous to keep around for field duty. It'll be the arena for you guys. So, if you don't want that to happen, do exactly what I tell you to do…and maybe pray."

Chapter 25

Jillybean

"I think I made a mistake coming back here," Jillybean said out of the corner of her mouth to Neil as the four women stared and whispered to each other. One made a joke and the other three laughed, cruelly.

"Don't be silly," Neil said, scowling at the women. When he scowled, it wasn't a pretty sight and the women quickly looked away. "Of course you belong here. People can be mean. I'm sure they'll, uh, stop, you know…" Neil struggled to come up with something positive to say, but then he brightened. "Deanna! How are the new people?"

Deanna had just come up, and at the question her eyes slid over to Jillybean before she answered: "Troubled. You know, the usual sad story: capture, enslavement, endless rape. But thanks to Jillybean, they're safe now."

Neil beamed and put an arm around Jillybean's shoulders. "Well, that's good, right?"

With another glance at Jillybean, Deanna shook her head. "It's not all good. They say she killed eleven armed men."

The smile on Neil's face faltered. "Eleven?" He rubbed his head as if the number had caused him to spring a headache. "Oh boy. Eleven? You killed eleven men?" Jillybean nodded reluctantly and Neil rubbed his head some more. "Any chance we can keep the ladies from talking about what happened?"

Ipes and Jillybean shared a confused look before the girl said: "But they were bad men who did very bad things. Why can't they talk about it?"

Neil dropped down to one knee so that he was eye to eye with her. "It's because people are easily frightened. You already have a reputation, Jilly and the fact that you killed eleven armed men…"

"They weren't normal, they were slavers and pirates. They were eleven very bad men and I didn't do nothing wrong. Not even Ipes thinks so and he's always telling me not to kill so many…" She stopped speaking abruptly and cast guilty looks up at the adults. "There…there were a few others, too, but they were all also bad. I promise they were."

Deanna looked down on Jillybean and sighed, a long, sad sigh. "I bet they were bad. I wish…" She gasped suddenly and her face spasmed. One hand went to her round belly and tapped it lightly but urgently as her eyes bugged and she showed her gritted teeth. "It's Emily! She's got…ow…she's got a grip of my insides and is pulling on something that shouldn't be pulled on."

Since this was an internal battle, Neil and Jillybean couldn't do anything but wait on the outcome in a nervous state. After a few moments of pained grunting, Deanna's breathing returned to normal and her smile returned. "She's a real fighter. She kicks so much I bet she'll be born knowing kung fu."

"Can I touch your baby-belly Miss Deanna, ma'am?" Jillybean asked, suddenly filled with a desperate longing to touch another baby. To her, babies were the ultimate in innocence and it still stung like acid on her mind to think about baby Eve.

It must have stung Deanna as well because she drew in another sharp breath and stepped back. "Um," she said, a tilted smile on her full lips. She glanced at Neil and there seemed to pass a season's worth of time until he nodded.

Deanna put a false smile on her lips and said: "Sure." As Jillybean stepped close, Deanna's fingers curled, looking like giant pale spiders dead on a windowsill. She kept them held just above the swell of her belly. They were at the ready—just in case.

Just in case I do something evil, Jillybean thought. *Just in case I suddenly pull out an eight-inch hunting knife and plunge it up to its hilt into that fat balloon of a belly.*

Jillybean wanted to cry out: *But I never would!* only she knew she wouldn't be believed. She had done too much evil in her past to be believed about anything.

Resigned to the presuppositions all criminals lived under, she bore the burden she deserved and only put out a delicate hand. Deanna's belly was warm…no, it was hot. The furnace of the Lord was creating a baby in that belly and it was hot!

She longed to keep her hand there for minutes, hours, days if needed until the baby was born. But she pulled her hand away after the first movement of the infant. "She moved," Jillybean said, affecting a lying grin.

"Yes," Deanna agreed, relieved that the hand…the same hand that had killed dozens? Hundreds? Perhaps even thousands, was removed. "I have, uh things, to take care of," she said and then left, her feet moving with indecorous speed away from the hotel.

Jillybean watched her go and did her best not to cry. Still her eyes watered and she had trouble catching her breath. It started a light hitching in her chest. "I shouldn't have come back," she said, again, unable to look up at Neil.

"That's nonsense!" Neil cried with forced cheer. "This is where you belong, Jillybean."

He's sweet, Ipes said, the sadness in his voice matching the overwhelming feeling bubbling from her soul. *He's always been sweet, but he doesn't see it yet.*

"Not yet," she agreed, in a whisper. Louder, she said: "I'm sure you're right."

"Of course I'm right. She'll come around. They all will. We just need to give it a little time. In a week or two, they'll see that you're doing much better."

But they didn't have a week or two. They didn't even have a full day. Like a lone wind, a whisper began to float through the valley. It coursed through the eaves of every house and along door jams and under stands of aspens, and it even spun out to the tremendous walls of stone that guarded the entrances to the Valley.

The rumor that Jillybean had come back to the Valley reached every ear and then that lone wind became a gale of gossip. Every Jillybean story, true or not, was retold and rehashed, and it was the true stories that were the most damaging:

I heard she poisoned the general and stood over him laughing as blood poured out of his eyes.

That's nothing. I heard she set two ferry boats on fire and that they were crammed with people. Women and children and everything.

Oh, yeah? Well, I was on the River King's bridge when she blew it up. She didn't care that there were like, three hundred of us packed in trucks crossing it when she blew it up.

That's not how it happened. She rescued us, Fred.

And what about New Eden, Kay? How many people did she kill there, just trying to save a baby? I heard she killed a thousand without blinking, so don't tell me she blew up that bridge to rescue us. She blew it up because she likes fires and blood and death. That's who and what she is.

They'd all heard the same thing and more scandalous rumors besides. With a lack of television and theater, Jillybean's exploits had become a form of entertainment in themselves. Two themes ran through them—she was absolutely crazy and she was dangerous to everyone around her. Everyone except for Sadie and Neil, both of whom supposedly had some sway over the girl.

The danger she posed was why a delegation came to the Stanley just as Neil and Jillybean, who had on a new dress of yellow and white, found for her by Deanna, sat down for dinner that evening. They were blowing on soup that had just come from the kitchen under a miasma of tomato-smelling steam when a soldier came bustling into the first floor dining room and leaned into Neil to whisper in his ear.

"A delegation? Really? Now?" Neil asked. "Is Trigg behind it? If so, tell him I'll talk to him in the morning." The soldier leaned in again, his eyes on Jillybean as he made hissing noises into Neil's ear. After a few seconds, Neil frowned and said: "Oh, I guess that's different. Jillybean, honey, wait here, I have to talk to some people."

The little girl didn't wait. The moment Neil left the room, she grabbed Ipes and scampered after, moving with practiced stealth along the dim corridors. It took no special genius to figure out that this "delegation" concerned her, and she wanted to hear what was happening first hand.

It wasn't much of a surprise to her that it really wasn't a delegation that stood out front, it was an angry mob. At least three hundred people had gathered in the fading light. They didn't carry pitchforks like Jillybean had seen in her cartoon movies from before the apocalypse, they carried guns.

At the sight of them, Jillybean slunk down, away from the window, afraid that if she was seen, the mob would turn on her and kill her. *We should get out of here!* Ipes hissed. *We gotta hide before it's too late.*

Jillybean didn't run or hide. She knew these people. As long as she stayed out of sight, she had time. They would talk and talk before they committed to any action. It was a weakness. "Not yet. I want to hear what they're saying."

Along the front of the Stanley was a wide porch, painted a brilliant white where guests once took their tea as they watched the sun set over the snow-capped mountains. Neil stood on the porch alone, looking small but defiant with his balled hands planted firmly on his hips. He was practically shouting at Fred Trigg and a little group of his friends who stood in front of the larger crowd. Because the crowd was loud and boisterous,

Jillybean couldn't make out anything more than an occasional word.

She had to get closer, and so she slunk down and edged right to the corner of the front doors.

She's dangerous.

She's a monster!

She murdered General Johnston!

And that baby. Don't forget she murdered her, too.

This was the background noise that Jillybean tried to filter out to hear Fred Trigg, who was speaking in a sad voice: "I wish it could be another way, but the people have spoken. They are afraid, Neil. This valley isn't the place to try to rehabilitate a mass murder, no matter how small and cute she is."

"I said I would vouch for her. I will personally watch over her and make sure…"

Fred threw his hands in the air. "Please! We don't live in a world where you can vouch for another person, not when murders have been committed. You say you can guarantee our safety, but you can't. Neil, you can't be governor at the same time as watching her twenty-four hours a day."

Jillybean was so entranced by the terrible words that she didn't hear Deanna slip up to the door, the carpet muting her footsteps. "Come with me," the woman ordered. "You can't be here." Slowly, with clear reluctance, she held out a hand to Jillybean.

"What are they going to do to me?" the little girl asked, as Deanna whisked her along, heading for a back staircase.

"Nothing. They won't do anything, trust me. They're just scared is all. They're…" She stopped. They were on the first landing which was wide and open. Even the back staircase was of such opulence that there was a French chaise along one wall of the landing and a plush, comfy looking chair in the corner.

Ignoring everything around them, Deanna bent down and looked into Jillybean's eyes, staring intently. When Jillybean finally got too self-conscious to keep up the sustained eye contact and turned her face downwards, Deanna asked: "Are you hearing any voices in your head? Like…like Eve, or someone else?"

"I hear you."

"Jillybean, you know what I mean."

"I'm not hearing nothing and that's the truth. You can ask Ipes. He'll tell the truth. He says he's like George Jefferson and can't tell a lie."

Deanna stared for a moment longer and then said: "Good," before pulling Jillybean along again, heading up and up to the third floor. Once there, she sped them along to the last room of the wing. It faced east where the mountains were just strange dark angles blotting out the stars.

"Neil won't let them hurt you," Deanna said, and yet at the same time, she locked the door and then pushed the bed in front of it. She laughed and added: "Just a precaution." The precaution also included a pistol which Deanna set on her lap as she faced the door and waited.

Jillybean expected to be there for a long time, but it was only a few minutes before someone lightly tapped six times on the door, three sets of two. Deanna shoved the bed away and Neil hurried in. He was red-faced and fuming.

"That Fred. Oh, so help me, I feel like…" Neil stopped what Jillybean knew was going to be a threat. "He's going to force you out of the valley, Jillybean. I'm sorry but he has riled up a few hundred people against you. It's not even close to the majority of the citizens, but it's enough to cause trouble."

The girl felt her legs start to shake and before she could collapse, she sat down on the bed, Ipes held to her chest, protectively. "Can I talk to them? If they saw who I really was, maybe they'd change their minds."

"It wouldn't work," Neil said, going to the window and looking out. For once, the view wasn't beautiful. It was far from it. The hundreds of people had not left. They stood in little clumps all around the hotel, bundled in coats and scarves. They talked, all the while staring up at the building.

Neil turned from the window and went to the door and listened with his partially chewed off ear. "It wouldn't work," he said again. "Fred is a master manipulator. He'll turn your words against you and whatever character witness you brought forward, he would impugn, ruthlessly."

He had used a lot of words that Jillybean wasn't so sure about, but she got the gist: there was no beating Fred through logic.

"I don't really see what he's gaining from this," Deanna said. "Is he really that afraid of Jillybean?"

"Yes, actually," Neil answered. "But that's really not the reason. He knows that this will end me if I protect her."

Jillybean's heart, what felt like a tired little stone, sank in her chest. "Do I have to leave tonight?"

Deanna leapt up from the chair she'd been sitting in, the pistol in her hand, waving as she hissed: "This isn't fair! We can stop this, Neil. I know my friends will stand up for her and most of the people you brought through…"

"And the soldiers?" Neil asked, cutting his eyes Jillybean's way. "I doubt they'll be persuaded. And that goes double for the civilians who had been here before we showed up. All they know about Jillybean are the rumors. So what does that leave us? A few dozen people who'll stand up for her out of five thousand."

Jillybean blinked in a slow way—it seemed to take the place of thinking just at the moment. Not a single thought entered what suddenly felt like an air-filled head. Right then she didn't think there was much difference between her and a balloon, and she was sure that a stiff breeze would float her right out the window and where she would end up, no one would know and certainly no one would care.

Involuntarily, she took three steps toward the door, her feet acting on their own, her eyes huge moist blue orbs. Neil grabbed her arm. "No," he said.

Deanna was slower and only reached out once Neil had stopped her. "Hey, sweetie, we'll fight this, somehow." Jillybean saw that her smile was all fakery, like the fancy front of a dirty saloon. Deanna had no idea what to do and she was just spouting nice sounding words. "Neil, tell her. We'll fix this. We'll find a way, just like as we always do."

Neil's teeth gritted together and he looked as though he were biting down on tinfoil. "No. There isn't a fix for this and the longer I drag this out, the worse it will be for you."

"For me?" Deanna asked, her bewilderment showing on her face. "What the hell are you talking about?"

"Yes, for you. Let me spell it out," Neil said. "Jillybean can't stay and I can't let her go out into the wilds by herself."

Deanna's brow crinkled, three little lines showing on her brow. "Then send someone with her."

It seems so simple for her, Jillybean thought. Just send "someone" as if there were a line of someones jumping at the chance to leave the safety of the valley with someone who was in all likelihood a murderer. Leave and never come back. It was a prison sentence.

Neil's face split into a pained smile for all of a second. "Who could I possibly send? If Grey or Sadie were here, maybe I could send one of them, but only because they love her. But they're not here and that leaves only me."

This statement—this near declaration of love—sent the airiness in Jillybean's insides twisting so that her stomach went one way and her throat went the other. It squeezed the air out of her and she could only make a high-pitched, squealing sound. If she was hearing Neil right, it meant that she might be exiled, but she wasn't going to be all alone! Neil would come with her. He would look after her!

As much as he can, Ipse said, quickly, trying to add an element of reality to what felt like fantasy to the lonely girl.

She knew that Ipes was right. Neil wasn't all that much of a guardian in truth, but he was a thousand, no, a million times better than being alone. She didn't know whether to cry or scream or laugh.

Deanna struggled for words as well. The three little lines had sprung two mates and now there was a row of them. "And… and…hold on. Wait. Then it'll be just me here alone? What if Grey doesn't come back? Or Sadie?"

Before anyone could answer, she laughed miserably, high in her throat and there were tears in her eyes, gleaming spheres that stretched until they hung pendulously from her lashes. "I didn't mean that. I don't know why I said that. It's only been five days. Sorry, I'm being silly. I was just hoping they'd be back by now."

She laughed a second time, high and gay and strange as if there wasn't an angry mob outside the window demanding blood and two frightened people right in front of her. "Isn't that stupid? I just…I just… I guess I've got pregnancy jitters or whatever they call it."

Neil waited until she had pulled herself together. "They'll be back soon enough, but until then, I need you to run things. You'll be acting governor until the next election, which is going to be sooner rather than later, especially when Fred lets it 'slip' that I blew all the supplies."

The three lines were back on Deanna's forehead. "He's going to make it miserable here for us, isn't he? He's going to try to drum Grey out of the army, I bet. I'm sorry, Neil but we should never have traded those supplies."

Jillybean felt like a bug flitting around a bulb, unable to land, unable to fly away. That one person wanted her, that someone wanted to take care of her in some way, in *any* way, was so great that she hadn't been following the conversation as close as she should have been.

Deanna's fear for Captain Grey caused her to focus, because she liked him very much. "You guys need supplies? I have a lots of gas and I bet you can trade it for all sorts of stuff. It's not with me, but I can get it for you."

"That's very sweet of you," Deanna said, "but we need more than what you have in your car."

"I know that, silly. Asides, my car can't carry it all. I need one of them long cylinder trucks. A fuel truck, right, thanks Ipes. I need one of them or maybe two and someone who can drive them. The sticker-shifters are too tough for me. I tried one once and the car hopped around a little like a rabbit and made a grinding noise that didn't sound good, not at all."

Neil's face froze in a contorted look, something between puzzlement and shock, as if he was shocked that he was puzzled, or puzzled that he was shocked. "You have that much fuel? For real?"

"For reals," she answered scratching her left butt cheek, absently. "But it's all the way in Missouri and that's a long ways away."

Silence settled over the room as outside, the undercurrent of voices picked up. Neil went to the window, stared out for a moment before asking: "Would that much fuel change people's minds about Jillybean?"

Just then he was spotted by the crowd and a rock was thrown, thumping off the wall next to the window. Neil quickly ducked back, almost running into Jillybean who went to the window and stood on tiptoes to look out.

"I don't think I want to come back," she said. "I don't like those people."

"You know they're not all like that," Neil said. "Fred's got them riled up, but perhaps we can use the fuel to change how they look at you, Jillybean. I mean, this was exactly why I gambled our supplies away in the first place. I knew that once you were free of all the danger and the constant running and the scrounging to live, you would be a force that we could, uh, harness for the greater good."

213

Jillybean looked back, confused. "Harness? Like a donkey? Or a slave? I don't like either idea. And why should I try to change their minds? You know it won't matter what I do. Fred didn't do this to them, I did. All the bad stuff I did is why they're like this, that and my craziness. That's all they'll ever see me as: a crazy girl."

Neil and Deanna shared a quick look, but the girl's logic was too spot on to refute. They both slumped, looking dejected. It pained Jillybean deep down to know that once again she was being the cause of trouble. It was because of her that Neil was being forced out of the valley, and it was because of her that Captain Grey was going to lose his job on the council and in the army. And who knew what was going to happen to Deanna and Sadie?

"I'm going to get the fuel for you," she said, "but I won't be coming back. You can have it all and then Fred won't be able to say anything about missing supplies and you'll be able to keep your job, Mister Governor, Neil, sir and Captain Grey will be okay, too."

"No," Neil shot back. "I won't have you out there all alone. We'll get the gas and then…"

Jillybean held up a tiny hand, silencing him. "I won't be all alone. There are people out there who like me and think I'm nice. I'll live with them." In truth, there was only Granny Annie, whom Jillybean wasn't all that keen to go live with. She was old and a little weird and her luck with the monsters wouldn't last forever. She would be eaten eventually and Jilly would be all alone again.

There were also Lauren and Tristyn in Scottsbluff, two people she had never met before but with whom she felt a certain bond with, all because of the perfect home they had left behind that Jillybean had slept in. She felt she owed it to them to try to find them and let them know that the dad of the family, Jack had never come back to read his letter.

Who knew if they would like her and Ipes, especially after she delivered such bad news. Either way, she would take the chance. It was better than living with so much guilt—it was sadly obvious to her that Neil wanted to stay in the valley. She saw that he liked it here, that he liked being the governor and she saw that he was good at it, too.

There was no way she could live with herself knowing she had forced him into a miserable lonely exile.

"I just need someone to come with me who can drive a truck," she said and smiled, in a sweet, lying manner. To change the subject, she said: "You know what else? One of my teeth is loose. See?" She opened her mouth and wiggled a molar with her tongue.

Chapter 26

Neil Martin

A part of Neil didn't believe Jillybean. He feared that she was making up this "old friend" of hers for his and for Captain Grey's sakes, but a larger part hoped that it was true.

If there were people who didn't know her violent past, then there was a chance she could eventually let all the evil things she had done die in a long forgotten memory. Hell, he could barely remember anything from when he was seven, a flash of an image here a flash there, perhaps that could be her as well.

"Ok, Jillybean, tomorrow we begin one more adventure together. Once we get the gas, however, we're not coming back here. I want to see this Granny Annie for myself."

"She's real, I promise. And she'll be glad to meet all of you, but she might try to steal some of your stuff. That's just the way she is."

Neil said that was: "Good," though he didn't know what he meant by that. He then settled her into the room and sent Deanna to fetch the last of their supper with instructions that Jillybean was to eat both portions. Her bones protruded at every angle which couldn't be healthy.

As Deanna went for the food, Neil sent for Fred and the rest of the council. "You want to have a meeting without Deanna?" Fred asked, a grin on his face, looking as though he had won some sort of contest.

"There won't be any votes being taken so there's no point," Neil replied. "I've just come to announce a few decisions. Jillybean will be leaving the valley first thing in the morning. I will be escorting her to the home of a women in Oklahoma who knows Jillybean and has offered to take her in."

"And who will be acting governor?" Fred asked, his greedy eyes all aflame.

Before Neil could answer, Colonel Mires, the acting Commissioner of the Army asked: "Why are you going? Shouldn't you appoint someone else to escort her?"

"Like who? Someone from the military? I think that would be abusing my authority. I'd send Fred, but he can barely take care of himself."

"Ha-ha," Fred laughed, sarcastically. "Why don't you ask for volunteers? Oh, right, that would just make you look weak when no one stepped up."

The colonel surprised Neil as he glowered at Fred. "Who could call braving the wilds for the sake of a troubled little girl, weak? I would volunteer myself, but Grey gave me specific instructions. I will ask around among the men to see if there are any who would go."

"There's no need," Neil said. "There's a second reason I am going." He paused to take a steadying breath. He hated to lie and wasn't good at it. "There have been questions concerning our supply situation. What many of you don't know is that the war with the Azael has left us in a very weakened state…"

Fred jumped in: "And Neil pissed away a lot of what we had left to find out where Jillybean was. He's put us in a terrible position, one that we may not recover from without a change in leadership…if you ask me."

"No one did," Neil said. "Fred is only half-right. We are in a tough spot and from a certain point of view it looked as though I wasted supplies unnecessarily, however. The money wasn't wasted, it was invested."

Fred's mouth fell open. "How?"

"That's none of your concern. A real leader takes calculated risks and the return on investment with Jillybean may be as high as five to one. The one stipulation is that I have to seal the bargain, personally. It's why Deanna Russell will be acting as governor in my stead."

Colonel Mires drummed his fingers on the desk for a moment before saying: "You can hardly be accused of abusing your power under these circumstances. Five to one seems like too much to be left unguarded."

Since Neil was lying through his teeth, he couldn't very well have an escort witnessing his perfidy first hand. It would undermine his standing as governor and he'd be out the door at the next election, besides, he hoped to have a guard.

"I'll be meeting Captain Grey and his team. They will guard the cargo on its way back to the valley. Now since there are no more questions, I need to get ready."

Fred jumped up. "No more questions? I have a hundred questions! What sort of timeframe are we looking at? Who's going to take Deanna's place on the council? Where are you go…"

"I guess, I should have said: since I'm not going to answer any more questions, I need to get ready." He left Fred fuming and almost certainly plotting. It was in his nature, or so Neil assumed.

As he marched away, a dreadful thought popped into his head: *Why hasn't Jillybean killed him?* Where that thought came from, he had no idea.

"We'll just pretend I never thought it," he whispered, heading down the stairs and out into the night. He really did have a hundred things to do.

The next morning, Neil rolled his dice. He wasn't much of a gambler and in dice terms, he didn't know what was a good roll and what was a bad one. *Snake eyes*, that is, both dice coming up with ones was about the only thing he knew for certain was bad…and he really wasn't all that certain about that.

He'd seen craps played on two occasions and the rules seemed to evolve with every roll of the dice. Once, he'd been in a casino where everyone went mad when a four and a five were rolled. People were jumping up and down, trampling Neil in the process. Five minutes later the same four and five were rolled and the place became as dismally sad as a funeral home.

He was gambling a lot on a deranged little girl who talked to a stuffed zebra and who had killed over a thousand people. When he thought about it, gambling seemed like too tame of a word.

"No whammies, how about that," he whispered as he loaded up a Jeep Wrangler. Jillybean's KIA wasn't built for mountain driving, especially when there was four inches of snow to contend with. The Jeep with its huge, heavily treaded tires, would be fine.

Jillybean didn't think it was fine at all. She went round and round the vehicle with a look of discontent on her face. "Can we put some armor on this thing? The plains are chock full of bad guys, that's what means there's a lot of them and armor will come in handy. I can solder stuff, you know, and I bet I could weld stuff, too if I could get some proper electricity. I could put some metal walls over the windows. I bet."

"We don't have time for all that. We need to zip up to Wyoming, find Grey and Sadie, and then zip out to Missouri to get the gas and then zip back before Fred turns the entire valley against us."

"That's a lot of zipping," Jillybean noted, without much enthusiasm. "I never was able to zip anywheres. There was always monsters and bad guys and people needing rescued and stuff."

Neil patted the side of the Jeep. "Well, that's not going to be us. We'll stay optimistic and good things will happen."

His actions didn't quite jibe with his words. The quickest way to Wyoming was to first head east to Denver and then north along I-25. In the old days, a trip like that would have taken three hours. In the old days there weren't bandits lurking in the ruins of the Mile-high City.

Instead of trusting to optimism, he chose to follow Grey's example and he cut north through the mountains, erroneously thinking that direction was safer. The sheer number of zombies changed his mind. They seemed to be everywhere and he faced the same early problems that Grey had.

Like horrid logs, zombies rolled down the side of hills at them, and they jumped off cliffs and formed a diseased barricade right in the middle of the road. "Is your seat belt on?" he asked Jillybean every time they came to a particularly large grouping of them.

"Yes, sir," she always answered and then pulled her sleeping bag up to her chin. She kept the sleeping bag near for "extra protection for when the monsters break the windows," was how she put it.

"They're not going to break," he had said. Forty-two minutes later the window right behind Neil was smashed with one punch by a fearsome zombie of great size. He was a huge thing with a bloated stomach and a mouth full of weeds that he growled through.

The growl was drowned out by a scream and a gunshot. "Sorry about screaming like that," Neil said. They had been skirting a boulder when the beast had come from out of the woods to slam into the slow moving vehicle. Now it was half in the Jeep and half out, bleeding down the interior of the back door. "It just surprised me how fast it was." Neil jerked the Jeep right and left until it fell out.

"It was fast," Jillybean agreed as she picked out the empty brass casing from her .38. She gave it an interested sniff before chucking it out the broken window. "And big, too. Have you noticed that the monsters are getting bigger?"

Just then, dodging in and out among a herd of them, they did indeed seem larger than usual, but he was sure that it was his imagination. "No, I haven't noticed, but it's unlikely that they've grown. Most of these things were adults before they became monsters. They've grown all that they're going to."

"Maybe, I guess. Though, then again maybe not, on account that they're not people no more—*any more*, jeepers Ipes, I'm not in school." She seemed to lose her train of thought as she slid a shiny new bullet into the gun and hid it away somewhere in the rags she always wore.

They passed another beast of monstrous size and Jillybean nodded at it. "When I woke up, I thought they looked different, scarier, you know? At first, I thought they had just been getting all fattened up, you know, because of winter and all, but they are definitely bigger."

Neil took his eyes off the road and stared at two of the creatures who still had the tattered remains of clothes on them. Both wore pants that were hitched high up on their ankles. "Great," he said. "Zombies that can heal themselves and who continue to grow. That's just what we need, giant zombies."

"I don't think we need giant zombie-monsters. Oh, careful, Mister Neil, sir." Up ahead was the same boulder where Grey's team had been ambushed. Jillybean had a nervous twitch to her eye as she looked at it. This more than the boulder caused Neil to stop a hundred yards down the road from it.

"Are you worried about an ambush?" he asked.

She shrugged her shoulders. "A little, I guess. It's the perfect spot. You could roll big rocks from up on that hill and squish anyone. Or you could wait around the corner with guns and spiky things in the road. I should go up that hill and check it out."

Even though it made sense for her to go since she was far stealthier, a better climber and a far worse driver, Neil felt embarrassed to send a seven-year-old out to do what he considered a man's job. But he didn't argue. He watched her slowly mount the snow covered hill until he saw a number of stumbling, slipping and sliding zombies advancing on the Jeep. Grumbling, Neil was forced to abandon the warmth of the Jeep time and again to deal with them. He left the M4 behind and grabbed his trusty axe, and after caving in a few skulls, he would glance up to make sure Jillybean was doing well and then duck back into the Jeep.

Coming back down for Jillybean was a piece of cake compared to going up. After a few minutes of walking along the ridge line and gazing down the other side of the hill, she produced a small blanket and a black garbage bag from her backpack. She fashioned a sled of sorts and was back down on the road in under a minute, her cheeks rosy and her smile going from ear to ear.

"I wish I had a real sled," she said to Neil, as she took the blanket from the bag, gave it a few shakes, and stuck it back into her pack. "Just think how fast I coulda gone if I had one."

Too fast, Neil wanted to say. His heart had been in his throat watching her fly down the steep hill. "If we only had time, but we don't, darn it. I take it you didn't see anything from up there."

"Nothing scary, but the angle wasn't the best. It's like a cliff or something on the other side. You wouldn't have liked it. I know how you don't like heights. And it was all slippery. One false step and then splat! Ipes was freaking out, too. You know, sometimes you and him are a lot alike."

He was being compared to a neurotic, chicken of a stuffed zebra that wasn't even real.

Instead of throwing away the garbage bag, she held it up for a quick inspection. There were a few minor tears in it and so she dug in her pack once more, pulling out a role of grey duct tape that she had smushed flat so it took up less room.

"In my experience, once a trash bag is ripped, tape isn't going to save it," Neil told her. "Besides, we can get more. The world is filled with bags and we don't really have that much in the way of garbage."

She laughed at him as if he had told her a joke. At first he thought it was a symptom of her insanity. After all, people laughing at nothing was usually a stereotypical action of the mentally ill. She folded the black bag once and put it up to the broken window. "You wanna do the holding or the taping?"

Finally, he caught on that she wanted to cover the broken window so they wouldn't freeze on the drive. "I'll tape, I guess."

Jillybean watched him with a raised eyebrow, her look indicating that he was doing a less than genius-level job at using tape. "It'll hold for now, I guess," she said, "but you'll need to stop at the first hardware store we see so we can put a real fix on it."

221

He wasn't about to argue, the tape job was sloppy at best. To be on the safe side, he ran more tape across the bag going in four different directions. It was noticeably warmer as they climbed into the Jeep.

"Let's see if we can get around that boulder," Neil said, growling the vehicle forward. It was nerve-wracking to skirt the huge rock since they had to go into the partially frozen-over river. Safe on the other side, their nerves were further tested when they saw the great mound of bodies piled at the base of the cliff.

Neil parked next to it with a screwed up expression on his face. The dead were stiff and oddly contorted as if they had frozen in the middle of rigor mortis. The snow only partially covered them and made it seem as if the bodies had been there for months, if not years. It was like something seen on the approaches to the summit of Everest.

"I hope they're alright." Jillybean couldn't seem to take her eyes off the mound of bodies.

"I'm sure they are," Neil assured. "I bet those bodies have been there for weeks."

She shook her head and finally turned away. "No. They've been there for five days. Miss Deanna said it snowed five days ago. These monsters fell just before it snowed or they woulda been eated by the birds. And they didn't just fall, neither. There's only one reason the monsters woulda been up there."

A lump gathered in Neil's throat as he stared up at the cliff face. He knew the one reason—they had been chasing someone. "We should hurry."

He pushed the Jeep through the twisting mountain roads as fast as he dared. It was a good vehicle, well balanced and sure footed. Despite the snowy roads, they made good time and it was an hour before sunset when they found the truck that Captain Grey had taken on his expedition. "Oh, God," he whispered, coming up on the vehicle slowly. "That's their truck."

For a moment, Jillybean's face showed her anguish. Then her lips drew into a line and her eyes narrowed into slits. Before he could stop her, she had slid out of the Jeep and was trudging through the ankle deep snow, slinging her pack and putting Ipes into an inner pocket.

"Their packs are still in the back, all except Sadie's, which is in the front seat. The truck is out of gas, but the gas cap is still on. There's no sign of a struggle, no bullet holes, no blood. Strange."

She stared around the truck and then looked back the way they had come and was silent for so long that Neil finally asked: "So what happened? They didn't just disappear."

A nasty look of contempt crossed her features before she gave her head a quick shake. "No, they didn't disappear. People don't just disappear. They were taken, but they weren't taken here. This is no sort of ambush site unless the bad guys were dressed as monsters and were mixed in with them, but…but that would be too risky for pirate types."

"Maybe it was dark when they ran out of gas and the bad guys snuck up on them as they were about to put more gas in the truck."

She shook her head. "Would Captain Grey let his truck run out of gas on a mountain road filled with zombies? I don't think so and neither does Ipes. But Sadie would." Jillybean walked once around the truck, touching the scratches that marred the sides. "These are new. There's no rust in them and no paint either. Sadie was driving last and she was in a hurry."

Neil also touched the gouges. They hadn't been there when the truck had left the valley. "Do you think they were ambushed back at the boulder?"

"Someone had allowed the monsters to chase them up the hill and over the cliff. My guess it was Sadie. She is super fast and relied on her legs. And while she was gone Grey and the others probably tried to hurry past the boulder only to fall into a trap. That boulder was the perfect spot for an ambush. They might have got them before they had a chance to react."

"But why leave a truck full of gas. That doesn't make any sense."

She shrugged, listlessly. "Maybe not all the monsters went after Sadie and they didn't have time to siphon the last of the gas from the truck. They took what they needed and left."

"So, Sadie might still be free," Neil said, jumping at the slim hope. "Get in. We'll find her and then we'll figure out what to do next."

Jillybean didn't get in. She was no longer so grim and focused; she looked sad and worn. "Will it ever be over?" she asked, looking down at Ipes. There was a moment of silence and then she nodded. "Until then, we keep going."

She sighed, climbed up into the Jeep and began digging into her backpack, producing a map of Colorado folded so that the section of mountains they were in was facing out. "If they left in the morning, they were likely aiming to get to Poudre Park by nightfall. If Sadie was on foot, I think it would be her only option."

"Then we'll go there. Get that bomb shooter of yours ready."

Chapter 27

Neil Martin

Twenty minutes later they struck Route 14. To the east was Poudre Park to the west were a number of rinky-dink mountain towns that were so small and stuck so far out in the middle of the wilderness that it made little sense wasting gas heading to any of them, and yet that was the direction in which they found tire tracks in the snow.

Again, Jillybean was out of the Jeep before Neil could get out, in fact even before he stopped she was down on the ground like a bloodhound going back and forth, gently touching the tracks with her tiny fingers. "There were two trucks and they were the *sorta* big ones, but not the really big ones. Bigger than Captain Grey's truck, you know what I mean? And they were pulling trailers. Those smaller tracks were made by trailers."

All Neil saw was a mash of tire prints. He stepped closer, standing over them—it was like looking at an alien language and he couldn't make heads or tails out of it. But since he had Jillybean with him, he didn't see the point of poking around in the snow further. He trusted her in these sorts of things. "Can you tell anything else from them? You know, like how many people they could have with them or what kind of weapons they had?"

Jillybean looked at him for a long moment as if she were looking at a bug she had never seen before. She then glanced down at the tracks, her brow crinkling. "They don't have artillery guns like the Azael had, if that's what you mean. Other than that, I can't tell what type of guns they had. All I know is that some of the tires are mismatched, which isn't, um, out of the normal? Is that how you say it? Is that what means that's how it is nowadays?" Neil nodded and she shrugged. "So, I don't know if that means anything."

Neil looked back and forth down the highway, seeing nothing but snow, tire tracks and mountains rising up like shark teeth. There wasn't much else to see other than the deepening shadows that stretched long across the road.

"Five day old tracks going deeper into the mountains?" It wasn't much to go on, but they had nothing else. "Maybe these bandits have some sort of hideout that they sneak out of to take people as slaves."

225

"Maybe," Jillybean said, with a shrug that couldn't have been more of a platitude if it had been spoken by a politician. Neil correctly read it not as a *maybe*, but as a: *definitely not*.

They decided to spend the night in Poudre Park since it was the closest shelter available and, hoping to find Sadie safe and sound, they drove through the not-so empty streets looking for any sign of her, however the zombies spilling out of the houses along the main drag made it difficult for them to do anything more than survive.

They dashed here and there, turning u-turns every time the road ended in a gulch, which seemed more often than not.

There were zombies everywhere and Neil ran many of them down as they frequently slipped and fell in front of the Jeep. He roared along in four-wheel low, smushing zombies into the snow. It was strange to see them pick themselves up again, leaving behind a body print…and usually some flesh and grey blood. It was like a horrible version of a snow-angel.

Since secrecy was well out the window by that point, they began to yell Sadie's name over and over, but in the end they had to give up. Not even Jillybean's sharp eyes had seen any sign of her.

Sadie hadn't been on the road, and there hadn't been any tracks in the snow left by her Converse sneakers, and now she wasn't in town; there was only one thing to conclude: Sadie had been captured along with the others.

Depressed, and with the dark bearing down quickly, Neil found a little house tucked off a side road where they made camp for the night, but only after Jillybean set traps and flares, and showed Neil two different escape routes and three hiding spots just in case of this or that evil scenario occurred.

There seemed to be a lot of these possible scenarios. She had walked around the house with her eyes slightly out of focus as she imagined all the possible dangerous situations that could befall them, and it was a little distressing when she started reciting them to Neil in a ghostly monotone. She seemed to go on and on and, coupled with his fear for Sadie and the fact there were bandits perhaps lurking nearby and zombies by the hundreds meandering all through the town, it was no wonder that he slept with one eye open and both ears actively trying to listen beyond the usual night sounds for the tell-tale creep of a slaver treading through the snow.

They woke along with the sun and after a quick breakfast, they were ready to go. Neil wanted to go west first, while Jillybean wanted another look at the town. Without argument, Neil turned east and drove once more around the town. It really wasn't much more than a hamlet and was so little that it took only ten minutes for them to go up and down every street.

Jillybean saw only one thing out of the ordinary: the trucks had apparently not begun their trip in Poudre Park as they had assumed, the tracks had come from somewhere east of the town.

"Which means what?" Neil asked.

Before she answered, Jillybean looked down at her handy map and seemed uncharacteristically uncertain. "I don't know. Maybe there is a secret hideout like you said, but it doesn't make no sense. I mean it doesn't make *any* sense, thanks Ipes. Why would they have their base so far from anything? It would waste so much gas coming up here all the time."

The two fell to thinking as the Jeep rumbled on and the morning sky grew bluer and clearer. Neil drummed on the steering wheel, thumping a beat that sounded like the hooves of horses. "Okay, if the people who made these tracks came from the east, then they probably don't have anything to do with capturing Sadie and the others."

"Yeah, I guess."

"And so we should go east." He jutted out his chin to see the map splayed between them. With his eyes, he traced the line of I-14 as it squiggled down out of the mountains. "If I was a slaver who had captured Grey and Sadie, I would head out to the lands of the Azael and try to sell them for top dollar."

"Unless Sadie mentioned who her father is," Jillybean said. "Then I bet they'd go to the River King's place and try to hostage her."

"In which case, they'd head straight east as well. And so shall we." With their direction set, they sped east, dodging rocks in the road, and zombies coming from all directions. By the time they came to the rock slide that had taken out the road, Neil's hands were stiff from white-knuckling it for so long.

The two stared at the destruction and both knew there'd be no getting around it. "Okay, maybe those guys with the trucks and the trailers were the ones who got to Grey and Sadie," Neil said as he spun the Jeep around and sent it racing back the way they had come.

He followed the tracks back through Poudre Park and then deep into the mountains until they came upon a road heading north; the tracks in the snow turned that way and Neil did as well. Hours went by and they stopped only to relieve themselves and to refill the gas tank using five of the jerry cans strapped to the top of the Jeep.

They drove until the sun disappeared behind the mountains and even then Neil, didn't want to stop. His heart insisted that he keep driving through the night.

The idea that Sadie had been in the hands of vile slavers for five days filled him with rage and fear. He knew Sadie. He knew that she could be fierce and headstrong. He knew that she would fight if they tried to rape her…and his heart broke at the thought of what would happen if she angered the wrong man.

"There's a place," Jillybean said, when the sun had been down for an hour and the stars were spilling across the night sky. "Look, Mister Neil, right there. Slow down, there's the drive…" She turned in her seat to look back. "You just passed it. That was a good place."

"We shouldn't stop. They've got a five day head start and we need to eat into their lead. I'll drive tonight and, hopefully, we'll get out of the mountains. You can drive tomorrow on the plains where it'll be open."

Jillybean squinted ahead into the dark, her little nose wrinkling in displeasure. "If you're going to drive in the night time, you might as well turn on your lights. With all these mountains, no one is going to see us except the monsters."

After so long, the idea of using lights in the night was now so foreign to him that he hesitated before flicking the switch. "Huh," he grunted as the headlights lit up the snow. "That's better. You should try to get some sleep."

"Can I make you something to eat first? We have a few apples or some soup. It'll be cold. Unless I take out part of the dash." A flashlight appeared in her hand so quickly that Neil's eyes were dazzled by it. She scooched off her chair and began to dig through her pack for tools, producing two different screwdrivers in seconds.

She had such a serious look on her soft face that it was at the same time sweet and sad. "It's okay," he told her. "I don't need anything right now. And maybe you shouldn't mess with that. You don't want to break anything."

"Actually, I think I'm going to have to break this panel off. The screws are on the inside of the engine compartment and so the only way to get at it is to either pry it away or cut into it. It'll be okay, Mister Neil, the panel doesn't serve much purpose except to hide the guts of the car."

"Maybe I don't want to see the guts. Generally, I don't want to see the guts of anything. Guts freak me out. How about you give me one of those apples?" The apples were getting on in their limited lifespans and were spotty in places and mushy in others. One trick was to eat them without looking and the other trick was for Neil to remember he wasn't living in the old days when grocery stores never ran out of anything. Nowadays, you took what you could and you didn't complain.

Jillybean put away her tools and took out her duct tape once more. She calmly taped a can of chili to one of the heating vents. "It'll be warm, at least," she remarked. While she waited for it to warm up, she fished around in the back of the Jeep and found a text book of enormous heft.

"Human anatomy?" Neil said, reading the spine. "Why are you reading that?" In his mind, a queer and somewhat evil image accompanied the question: Jillybean huddled over a body, a scalpel in one hand, a candle in the other, hot wax dripping down into an open chest cavity. On the floor around her were organs and pools of blood and on her face a nasty smile.

"I might want to be a doctor when I grow up," she explained. "There doesn't seem to be a lot of them and I've discovered that when something is scarce it is worth more to people and if I'm worth something to people they'll want me around."

Neil felt immediate guilt. It formed a lump in his throat that he had trouble choking down. At last he said: "That's an admirable goal. Is there's anything I can do to help?"

She didn't think there was and told him so before pointing her nose back into the book.

The guilt remained in him, churning his stomach. He had failed her time and again and here, once more, she was trying to do good, and once more, someone was judging her…he was judging her.

"You'll be a great doctor. In fact, I'll be your first patient. I'll let you know when I'm sick and you can fix me."

"I'm sorry, Mister Neil, but being a doctor is not that easy. From what I gather, it can take a person years to become one.

But, I guess if you're sick and no one else is around, I could take care of you like my mom took care of me. I always got better so she was a pretty good almost-doctor."

She read until her eyes began to water and her mouth stretched into a yawn every other minute. Then she slept in a cocoon of blankets with her .38 within reach and her grenade launcher propped against the door.

Neil watched her nearly as much as he watched the road. He found her soft child-features to be beautiful. With her mind finally shut down and her cares hidden beneath dreams, she seemed free for once and it showed on her face. The dark circles under her eyes faded and the creases on her forehead disappeared.

It was how she was supposed to look.

"One more adventure," he said, hoping that he wasn't lying to himself.

The night turned cold and the snow on the ground deepened. It was after two in the morning when he saw the truck tracks turning into a driveway and then coming out again and rejoining the main road he was on. His eyelids were desperately heavy. Too heavy for one man to keep up for longer than a few seconds. Twice already he had been jolted awake abruptly to find the Jeep veering off the road. He decided it would be best for them to take the turn and hope it led to a mountain cabin in which they could rest.

Jillybean didn't stir when he pulled up to the front door and stepped out. Alone, he crept in, his M4 at the ready. The gun wasn't needed. The cabin was a mess, but it was empty. There were serviceable mattresses on the floor, five or six blankets and enough wood to get them through the rest of the night.

He waited until the fire had thawed out the house before he went back to the Jeep and lifted Jillybean out. She barely stirred and was back asleep on one of the mattresses in no time. It didn't take too long for him to fall sound asleep as well.

There were no traps and no escape routes and no alarms, and yet Neil slept soundly for four straight hours and didn't wake until after six with Jillybean shaking him.

"I think there are six bad guys and they stayed here for two days," she stated before his eyes had completely focused. "They were definitely here longer than one day. That's for sure. Here you can see where they kinda cleaned up after that first day."

She hurried to the window and pointed to a garbage bag that was partially covered with snow. "See?"

"I don't know if I do," Neil answered. He saw the bag. It was mostly torn in half and a couple of empty cans were laying here and there. Next to it was a mishmash of tiny prints. "Ah, I get it. The bag had to have been left by the slavers otherwise the rats or whatever would have gotten to it before the snow. And... and..."

He really couldn't go on. What else did a ripped up bag mean? "And they ate a lot? Enough for two days? Possibly. With those cans and what's scattered around here, it seems a little light for two days' worth of food for thirteen people."

"I don't think they fed their prisoners much." She went to stand in the corner of the room furthest from the fire. It was the only part of the front room that wasn't littered with a mess of garbage. Next to one of her shoes were two cans of corn that looked to have been licked clean. "I think they may be starving them."

"Then we better hurry. Five days is a long time to go without food." They ran to the Jeep, with Neil heading for the driver's side. The four hours of sleep had left him with enough energy to get them out of the mountains and maybe beyond.

He wished he had some coffee to help keep him awake, but it was a luxury that was rarely found. "And where would I get cream and sugar?" he muttered.

"Sugar comes from a plant and cream comes out of a cow, but you gotta do something to it," Jillybean informed him. "Like stir it real fast or something."

She went on for some time explaining the nature of milk and then cows and then bull and buffalo, and Neil didn't interrupt. He liked her little voice and he liked how animated she became when reciting a litany of facts, one fact jumping to the next, sometimes with the most tenuous of bonds.

For an hour, she prattled on about everything under the sun but slowly she began to tire and eventually she pulled out her anatomy book and took to reading. Neil took to yawning and gazing with dull eyes at the majesty of the Rocky Mountains— just then, he was heartily sick of them and he was sick of the snow and the constantly winding road, and the zombies that were funneled onto the road by the steepness of the walls of rock that surrounded them.

It was all very annoying, and yet when they finally broke free of the mountains and sped down into the plains, he knew this was worse. The land was vast and desolate, so dismally and utterly empty that it was hard to comprehend.

Neil slowed the Jeep and stared as far as his eyes could see —there wasn't a tree or a house, or even zombies in sight. The earth was a relentless brown and above, the sky was a uniform grey, a vast ceiling that was cold and oppressive.

Next to him, Jillybean grunted once at their surroundings and put her nose back into her book, which was far more interesting and colorful. Neil grunted as well—there wasn't much else to say to such an expanse of nothingness.

He drove on at reckless speeds trying to make up time. Eventually, he saw a herd of zombies grazing like cattle, and then a few miles later he drove next to a double line of trees that ran on either side of a small river, and once he sped through a town that consisted of nothing more than a handful of buildings and a seventy foot tall grain silo.

Jillybean grunted at that as well and eyed it close, very likely recalling how silos had been used as guard towers by the fanatics from New Eden.

They saw some hawks and some derelict cars and deer, but for the most part, the landscape didn't change at all that day. It wasn't until four in the afternoon that they saw something that truly got their attention: Parked along the side of the highway were seven tremendous armored vehicles.

"Traders," Neil said, a nervous twist in his gut. Traders could be dangerous people out on the plain where there wasn't anything close to real law. Had they not been on a quest, Neil would have skirted wide around them, but there was a chance that Grey and Sadie were in one of the vehicles.

Jillybean reached for her grenade launcher, but Neil stopped her. "Let's try talking to them first….but just in case, keep it handy." She reached for the door handle, but he stopped her. "No, it's too dangerous for you to go. Stay low but keep the gun aimed their way. They're probably watching us right now and maybe a grenade launcher will make them second guess any shenanigans they may try to pull."

Neil climbed out of the Jeep as Jillybean threw a blanket over her head to minimize her exposure. "If something goes wrong, I want you to promise me, Jillybean that you'll go back to the valley and tell Deanna what's happened. She'll arrange a fair trade for Grey and Sadie."

"I don't know if I can make that promise. It won't be her, it'll be Fred and he'll be making a trade with *my* gas and then he'll kick me and you out of the valley. If something goes wrong, I'll handle it."

"Oh boy," Neil said, turning away. He saw there was no use arguing with her. She had a look in her eyes that could melt steel. "I hope Ipes can control her."

With his hands raised, Neil approached the huge vehicles. The men scattered on them didn't see him as much of a threat and only gazed down with mild curiosity. "Who's in charge?" Neil asked.

Arms stretched and fingers pointed towards the third vehicle to a man who was supervising a tire change. He was round and hairless, save for curly sideburns that started just above his ears and ran down the side of his face.

"His name is Rodriguez," one of the men said.

Rodriguez stared at Neil with a look of disgust, both at Neil's face and at his scrawny size. "You're a lucky one," he said, drawling out the words in a thick Kentucky accent. "You're too small for the arena and too weak for the pits. I guess that means you can remain a free man for the time being."

This was their version of luck? "Thanks...I guess. I was wondering if I could take a look at your people, you know, the slaves. I've been looking for some, uh...uh, action."

"Action? I suppose I can spare five minutes." He chortled at this, as did the men who were changing the tire. Neil wasn't in a joking mood. He was too nervous and the insult went right over his head.

"I just need two minutes, three at the tops," Neil said, causing the men to laugh harder.

The leader laughed with both hands on his round belly and when he could, he said: "However long it takes you to do your stuff, it's a flat fee of a hundred, paid up front. Kinky stuff is extra."

A hundred was too steep just to get a look at who the trader had imprisoned in his vehicles. "Do you have any younger girls in there? Say around seventeen? Black hair? Kinda feisty?"

More jokes sprang up from the group of men; however their leader only stared at Neil with shrewd eyes. "Feisty?" He said the word as if he didn't know its meaning. "I don't know about feisty, but I got a couple of girls that might fit the bill."

"I also want them new...pretty much untouched."

Rodriguez rubbed the swell of his belly, musing quietly. Finally, he said: "I got some that have only been on tour for a few months. Practically fresh in this day and age. They're pretty special, though. They might run you one-twenty."

Neil shook his head, feeling the exchange on an almost psychic level. He was born to negotiate and now that he was in it, his nerves calmed. Unfortunately, he had hit a wall. Rodriguez didn't have Sadie.

"No. That won't do. I'm very particular. I'd pay...say five for any information on where I could get a girl like that."

"Ten," Rodriguez replied immediately. Neil pretended to think it over and Rodriguez added: "She's perfect for you: young, hair the color of night, a perfect ripe body."

Neil dug in his pocket and held out ten 5.56 MM rounds. "Where?"

"The Colonel has her."

Chapter 28

Captain Grey

The following morning, as Jillybean and Neil left the mountain cabin to begin a long day of driving under a ceiling of heavy cloud, Smitty lined up his prisoners and inspected them. He didn't like what he saw. "You are all disgusting. Pecos, Doug and Bill, we're going to need a lot of water. Find some buckets and fill up the bathtub. The rest of you get enough wood to get a fire going."

"I'll bathe the girl," Doug whispered. He was too loud and Smitty heard. The leader of the bandits kicked Doug in the thigh hard enough for him to curse and limp away.

"No one touches the girl! If she turns out not to be who she says she is, we'll all get a shot at her. Until then we play it smart."

The cold made fetching water and wood unpleasant, however the men didn't complain all that much. They repeated things like: "Top dollar," and "It's just about payday."

The prisoners were bathed without regard for any modesty and then the soldiers were told to shave. At the same time, their clothes were cleaned in new water and set to hang over the fire to dry. By noon, they were ready to go.

The Colonel had moved his base of operations from a boggy, mosquito filled island to Rock Island, what once had been a military installation sitting smack dab in the middle of the Mississippi River. It had many advantages over the previous base. It was far easier to defend, it allowed the Colonel to control river traffic from the north, and, with his three ferryboats running day and night, he could charge people looking to cross the river.

He was a direct rival of the River King and, from what Grey had seen and heard of him, he was a dangerous man. Even the bandits feared him. There was no law in the world beyond *might makes right,* and this close to the Colonel's base, he was definitely the mightier.

Smitty, the leader of the bandits, sent Matt to begin negotiations as the rest of them hid on the west side of the river in the city of Davenport. Not only was it a possibility that the Colonel would try to snatch Sadie without paying for her, they also feared he might try to take the men from Estes. As Smitty put it: "He's a soldier, they're soldiers, who knows if they got some sort of weird bond."

Since trust was such a difficult commodity to come by, the Colonel sent his own team out to check that everything was on the up and up. Only then did he leave his island with a heavy escort to meet in a Davenport bar. His soldiers came in first, their weapons at the ready.

The Colonel came in last, walking slowly, making an entrance, Grey thought. He swaggered right up to Sadie, lifted her chin, and then made a face. "She's not one of mine and neither are these men. You've wasted my time."

He turned to go and that was when Captain Grey ordered him to stop in a voice that was like thunder. "You would be wise to turn around. We're not just any soldiers."

This piqued the Colonel's curiosity and he did just as Grey commanded. He came right up to Grey and stared him in the face. The Colonel was a tall man, taller than Grey, though not nearly so thick with muscle. He had intelligent blue eyes that bored into Grey.

"I know you…Grey, isn't it? You came this way about six months back. You tried to recruit me into Johnston's division, hiding up in the mountains. In fact, didn't you try to *order* me to go?"

"In the general's name, sir. I had my own orders to follow."

The Colonel continued to stare. "And how did that work out for either of you?" Grey had been standing at attention, now he glared at the Colonel, who suddenly smiled easily and smacked him on the shoulder. "I'm sorry, son, Johnston really was a good guy. Sorry to see him go. And I should be thanking you Estes boys for giving the Azael such a fine whupping. They needed to be brought down a peg or two."

"We would have preferred a peaceful solution," Grey replied, still stiff with anger.

"That was always the problem with Johnston," the Colonel said. "He was always too much of a wimp. It's no wonder he went and got himself assassinated. How'd they do it? I heard all sorts of things: poison, strangulation, I even heard it was a knife in the back, Brutus style."

This morbid talk was fascinating to everyone except Grey's squad. They glared, while the rest leaned in to hear Grey's answer which wasn't what the Colonel was expecting. "Why do you ask, Colonel? Worried about your own neck?"

"Just curious," he answered. "I'm curious about a lot of things. Like, who's in charge over there? I heard it was a civilian."

Before Grey could say anything, Smitty suddenly barked: "Don't answer that! Sorry, Colonel, but we're not here to reminisce or gossip about crap. We're here to make a sale. Do you want these people or not?" He was clearly put out that they had lied about Sadie and didn't want to waste another second.

The Colonel shrugged. "Not really. I'm just trying to be polite. It's a quality that you should consider cultivating. For your own good, of course." There was an underlying current of danger in his cool words.

"Of course, sir. My apologies." Smitty's anger dissipated and now he was practically groveling. "It's just I've got supplies to purchase before we get moving and the sun is uh, you know, it's getting late."

"Sure," the Colonel said. "I understand. Grey, good luck." Again, he turned to leave and again Grey stopped him.

"You're making a mistake," he said, "and so are you, Smitty. Give me a minute alone with the Colonel and I'll get you a sale today." Smitty made a show of eyeing Grey and looking even more put out, but everyone knew he wanted to make his sale and go.

When he and the others left the room, the Colonel only raised an eyebrow, suggesting by it that Grey should make his sales pitch and be quick about it. "You wanted to know who the new leader is in Estes? A personal friend of mine. We're so close that he's made me Council Minister of Defense. I run the military in Estes."

This statement had the Colonel reappraising Grey. "Interesting," he said after a time. "And what am I to make of this? Will your president, or whatever he is, reimburse me for what I pay this slaver? If so, it would have to be with interest. As we're both fellow soldiers, I would think thirty percent to be proper."

Grey hesitated. There wasn't any money in their treasury to pay ransoms, interest or no interest. "Actually, we're in a bit of a financial bind. The war with the Azael really made things tight. I was hoping you would free us as a way to facilitate diplomatic relations between our two people."

The Colonel groaned: "Please. Whatever pathetic, rural, let's all get out and vote, government you have there now won't last and then what? My money will have been wasted and I'll be asked to suck up to someone else."

"What about doing it for my men and the girl. Colonel, you're a soldier first and foremost…an American soldier. That used to mean something. It used to mean we were the good guys. It used to mean we sacrificed for the weaker among us. It used to mean…"

"I know what it *used to* mean to be a soldier, but those times are gone. Hell, America is gone. Sorry, but we live in a different time. It's survival of the fittest and there's no room for charity in this undead world, Grey."

Grey wasn't naive, he knew how evil the world had become, just as he knew that Sadie and his men would suffer horribly because he had led them into the simplest of traps. If he could keep them safe he would, no matter the consequences.

"Then do it for the bargaining power," he suggested. "The River King has a score to settle with me and I guarantee he'll pay top dollar for me. Please, buy us all and then sell me to him and let the others go. You'll make money and you'll be the good guy."

The Colonel rolled his eyes. "I really doubt you're worth that much. The girl alone will probably set me back three grand. What could you have possibly done…oh, wait. Were you with the team that blew up his bridge? We heard rumors that there was some sort of military strike."

"Yes, I did it, sir," he lied, "and I know the River King will pay a good deal to string me up, but he won't care about my men. He'll just use them up in his arena. They're small potatoes. Please, be the bigger man, set them free."

He looked to think it over for a few seconds, tapping his chin, as if weighing the pros and cons. But he had no intention of doing the right thing. "I think I'll be the richer man instead. Thanks for the heads up concerning the River King." He was about to leave when he caught Sadie glaring at him and something clicked in his eyes.

"Hold on. Do I know you from somewhere?" Sadie immediately dropped her chin to her chest once again, but he took her by the hair and hauled her face upwards. She came up spitting and at first he grew angry, however his eyes crinkled in amusement a moment later. "You're that goth-chic! The zombie killer…no it was a zombie hunter you pretended to be. The last time I saw you, you were dead, drowned like a rat. Well, this is a small world. Whatever happened to that runt you were hanging around with?"

Sadie glanced toward Grey, who warned with his eyes. "Dead," she said without adding more.

"Well, that's too bad. You two were a hoot." He gave her a closer look and was just sniffing her hair when Smitty pushed in exclaiming that the minute was up a long time ago. The two men took to arguing over the price of the prisoners.

Smitty was no idiot. He knew something was up and drove a hard bargain, trying to get the Colonel to take all of them at once. He tried to sell Sadie on her youth and pretty face, to which the Colonel only laughed: "I actually know this girl. No, she wasn't one of mine, but I met her twice last year and I pity the man who tries to bed her. He'll end up with his throat cut."

The slaver had seen some of Sadie's fiery nature and now his face fell. He cut his asking price, and a minute later they concluded their deal. Smitty was suddenly relieved and jovial. "Good luck," he said to Grey as he left.

"It's nice that everyone wishes me luck," Grey said, feeling as though he would need a healthy dose of it if he were to live out the week.

"None of us really mean it," the Colonel said. "It's just some leftover niceties from the old days." He turned from Grey and spoke to one of the men who had accompanied him. "Gilmour, I need you to find out if any of those bounty hunters are still around. I want to see if there's any money on this guy's head. Also, see if that slaver is still in Moline, maybe we can unload the rest of them, tonight."

The group of prisoners were escorted to a waiting truck by sharp-eyed guards and soon they were whisking east through the perfectly cleared streets of Davenport. They sped right up to a dock where a small boat waited to take them across the Mississippi. It was a twenty foot pontoon boat that looked like it had been pulled out of a far-off lake and was now thrust into the role of ferry.

There wasn't any shelter from the stinging wind raking across it from north to south. The prisoners were without coats and so they huddled together against the cold. Sadie sat in the middle, tears dripping off her chin. "So, do I tell them who I am?" she asked in a frightened whisper. "Which will be worse for me, being a sex slave or being brought back to my father?

239

He'll kill me, I know it. I just know it. The only question is will he do it publicly or privately?"

Grey spat over the side of the boat. "With him it'll be whatever way benefits him the most. Sorry Sadie, but if I get the chance to kick him in the throat, I won't hesitate."

"He needs to die," Sadie said, rubbing the tears from her eyes with her cuffed hands. "I'd kill him if I could and the only way I can do that is by getting close to him." She smiled at Grey. It was a sad, wan smile that was nowhere near the usual impish one she wore. "I don't want to be a sex slave, Grey. I can't do that. I'd rather go down fighting."

Lieutenant Wilson, who was crushed up next to her left side, said, "But you won't be fighting. After all the escapes and the bombs and what have you, he won't give you the chance. Hell, you can't even escape now. And it'll be worse in Cape Girardeau. Do yourself a favor, do the slave thing, bide your time and wait to get lucky and then go…go back home and never leave the valley."

He didn't look at her as he spoke; he looked down at his shackled hands. The other soldiers were equally glum. Before, they had been prisoners, but they had just been bought. It made them slaves. It changed them.

Grey didn't like the look in their eyes. "Okay, all of you listen up. You are soldiers of the Valley, but you are also soldiers in enemy hands. What were we trained to do in captivity? Escape. You do not give up that attempt, no matter what. Each of us will persevere. Each will take what they dish out with the goal of escape always in the front of our minds. Those are your orders. Escape, evade, and survive. I have faith in each of you that you can do this."

The soldiers nodded, each muttering: "Yes sir," under the sound of the wind and the twin engines pushing them slowly toward the island.

Only Sadie didn't answer like the rest. The wind had dried up her tears and seemed to have blown away any evidence of her momentary display of cowardice. "You already know what I want to do and it doesn't involve escape. In fact, if I could I'd start with that jackass."

She glared at the Colonel until he noticed and came strutting over. "Lovely day for boating on the river, isn't it?" he asked, snug in his cold weather gear.

"You are a slave master," Sadie declared. "I remember last year you said all your slave women were free to come and go. You said they were providing a 'service' of their own free will. What a joke. Are you still going to stick with that crap? Are we free to come and go?"

The Colonel smiled easily, as if he had been hoping Sadie would say something along these lines. "It must be nice to be so amazingly ignorant."

"Yessa massa," Sadie shot back. "It is nice, massa. I loves being ignorant."

"I'm willing to bet that your ignorance is what is going to get you killed. Oh wait, you were already killed and why? Because you blundered about ignorantly. You didn't know how to fight. You didn't know Cassie could swim. You didn't know that practically everyone in New York was your enemy. I could go on, but why bother? You're still so ignorant about so much."

"And what does any of that have to do with you being a slave master?" Grey asked. "You can't deny that's what you are."

"Oh, please, Grey. You act like slavery is a new invention. Let me tell you that it didn't start with America. People have been enslaving one another since time began. Every race and every people enslaved each other and they were still at it even before the apocalypse. There was still slave trading in Africa, in Saudi Arabia, in Pakistan and the far east."

Grey looked around with wide-eyed astonishment. "And is that where we are? Is this Pakistan?"

The Colonel surprised Grey by his answer. "It might as well be. There's nothing special about this land, or this river or the people who used to live here. Americans are and were no better or smarter than anyone else in the world. Supposedly, we were 'civilized,' but in reality we were nothing but human animals doing what animals do. They survive. The strong survive at the expense of the weak. They thrive on the weak. And you are the weak."

Grey could tell that Sadie wanted to reply with a snarling, cursing comment. He told her: "No," in a soft yet commanding voice. Now wasn't the time. He could tell that the Colonel had worked himself up and was on the verge of displaying his "strength" or his "greatness." It might have been why he had come over in the first place.

The Colonel stood over his slaves for a minute before saying: "Weaklings, pathetic weaklings."

The ride across the river was over soon after and the Colonel all but ignored them. They were marched to what had been the base military police headquarters and were placed behind bars, two to a cell, except for Sadie, who was given her own.

To their delight, the handcuffs were removed and they were fed and watered, but not spoken to. No one would look them in the eye, except for Sadie. She had plenty of visitors who came in to stare, including a trader named Rodriguez who was bald and fat and smelled of woman's perfume and diesel fuel.

"Take off your clothes," he said to Sadie from outside the bars. "Let me have a look at you."

"Go fuck yourself," Sadie answered.

He made a grumbly sound in his throat as he appraised her through narrowed eyes. "How about this, take off your clothes or I'll have the guards come in here and take them off for you. I'm willing to bet they won't be gentle and they may take some, how should I put it delicately? They may take some liberties with you. In fact, they'll like it if you fight them. They'll like it a lot. They might even like it so much that they come back for more. Do you want that?"

Sadie shook her head and the trader said: "Then do this the easy way. I just want to see what your value is and I can't do that with you in that silly dress. It's awful, by the way."

"I didn't pick it out," she answered through teeth that barely parted to spit out the words. To Grey, she didn't look spitting mad, she looked biting mad.

"Just take it off and get this over with."

Sadie glanced around. There were no real walls between the cells, only bars, which meant every one could see her. Although it wouldn't be the first time the men had seen her naked during the humiliating trip, she seemed uneasy and so Grey ordered: "Eyes right!"

No one but Rodriguez looked as Sadie dropped her dress. "So skinny. Why do all the girls have to be so skinny? Turn around. Oh, well that's better. Nice tush. Okay, put your clothes on. I can use you if the price is right."

They spent the night wondering if the price would be right. It turned out it wasn't. They were fed at the break of dawn, given coats, hats and gloves, and were reshackled, this time, not just in handcuffs, but with leg-irons as well. They made getting on another boat a bit of an adventure.

This one was larger, but not any better from a comfort standpoint. It was wide and flat with a small pilot house in the rear. It was loaded with goods of all sorts, all stacked on towering pallets that were roped and chained in place, making any walk along the boat a dangerous obstacle course.

The little group of seven prisoners were the only human cargo. They were given a small square of deck directly beneath a pallet that was stacked twelve feet high with bundles of cord wood cut in eighteen inch lengths. They huddled against the wood which kept the worst of the wind off of them.

Fifteen men accompanied the boat, each of them armed with an M4 and each looking very capable. At all times, two of them were stationed fore and aft, two more were on either side and one stood vigil over the slaves.

"Where's the Colonel?" Grey asked the young man who watched over them first. He was covered from his lower eyelids on down in layers of green camo. "He's not going to see us off?"

"I'm not supposed to talk to you."

"Fair enough. Can you at least tell me where we're going?"

The young man was silent for so long that Grey didn't think he was going to answer, but then he spat out: "Cape Girardeau. It turns out that you're worth quite a bit of money."

Grey wasn't surprised. He knew his fate and had already accepted it. "What about my friends? What's going to happen to them?"

The soldier turned to watch as the boat began to push down the river. Again, he was quiet for a long stretch. After miles of empty river bank swept by, he simply said: "They'll be sold at auction, probably destined for the arena. They like their blood."

Chapter 29

Jillybean

Two days later, Neil and Jillybean, looking like a pair of small and somewhat timid monsters, moaned their way down a road which ran parallel to Highway 74. It was as direct a route to Rock Island Arsenal and to the Colonel as Neil would allow.

He was nervous and wanted to make a complete circle of Davenport before angling in toward the base. Jillybean, who trusted her acting skills and her monster makeup, saw it as a waste of time, while Ipes thought that making two circles of the base was the safest course.

Maybe even three, he said. *Heck, I might even do four just to be on the safe side. Why take chances with safety?*

"You're going to get wet one way or the other. You might as well get it over with." It was an island after all and both Neil and Jillybean felt that they couldn't exactly just walk up and ask for a ride across the river without incurring disaster. Neil had used that word: incurring. Jillybean had inferred its meaning and didn't want an *incurring* though she fully expected one.

She had heard from Neil, Sadie, Deanna and all the ex-prostitutes what sort of man the Colonel was—he was a bad man, a very bad man. And she knew what she was supposed to do with bad men.

"I execute them for their badness," she said in a whisper. She had to whisper. The words were taboo. They were utterly and completely true, but they were also taboo. Neil wouldn't understand and neither would Ipes. And the monsters would certainly not understand how one of their own was suddenly talking.

Oh yes, there were other monsters about, but not many, not enough in Jillybean's opinion. In a crowd, the two of them would have been basically invisible. Now, they stood out because of their size. The corn-fed monsters were big ones. They had thought the mountain monsters subsisting on pinecones, stiff grasses, roots and the occasional columbine were big, but these ones were giants.

It wasn't just the boy-monsters. The girl-monsters thundered along, almost as loud and almost as scary.

Jillybean made sure not to look at them except out of the corner of her eye. To look directly at them would cause her to shudder and her shoulders to twitch. These weren't exactly the moves a monster would make.

Tell me why we have to get wet at all? Ipes asked.

"Because of the water. Now hush." He knew why, he was just being a pain in the rear, Jillybean thought. After all, he had been there when they had hashed out the choices before them which had boiled down to just two: ransom or rescue.

All three of them wished that ransom was the better of the two options. It would have been neat and simple to march up, negotiate a price for Sadie, Grey and his team, and then get back to the valley before any more damage was done.

There were two main problems with the ransom scenario, namely Neil and Jillybean. "I'm the governor of Estes Valley, for goodness sake's," Neil had said, once more drumming his fingers on the Jeep's steering wheel. "I've got enemies from Denver to New York, and if the Colonel is willing to throw away diplomatic protocol by buying Captain Grey, the head of our military, he wouldn't hesitate nabbing me as well. And you are likely the most wanted person on the planet."

She didn't think she was the *most* wanted person. The people of the valley didn't want anything to do with her and everyone else only wanted to do bad things to her. All except for Sadie. Her big sister had always been there for her. From the first second Jillybean had met her deep underground in the evil church of New Eden, Sadie had tried to protect her.

To Jillybean, Sadie was the most wanted and loved person on the planet and she would do anything and everything to free her from the evil, bad colonel.

With ransoming out the window, they turned to rescue and that meant Neil turned to Jillybean. "You're the expert, what sort of plan do you have cooking?"

"Cooking? I don't have a plan cooking or food or nothing. I don't do plans from this far away. I have to get close and see stuff." And that was why they were moving in, dressed as monsters, their weapons and bombs hidden under their ragged clothes.

It had taken two hard days to get where they were. The obstacles in their path hadn't been easy: monsters by the millions, land pirates that almost had them in Nebraska, and a sleet storm that swept down on them out of the blue in Des Moines.

It was after three in the afternoon when they got to Davenport and both of them were so eaten up with fear that neither would wait even a minute. They had changed into their monster clothes in the car and within minutes were on their way, hoping that this would be the last mile of their long chase.

For Neil, it was almost the last hundred yards of the chase. It had been months since he had last pretended to be a monster and it showed. He walked, stiff with fear and he wouldn't stop making eye-contact with a monster that was strangely colored: from the waist up, he was green, but from the waist down, he was yellow. It looked as if the monster had been dipped in dye like an Easter Egg.

Jillybean couldn't understand how it came to look like that, but, regardless of its coloration, she knew enough not to look at it. She tried to warn Neil to stop looking, but since he wouldn't stop looking he didn't see her furtive attempts to tell him to stop looking.

The monsters began staring right back, which turned Neil's moan into a high-pitched whine. *Neil's going to get eaten!* Ipes cried. *Don't look it's going to be messy, and make sure I don't get any blood on me. You know the sight of blood gets me si…sick. I think it's happening already…*

"Oh hush. You're fine," she mumbled under her breath. Ipes was right about one thing: Neil was about to get eaten. She reached into one of her deeper pockets and pulled out an oddly shaped and bumpy ball. It was one of her MSDs—monster distraction devices. It was a small, battery powered Bumble Ball.

Flicking it on, she dropped it. Immediately, it began to bounce around going in completely random directions, its led lights blinking away like crazy. The two-toned monster turned and stared at it in amazement. All the monsters did. They came and stood around the bouncing ball in a perfect circle.

"Thanks," Neil said. "That was clo…" Jillybean grabbed him and hauled him into the closest building: an IHOP. It appeared to have been searched by someone with anger issues or had been the sight of a one-restaurant riot. With all the broken glass and the trash strewn everywhere, it was the perfect spot to re-teach Neil how to be a monster.

"Like this," she said and then went through her routine, showing just how easy it was. When he tried to imitate her, she groaned and stuck her hand on her forehead. "You're missing something."

Yeah, like a brain.

"Not now, Ipes. I think it's your hands, Mister Neil. You don't seem to know what to do with them. You can't just hold them out like that. You're not a praying mantis. That's what means a weird bug. They hold their arms like that, but the monsters don't. You should try being natural."

"That's not easy since I'm not naturally a monster and besides, it was a little freaky this time. I don't know why." Despite the chilly day, Neil was sweating, especially around the eyes, which Jillybean found odd.

"Just remember, they won't hurt you as long as you seem to belong. Come on, try it some more."

She carved away the bad parts of an apple and then munched on it as he stumbled around the restaurant. When she had chewed down to the core and there were little brown seeds showing, she declared Neil much improved, even though he was only sort-of improved and they moved out once more.

In order to keep an eye on him, she let him lead the rest of the way. *Thankfully monsters aren't all that bright*, Ipes remarked, after watching Neil for a time. *He looks more like a robot. Sort of like a really scared robot.*

The zebra wasn't wrong, Jillybean thought as they made their way down to the waterfront. She couldn't understand being afraid of the monsters, especially when they weren't being attacked. It was sort of like being afraid of sharp knives *sitting* on a counter.

Neil was still sweating his way through his routine when they reached the river. As they traveled, Jillybean had been picturing the island in her mind. She had imagined that a place called Rock Island would be well, more rocky. It was a bit of a surprise to see that almost the entire east half of the island was taken up by an eighteen-hole golf course and a cemetery; it was flat and faded, but still green. The western half of the island was crammed with buildings, and barracks, and warehouses of all sorts.

And there were people, a lot of them. Some walking around the golf course pulling golf-bags on wheels, some marching in formations and some seeming to just wander. A number were at the river wall holding long poles. These were much longer than spears and at first, she couldn't tell why they had them.

Although the monsters that had marched down the road with them were now staring intently at the river floating by and wouldn't have noticed if the men at the wire emplacements had done cartwheels, she stayed perfectly in character as she went to a pub on the bank of the river called the Driftwood.

It was nautically themed as she knew it would be and was as horrendously trashed as the IHOP had been. Ship steering wheels had been ripped from the walls where, in her opinion, they didn't belong in the first place, and stiff plastic looking fish that had been mounted about the place were now strewn among the shattered crockery. Tables and chairs were more often than not flat side down with their legs pointing at the ceiling.

All of this mayhem was just fine with her. It made for good cover as she pulled out a heavy set of binoculars and set them to her small face so that her nose was just a tiny bump set in a black V of plastic.

The soldiers with the long poles sprang into her vision. She watched one of them point further along the river and she swiveled the binoculars to see a monster attempting to climb out of the river. The men sauntered over and began poking at the thing until it fell back in the water.

They were extremely casual about it, and for good reason. In order to be any threat, the monster had to climb six feet straight up and then would have to overcome a tangle of concertina wire. It wasn't likely that too many would make it onto the island.

"Wire cutters," Jillybean muttered. "Don't let me forget them, Ipes." She went back to scanning, her eyes sometimes focusing with the intensity of a laser and sometimes drifting as her imagination took over her mind.

She could see a host of possibilities and problems. The first being the river itself. Yes, there were many, many monsters in it, but they didn't frighten her so much. She had been in the Mississippi before and it had been a far from pleasant experience, but she had learned from it. She knew the river's dangers and she knew how to combat them.

In fact, she considered the river to be an asset. The soldiers would never expect anyone would be crazy enough to use a river full of monsters as an access point. If they watched at all, it would be for stray monsters who had somehow climbed the wall and were hung up in the wire.

So getting on the island wouldn't be an issue, however staying on the island would be. Neither she nor Neil looked anything like a soldier and no amount of makeup or costuming would change that.

The next problem would be in finding the prisoners and freeing them. They could be anywhere on the island. Once they did find them, Neil and Jillybean would have to somehow free them and escape without alerting the entire island. There were so many problems wrapped up in doing so, that it was mind-boggling even to Jillybean.

"One issue at a time," she said as she ran the binoculars back and forth. Neil waited patiently until he couldn't take it anymore.

"How the hell are we going to do this? Two people taking on thousands?"

Jillybean looked at him with a queer light in her eyes and a cold feeling deep in her soul. It was the—*someone's about to die and it's not going to be me*—feeling she got when she started to plan an attack. "We aren't going to take on thousands, silly. That would be the same as suiciding ourselves."

"We aren't?"

"No, of course not."

Ipes made a dismissive noise in his throat. *Sheesh! Neil can be such an idiot sometimes. Take on thousands of soldiers? What a maroon. Am I right, or what? Ha-ha…say, Jillybean, he is right about one thing, there are thousands of bad guys. How are we going to take them on?*

"By shopping and being quick about it."

Chapter 30

Neil Martin

The smell of burning wood drifting from the island brought
with it a touch of nostalgia for Neil. It reminded him of deep
autumn in New Jersey, when the trees were red and gold, the
days cool and the nights pleasantly chilly. Neil missed those
simple times with an ache of longing that would never be cured,
because those times were dead and buried.

Neil took in one more breath of the smoke on the night air
and turned his mind back to Rock Island, where not a single
beam of light was visible. From where they stood on the river's
edge, the island was darker than the night and darker even than
the shimmering river that flowed by. The stars danced on its
surface, except of course, where a zombie floated along, and
there were many zombies.

The river wasn't nearly as clogged with them as it was
down south in Cape Girardeau, but there were too many for
Neil's tastes. They moaned, quietly, and gently splashed the
water, not yet in a feeding frenzy, which Neil was secretly afraid
would happen the second he got in. The idea of stepping down
into that dark water made his balls shrivel.

And the shriveling has only just begun, he thought. The
water was not only infested with zombies, it was also sharply,
deeply cold. Perhaps even deadly cold. Neil had no idea where
the waters of the Mississippi originated. He had never bothered
to look it up. As far as he knew, it flowed down from Canada,
where it was always stupidly cold.

It wasn't a good sign that there was already ice on the edges
of the bank. Yes, the planes were thin, unable to hold even
Jillybean's weight, but it was still ice. Jillybean's first stop had
been to a marina that sat a quarter of a mile away from the
Driftwood Pub.

They picked up neoprene wetsuits to insulate themselves
from the cold, thin life jackets, a square of heavy netting ten feet
on the side and a number of floatation devices. Despite this, the
pair didn't look like divers at all. Over the wetsuits and the life
jackets, she had draped them in the shredded camo they had
picked up at their next stop.

An army surplus store had given them the camo as well as
other interesting items that the little girl had snatched up. Then

they were off to three different pawn shops, a Radio Shack, two police stations, a library and the Davenport Historical Society.

For the most part, Neil had tagged along acting as a human shopping cart and *not* asking questions. When he asked questions, it seemed to set Jillybean on edge. "We don't have a lot of time for questions," she would say and then follow it up with: "Here, hold these."

Time seemed to be her enemy. Along with the running around, batteries had to be charged, explosives had to be prepared, everything had to be bagged and double bagged, the Jeep had to be emptied of their belongings, the gas drained, the battery pulled, and the jerrycans of fuel had to be sealed with wax.

All of their belongings went onto the net which barely floated, despite the buoys tied every two feet. "It'll be fine," Jillybean had said when the car battery had caused it to sag, but where she got her assurance, he didn't know. He was scared to death at the prospect of invading the Colonel's island fortress, and his fear only ramped up when she started prying open one of the claymore mines.

"I won't ask," he had said. His testicles had shriveled then as well. Now, with midnight fast approaching and him waist-deep in the frigid waters, he worried that the shriveling would be permanent. Even with the wetsuit, his teeth were chattering, while Jillybean's lips had a blue cast to them.

But she said nothing, not a word of complaint, as she slid into the water and covered her head with her hat. The ice in the water matched the ice in her veins. The only time she showed the least sign of weakness that night had been an hour earlier as she was putting grenades into various pockets. She had stopped for a moment, hefting a weighty little green bomb in her palm and said: "I hope I forget tonight, Ipes."

Neil didn't like the sound of that and demanded answers. "Sure," she said, in a vague way, and started talking, ticking off her plan.

"We go for the boats first. The small one will be the getaway vehicle and we'll booby trap the two big ones. Next, I'll move up to the Joint Manufacturing and Technology Center. According to that pamphlet we got from the Davenport Historical Society, it's the biggest building on the south end of the island. From its roof, I'll be able to guide you to the MP station that's marked on your map. If Grey and Sadie are anywhere, it'll be there. You will go in and rescue them, and then I'll guide you back to the boat."

"Oh, that's simple enough," he had said, although it didn't sound simple at all. In fact, it sounded dangerous as hell, especially the part about him having to go into an MP station alone.

But he had known the job was going to be dangerous going in—he just hadn't know it was going to be this cold.

Going into the river up to his neck was one of the hardest things he had ever done. It physically hurt. "Your hat," Jillybean said. His hat, like hers, had once been a lady's beach hat, white and gold, with a brim nearly three feet in circumference. It was ridiculous in size and, now that it had been decorated in strips of camo, wet cardboard, and fake seaweed from the Driftwood Pub, it was heavy as well.

But it would do the job. Neil, Jillybean and the net filled with their belongings and necessities had been expertly camouflaged to appear as nothing more than floating river trash.

They pushed off into the sluggish current, both kicking with their flippered feet—the scuba fins were another of the many items that Jillybean had the foresight to pick out.

Even with the flippers, they grew tired, fast. The river was three hundred yards across and soon they were breathing too heavily for their own good, attracting the wrong sort of attention. Soggy river zombies had begun to turn their horribly pruned faces toward the floating pile of trash.

"We can rest and drift for a bit," Jillybean said in a whisper. "We're ahead of schedule."

They would kick for a minute and then rest for a minute and gradually, the island drew closer and closer. Even with the dark, Neil could see men walking slowly along the sea wall. They were guards patrolling the island. *Had Jillybean taken them into consideration?* Neil couldn't help wonder.

She seemed to read his mind. "For them, the threat is external. They'll be watching outwards, if they're even doing much watching. Once we penetrate their defenses, it'll be like we're not even there."

Penetrating their defenses started with getting to the boats on the southern side of the island. As they got closer, it didn't seem as though it was going to be all that difficult. There were three rather small docks in a little cove and birthed next to each dock was a boat.

Two of the boats were bigger than the docks they were tied to. They were ferries though smaller than any ferry Neil had ever been on. The third boat was a pontoon that bobbed on the river like a piece of styrofoam.

"Keep us from going any closer," Jillybean whispered. She pushed back her hat so that it sat at a jaunty angle. A bag was stuffed down the front of her wetsuit. Carefully, she pulled out a clunky black object that looked like it belonged on a high-powered rifle. For a minute, she stared through the small end, spending most of her time eying a beige-bricked one-story building that stood fifty feet from the land side of the docks.

"Okay, we got at least one bad guy in that building. He's watching the docks, or rather, that's what he's supposed to be doing. I think he's reading a magazine or something."

"May I see?" Neil asked. When she handed over the scope and he looked through the eye-piece, he was rather amazed at the clarity. There was a man sitting at a window that overlooked the docks and yet he didn't look up once from a magazine he was reading by way of a small hooded flashlight.

Neil then scanned the shoreline, looking for one of the patrolling guards, and saw one moving away. He had to be seventy yards off.

"This thing is cool," he said, feeling a touch more assurance that they might actually live through the night. He held it out to her, but she shook her head.

"Watch the man, and try not to get it wet, okay? It says water resistant on the side, but Ipes doesn't believe it and neither do I. Whistle if anyone comes or if the guy looks out, K?"

Jillybean started kicking, moving the entire net towards the pontoon. As much as Neil needed to watch the guard in the building, he was utterly curious as to what Jillybean was up to. She was going to sabotage the two ferries, but how? And she had dragged away all of their stuff. How was she going to get it all onto the pontoon? It was far too heavy, almost too heavy even for Neil. And how was she going to deal with the chain and lock running from the boat to the dock?

Neil had scanned the boat and the dock. The metal of the chain looked like a line of white silver through the scope, and the heavy cleat on the dock looked just as new.

Movement to his right had him gasping as he swung the scope. When he saw it was just Jillybean he felt a stupid sense of relief. She no longer had the net and was only hauling a duffle bag along. It was supported by two buoys and yet rode very low in the water. When she got to the rear of the first ferry, she didn't try to bring it up with her, she only reached in for something in a plastic ziplock bag.

Then she disappeared for a minute. When she came back, she was empty handed. She repeated the same thing at the next ferry and then swam back to Neil, who hastily scanned the building and the shore. The man in the guard shack hadn't budged and the man patrolling the closest section of seawall was leaning against a squat little building, smoking a cigarette.

"Everything good?" she asked.

"Bad guy." He held out the scope and pointed. She picked him out easily, nodded once and then started gently kicking *towards* the man. He followed along thinking that her crazy had gotten the better of her, however as they got closer, the man flicked his butt out into the river and walked off.

Two minutes later, they got to the six-foot seawall and once again Jillybean began digging in the duffle bag.

"How'd you know he was going to leave?" Neil asked.

"Because he's a walking around guard," she answered, opening a new ziplock that held steel tent-pegs which she started shoving into the small gaps in the rock wall, reaching up as high as she could. "I knew he wouldn't stay, but I didn't know which way he would go, so going right at him seemed ideal. Now, hush and hold me steady."

The seawall was in truth closer to a twelve-foot seawall with half jutting straight up out of the water.

Jillybean used her tent-pegs as hand and foot holds, jabbing new ones in every foot or so. When she made it to the top, she didn't try to take on the concertina wire, instead, she retreated back down, dug once more in her bag and handed Neil a pair of wire-cutters.

He went up, almost falling with every foot hold. He had jettisoned his flippers and now had rubber water shoes on his feet. The thin steel pins dug in painfully, but he remained stoic, after all, Jillybean hadn't complained.

In fact, he was just happy to have the pins. Before getting into the water he hadn't even considered the wall as an obstacle. He figured he would scamper up it, no problem, not realizing how few holds there really were or how slick and mossy the rocks would be.

Thankfully his feet held out and then it was just a matter of cutting the wire. It wasn't difficult at all: four little *snicks* and the wire sprang apart.

"We're good," he whispered. He expected her to hand up the strap for the duffle bag, but she held out the scope instead. Quickly, he looked in every direction and, to his relief, saw nobody. Only then did Jillybean toss the strap to him.

The bag was heavy, but grew lighter as the water drained away. As only a little kid could, Jillybean easily followed the bag right up, going up the wall as if she were on a ladder. She pointed him across the street to the closest building. "Keep an eye out," she whispered and gave him a push. Instead of following him, she ran to the right.

Neil stopped, wondering what she was doing, and she shooed him on. "Hide!" she hissed. As he lugged the bag next to a bush, she ran to grab one end of the cut wire and dragged it to the center, pegging it into a crack of the seawall. She then got the other side and pulled the two together, using their own barbs to hook them so that it looked as though the wire had been untouched.

"Genius," Neil said. He hadn't thought about the wire, either. He liked to think he would have, but he was hyped up on fear and was having trouble thinking beyond Run! Hide! Breathe!

She joined him seconds later and immediately dug into the duffel once more, bringing out the larger garbage bags that held their clothes. "Can you turn around, Mister Neil, Sir?" she asked. "I have to get dressed and you're not aposed to look."

He hadn't planned on looking and for some reason felt the need to tell her that, but it didn't seem to be the time or the place, and so he turned. They peeled away the neoprene like it was a second skin and donned dry clothes.

Jillybean had bluejeans, her usual keds, pink socks and a white shirt with red carnations stitched on it. Over this she put on a pink coat that clashed with the carnations but went with the socks.

Neil had picked out a mottled new style of BDUs, black boots…and a yellow sweater vest because of the cold. He gave it a pained look and for once, tossed it aside. The last thing he put on was green paint, smeared across his face. It was supposed to both add to his camouflage and make him look fiercer. Without a mirror, he was afraid he looked like a sad, green clown.

When they were dressed, Jillybean dove once more into the duffle. She handed Neil three sets of handcuffs, a two-way radio, a police X2 Dual Shot taser, a 9mm Beretta with two extra magazines, and a grenade. He took this last with two hands, afraid to drop it.

"Just use the taser if you can," she said, seeing his fear. "The bomb is for a just in case emergency. But you should really try to be quiet and the bomb is really loud. Oh, and keep your radio on, okay?"

"Sure… I'll just walk right into the MP station, overpower all the guards and rescue everyone. No problem." That was the very simple plan Jillybean had concocted, but there was definitely a problem with it: Neil wasn't an overpowering kind of guy.

Also he was afraid of the grenade. What if it just went off on its own? What if the pin got pulled by accident? What if the timed fuse was broken and it went off before he could throw it?

"You should put that in your pocket," Jillybean suggested, as she pulled out another double-wrapped trash bag. Inside was her backpack and right on top was a white ski hat with a red pom-pom looking like a giant cherry sitting on a cake. All in all, she appeared like a second grader on her way to school.

It was odd to see her so—normal.

"You're going to stand out," he said. "What happened to those BDUs you had before?" Earlier, she had taken a pair of shears to the smallest set of BDUs they could find at the army surplus store. She had hacked off most of the fabric of the sleeves and pant legs, and then safety-pinned the rest so she would look half-way normal.

"They didn't go with my socks. Hey, can I have the scope, now? We gotta get going."

After taking one last look around with it, Neil handed over the scope and they split up. Jillybean made her way through a parking lot and then hurried across the main road that ran down the center of the island. Her destination was a four-story building a block down the road. From a tower on its roof, she would have an excellent view of most of the island, including the direct approach to the MP station a half mile away.

With her rifle scope, she'd be able to warn Neil of any danger coming his way. It wouldn't give him a free pass, but having her as his "eye in the sky" would help.

Crouched between two cars, he waited in a growing sweat for her to get into position, and it seemed like an eternity before the radio crackled: "Bird's in the nest."

"Roger," he said into his radio. They hadn't discussed any sort of code names, or any procedure or really anything beyond the plan's outline. Was he supposed to wait for her or get detour directions if there was a bad guy...

"The road is clear. You can go."

He supposed that answered at least one of his questions. "Roger," he said again before taking a deep breath and slinking along the parking lot until he got to the road where he paused. It seemed like a very long stretch of open asphalt. Anyone looking out a window of one of the many buildings lining the road would be able to see him, no problem.

"Why am I going this way?" he muttered. "Wouldn't it have been better to take a side street?" More than likely, but it was too late to change the plan, so he continued in his slinking manner, keeping very close to the first building which turned out to be the base commissary. Like a burglar in an old time movie, he kept his back to the wall until he came to a window and then he crawled past.

"What are you doing?" Jillybean asked through the radio. "Just walk normal. You look like a suspicious and that's what means people will look at you weird and ask questions."

"Walk normal, easy for you to say," he muttered to himself as he left the "protection" of the building and went to the sidewalk. He tried, but he just couldn't make himself walk normally. It was almost as if a pole had been shoved up through his spine. He couldn't seem to turn to look in any direction.

His feet moved but the rest of his body was fused in place. His eyes bounced from one side to the other trying to see in his periphery without being obvious. He could only hope that Jillybean was doing her job.

In this odd, disjointed fashion he walked two blocks through the midnight streets of Rock Island. He wasn't the only one out, however. Just when he was getting comfortable, Jillybean hissed into the radio: "Hide!"

Neil froze for a full three seconds as he stared around. How was he to hide if he didn't know what or who he was hiding from? Finally, he ducked down next to the back bumper of a parked car. Not a second too soon, either.

A kicked rock bouncing on the sidewalk just in front of the car sent Neil's heart into his throat. Whoever it was, wasn't more than ten feet away. Close enough for Neil to hear the man's lighter as if he had thumbed it himself.

Neil reached for his pistol, wondering why he hadn't had it out to begin with. It was halfway out of his pocket when he remembered that he was supposed to be stealthy, so he switched the Beretta to his left hand, nearly dropping it in the process. He froze again, his right hand on the butt of the taser, not really in any position to use either weapon.

Slowly, he ducked down until he could see the man's feet—he was wearing boots. Did that mean he was a guard? If so, which way would he turn?

He turned to the right, towards Neil, strolling down the sidewalk which was just feet from where Neil cringed with his head turned and two useless weapons clutched in his fumbly hands.

The man was a guard. He carried a rifle slung loosely over his right shoulder and a cigarette in his left hand. If he had even average speed, he'd be able to have it pointed at Neil before Neil could get one of his weapons in a proper grip.

Neil almost went for his weapons as the man drew abreast and lifted a hand. He thought he'd been seen but the man was just raising his cigarette to his lips where it flared like a red star, illuminating the tattoos on the man's face.

And then he was past the car and the cringing man, walking slowly away. When he passed the next intersection, and was just a shadow, Neil took better hold of his weapons and hurried on.

The radio, now stuck deep in a cargo pocket crackled: "You're in the clear."

"That's what you said before," Neil muttered, feeling the shakes invade his arms, his hands and his chest. His breath rattled in his lungs as he walked and he was still so freaked by nearly getting caught that when Jillybean contacted him again, he jumped.

"Don't walk with your guns out. You'll be a suspicious again. Just walk normal."

He understood. There was still a slight chance that he'd be mistaken for just another soldier going about his business, but a soldier going about his business with a drawn Beretta and a taser would be too suspicious to ignore.

The Beretta went in one pocket and the taser the other, and now Neil walked with his shoulders hunched almost to his ears, his hands itching to grab his weapons. In the next quarter mile, there was no need to draw either, but once he was at the MP station he took both out.

The building was two stories high, about forty yards long, but not very deep, making it somewhat of a rectangle set in between two other buildings. The front of the building didn't face the street. Neil had to walk along a sidewalk where his presence would most certainly be questioned if he were seen.

He went to the side of the building and put his back to it, listening intently for any sound, however he could hear nothing. Either the construction was too good or the building was deserted, and he didn't believe it was deserted. It didn't have that sort of feel.

Creeping, sweating, and trembling, he went to the front doors. They were glass, but nothing could be seen because of the blackout curtains. "Definitely not deserted," he whispered.

His own words reminded him of the absolute need for silence, so he took out the radio, turned it off, and he placed it in the shadows next to the building. Now, if he was caught, he could claim to be acting alone. They probably wouldn't believe him and they would possibly torture him, but he'd hold out long enough for Jillybean to get away.

There was nothing left but to enter the building. Fear made him pause on the front steps and stark terror turned the pause into a hesitation that was on the verge of becoming a faltering.

"Shit," he whispered and went through the doors, pushing past the blackout curtains. He found himself in a candle-lit lobby that had been repurposed into a cubicled set of offices with a manned desk at the very front.

The man behind the desk: tall, slim, dressed in BDUs and with a natural military air blinked in surprise as Neil raised both weapons.

"Yes?" he asked. "May I help you?"

"Where are your prisoners? Six soldiers and a girl of about eighteen. Where are they?"

The bewilderment in the man's eyes finally left to be replaced by a sharp look. "They're gone. They were sent down river two days ago."

The reply smote Neil hard. A wave of anguish almost overcame him, but then suspicion set in. "Let me see your cells.

Come on, get up. And go slow or I swear I'll splatter your brains all over the place." He had both weapons pointed at the man's head.

With his hands up, the soldier got to his feet and then led the way around the cubicles, through another set of offices and to a heavy steel door that was wedged open. The cells were past the door and they were undoubtedly empty.

Now, anguish really did sweep over Neil. He had been too late. They had been sent downriver and that meant they had been sent to the River King. It was hard to believe, but the River King was even more of an evil beast than the Colonel was.

Neil's fear for his best friend and for his daughter was heavy on him and he was slow to perceive the danger as the soldier spun so fast that he was a blur.

Chapter 31
Neil Martin

The guard moved so fast that before he knew it, Neil found his gun-hand thrust upwards so the barrel was pointed at the ceiling and at the same time, the man was reaching for the taser with his other hand. Instinctively, Neil pulled the trigger.

The twin tasers shot out and struck the man directly in the forehead, discharging 2,000 volts of electricity. What happened next was haunting. The guard fell to ground in some sort of hyper-epileptic fit, his muscles curling his arms into unnatural positions, like two caterpillars tossed onto a frying pan. His legs shot straight out stiff as boards, his heels thudding onto the tile in a disgusting drumroll. His eyes rolled back in his head so that only the whites showed and his teeth were locked so tightly together that Neil was sure they were going to crack and shoot out of his mouth.

"Oh, God," Neil whispered and tried to pull the tasers out of the man's head without touching the wires, but they stretched and stretched. Neil was halfway across the other room by the time they came out and by then the man was no longer being shocked. He laid on the floor, drooling, his muscles twitching, his eyes going in two different directions.

"I'm so, so sorry," Neil said coming back to stand over him. "It was an accident. I never would have…" He stopped as he saw urine flowing from beneath the man. The apology wasn't being heard.

Completely clueless how to help the man, sickened by what he had done and afraid of the consequences of getting caught, Neil turned and headed for the door, the long wires trailing behind. He didn't know how to detach them and he wasn't about to touch them, fearful of any residual juice left in the little boxy gun. They snapped off unexpectedly when he was twenty feet out the front door, which had shut on the barbed points.

He almost didn't run back for them, but he felt there was a chance that he had accidentally fried the guard's brains enough that he might not even remember that Neil had been there—if he recovered that is.

With the wires detached, Neil's fear of them disappeared and as he hurried away from the MP station, he tried to wind them up and stuff them into his pocket. It was like trying to stuff live snakes into a bag and he was so involved with the process that he didn't see another guard standing in the dark leaning on a tree, until he was right on top of him.

"What are you doing out so late?" the man asked causing Neil to jump and squeak in fright.

"Me? I—I was just. I was just…" He couldn't come up with a lie. His brain felt as scrambled as the man he had just left. His first coherent thought was more of an internal aggravated whine: *Why hadn't Jillybean warned me this guy was right there?* His next thought was: *I left the radio back in the bushes!*

The soldier went on: "Curfew is long gone and you had better have a good… what's that on your face?"

"My face?" Neil had forgotten about the war paint. He had begun making nonsensical "Uh, uh, uh," sounds when the light from the soldier's under-barrel flashlight blinded him a second later.

A real fighter might have pulled his gun, but Neil still had his useless taser in his right hand, while his left hand was frozen half-in and half-out of a pocket filled with wire.

"What the fuck?" the soldier cried. "Who are you? And drop that…that gun or whatever it is."

Neil was caught, dead to rights, and there was nothing he could do. The taser fell to the ground and was kicked away and then he was shoved against the same tree the soldier had been leaning against and then searched.

The grenade and the Beretta were discovered. When the cuffs were found next, the soldier slapped them on Neil's wrists and then turned him around. "A grenade and a gun? Tell me what you were doing here, or so help me." He shoved the bore of the M4 into Neil's face, pushing it hard against his cheek.

"Uh, stealing," he answered, thinking on the fly. "I was uh, hoping to get some stuff. You know like cool bombs or something." His one hope was that he could stall long enough for Jillybean to rescue him. He looked past the soldier out into the night as he said: "Everyone says the Colonel has the coolest gadgets. Is that true?"

"I'm not going to tell you jack shit. Do you think I'm stupid?"

Actually, Neil didn't think he could be all that smart. He was pulling guard duty in the middle of the night. Those slots weren't likely given to the best and the brightest. Neil just had to keep the guy occupied. How long would it take Jillybean to climb down from the four-story building and scamper two-hundred yards down the street? Five minutes? Six? So far it had been barely one minute.

"No sir. I don't think you're stupid at all. Not at all. I just, uh, figured that you were up there like a captain or a major and might know a lot more than just a dumb schmuck like me. The stories we hear about you soldiers here on the island, well, they are, uh, something else. Adventures and fighting and, uh, stuff. And the women. We hear you have tons of women."

The soldier wore a screwed-up expression. "What are you talking about? There aren't a ton of women here. And shut up, I gotta think." He was quiet for at least half a minute before saying: "Sergeant Martinez will know what to do with you. I was supposed to call him anyways."

He produced his own radio. "Charlie one this is Charlie six, over." He waited a few seconds and then repeated: "Charlie one this is Charlie six, over."

As they waited on a response, Neil grew tense, his eyes darting out into the night. How close was Jillybean to showing up, pistol in one hand, a taser in the other? It had to have been at least three minutes since Neil was captured. *I just need two more minutes*, he thought.

Charlie six wasn't going to give it to him. "Something's wrong," the guard said, turning from Neil and shining his flashlight out into the night. The light made the shadows darker than before, which seemed to unnerve the soldier.

He grabbed, Neil's arm and started pulling him back the way Neil had come. A third time he tried to raise Charlie One, and when that didn't work, he grew panicky. "This is Charlie Six, is anyone out there?"

"Get off the net, Six, shit."

"Who is that? Dinkins is that you? I caught an intruder but Charlie One isn't responding. There may be something up."

A new voice broke in: "He's probably taking a dump."

The first voice: "Shut up, Roy. Charlie Six, take him up to the big house. I'll go check on Charlie One. Everyone else stay extra alert. If anyone else gets on the island, the Colonel will have our asses strung up in the trees."

Extra alert, Neil didn't like the sound of that. Had it been four minutes, or was time just seeming to fly by? "I'm all alone. Here, check my other pockets. You'll see…"

"Shut up." Neil was yanked along by the soldier, who kept his gun trained outwards swiveling it towards any sound or overly suspicious shadow. They walked past the MP station and fifty yards further on, they were on the less built up side of the island. On their left was the third hole of the golf course and on their right were strange insect like hunks of metal arranged in a great semi-circle.

In the dark it was hard to tell what they were until Neil saw a sign that said Artillery Park. "How pleasant," he said to his captor. When he didn't receive a response, Neil fell saying: "Ow! My ankle," in a bad bit of acting.

The soldier knelt down, not next to Neil, but on his back. Neil could only breathe in tiny sips as again, the man pointed his rifle outward as if expecting the rescue that Neil was hoping for.

"Can't breathe," Neil said. The knee crushed down harder and now even sipping air was out of the question and the night grew blooming black clouds that pulsed along with his heartbeat.

The radio saved Neil from blacking out. "Charlie 6, this is Charlie Two, over."

The knee had to be shifted for the man to get to his radio. "This is Charlie Six, any word from Charlie One?"

"Yeah, he's fine. He wasn't at the desk. I found him upstairs getting dressed and acting like he was drunk, but I didn't smell anything on him. He said he must have fallen and messed himself up, but I don't know about that. I'm going to have to wake up Captain Cornell, and he's going to be pissed."

"I wouldn't worry, we'll probably get medals. Six, out." He put the radio away and pulled Neil to his feet. "I'm going to get a medal, at least. They'll probably string you up by your thumbs. Come on."

"My thumbs?"

"Yeah, it's not pretty."

Neil was half-dragged to a stately home that sat at the edge of the golf course. Its windows were blackened but there was a curl of smoke rising from the chimney, making the stars blink in and out. They went up the porch stairs and Charlie Six knocked lightly on the door.

It was opened a moment later, but not by the Colonel. Another soldier stood in the gap. He didn't speak. "Private Blazek, sir. I was on security patrol and I caught someone sneaking around. He's not from the base. And there might have been another incident at the station. Captain Cornell is being called in, just in case we need to go to full alert."

As the eyes of the soldier in the house started to narrow, Charlie Six added: "They told me to come straight here, just in case there were more of them. We thought the Colonel would want to know right away."

The soldier thought it over for a moment and then said: "Take the magazine out of your weapon and clear it." The door was opened as Blazek made his weapon safe. He did the same thing with Neil's Beretta and then handed the grenade over before stepping into a beautifully decorated foyer.

The soldier, who sported a name tag that read: *Haigh,* took the grenade and the weapons into another room. When he came back, he was accompanied by yet another soldier. They looked at Neil as though he were some sort of new breed of asshole that wasn't nearly as pleasant as the old version.

"We should wake the Colonel," Haigh said. "If there are more of 'em, he'll be pissed if we don't."

"I'm by myself, really," Neil said. "There's no need to wake him. It's late, after all. And it's not like I'm going anywhere." He held up the cuffs and although they twinkled in the light of a few lanterns, all Neil could see were his thumbs.

If they strung him up, how long would he be able to hold out before he told them everything they wanted to know, including where Jillybean was? Would he last ten minutes? Would he last even two?

"It's good that you like to talk," Haigh said to Neil. "Because you'll be talking a lot here pretty soon." He left them and was gone for a surprisingly long time given the situation. Or at least it felt like a long time to Neil, who sweated and shook, and couldn't seem to think of anything except getting strung up by his thumbs. Did they use piano wire for that sort of thing?

When he finally heard the Colonel's boots heading down the stairs, Neil was so light-headed with fear that he thought he would faint. The Colonel looked the same to Neil: tall, with sandy blonde hair, and a cruel twist to his lips.

"Get the paint off him. Let's see who we're dealing with." Haigh used a rag, not as though he wanted to wipe the camo off of Neil's face, as much as to smash it off. He ground the rag into Neil's flesh, causing him to fall over. Haigh followed him to the ground and kept going until Neil only had green at the edges. He was red everywhere else from the friction.

The Colonel looked down at Neil and failed to recognize him. *It had to be all of the scars*, Neil thought.

"Who are you and what are you doing on my island. And where are your friends?"

"I came alone," Neil lied.

"He's not alone," the Colonel said. He looked evenly at Neil for a good minute before he turned to Private Blazek. "Find them. Wake up both MP companies. Tell Captain Cornell to secure the perimeter and then go building by building from one end of the island to the other. Flush them out and if you can, try to take them alive. I want to make an example of them."

The soldier snapped off a salute, rushed to get his weapon and was trying to get the magazine in place and leave the house at the same time only to be confronted by Jillybean as he opened the door.

The little girl with the pink jacket and the white hat with its pom-pom sitting gaudily on top stood in the doorway with an aimed pistol in one hand and a live unpinned grenade in the other.

"Don't move or I will shoot you." She was absolutely stone cold. There wasn't a twitch in her. For emphasis she cocked the gun. "Drop the weapon and step back." Her .38 never budged and the look in her eyes was altogether ice.

Blazek stepped back, fumbling both the weapon and the magazine so that they thudded to the floor. Trying to take advantage of the distraction Haigh reached for his holstered pistol quick as lightning, but Jillybean was faster. The gun was pointed at him in a blink.

Slowly, she raised the grenade, and with a deadly smile on her impish face, said: "I really, really wouldn't if I were you. I've killed lots of bigger guys than you, and that's what means I could kill you if I wanted. And I kinda want to. You're a bad guy and everyone knows it's ok to kill bad guys."

She moved into the room, shifting the balance of power, and Neil didn't know whether to cry in joy over his imminent rescue or in sadness over what he was, once again, forcing the little girl to do…and to become. She would kill these idiots if she had to. She would gun them down without blinking.

And what would that do to her? How many dead bodies could she leave in her wake before she broke, once more? How many bodies would it take to permanently fix the idea within her that that she was a killer and that it was right and good for her to kill?

Chapter 32

Jillybean

From her perch, high on the four-story building, she had seen the guard lurking in the dark and she had keyed the talk button on the radio, just a tap. Then she had keyed it again and again, in growing fear, until Neil came blundering around the corner.

"Stop," she whispered into the radio. "Neil, stop. Stop! Neil!" He didn't stop and he'd been captured and, just like that, her fear turned to frustration. Nothing was going right, starting with the fact he had come out of the MP station alone and now he was captured as well.

"Son of a…"

Jillybean! Ipes snapped. *You do not say bad words, ever.*

A few minutes earlier, the zebra had finally been freed from his triple ziplock bag imprisonment and, after making a great deal of noise gasping for breath and saying: *Finally, finally I can breathe,* over and over again, he had climbed up on her pack. She had asked if he wanted a turn on the scope, but he said he had the eyes of an owl and didn't need a scope and that he was fine guarding the backpack.

"And what are you guarding it from?" she had asked.

Mice, duh. We have valuable items of a yummy nature in here. The cookies alone are worth millions.

She had grinned at that then, but now she glowered at him. "I was going to say: son of a gun and that's not bad at all. But you know what? I am mad enough to say bad words. What's wrong with Mister Neil? Is he blind? Is he deaf?"

Don't be too hard on him. Very few people are cut out for this sort of operation. Only spies and top military guys are allowed to do covert ops and that's for a reason. Normal people lose their heads or make mistakes.

"Yeah, and now I gotta fix them," Jillybean griped.

How? We'll never get down there in time, especially with you just sitting here, complaining.

"I'm sitting here *because* I can't get down there in time. From here, I can see everything, or most of everything. All the important stuff, at least, like where they'll be going."

As Neil was handcuffed by Private Blazek and then led away, Jillybean scoped the island as far as she could see, noting the things that would hurt her and those that would help her, and she had a simple plan worked out in no time. Preparing for it took only minutes and she was basically done by the time Neil was brought to the first stately house on the edge of the golf course.

The house was too nice for a plain old soldier. It had to be an officer's home and she could only hope it was the Colonel's home. It would make everything much easier if it was.

Within seconds of Private Blazek knocking on the door, she had her backpack zipped tight and was running for the ladder that zigzagged down the back of the building to the ground. Instead of heading straight for the stately house, she pulled the wire cutters from her pack and made one stop.

She lacked the arm strength to cut the chain-link fence, but her weight was enough. Once through, it took only seconds to slap a gadget onto a steel cylinder with a bit of duct tape.

Only then did she jog for the stately house with her pack flouncing on her back and a taser thrust in her pocket. She couldn't have been more obvious, but she had no choice. She had to cover as much ground as she could before the base came alive with search parties.

The soldiers would never believe Neil came alone and if they knew the truth: that he had invaded the island with only a seven-year-old and a zebra as back up, they wouldn't have believed that either. They would search and if they caught her out in the open the only tiny chance she would have against an armed man was the element of surprise.

Surprise was the real reason she had ditched the poorly altered camouflage clothing she'd had on earlier. Not only was it silly, it would look automatically suspicious. But what did she look like in her jeans and her pink jacket and her hat with its pom-poms? She looked like a little kid. In fact she looked like a harmless little kid straight out of the past.

Who could think a sweet little girl could be dangerous? She hoped that if she ran into anyone, her unexpected look would buy her enough time to shoot her taser. Thankfully, she hadn't met anyone on the way to the stately house, and now, stepping through the Colonel's doorway with a gun in one hand and a live grenade in the other, there was little question she was dangerous.

"Nobody move," the Colonel ordered, his face set and grim. "There are some crazy bitches in this world. Trust me, when one shows you a grenade she just might use it, even a crazy, little bitch like this one."

"Do you want to see crazy?" Jillybean asked, the smile widening. She nodded to Neil. "There are keys to the cuffs in my pocket. Unlock yourself and take the gun and the bomb." He slid around Jillybean and, moving gingerly so as not to disturb her aim or so she wouldn't drop the grenade, he fished out the keys and took the grenade from her. He held it, ready to throw, even though the room wasn't all that large. When he took the gun as well, Jillybean unzipped her monster jacket.

Strapped to her skinny body was a claymore mine with the words FRONT TOWARDS ENEMY clear as day printed across the front. She held the clacker in her right hand.

"Crazy as fuck," one of the soldiers said.

"I'm not done." Jillybean's smile was now a hellish thing and Neil recoiled from it, looking as scared as the others. With her left, she dug out a second device. "Colonel, you don't want to know what this one does, but you'll find out if you call me any more names."

"I highly doubt that," the Colonel said, evenly. "It's one thing to offer a *MAD* scenario…" Her blank look had him explaining: "It means: mutually assured destruction. That's what you're threatening with that grenade and that absurd mine. I understand, of course. You've come to my island to steal, or what have you and now you're caught. You have no other choice, but blowing us up or blowing something of mine up for name-calling? I have to say that's rather childish."

"Childish?" she asked. "Did you just call me childish?"

You know you are a child so anything you do is, by definition, childish, Ipes said. *So that makes it not a really, really bad name. I say you give him a break this one time.*

A part of her agreed with Ipes, but at the same time, there was an undercurrent of expectation in the room. There was a fearful expectation coming from Neil and Private Blazek, but from the colonel there was a different feeling. It almost seemed as though she were being tested.

Which way to go? she wondered. She only had the one bomb planted…but they didn't know that.

"I'll let it slide for now," she said. "I won't blow up the bomb out of anger." Neil and Blazek looked relieved, while the Colonel had a tiny smile on his lips telling her she had chosen wrong. She could fix that with a push of a button.

"Instead, I will blow it up to teach you a lesson, Colonel."

He peeled his smile back to show his teeth. "And what lesson is that? Not to trust this imbecile to guard my island?"

"No. I want you to know that I'm in charge." She pressed the button. There was a second where the room held its collective breath and then came a thrumming explosion from somewhere to the east of them. It seemed to go on and on, like chain thunder, shaking the windows.

Jillybean felt the explosion on a deeper level than anyone else. On the surface, she felt a strange fear, almost like a horrible memory or stomach-churning déjà vu.

She knew what it was—the same fear she'd been living with for over a year now. Her tongue tasted like pennies, and a cold sweat crept over her and her stomach curled on itself like a snake.

And yet, there was another part of her that saw the sudden alarm in the Colonel's eyes and saw Neil cringe, and she caught the two goons who'd been in the house with the Colonel look at each other, not knowing what to do.

Deep inside, she liked the looks of fear, but even more, she liked the fact that she had caused the fear. It meant she was the one with the power, and she craved more. It was an evil, Eve-like feeling.

"No," she whispered, clamping down, not just on the evil but also the fear in her. Before, when she had executed Dave and Perry and killed those men who had followed her in the night and shot Jimmy with his big Adam's apple and Kevin, the fat slaver, she had just turned cold and deadly. It had just happened. Now she clamped down on her emotions on purpose. She would be like the first bounty hunter who had killed Sarah, shooting her in the chest. He had been purposefully cold and she would be, too. She could be Jillybean another time.

"There's another lesson you could learn," she said to the Colonel. "Don't store all your fuel so close together." Although she had planted only a single remote controlled bomb on a single fuel truck, it had been parked between two others.

"You bitch!" he hissed and then ran to the window. When he pulled back the curtain, the night was startlingly bright.

"What did I say about name calling?" Jillybean asked, producing yet another remote control device.

That this one wasn't connected to anything didn't matter. The Colonel took one look at it and reined in his fury. He held out his open hands, palm up. "Okay, fine. No name calling. Damn it!" He turned back to the window and then back at Jillybean. "Look at what you did. You know what a waste that is? We don't get that back, you know."

"I know," she said. "It's a pity. That's what means it's sad. Now, turn around and lay on the floor. Go on. One at a time. All of you turn around."

"Have them put their hands on the backs of their heads," Neil said. "Oh, I guess I could have told them that. Hands on your heads." One at a time, with Jillybean covering him, Neil frisked them and took their weapons. Since they had three sets of handcuffs and four prisoners, Jillybean daisy-chained them so that they looked like school children holding hands.

The Colonel and Haigh were considered the most dangerous and so they were stuck in the middle of the line, both of their hands connected to the man in front and behind. To add a last incentive to compliance, Jillybean duct taped a grenade to the Colonel's throat and attached a stiff wire to the pin. She looped the other end of the wire around a toothbrush which she held like a leash.

She could kill him with a tug of the brush.

"Now that you've got us all trussed, what do you want?" the Colonel asked.

Neil leaned in close to Jillybean. "Our friends were sold to the River King. They're probably there by now, or very close. We should hold the Colonel hostage until we're far enough away."

That seemed like the only sensible plan, but something about it nagged at Jillybean. "Wait, if we leave empty handed he'll guess we were here after the prisoners. He'll know exactly where we're heading and if we let him go, we'll get caught for certain. We should take some stuff with us, that way he'll just think we're stealer people."

"Good plan," Neil whispered. Louder, he addressed the Colonel: "We want access to the armory."

The Colonel didn't seem surprised. "What are you looking for? Guns? Ammo?"

"C4," Jillybean answered, rattling off: "Detonators, blasting caps, grenades, claymores, M79 ammo. And do you have any bullets for that big cannon out there? It said it was a nuclear cannon."

"No, they don't make them anymore, but we have the rest. If you give me a list, we can call ahead and have it all gift wrapped and ready to go."

Jillybean's cold heart wouldn't let her laugh, all she could do was smile. "No, but you can call whoever is with security. You'll tell him that you've caught the guy who blew up your gas and are questioning him. Tell him to send his men to help put out the fire."

Neil added: "And tell them that it's a crime scene and that you want it guarded until morning."

Under their watchful eyes, the call was made. Jillybean then hustled them outside. "Where's the armory?"

Before the Colonel could answer, Neil shoved Blazek's M4 into his ear and growled: "Don't get cute and don't play games or you'll be the first to get it."

The Colonel cocked an eyebrow at him and scoffed: "You don't scare me, little cowboy. The girl yes, but not you, so why don't you wave your gun someplace else?"

Neil looked cowed for a moment and then spluttered: "Well…you are…just show us to the armory."

"Gladly, if it will get you out of my hair." True to his word they wove behind the buildings, which were alive with soldiers staring out at the fire or talking to each other from adjacent windows. The little group was hardly noticed as Jillybean kept them in the deepest shadows and kept herself hidden by the larger men.

The armory turned out not to be a classic armory that she was used to. It wasn't situated in a half-buried bunker, it was right out in the open in what once had been the *RIA Auto Skills Shop*, or so the sign in front read.

"There's a coupla guards in there," Blazek warned in a whisper. He was the last in line behind the Colonel and with the grenade so close, he was visibly freaked, holding his cuffed hand as far out in front of him as he could.

His admission earned him a glare from the Colonel, who stared hard at Blazek as he growled to Jillybean "Don't worry, they'll listen to me. Just let me do the talking." He hammered on the heavy door and barked: "Open up. It's Colonel Williams. I need access right this minute."

A slot in the door slid back and a pair of nervous eyes looked out. The Colonel was very close to the door, basically taking up the entire view. "Open up, son. I need some special items."

The door was cranked back and the soft glow of lit candles leaked out into the deep night. Two men stood at attention; both carried M4s and wore matching looks of befuddlement as the four prisoners filed past. There was no hiding the cuffs even under the dimness of the light and yet they didn't reach for their guns until it was too late.

"Don't move!" Neil snapped, his own M4 up to his cheek and aimed.

"What's going on?" one of the men asked, unable to figure out the obvious and still standing at attention despite the gun pointed at him.

Haigh answered: "We're being robbed."

"That's right you are," Neil said. "Put the weapons down, very slowly." They looked to the Colonel, who nodded his permission. Now they had two extra prisoners, but no cuffs and no very good way to keep them tied up.

Jillybean's wires and strings were too thin to do the job and the only wiring in the armory was designed with explosives in mind, not trussing up grown men.

"What do you think?" Neil asked Jillybean. Her eyes were half-lidded as she slowly spun to stare at the crowded warehouse-like building.

"I need another grenade and the shoelaces from one of their boots." Neil had them both in no time. She had the men sit back-to-back against a support beam. "You see this," she said, showing them the grenade. "I'm going to knot the pin to one of your hands and the grenade to the other. Do you understand what will happen if you try to escape?"

They nodded vigorously and she patted the closest one on the head and asked: "Where's the C4?"

Jillybean was like a kid in a candy store. While Neil guarded the prisoners, she went up and down the aisles, shining her flashlight at all of the crates and boxes. It was all so neatly laid out that she found everything she could ever want or need in no time.

Ipes was like a very small zebra in a building filled with bombs. *What are you doing? All we have to do is escape. You don't need all that stuff. Like that...that AT-4. What is it and why do you need it?*

273

"It's like a *LAW* rocket, I think, and I don't know what we'll need it for. We aren't done with this. Sadie is in more danger than before. Now, hush. I got to concentrate."

The workings and uses of the gadgets and bombs were all obvious to her except for the items sitting in a cage within a cage. A section of the warehouse near one wall was caged off and in the cage was a second cage. Within it was what looked like a small carry-on suitcase and inside that, sitting in a bed of soft grey foam were ten steel cylinders, each only six inches tall, and each marked with the skull and cross-bones, a symbol even she knew meant poison.

"Mister Colonel, sir, what is *Venomous Agent X?*" she yelled from down the row and pointing back at the cage. "Is that snake poison?"

His eyes widened for just a second and then a strained smile jumped onto his face as he tried to conceal his fear. "It's bad news. Don't touch that, whatever you do. It's VX gas. It's a chemical weapon that could kill all of us in seconds if you release it by accident."

"He's right. Don't touch it," Neil warned. "I read about that stuff. It could end up contaminating this entire island, killing everyone. You can have anything else, but not that."

Jillybean stared at the cylinders, wondering how anything so small and innocent looking could be so deadly. "The entire island?" All of the men nodded, the guards included. "That's all the more reason we should take some."

This caused an uproar from everyone, Ipes included. His voice in her head drowned out everyone else. *Jillybean, what are you thinking? Poison gas that could kill thousands? Using it would be the worst thing you ever did. Think about it, not everyone on the island is guilty. Remember the sex slaves and the workers? If you kill innocent people it'll make you a murderer. You, Jillybean. It wouldn't be Eve this time. It would be you and this time you won't have any real excuses.*

The little girl turned away, hunched over the zebra as she scurried down one of the aisles so no one would be able to hear her answer him in a whisper: "The River King has Sadie and Mister Captain Grey, and the only thing that will make him turn them over is a real threat."

And what happens if he doesn't believe the threat is real? What will you do then? He didn't believe Captain Grey would blow up his bridge, remember? What happens if he doesn't believe you, will you use it on someone?

Her eyes slid to the little group of prisoners and the coldness in her heart intensified to the point where it was entirely ice, incapable of a single emotion, not even hate.

Speaking in a monotone like a child giving a book report in front of the class for the first time, she said: "Those grode-ups are evil. You heard all the stuff Deanna and the other ex-prostitutes said about the Colonel. What they did to her and to the other girls and to the people who he didn't like. It was horrible and sad. And you heard Neil tell the story about how the Colonel stole everything from him and Sadie, and kicked them out among the monsters."

But that was just the Colonel, Ipes insisted.

"All by himself? You know that's not true. Those men helped the Colonel do all that bad stuff and they deserve to die."

Maybe they do, but not like that. You executed Dave and Perry and the others and I didn't say a thing because it had to happen, but you did it humanely. This would be awful. I think…I think if you do this, you do it without me. If you take that VX stuff, I'll go away and never come back.

"And you don't care how the Colonel made naked women walk out among the monsters because they wouldn't sleep with him? And you don't care how he would string people up over the monsters and let them get eaten alive starting at their toes?"

Ipes' stripes crinkled down in anger. *Of course I care, but I also care about you. If you do this, you'll be as bad as the Colonel. And maybe you'll turn into him.*

"That's not possible. I'm a good guy."

A good guy with a heart of ice? A good guy who is willing to gas a city to death? I'm afraid a person who does those things isn't good and it's not a person I will associate with. Put me down, Jillybean. I don't think we can be friends anymore.

Chapter 33

Jillybean

She was silent for a minute, staring through the bars of the two cages at the cylinders sitting in their foam coffins. The cylinders represented real power. It was why the Colonel had them in the first place. With them he could threaten any city in the world. He could even threaten the Valley.

That was a fact. The Estes Valley would never be safe if the cylinders remained in his possession. Did Ipes care about that?

And did he care what the cylinders meant to her? With them, she'd finally be able to live free. In one sense, power equaled safety and that wasn't something a little girl should give up so easily. And why would Ipes want her to? Wasn't it his job to protect her and to help her?

If she had the cylinders, people would no longer laugh at her or look down at her. In fact, she could make them bow down to her if she wished, and boy, a large part of her wished for just that.

She could be queen!

"But I would never be like that stupid Colonel, Ipes. I would be a good queen. I would help people."

How? Tell me how you'd help people with your VX gas? Would you do it by threatening them? Or by using the gas? Think about it. The only power in that gas is an evil power.

A sudden perfect image slipped into her mind: a grey city filled with grey bodies, lying in horribly contorted positions, their faces frozen in looks of utter terror and pain. The corpses carpeted the city streets as far as the eye could see, and in the middle of the dead city was a little girl with a crown on her head.

You'd be queen of the dead. And your only power would be the ability to kill more people than anyone else. Is that what you want?

"No," she said in a whisper. "But that's me already. I've killed so many. I'm a murderer."

No, Eve was a murderer. The people you killed were all justified. Every one of them was killed in order to save your life, a life of another or there was a clear and present danger. Those should be the only criteria in which you take a life. Any other reason is murder.

Jillybean went to the bars of the first cage and ran her index finger along them as if testing her reality. A part of her wondered if they would part like smoke. Sometimes she didn't know if she was in a dream, a hallucination or a terrible reality.

"Okay, Ipes. I won't use the VX, but I won't let the Colonel keep it either." She announced this to the room at large when she came back to the others. "We'll throw it away or bury it or something. Where are the keys to those cages?"

The Colonel glowered at the guards when they told her and then said, "Don't expect me to carry that box."

"One of you has to," Neil said, "and since you were probably all gung-ho about getting the stuff in the first place, Colonel, I think it would only be fair for you to be the one carrying it."

"I wasn't going to use it," the Colonel replied, feigning an innocence that Jillybean didn't believe. "I only wanted to keep it out of the hands of people like the Azael, or the River King, or... or Yuri." He faltered as he said this, his eyes flicking to Neil, but he recovered in half a blink. "Those are the true bad guys."

Neil didn't notice the stumbled word or the look. "And now, no one will have it. You should be happy."

He wasn't happy. Ten minutes later, the group left the armory, each of the four prisoners carrying a load of weaponry— the Colonel held the box of VX in his arms. In the light of the still glowing fire the sweat on his face glistened as though he had been doused in oil.

With the fire roaring on the eastern end of the island, they made their way along the west side and only had to duck away from a single man on patrol, before they made it to the docks.

Jillybean scoped the area and when she saw that there was still only the one guard in the boat house, she said to Neil. "We'll head down to the pontoon. Chances are, he'll come down to investigate who we are, when he does, you pop out and get him. Can you do that?"

Things happened just as she had foreseen and in one minute, they had another prisoner on their hands. Thankfully, he was very cooperative and showed them where the extra fuel was kept and even helped to load the pontoon up. Neil wanted to take him along, not only to act as an extra hostage, but also because he was very knowledgeable about many aspects of boating and the river in general.

"No. He stays, and so does Mister Private Blazek," Jillybean said. "They're innocent."

The boat guard and Blazek beamed as the Colonel grew hot. "What's that supposed to mean?" he demanded. "Who are you to decide who's innocent and who's guilty?"

She didn't answer him except to narrow her blue eyes. Haigh, who had trouble looking at anything beyond the grenade duct taped to the Colonel's neck just five feet away from his face, said, "I didn't do anything wrong, either. I'm just a bodyguard. I've never shot or killed anyone or…"

"I don't believe you," Jillybean stated. "Now everyone get inside so I can tie these two up." She tied them the same way she had tied the armory guards: showing them the grenade and explaining what would get them killed.

When they were trussed and sitting as stiff as boards, afraid to move even a muscle, she pointed Neil and the last three prisoners to the pontoon.

"You don't need us anymore," the Colonel said as he stood on the dock next to the boat. He didn't want to get on the boat; he was afraid to. Jillybean saw it in his eyes. "You could tie us up just like you did those guys."

Neil paused behind the Colonel. He gave a glance back at the base where the fire still glowed and for the most part the streets were still empty. He mulled over the Colonel's words but didn't act on them. "I don't think so. You'll have your men after us in no time. We can't take the risk. What do you say, Ji…"

He caught himself from saying her name just in time, but it wouldn't have mattered if he had. "He knows who we are," Jillybean said, moving up behind the Colonel and shoving him so that he practically fell into the pontoon. With only three prisoners, each had his own set of cuffs, pinning their hands behind their backs and their balance wasn't the best on the rocking boat.

"I don't, I swear," the Colonel said, doing his best to feign innocence.

The cold feeling had such a hold over Jillybean's heart that she walked past without looking at the man. As he went on lying, she went to the pilot's seat and sparked two wires together that she had cut earlier that night, back when she didn't know if she would have the keys or not.

The twin engines rumbled, good-naturedly. Neil shoved the pontoon from the dock and hopped onto the flat deck, lost his footing and nearly fell into the river where the zombies were thrashing about.

"Jeeze, that was close," he laughed, looking embarrassed. When he got to his feet and had a good hold of the low railing, he said to Jillybean: "Okay, punch it, Chewie."

"Punch who?" Was this the name of one of the men? And why would she want to punch them? She was sure they deserved a good punching, however her wrists were narrow and particularly weak. If she punched one of the goons, she was sure she would end up hurting herself more than them.

"That means drive the boat kind of fast," Neil explained and then amended his explanation a second later: "But not too fast. We don't want to crash. And go left! There's a whole mess of zombies in front of us. Maybe I should drive."

She thought that was a good idea since she couldn't see a thing. After setting the throttle to neutral, they quickly changed positions. Jillybean sat at the front of the boat, training a spotlight outwards over the river, trying to spot the bobbing heads of the monsters.

When she did, she would call out left or right, or LEFT! or RIGHT! depending on how close they were. Running over a monster didn't hurt the boat, but there was a chance it would hurt the propellers or, more likely, get caught up in them.

The pontoon came with an odd device that looked to Jillybean like a saw on a pole. It had been designed for trimming high tree branches, but its use onboard the boat was obvious and disgusting. They hadn't gone two miles before Neil had to put it to use, sawing away the parts of a monster that had got sucked up in the propeller.

He was as white as the moon as he sawed. It seemed to be taking a long time and so Jillybean looked over the edge. "It would go faster if you killed that thing first," she suggested. There was a separate tool for that as well—the longest handled axe she had ever seen.

She wasn't about to watch this part, either, and so turned to look at the prisoners, who were whispering with their heads bowed close together. They stopped when they saw her looking.

"You know who we are, or at least you know who he is." She turned her chin partially toward Neil without taking her eyes from the men. They were sitting on the pontoon's cushioned benches. All around them were the boxes of armaments they had stolen, while in the back was the net filled with their belongings.

Hauling it out of the water had turned it into a complete jumbled mess.

"I don't think it matters what I know," the Colonel said. "You have maybe five more minutes of running before my men come after you, and when they come they'll be coming in force. And when they catch up to you, if I'm dead, they shoot you on sight."

Jillybean's eyes drifted back the way they had come as she pictured the mayhem they had left behind. She knew that a search for the Colonel was already under way. For the moment, his men would be looking for orders, not because anyone would think he had been kidnapped. She also knew that someone, a patrolman probably had to have seen or heard the pontoon leaving.

How long before that was called in? Would it be investigated? And if so, with everything else going on, how much of a priority would it be given? Once they decided to start searching for real, how long would it take until they cut through the locks chaining the other two boats in place? Jillybean had taken the keys from the boathouse and had tossed them into the mighty Mississippi.

This led to the question of how long would it take them to hot wire the first boat? And lastly, how long before they accidentally detonated the first trap Jillybean left behind?

"I say we have closer to twenty minutes," she decided. But in this, the Colonel knew his men better than she did. Five minutes later, as they were once again chugging downriver, the skyline to the north was suddenly lit with a brilliant orange and black light, and seconds later a rumble like thunder rolled over them.

"You can slow down," she told Neil. They had just triggered the first of her booby traps and she was sure that if there were men on the second ferry, they'd be running to get off of it as fast as possible. It would be some time before anyone would venture taking a boat off the island.

She went to her backpack and, squatting down in front of it, pretended to look for something within it. "Ipes," she whispered. She was still filled with ice, but there was a whisper of fear in her that she guessed stemmed from the proximity of the VX gas. It was the very nature of temptation for her and she had to guard against it.

Still, she knew what had to be done, but she didn't like it. "Please, make me forget this," she whispered to the zebra.

That's up to you, he answered. *Maybe you won't do anything that you will need to forget.*

"I don't think that's possible." The little girl stood up with the .38 in her hand. She let it hang against the side of her blue jeans where it wasn't obvious. With a deep breath, she went to the prisoners. "What's his name?" she demanded of the Colonel, pointing with her free hand at Neil.

His grey eyes locked on her blue ones. "I don't know. It doesn't matter. You've stolen my stuff and you've made your getaway. You can let us go now. That would be the smart play, get out while you can."

There was no getting out now. She was in neck deep and so was Neil…and so was the Colonel, though he didn't seem to know it. "It does matter or you wouldn't be lying."

"Okay, it doesn't matter to me, but I suppose it matters to you. Either way, let us go. Keeping us would be…"

"His name is Neil…"

The Colonel was wild-eyed and wanted to scream. Instead, ever mindful of the grenade at his throat, he said, quietly but intensely: "I don't care what his name is! If you care that it remains hidden, then don't say it."

"Please, don't say it," Neil pleaded.

"Because if I say it, we'll have to kill them?" she asked. "He already knows. Remember, he had Sadie prisoner and when he was naming off the 'real' bad guys, he faltered saying Yuri's name. He faltered and looked at you, Neil. That's when he put it together. He knows you and Sadie were together. And since Sadie came here with men from the Valley, it would be nothing to figure out that's where you came from."

Neil was staring intently at the Colonel, who was staring with gritted teeth at Jillybean. Finally, Neil dropped his head and sat back in the pilot's chair. "It's done now, so I guess it doesn't matter."

In the space of one clunking beat, sudden rage melted the ice holding Jillybean's heart. "No, it does too matter. He knows you, Neil. He knows where you came from and if we let him go he plans on doing something about it. That's the reason he has to die."

"You were going to kill him one way or another, weren't you?" Neil asked, in a soft voice.

Her little mouth came open in an instant denial, but the lie wouldn't come. She hadn't planned on any of this. The Colonel had just fallen into her lap, however from the moment she had set eyes on him, she knew that he would have to die.

He was a deadly scorpion, but then again, so was she and when two scorpions came together, there was only one winner. That was the base, deadly nature of the world…and yet, despite having a million reasons to kill him, all she could feel was the guilt of a murderer. And this was only made worse with Neil looking at her with despair in his blue eyes.

"I worry that you haven't changed," he said, his voice still quiet, still filled with sadness.

"I have," she pleaded, her soul still mired in guilt.

He shook his head, gazing at the prisoners as if the sight of them caused him pain. "I don't know. You have a mine taped to your chest. Honey, that's not normal. And what you did to those men, tying them up with live grenades, that's cruel. What if one of them slips? What if one of them flips out? You will have killed them."

For a moment, she didn't know what he was talking about. Hadn't he been watching? "But I didn't do it for reals. Didn't you see? I showed them the grenade but didn't attach it. I lied. See, this is the same grenade." She showed him the one grenade she'd had all night. "I thought it was a waste of a perfectly good bomb. And the mine on my chest isn't real, neither. I took the guts out of it to make the remotely detonated bomb. This is just the cover."

She tapped it and a hollow sound popped out of it as if she had struck balsa wood with a xylophone hammer. She even peeled away the tape to show him the empty mine.

The Colonel cursed, but Neil laughed at the sight of it, but it was only for a second. He grew serious and asked: "But you were going to kill him no matter what, weren't you."

The answer was a resounding YES, however she couldn't say that feeling the way she was, that is, feeling human and vulnerable. She let the ice fall over her soul again, masking the real Jillybean. "Yes, because I do what I have to do. Ipes says it's okay. The Colonel is a clear and present danger."

"Yes, you're right, he is," Neil answered. With a long, dreadful sigh, he reached down and picked up the giant axe. The Colonel glared at it, however the two body guards began yammering about fairness of all things.

Neil, the pained expression hanging on his face like the drapes on a hearse, said in his most authoritative voice: "Colonel Williams, for the attempted murder of Sarah Rivers, I sentence you to death."

In answer the Colonel only clenched his teeth, locking his jaw tight and staring at Neil as if he could kill him with his gaze alone. Neil ignored the look. He sighed again as if it was a preamble to every statement. "And you two," he said addressing the bodyguards, "You two are hardly innocent. You were both in New York. I remember you. You were there when Sarah was raped and when Sadie drowned, and you did nothing to help."

"That's not a crime," one said, while the other cried: "I was following orders!"

The whining washed over him, leaving nothing but pain. Another long sigh. "Stand at the railing and we will make it quick," Neil said. He swallowed with a clicking sound that everyone heard. "You'll get a bullet to the head, which is better than your victims ever got. But if you stay where you are and keep whining, I'll use the axe and throw you over in pieces. It's your choice."

Even Jillybean with her ice-cold soul was taken back by the pronouncement, but she stepped up, showing the .38 to the men. Neil's eyes widened and he gave her a look and a tiny shake of his head that said: *Please put that away.*

She wished she could, however, she simply didn't trust Neil. Mutilating a bound man with a giant axe was, sadly enough the only thing she could expect him to accomplish without hurting himself or falling in the river.

Jillybean stepped up next to the rail, clicked open the six-shot police special to show the prisoners that this time, she wasn't playing around.

"You, Haigh," Neil said. "Come on. Let's get this over with." He was almost begging for Haigh to take his death like a man. It was a terrible thing to ask and Haigh didn't comply.

He knelt with his hands behind his back pleading in an incoherent babble, tears dripping down his once tough face. Neil raised the axe and gave him a whack with the blunt end, striking him on the shoulder near the neck.

"I'll turn it around, I swear," Neil almost screamed. It was hard to tell who was more afraid.

Haigh and the other guard huddled on the flat deck of the boat which was carpeted with a green bristle, like a fake putting green. They tried not to look at the axe in Neil's trembling grip, but their eyes went to it time and again, drawn uncontrollably.

The Colonel didn't blubber or whine. He alternated between making overtures, promising great sums, and stating with complete confidence that Neil didn't have the balls to kill him.

"Ipes?" Jillybean asked. The ice was on her like a block, thick, heavy and unmoving. The men had to die. They were whining and cringing now, but that would change the second they had the upper hand. They would become deadly and cold, themselves.

Ipes sighed exactly as Neil had and said: *They are a clear and present danger. I wish it was easier.*

"Me too." She closed her eyes, took a deep breath and fired the pistol at the two guards without really aiming. She was so close there wasn't much of a need to. Along with the thunder from the little gun, there was a very unmanly scream.

"Fuck…fuck…fuck!" Haigh shouted. There was a splotch on his BDU shirt inches from where his bellybutton sat. He looked down at his stomach as the splotch spread downward, pulled by gravity.

Neil had a grip on the axe-handle as if hiding behind it, as if it alone could protect him from the loud sound. Upon seeing that he wasn't the one who was bleeding, he recovered. "Please get up. This is going to happen one way or the other. Okay, so please."

Haigh, weeping like a child, made his way to the railing. He knew he was a dead man. He'd been shot. Infection was already setting in. It happened in seconds, and they all knew how it would go. How, even if he lived through the night, it was only a matter of time before his insides rotted into green mulch.

"Lights out, okay? Lights out?" he begged as he groaned his way to the edge of the boat.

"Yeah, lights out," Jillybean said. Haigh was shaking all over as he stood at the railing, leaning on it with most of his weight. His lip trembled and he had his eyelids crimped shut as hard as he could.

This time, Jillybean took careful aim even though she was only two feet away. When she pulled the trigger, Haigh flopped into the water, causing the monsters around the boat to go nuts, thrashing like crazy. The other guard began to whimper.

"Colonel?" Jillybean asked. He refused to look up. "My name is Jillybean." She paused, waiting for any response, but he kept his face down showing the thinness of his hair at the top of his skull. She shrugged. "And his name is Neil Martin. He is the Governor of Estes Valley."

"I don't care," was his only answer.

"I'll shoot you right there." He shrugged and the other guard just quivered like a jello. She glanced at Neil and he sighed as he had been. It was an uncommitted sound as if he were waiting for her to do something; as if he were waiting for her to take charge...or for her to take the blame.

For a moment, the bile built up in her stomach until the burn was more than she could take, but then she swallowed once and it was gone. Just like that, the cold covered her more completely than ever. She had a job to do, one she wished could be passed to someone else, a grown-up, perhaps. Neil, perhaps.

But Neil hadn't recovered from the death of Haigh. His eyes went to the body as it floated face down. Jillybean could tell he was about to cry—she was about to cry. Deep down, a part of her was crying over what she had to do.

This time she didn't waste bullets; they were too precious. She shot the guard in the back of the head. He flopped like a slab of rubber and was a bitch to drag off the boat because of his great weight.

"Not like this," the Colonel muttered, breathing heavily and leaning to one side. He wasn't talking to Jillybean. He was addressing fate or God. "I can't die like this." Jillybean proved him wrong a moment later.

Chapter 34

Captain Grey

At the moment, Jillybean put a bullet in the Colonel's head, the ferry-turned freighter was slipping into a mooring channel next to the western bank of the Mississippi. They came to a rest about a hundred yards from the current bridge at Cape Girardeau. It was an incomplete string of floating pontoons stretching across the water.

Every hundred feet or so, there were gaps to let the zombies float by. These gaps were created by partially unchaining a few of the pontoons so that they slid back, pushed by the current.

Beyond the pontoons were two monuments to a seven-year-old's fury. The crumbling remains of the original bridge jutted up out of the water, and then, further on, barely visible in the darkness, was the ass end of the River King's barge that Jillybean had destroyed.

Sadie marveled at the sight. "This is the first time I've ever seen the boat," she said. "And this is the closest I've come to the bridge. I heard the stories, but they are nothing compared to being so close. I...I kinda wish she were here, now."

"For your sake, I do too," Grey answered. "But if it was just me, I'd rather that she be far away. She doesn't need this."

They went quiet as one of the guards came by, checking their cuffs and then checking the perimeter of the boat. The guards were very careful and had been during the two day trip. The ferry had moved down the river at a snail's pace. Many times, when there were too many zombies around, they turned off the engines and drifted with the current.

Even when they found long stretches of the river relatively open, they didn't rev the engines and fly down the waterway. There were too many obstructions hidden beneath the black surface of the river for them to do anything so foolish.

Grey was impressed with how careful and prudent the boat's captain was. He always had a sharp-eyed guard up front, keeping watch, just as there were always guards staring intently at the banks.

According to the talk on board, there were thousands of bandits operating between Rock Island and Cape Girardeau, just like there were thousands between New York and Rock Island and thousands more between Cape Girardeau and the Estes

Valley. With certain valuable items becoming more and more scarce, banditry was a growing profession.

They preyed on anything that moved, including each other. It made travel by boat one of the safest ways to go; only a fool or someone desperate would ever dare swimming the Mississippi. Grey had been in the river once, jumping off a bridge with Deanna to avoid capture. It had been a horror he hoped never to have to repeat.

When they reached Cape Girardeau, it was still full dark and men on shore with flashlights guided the captain into position. His skill at handling the ungainly barge was such that they docked with all the violence of a gentle kiss. Just like that, the guards switched from watching all sides to concentrating solely on the shore and the dock. Some even crouched behind the pallets with their weapons trained outward—there was no love lost between the Colonel and the River King. They were rivals for the east-west bound traffic. And yet, they were also, out of necessity, trading partners.

But that didn't mean there was an iota of trust between them. Unarmed men from the bank came down the dock with their hands up. As the new slaves watched and listened, there was a brief discussion between the captain of the boat and the "Trade Master" of Cape Girardeau.

They talked about the load they were carrying in very dry terms: "Eighteen hundred pounds of cord wood, three hundred pounds of coal..." And so on until they came to the seven prisoners. "...five male slaves, one female and a bounty."

"Who is it?" the Trade Master asked with more than a hint of interest in his voice.

The captain walked around the pallets and shone a light down on the slaves. "His name is Grey. Supposedly, he was part of the team that did that." He stretched out a long arm to point at the ruins of the bridge.

"I remember him, yes," the Trade Master said the anger palpable in his voice. "And, who is this?" The light shifted from Grey to Sadie, who squinched her face and turned away. "Don't be like that, darlin', it just makes everything more difficult. Now there's a good gir..."

He broke off in mid-word and gaped for a moment before recovering. "She's, uh young. Good. Young is good." The anger was gone and, to Grey, he was suspiciously neutral in his tone. The Trade Master had recognized Sadie.

The captain had heard the stumble, but didn't attach the correct importance to it. "She's sixteen," he said. "Very nubile and untouched by the general population." By this Grey guessed it meant she hadn't been used as a whore.

"Also, good," the Trade Master said, though this time he spoke with even less enthusiasm as if he were losing interest in Sadie. His intense gaze told a different story, however. "I could do, I don't know, maybe three thousand for her. She's cute, but a little scrawny. The bounty for Grey is also three thousand, I think. I'll have to check on that. And I can give you two hundred a piece for the others, for a grand total of seven thousand."

Adding body language to the conversation, the captain took a defiant stance, folding his arms across his chest. "I've been told to accept nothing less than ten thousand for the lot of them. I don't know if you realize it, but those soldiers are soldiers of the *Valley*. They're in top physical condition, and, if the rumors are true, they're the best fighters in the world. And the girl cleans up well, and she's young. You really can't tell with the way she's bundled up, but she's really a fine-looking girl."

"But she's not worth ten thousand," the Trade Master insisted, "not even half that. Maybe I could go thirty-five hundred if she's got a nice rack."

"Thirty-five hundred for her is fair," the captain agreed, "but I still can't accept less than ten thousand for the group. This Grey is an officer, and like the others is a soldier of the Valley. The Colonel believes that if we get anything less than ten thousand, it would be better to send them back to the Valley."

The Trade Master gave him a sharp look. "Do you mean to ransom them back? Will they really pay that much for a few soldiers?"

"Unlikely, but we wouldn't be selling them back, we would just give them back. The Colonel feels it would go a long way to cementing a proper relationship between our two peoples. Perhaps it would be the basis of an alliance, I don't know, but it would definitely go a long way to creating an exclusive trade and passage agreement. That right there is worth far more than ten thousand."

A shrug from the Trade Master suggested he didn't think so. "Maybe, but either way I can't authorize that amount. I'll have to talk to the River King, personally. We'll catalogue the rest of the goods tonight and I should be able to have an answer by morning."

This meant another cold night shivering on deck for the slaves, but it helped that they had some tiny hope that they might be released by the Colonel.

The little group of slaves prayed fervently, holding hands as the Trade Master's men inspected every inch of the boat, watched by the guards, who were extra attentive, not willing to risk any last moment loss in their profits.

No one got much sleep and in the morning, the slaves sat on the flat deck, shivering and watching the steam lift off the captain's mug as he waited on the return of the Trade Master.

"I don't understand your bargaining position," Grey said to him. "I offered almost the same thing to the Colonel. We could have cemented a very promising relationship three days ago. Both of our societies are mainly made up of soldiers, after all."

The captain blew on his mug for a moment, never taking his eyes from the city of Cape Girardeau. After a sip, he said: "We don't need an alliance with you fucks. Especially now that you have so many enemies. And as for trade and passage, who else are you going to turn to?" He lifted his mug toward the remaining pillars of the old bridge. "You literally burned your last bridge, so all you have is us. No, all of that was a smoke screen to get a better price."

This sent their spirits plummeting and more than one of the soldiers blinked back tears, not showing any of their normal grit. "Let's look alive," Grey said in a savage whisper. "We aren't done yet. I want to see a little fire in you men. You'll need it when the time comes."

Almost soon as he said this the River King showed up in person, as small, lithe and deadly as always. The slaves were ordered to their feet and told to stand straight. There was no need for anyone to order Sadie. She stood like a queen with her dark eyes flashing.

The River King barely gave a look in her direction. He went down the line of slaves to stand in front of Grey. "You look unwell, Captain. Not quite the robust hero that I remember."

"I'm fine," he answered, and in a way, that wasn't a lie. Despite the cold and the wretched conditions, he didn't feel nearly as bad as he had before they had left on the mission.

"We'll see about that," the king said. Turning to the captain of the barge, he smiled without any mirth or kindness. It was the smile a fox gives to a rabbit. "My Trade Master told me that you threatened to release these…people, back to the Valley."

"Yes, your Highness. It is an option that the Colonel is seriously considering."

The River King laughed loudly causing the zombies in the water to thrash. "Oh my. I had a good chuckle when he told me, but it's much funnier in person."

"It's not a joke," the captain said through pursed lips.

"Well, then that's just sad. You must not know what goody-two-shoes the people of the Valley are. They would never ally themselves with your boss. The idea is sheer idiocy. And I'm not all that worried about you getting exclusive trade rights. They don't have anything to trade and even if they did, for the most part they're too chicken to come out of their little mountain paradise. They'll trade with anyone just so long as you go to them. I'll give you eight thousand for the lot. That is my final price."

The captain appeared to deflate. His defiant stance wilted and his face drew downwards. He opened his mouth to answer, but before he could Sadie spoke out: "If you let these soldiers go I'll make it worth your while...your highness."

The two, so obviously father and daughter, stared hard at each other in a battle of wills. The anger and the hatred seemed equal between them and seemed to grow, but then the king smiled, toothily. "I might want to hear this," he said to the captain, tipping him a lewd wink. He ambled over to the girl who was not three inches shorter and leaned in close.

"Free them or I'll tell the boat captain who I am," she whispered into his ear, matching his smile tooth for tooth. "What do you think the price will be then?"

"Such a child," he answered, snorting out a quiet laugh of contempt. "And how will that work, exactly? Will they remain on the boat? How long do you think they'll be free once the boat leaves? Or do you want them to walk straight through my city alone and unarmed? Do you really trust me to just let them leave once I've concluded my deal here? And even if they did get away, how long will they last against every bounty hunter in Missouri?"

He was about to go on when the captain, a lusty leer on his face, called out: "What's she offering?"

"It's nothing I haven't heard before," the King replied before leaning into Sadie once more. "Here's my counterproposal: say anything at all and you'll regret it and your friends will regret it. They'll bleed and scream because of you and I'll make you watch. That's a promise."

"So?" the captain of the boat called out, his growing impatience obvious.

"So what?" the King shot right back, turning from Sadie. "The girl was hardly inventive. My offer of eight thousand stands, take it or leave it." He walked to the gangplank and gracefully stepped along it without fear of falling.

Grey glanced at Sadie and saw the tears in her eyes. Others probably mistook them for sadness. She wasn't sad. She was enraged. "I'll kill him. I swear to God, I'll kill him."

Although Grey was thinking the exact same thoughts and a vein pulsed in his neck with the intensity of his anger, he advised: "Keep your cool. Bide your time and don't give away your hand. If you get the chance, take it. If not, live to fight another day. That goes the same for all of you. Remember your mission: escape and evade."

Unfortunately, there was no chance at escape. The dickering over the price of the prisoners gave way to dickering over the rest of the merchandise and it was after noon before a deal was reached. In all that time, the prisoners were carefully guarded.

They were even moved to the center of the barge, perhaps as a precaution against one of them jumping into the river. If Grey knew what the River King had in store for them, he might have considered it. But he didn't find out until the deals were struck and the slaves marched into the center of the fortified base.

In the months since he and Sadie had escaped, the walls had been pushed back to encompass more of the town, including a once open field. It was now arranged with bleachers circling a raised stage and in the center of the stage was a metal cage. It was a fighting cage. The seven prisoners were shoved through the single door.

"Don't expect us to fight each other," Grey said to the Trade Master as he locked the door. "It'll never happen. I'd order my men to strangle me before I lifted a finger to harm them."

"Your days of fighting are over, my friend," the man answered and then walked away, leaving the seven alone, except for two guards who stood at opposite sides of the cage, well back from the bars.

"What did he mean by that?" Lieutenant Wilson asked. Grey guessed it meant he'd be executed, probably in some public fashion, but he couldn't bring himself to say it. He only shrugged and tried to pretend he didn't feel the fear crawling in his belly like a giant worm.

Wilson, who was pale and had a jitter going in one eye, wanted an answer and asked the guard the same question. "I don't know," the man said, "and if I did know I wouldn't tell you, because I ain't allowed to talk to you."

The guard, a ferret-faced man who squinted at everything, stood for a moment with his slitted eyes aimed up at the sky before adding: "But if I could talk to you, I'd tell you to start praying real fast."

The soldiers glanced from one to another until PFC Keene said: "But we didn't do anything to you guys."

Ferret-face stepped closer to the bars and whispered: "That's not what I heard. I heard you were the punks what blew up our bridge. That's what everyone's been saying. So, did you do it?"

"They had nothing to do with it," Grey said. "It was just me." If the River King needed a scapegoat, Grey would be that man if it meant allowing the others to go free.

At Grey's confession, the guard made a face and blew out a short note of disgust. "They's gonna do some bad stuff to you, my man. I'm talking real nasty…" He clammed up as the River King led a twenty person entourage through an opening in the bleachers. Behind them was a veritable parade of people.

Hundreds of people followed and when they got through the opening, they dashed for the best seats. As the improvised stadium filled, the River King went to the front of the stage where there was a small podium. He didn't look back at his prisoners.

Soon the place was filled, packed with at least two-thousand people. There was an excited buzz in the air that made Grey's pulse race. They were eager for a show and eager for blood. The people of Cape Girardeau had been living off blood sports for a year now and their appetite for it was like a drug.

"Ladies and gentlemen," the River King's voice boomed over a dozen loudspeakers. "Thanks for coming out on such short notice. This is a very important day for us. Today is the day we finally get some *revenge!*" He screamed the word so that it could be heard from one end of the base to the other.

"These are the pieces of filth who destroyed our bridge. They blew it up as an act of sabotage against, not just me, but against all of us. Yes, we have killed the men who paid them for their treachery, but now it is their turn!"

The crowd cheered this with such enthusiasm that for a few seconds, Grey thought that they would rush down in a giant mob, tear down the cage and rip them to pieces.

The River King waved his arms, yelling: "Hold on, hold on," until they were quiet enough to hear him speak in a normal tone. "I know you are excited, but you'll have to wait just a little longer. As you can see, there is a girl with them."

A hiss erupted from the crowd and cries of "bitch" and "slut" rained down on Sadie.

"Yes, she is a nasty piece of work and, regrettably, she is my own daughter." The crowd emitted a collective gasp and then began whispering to each other in amazement. The River King spoke over the noise. "I can not kill my own daughter. It's a failing of mine as a father. I love her too much to kill her."

There was a smattering of jeers and boos from the audience. "Yes, I deserve that," he said, shaking his head in theatrical sadness. "She won't go unpunished, I promise you that. She will be sold in the slave auctions in New York and the proceeds will go to help the disadvantaged here in Cape Girardeau."

"She's cute! I'll buy her," someone called out, causing the crowd to cheer and catcall.

"Okay, sure," the king said, easily. "The opening bid is seven thousand." The crowd oohed and ahhed over this amount which seemed deliciously extravagant. The man who had offered to buy her sat back down, disappointed. "She leaves tomorrow on the next caravan east," the River King went on, "you have until then to scrape together any money…"

Sadie interrupted him, screaming: "You are such an asshole!"

He turned on her with hate in his eyes. "And you are guilty of collusion, as well as aiding and abetting enemies of the state. Your friends, on the other hand, are guilty of treason and the penalty for that is death!"

A snarl rose from the crowd and once again they seemed on the verge of turning into an uncontrollable savage mob. The River King called for quiet. When he got it, he bellowed into the microphone: "Iiiiit's time!" This caused the people to go nuts and they began stamping their feet on the bleachers, making a sound like thunder. He let them carry on for a few minutes and began to tire, he asked, "Who wants Skinner?"

293

The cheers were deafening as a giant of a man came down through the opening in the bleachers. He was dressed in scarves and rags that were brown with old blood, and across his face he wore a fearsome leather mask. In one hand he carried an axe with an immense blade and in the other he carried a whip that had eight heads.

He carried his instruments of torture raised up high as if he had earned a victory with them. The River King beamed at him as though he were a favorite son.

"To celebrate the capture of the saboteurs, we will have a three day party and Skinner will be our star attraction. But all of you will get to participate as well. At noon and nine, you will get to pick the winners for the day."

The River King snapped his fingers and said something to one of his flunkies, who then snapped his own fingers and a squad of guards went into the cage and dragged out the prisoners who were lined up in no particular order. Grey was happy to see that his men didn't shy back or whine. They stood tall and proud.

"We'll pick the first of today's winner by applause," the River King said, heading to Grey, who was furthest to the right.

"What's the winner get?" Grey asked, though he knew the answer.

At first the River King wasn't going to answer, but then he smiled right into Grey's face. "He gets to die. Trust me, being the first to die is really a plus."

"Because he doesn't have to look at your ass of a face any longer?" The squad grinned at Grey's display of bravado.

"No," the River King answered calmly. "Because he doesn't have to come back here every day with a ball of ice in his guts, afraid he'll piss himself if he's called and sickened that if he isn't, he'll have to sit through the torture of knowing that everyday could be his last. You'll be the final man chosen, Grey. I'll make sure of it. I want you to watch every one of your men get skinned alive."

Grey had no comeback for this. The hate was so strong in him that he could taste the bile in the back of his throat.

"Back in the cage with him," the River King said to his flunky. Louder, he addressed the crowd: "That one is special. We want to save the best for last. Now, about these. Who wants this one?" He came to stand behind Lieutenant Wilson, who calmly turned and spat a yellowish loogie square into the River King's face.

Rage turned him red in an instant, but he refrained from violence. He wiped away the spittle and declared: "It looks as though we have a volunteer."

The crowd roared approval as the others were led back to the cage while Wilson, spitting and kicking in a fury, was dragged forward to where a six foot tall pole was cemented to the ground. His hands were uncuffed from behind his back and then recuffed to the top of the pole, where a metal ring had been welded. His clothes were cut away so that he stood in only his boots and his underwear, shivering and not just from the cold.

Grey's heart melted for his friend, but he found he couldn't say a word in support. It felt as though his tongue had been glued to the roof of his mouth.

At a safer distance, the River King walked around the man, appraising him. Finally, he said: "The toughness of the Valley soldiers is legendary. I say eighty. Do I have any takers?"

He had many. The place went nuts and the noise grew even louder than ever. It dragged on for half an hour and during that time Grey had an opportunity to ask the ferret-faced guard what was going on.

"They're betting on how many lashes it'll take before that dude dies or goes unconscious. I seen some go a hundred and twelve. Yeah, it was pretty gnarly. You couldn't even tell what Skinner was whipping at the end."

Stunned, Grey could only stand there with his forehead pressed against the bars, his eyes seeing nothing. The River King's voice brought him around. "Two minutes until the betting is closed."

The first lash landed exactly two minutes later. Skinner raised a muscled arm and then brought his whip across Wilson's back and slashed eight red lines through his flesh. To his credit, Wilson didn't scream. He jerked and grunted, his body going rigid from the pain.

It took seven lashes before he finally cried out, which only made the crowd more bloodthirsty. Their cheers were beyond anything Grey could have imagined. They were animals, jumping up and down in an ecstasy of evil.

It triggered something animalistic in Grey. He attacked the door of the cage, stomping it with a heavy-booted foot. A second later, PFC Keene joined him and they alternated hammering on the door until they were too tired to go on. Two more soldiers quickly stepped up the second Grey and Keene fell back.

As he caught his breath, Grey's eyes were pulled toward the horrible execution. Already the skin across Wilson's back had been completely stripped away so that white bone stood out in a field of red gore.

"Fuck!" Grey raged, getting up again. He knew that kicking the iron gate was useless and futile and yet he couldn't just sit there as Wilson's screams drilled into his head.

At first, the screams were piercing with the vibrancy of his pain, but by the fortieth lash that tore away the last thread of his underwear, his cries had dropped in volume. By the sixtieth, he lacked the strength to do more than blubber.

As the eightieth lash drew near, it was hard to tell if Wilson was still conscious; both of his eyes had been exploded out of their sockets. A ghoul of a doctor checked him after each lash and by the eighty-third, the doctor waved off the bloody figure of Skinner.

Wilson was unchained and allowed to flop into the stew of flesh and blood underfoot and then Skinner was back having exchanged his whip for the huge-bladed axe. He turned his masked face to the River King, waiting for the signal to strike off the head.

Grey couldn't watch and turned away, however the River King ordered him to turn and watch. "I have all day," he said when Grey started cursing in an incoherent rage. "I can let that poor bastard suffer until the cows come home. Good boy. Your men, too. I want everyone to see who is really in charge around here."

"You're not in charge around here," Grey shot back. "You're afraid of the crowd. You're afraid of your own people. That's why you do this. You're a weak little coward."

The king only raised a single eyebrow, affecting a bored expression and finally Grey ordered his men to face forward. They stood at attention, their eyes forward as Skinner took Wilson's head off with one stroke.

Chapter 35

Neil Martin

It took both of them straining with all their might to heave the bodies to the edge of the pontoon and shove them off.

"That was a gentler death than he deserved," Neil said, taking a water bottle and rinsing his hands. There was blood on them and as long as it was there, his face had a curdled look to it.

"Deserves is a dumb word," Jillybean said in something of a monotone. She looked exhausted and it was no wonder. They had been charging hard for four days now. "No one gets what they deserve. I used to be a really good girl, but I didn't get good things. I just got people dying like Mister Ram and Miss Sarah and Nico. Then I was bad and I got to end the war with the Azael, which was good. You see how nothing makes sense?"

Neil wanted to smile at Jillybean to reassure her that everything would be okay in the end, but the body of the Colonel and his two bodyguards were floating placidly next to the boat and his lips wouldn't move in the direction of a smile. The bodies were proof that the only thing they could really count on was death.

"I guess it is a dumb word," he conceded.

She nodded, looking out over the bodies and not seeing them. If one didn't look too close, they seemed to blend in with the rest. The boat was surrounded by bodies, most thrashing in a futile attempt to get at the two humans.

"We should go," Neil said, at last. "We don't want to be around when the Colonel's men find his body. Our goose would be cooked."

"Huh? Isn't a cooked goose a good thing?" Jillybean asked. "I could go for some goose right now."

Neil nudged her towards the front of the boat with his now clean hands. "It's just an expression and I guess I really don't know what it means. Either way, we have to get away from the scene of the crime."

She gave him a sharp look at his poor choice of words, but the look faded quickly, replaced by the tired one again. "Sure, but they won't find his body. It doesn't even look like him, you know what I mean? He looks kinda fake, and in a day, he'll start to puff up and turn green and stinky…"

A sudden wave of queasiness had Neil breathing heavily just to keep his stomach from turning inside out. "Just go to the front and keep a look out, please. We should get as far down river as we can before dawn."

It was a difficult trek. Zombies clogged the propeller so frequently that Neil wanted to tear his hair out in frustration. He spent half their night sawing away bleeding bodies.

Jillybean finally came to look at the situation and suggested altering the angle of the engine that stuck down into the water. She pressed a button and the entire engine shifted.

"Hey, which button was that?" Neil asked coming to stand over her as she sat in the pilot's chair.

There were only three buttons on the entire console and she pointed to the one on the right. "It's not going to fix everything, but it'll help until I can get some proper welding supplies. Can we stop and get some? There's a little river coming up that like, smacks into this one. Just up it a few miles is a town that gots to have all sorts of stuff for us."

"Sure," Neil answered, wondering how she could possibly know the first thing about welding. For a good hour as they trundled down the river, Neil watched the girl sitting like a shadowy lump at the front of the boat.

She only spoke to point out better routes around the "monsters." She wound them in a curling course that sometimes made Neil wonder if they were still traveling downriver. He had to watch the slowly drifting zombies in order to tell.

When they finally reached the tributary, he slowed until they were going at walking speed. "This is the one, right?" he asked.

Jillybean jerked as if waking up, even though she had just called out a change in their course. "Right one what?" she asked. She stood suddenly and almost lost her balance. "Neil," she said with fear in her voice. "Where are we? Where's Rock Island?"

"What do you mean? You're not lost, are you?" Neil knew that it was almost impossible to get lost on a waterway that went in only one direction, but he also knew that if anyone could, he'd be the one.

"No, I don't think so. This is the mighty Mississip...I think." She spun, going in a circle, tottering slightly as if she hadn't been on the boat for the last few hours.

"What do you mean, *you think?*" Neil turned the pontoon in a gentle turn. "Do you remember what happened? I heard you talking about forgetting. Is that a thing? Did you forget what we did?"

Her eyes were big and shiny, the stars glinting on what Neil suspected were tears welling. "We did some…" Her wet eyes fell on the deck of the boat where the Colonel's blood had soaked into the bristly green carpet. In their world, the splotch couldn't have been anything except blood.

"What did we do?" she whispered. "And where is Sadie and Mister Captain Grey? I-I didn't kill them, did I?"

A shiver ran up Neil's back. What deadly strangeness swirled in her mind for her to even ask the question? "Why would you do that?" he asked and then immediately regretted the question. What if she answered? What if he was invited into her deranged mind and saw a glimpse of something he shouldn't see? With anyone else, he'd take the risk.

"I wouldn't…I think," she said. "But you never know. I mean, I've done…" She broke off and the tears were now on her face slipping down her cheeks.

"You didn't do anything," he said, quickly, but then immediately started yammering: "You didn't do anything to Sadie or Captain Grey, but we did something to…wait, never mind. It doesn't matter. Grey and Sadie are already downriver, sold to the River King."

Her eyes hung on the bloody splotch as she tried to makes sense of a world suddenly and inexplicably turned on its head. Neil couldn't possibly understand this, except to come to grips with the fact that this was Jillybean and there was no understanding any part of her mind, the sane or the insane.

He explained *most* of what had happened earlier, leaving out the executions, saying instead that they had left the Colonel alive and tied to a tree. "He'll be able to get free?" she asked, and he could tell that she wasn't sure if this was a good thing or a bad thing.

"We don't have to worry about him anymore," Neil said. "Our focus should be on the River King…hey, you can still weld, right?"

"Still? I've never welded nothing. Oh, sorry Ipes. I've never welded anything, but it's not that hard. I read about it in this 'do it yourself' book that lets you do all sorts of things."

Neil pulled her to the back of the boat and pointed down at the engine. "Can you weld something to fix this?"

She rubbed the last of the tears away, forgetting or perhaps never knowing why they had been there in the first place. "The engine's broken? But it was just working."

"It's not the engine. The zombies keep getting caught up in the engine. It's kind of slowing us down a lot."

"Have you tried varying the pitch of the engine? You know pulling the propellers up a bit? There's a button that…"

"I know the button, but you said something about a weld that would fix the issue."

She stared down at the engine her brow wrinkled. It cleared a second later. "Okay, I see it. A weld isn't going to help, but putting in twin steel plates in a V would divert any of the monsters around the propellers."

Neil could only say: "Oh," once again in awe of her intellect. He didn't feel bad for not thinking of that, however, as none of the Colonel's men had thought of it either and they had been using the boats on the river for a lot longer than he had.

Now he just had to make sure she didn't forget how to weld. He turned them up the small tributary which was far less congested with corpses. They buzzed right up the river and though it was shallow in spots, the pontoon floated so high in the water that they barely scraped the rocky bottom, but when they did, it was with a hair-raising screech and a sudden deceleration that would, on more than one occasion, throw them to their knees.

Just before dawn, they reached the town. Jillybean was all business. The first thing to do was to hide the boat. Neil started to look around for a secluded dock or a boathouse jutting over the river.

Jillybean would have none of that. "If the colonel is looking for us, those will be the first places he'll check. We need to really hide it."

Neil gazed around as the sky went from black to the deepest purple. There didn't seem to be many places to hide a twenty-foot pontoon, not with the banks so steep. "We could cut some of the foliage overhanging the river," he said, knowing right away that she would make that face of hers, the one that suggested he was an idiot. "Or…or we could…"

He trailed off. There was simply no hiding the boat on the river. Their only choice was to sink the boat or somehow get it up on the bank. With Jillybean, the idea of purposely sinking a boat was hardly far-fetched. In fact, drawing the boat onto shore, as difficult as that seemed, was so minor league that he was sure she had a sinking in mind.

"We could fill the, uh pontoon things with water, sink the boat and then pump the water out when it's time to go." As his sentence ended, each word grew quieter and quieter. Her raised eyebrow was all that it took to kill the idea.

She then smiled a bit of a crooked smile, high on the left and sloping down to an embarrassed grin on the right. "We could do that, but we'd need an air-compressor. There might be one in the town, I guess."

This was her way of saying: *there might be one, but it would be a waste of time looking for one*. "Or we could use that car battery to get a car moving and just drag the boat up. I think it might be easier, but I don't know."

Of course it would be easier, Neil thought. There were cars everywhere, but who knew where they'd find a compressor. There could be one in the local hardware store or it might have already been looted. And if they even found one, would pulling a boat out of the water really work? Would the engine run, would the electronics on the boat be ruined? Neil was pretty sure they would be and he was convinced that she knew it too.

"Or we could get a car going and pull the boat up. Good plan, Jillybean."

The smaller river had a creek that flowed into it and the creek was just wide and deep enough to handle the pontoon. Its banks started as steep as the river, but gradually leveled off. When Neil found a spot that he felt he could climb without falling in, he tied the boat to a half submerged log and the two of them climbed up the slope to stand where farm country butted up against small town living.

The town wasn't large and when they had trouble finding a suitable vehicle, Neil fretted that there wouldn't be a hardware store either and suggested that they try somewhere else. However, Jillybean was certain the town would have everything they needed and pressed them on, though in no sense did they hurry.

There were zombies about, moaning here and there among the dark buildings.

As Neil was the one carrying the heavy car battery, it felt like forever before they found a decent truck. As Jillybean used the red-dot laser from one of the scopes she had taken from the Colonel's arsenal to distract the zombies, Neil went to work switching out the truck's battery, giving it a quart of gas and praying that the engine would turn over.

It did on the fifth try, just when the battery had begun to sag. In a flash, Jillybean jumped in and they pelted back the way they had come just as the sun cracked the sky.

With the rope from the pontoon, they pulled the boat clear of the creek. Neil worried that it would make a hell of a racket coming up, but it slid across the grass, making less noise than the truck. They did not need to take the boat deep into the underbrush. Thirty feet was all that was needed.

This time, Neil kept watch for zombies, while Jillybean raced around covering the tracks the boat had left. She then grabbed a number of explosives and weapons.

"Look at all this stuff," she said, in awe of the very weaponry she had taken earlier that night. The look in her eyes, a sort of manic joy, made Neil nervous.

"We probably don't need all this stuff if we're just hiding out for the day."

The mania faded from her face and she took on a purposefully neutral expression that scared Neil even more. She was hiding something…something horrible. "Sometimes you need this much stuff," she said. "You never know who's watching."

"Maybe we should get out of sight," Neil said as he started glancing nervously around. Jillybean was, unfortunately right. You never knew who was lurking and what their intentions were.

The two found a house on the edge of town, which Jillybean fortified with bombs and booby traps in such a frightful way that Neil was afraid to even use the bathroom. He slept with a full bladder, his ears perking up with every sound.

Jillybean must have had full trust in her traps, because she slept deeply until after four in the afternoon when she hopped up, full of energy.

As Neil stared blearily around, his eyes red and scratchy, and his brain still in a fog, she went about the house dismantling her traps and talking nonstop about the dreams she'd had. They were so convoluted that he was quickly lost, and he found himself saying: *oh, yeah?* and *really?* whenever she paused for a breath.

"Yeah, it really was blue. Okay, I'm done with all the bombs. You can come out of the room. We can go get the weldering stuff now."

"Hold on, I wasn't hiding in there. I-I was just getting some different clothes to wear, you know so we can blend in with the monsters." In truth, he didn't want to be anywhere near those traps when he didn't have to be; that was just being prudent.

She glanced down at her blue jeans and her white carnation-covered shirt and sighed. "Yeah, I guess that is a good idea." It didn't take her long to find a pair of scissors, but she didn't use them on the outfit she had picked out. Instead she used the scissors, a stapler, some glue and some string to turn a green curtain and a brown coat she'd found in a closet into a very strange looking ghillie suit.

She was spiked and mottled and somewhat alien appearing. The zombies that had wandered into the front yard, barely gave her a second glance though they did give Neil a very close inspection, causing Jillybean to zip her red dot at their feet to confuse them long enough for Neil to get in the truck.

They tooled into the central part of town and found a hardware store that was small but packed floor to ceiling in a maze of goods. "So far, I've found these little town stores carry practically everything," she said, running the beam of her maglite around. "Who wants to drive an hour into Davenport just to get…" She squinted at the nearest item: an aluminum J-tube. "Uh, one of these things?"

She was not wrong and in no time, they stood in front of a fully stocked shelf of welding equipment. "Hmm," she said, looking at a little boxy device. "We would need a generator with one of these and it'll be loud. Better to go with straight fire, don't you think, Mister Neil?"

He thought that all welding machines used fire, but was tired of feeling stupid around her and so he only said: "I trust you to pick out the right one. I'm sure you'll do great." She beamed at him and then forced him into a servant's role. He lugged a heavy metal bottle of acetylene, another of oxygen, the welding torch, rod fillers, protective equipment and squares of precut metal out to the truck.

Once the items were brought back to the pontoon, Jillybean noted right away that the metal squares were too big. For some reason, this seemed to please her. She grinned in anticipation as she donned the leather apron and stuck the heavy welder's mask on her head. To Neil, she looked like a kid playing dress up—right up until she lit the torch. The sound of the flames reminded him somewhat of the sound a fuse makes when it burns towards a bomb.

"I'll go keep the monsters away," he said stepping back...to give her room, he thought to himself. "Unless you need my help here?"

"No, I got this," she answered, dropping the heavy visor down in front of her face. Her first order of business was to cut the metal squares to fit. Since it didn't take much muscle, she was able to do it on her own. Neil watched her from on top of the truck. From there he could see any zombies coming and keep an eye on her just in case anything went wrong.

The torch blazed bright enough to light up the clearing. The afternoon was growing dark as heavy clouds rolled in. He was sure that it would begin raining soon and he worried how moisture would effect a welder's torch. "It couldn't put it out," he said to himself, but wasn't certain.

The process of cutting through metal was very slow and she only just beat the rain, scurrying beneath the pontoon as the first drops landed heavily.

Neil thought she'd need his help to attach the two metal pieces to the underside of the boat, but again she managed on her own. Using a shimmed log, she braced the first square of metal flush against the underside of the deck, at an angle, three feet from the propeller. She then picked up a long rod and blasted it with the flames until it began to glow.

Seeing as she hadn't blown herself up and it was warmer and dryer under the pontoon, Neil crawled beneath it and watched through squinted eyes as she basically used the melting metal of the rod as a glue to hold the square to the boat.

It wasn't a professional weld by any stretch. There were gaps and odd bubbles here and there, but she went over it twice before going to work on the inner aspect. When she saw him watching, she flipped up her faceplate. Although Neil was beginning to shiver, she had sweat dripping into her eyes.

"You can't watch this!" she scolded. "You'll go blind and that's what means you won't be able to see no more. Also, the monsters or bad guys could see us, on a cuz of the light. You need to go watch, for reals."

That she was right didn't help much as he got soaked to the bone. Two zombies came stumbling up not long after he climbed back up onto the truck. It was getting so dark that he didn't see them until he noticed a shadow cast by Jillybean's torch that was moving.

"Oh boy," he said, sliding off the truck. At first, he grabbed the M4, but then thought better of it. There were only two of the beasts, after all. He hurried for the giant axe that he had used to threaten the Colonel and his men.

The rain made it slick and its over-sized head made it ungainly. It clanked right out of his numb hands on the first swing. It lodged in the neck of a gruesome zombie that was well over six feet. Once, it had been a woman. Now it was missing both breasts and had arms that were longer and stronger than Neil's.

She reached out with one of these great limbs and snagged Neil's wrist. "Oh, jeeze!" he wailed and leapt about, only freeing himself by shrugging off his jacket. The closest bit of safety was the truck and he climbed in one door, slid across the bench and was out the other side before she could smash in the window.

The second zombie, another female, charged around one side of the truck while the first went around the other. Neil dropped to the muddy earth and wriggled under the car. He was halfway to the temporary safety of the far side when something grabbed his foot and hauled him back.

It was the larger of the two zombies, still with the axe buried in its neck. The creature dragged him out into the rainy evening and dropped down to feed on Neil, only to be brought up short by the long handle of the axe, the bottom of which was planted like a flag pole in the soft earth.

She flailed her arms and as long as they were, they weren't longer than the axe handle and Neil was able to crawl again under the truck. When he looked back, he saw dark blood coursing down the handle to puddle in the mud.

Once on the other side of the truck, he found his limbs shaking so badly that he had to use the truck's frame to get to his feet—and then he was running again. The smaller of the two zombies rushed around the truck with frightening speed.

Neil's speed fell into the "frightened" category and he outraced her around the truck, where the larger zombie was still hung up on the axe. He sped around her and noted she didn't even look in his direction. With her insane desire to eat him, she had managed to nearly decapitate herself.

Thinking he would use the axe better if he got a second chance, he gave the zombie a kick which sent her flopping lifelessly onto her side. He grabbed the axe in passing heading to do another lap of the truck. He felt like he was starring in some absurd black and white comedy from the nineteen twenties and would have been embarrassed to know what he looked like.

But as no one was around, it didn't matter that he was so out of breath that he nearly fumbled his next strike with the axe. The metal was wet, cold and slippery and he thunked the smaller zombie on the head with the side of the axe.

It was enough to trip her and he was able to take a better grip on the axe as he gave her another whack.

"Ha!" he cried, in triumph. He gazed around as the grey rain fell. The clearing was empty of adoring fans. "No one's ever around for my victories."

He went to the pontoon and told Jillybean but she only brushed him off saying: "Good for you," without looking away from the flame.

"Good for both of us, really," he said. "Without me, we'd be..." A gunshot stopped his lips from moving and he stood completely still waiting for a second. The sound hadn't been close and yet, the fact that he heard it at all, meant it was way too close for comfort.

"Did you hear that?" he asked Jillybean.

She nodded, her mask slipping down her face as she did. "We should get going soon," she said after re-adjusting the faceplate.

"Just waiting on you."

A confused look crossed her face. "Really? You've pulled the battery from the truck, drained the last of the gas and transferred all of our stuff to the boat?"

"I was just finishing up," Neil lied. He left to "finish up," grousing because of the wet and the cold. There wasn't a second shot, but the first was enough to make them both nervous and they completed their tasks almost at the same time.

Then they were off, heading back down the tributary. Jillybean's metal V, welded just in front of the propellers, worked perfectly to keep the zombies from getting caught up in them. It wasn't perfect in other regards, however.

The V created a zone of turbulence in front of the propellers that caused the water to froth as if they were being run in a bathtub and for some reason, the sound of the engine seemed magnified—alarmingly so. Worst of all was the steering.

Pontoons don't change direction by use of a rudder, instead the entire engine pivots. The V didn't stop the pivot, however it did change the water flow around the blades and the boat, never nimble to begin with, now handled like a blimp in a thunderstorm.

At high speeds, the steering grew mushy and tended to slide left or right across the water, while at the same time careening forward. As he tried to pilot the boat, Jillybean leaned far over the back of the boat to see the action of the propellers and saw a solution.

"Pull over, Neil. I'll use the torch to cut holes in the metal planks. It'll create a more natural flow of water."

Neil was still too nervous over the gunshot to allow it. "We'll be fine for now. The river is really wide and I'm sure I'll get the hang of steering this thing, soon."

He never really did, yet because the river was a mile wide in spots, they didn't hit anything besides zombies and floating logs which, thanks to Jillybean's V, were kept from ruining the engine.

It was a bumpy, wet and ferociously cold ride. Jillybean's fix worked well enough for Neil to open up the throttle and they raced down river into a rain that was half sleet. They were both soon soaked to the bone and the cold went right to the marrow. They persevered as long as they could and the miles slipped away under them.

The fear of what could be happening to Sadie and Grey carried them beyond the point of sanity and deep into the territory of hypothermia. The cold was so intense that by midnight, Neil couldn't take it anymore and looked for another tributary for them to hide in. Jillybean had long before ceased to even talk. She had wrapped herself in so many now drenched blankets she didn't even notice when he ran up on a sandy bank. She simply fell on her side, much like the giant zombie Neil had fought earlier that night.

"Jillybean?" he asked. She didn't answer. "Hey! Jillybean!" She didn't budge when he shook her.

Feeling a crazy desperation, he carried her up the bank and across a long field to the nearest house and, after stripping her down to her dreadfully frail and icy flesh, he bundled her in dry blankets and then built a fire. Leaving the boat where anyone could see was terribly foolish, but he feared for the little girl: she was lethargic and her limbs were stiff. Her zebra had fallen from her hand and sat like a black and white sponge, staring at the ceiling of the little home.

Somewhere in a dark spot of his mind he had a half-forgotten memory about not rubbing the limbs of a person with frostbite, but he took the chance anyway and soon her eyes were able to focus enough for her to ask in a drunken voice: "Are we there yet, daddy?"

"Not yet," he answered, "but you can rest for now. Go to sleep, hon." In seconds, Neil found himself crying over her as he realized that if he kept this up, he was going to get the little girl killed.

That he was going to get himself killed as well only brought a shrug.

Chapter 36

Sadie Walcott

As Jillybean slowly recovered from hypothermia, sleeping beneath three dry blankets, cozied up to a fire, Sergeant Hendricks was whipped to death in front of a crowd of three thousand people. They came out despite the cold rain to see if he could last longer than the hundred and two lashes Private Raoul had endured the night before.

He didn't come close. The crowd left, disappointed after only sixty-one lashes. Depression and the miserable cold hastened his death, and in only ten minutes, he was a headless pile of bloody meat at the feet of Skinner, who walked over him as he left with the River King, the big axe hefted easily on one shoulder.

Once the bleachers were empty, the four survivors were marched back to the same prison Sadie and Neil had rescued Grey from months before. Not much had changed, except the number of guards which had been doubled. Having been threatened by the River King, personally, the guards watched over their prisoners with hawk eyes.

There would be no escape this time and no chance for revenge, at least not for Grey and his men. They would be killed one by one to the roar of the crowd. That thought was acid to Sadie's heart. She tried to keep it at arm's length. She tried to pretend it wasn't real and yet three times now she had been forced to stand at attention at the end of the gradually shrinking line as her friends died.

She never watched. Yes, she faced the torture as it happened, but she kept her eyes shut tight and if she could have driven spikes into her ears to keep the maddening screams from creeping in, she would have done that as well. When the horror was finally over, she kept her eyes from the mess that was left behind.

It was dreadful to contemplate, but she looked forward to when the traders in their tremendous mastadonian trucks finally made their way east from the river. The five trucks were deemed too large for the pontoon bridge and so none crossed. There were western traders and eastern traders and all were under the employ of the River King.

The eastern traders had come in the night before and most of the town of Cape Girardeau had crossed the bridge to see what there was to be had. Grabbing the bars and pulling, Sadie had hoisted herself up to the little rectangle of a window that faced east. She could just get her chin to the ledge and hold herself for half a minute at a time.

"They're here," she had said.

Grey, who was sitting against his cell wall, nodded without looking up. A languid depression had smote all of them, including Grey which had been a surprise to Sadie, however at the mention of the trucks, his hands had balled into fists.

"Play the game, Sadie. Escape and evade. Do what you have to do to survive and, yes that means take the rapes, right up until you can get that chain around some guy's throat, then kill without mercy."

The others in the prison all nodded. Besides the three remaining valley soldiers, there were seven cage fighters, all of whom were raggedy and weak. She didn't recognize a single one; few had been there even a month.

That was the extent of the conversation for the last seven hours since Sergeant Hendricks had been murdered. What else was there to say?

Besides being able to fulfill Grey's wish for her to escape, Sadie's one hope was that the traders would leave before Grey was killed. She didn't know if she'd be able to live through that. A part of her guessed that her heart would simply give out.

When her father finally dared to show his face in the prison, she knew she would get her wish. He would want to get one last dig in before she was shipped off. That was his way. That had always been his way.

"My daughter, you have embarrassed me for the last time," he said to her. The other prisoners kept silent and well back from the bars. The River King had come with four guards, and if their impressive size and ugly demeanor wasn't enough they were each armed with tasers and baseball bats. No one bothered to test their resolve with spit or curses.

"You must have me mixed up with someone else, your Highness. My father is dead, or soon will be."

He smiled, but it was sour and angry. "One of us will be dead soon, but knowing your temper, it's going to be you. And I wish I could tell you that I'll be sad when I hear the news, but that's just not likely. Not with the way you've treated me."

"The way I've treated you!" she shouted, showing some of her vaunted temper. She looked ready to tear down the bars between them and her head felt as though it was filled with nitroglycerine, needing only another jolt before it exploded.

Unruffled by the outburst, he regarded her calmly and said with casual serenity: "Yes. But I have not come to argue. I've come to say goodbye. Do yourself a favor and treat your new master better than you treated me."

"I'll give him everything he deserves," she answered in a quiet voice. Grey had caught her eye and had glared her into behaving. She could practically read his thoughts: *Play the game, Sadie. Escape and evade. Do what you have to do to survive.*

The River King caught the look and smiled a greasy smile that was an act that fooled no one. "I'm glad she listens to you, Grey. Hopefully you've taught her more manners than she displays in my presence."

He shrugged. "Her manners are fine when her life isn't being threatened, but I can't take any credit. Neil Martin is the only father-figure she ever had or ever needed."

A scowl momentarily replaced the greasy smile. "Touché. With comments like that I don't know if I should give you the gift I had brought." He waved to a man who had lingered by the door. He came forward with a brown bag. "I brought you a sandwich and some chips. You've got to keep your strength up."

"For what? Wait, don't bother lying. You're betting on me to what? Take a hundred and ten lashes?"

The greasy smile was back. "Something like that."

"Well, thanks," Grey said, reaching through the bars and taking the bag. "But I don't think a lash is what is going to kill me."

"Really? Are you expecting some sort of rescue? That would be something since no one knows you're here. And yet… stranger things have happened. It's why I've ordered extra guards on both banks of the river and the fence line. And I have three radio scanners going at all times. And, just in case, as an extra precaution, until you die, I'm bringing in the bridge every night."

Grey's face had gone tighter and tighter as the River King spoke; still he managed a smile as he said: "A squad of my men could tear this place up."

"A squad would be a nuisance if they were here, but they're not so it's just a lot of talk, which, sadly I don't have time for. Don't forget to eat up." He left without looking at Sadie or her extended middle fingers which was all the goodbyes she was going to give him.

"Do you really think we're going to get rescued?" one of the remaining soldiers asked.

Grey's answer was a simple: "No, there's very little chance. I was just giving him a false front. He's going to bet big that I can last a hundred lashes, but I'm going to see that I don't. I want to be as weak as possible going in. From now until then, I won't eat, sleep or drink."

That he had, in essence, just signaled he was surrendering, cast a gloom over the room. Silence held sway for a few minutes until one of the cage-fighters asked: "If you ain't gonna eat it, can I have that sam-ich?"

The captain glanced over at his soldiers and offered them the sandwich but they were both white-faced with hollow haunted eyes. One of them would be dead in five hours and the other in seventeen.

"It's yours," Grey said to the fighter. The words were quiet and lackluster. He threw the bag without any strength. It fell short and the fighter had to stretch out a skinny arm to snag it.

"What happened to escape and evade," Sadie asked, trying to make her voice sound tough, trying not to cry. "What happened to making it back to the Valley? And what about Deanna?"

He dropped his chin. "She'll understand. If she knew there was no other way, she'd want me to go quickly."

"Yeah," Sadie said. The conversation ended and nothing more was said as the gloomy afternoon faded into the dark of evening. It wasn't until the traders came with chains and a neck collar that she spoke again and the one word was: "Bye."

He only nodded.

She was pulled along by her chains down to the pontoon bridge, where she saw the extra guards patrolling. There had to be fifty of them within sight, each carefully eyeing the zombies floating by. Sadie crossed the bridge, hoping that at any moment twin explosions, one behind her and one in front, would cut her section of the bridge and she would just float away to be rescued by Jillybean or Neil or soldiers from the Valley. She even slowed her pace, pulling back on her chains to give the explosions a chance to occur.

But none did and the shock that none did brought tears streaming out of her eyes. Was she truly alone? Was she really going to be sold into slavery? The answer seemed to be a resounding yes as her foot touched the east bank of the Mississippi and she saw five trucks arranged in an angular circle. A small mob of people stood waiting for her. They crowded around and stared with bright eyes at her as she was brought into their midst.

"So we got a celebrity with us," the lead trader said. He was tall and other than the fortune in diamonds he wore, was average in appearance—neither handsome nor ugly, neither muscular nor skinny. He really only stood out because of the diamonds. The studs, three in each ear, were huge and gaudy and probably real, as were the diamonds he wore in his many rings and on the rather feminine necklaces draped about his neck.

"I'm no one," Sadie said, and the meekness in her own voice surprised even her. Tears were one thing. They came from a place of fear, yes but also frustration and burning anger, but the whipped quality of her own voice was hard to explain.

"Wrong, sweetheart, you're my star attraction. You're the River King's daughter. Who wouldn't want to fuck the River King's daughter? I'll have them lined up five deep."

"Weren't you supposed to sell me?" The idea of being *used* in such an appalling manner made her suddenly want to beg to be sold to one man. A single man would get tired. If she was being used as a rental, the torture would never end. Day after day, hour after hour, until she was diseased and all used up and no one would give a nickel for her.

Would they kill her then? Or would they let her go to wander the earth, forever alone, because who would want her? She wouldn't wander far, only to the nearest tree, where she would hang herself.

"Oh, I will eventually. Come inside where it's warm. My name is Diamond Dave. While you're with me, you will do everything I ask, exactly when I ask it, or I'll give you a few zaps with the machine. Trust me, you won't like it much. Do you know what electroshock therapy is?" She'd been following him up what was essentially a gang plank, but now she stopped and stared in horrified wonder at Diamond Dave. He seemed to tower over her, loomed in fact like a hungry giant.

The look on her face caused him to chuckle. "Yeah, I get that a lot and yet people still test me. It's almost like some of you bitches almost want your brain fried. Do you, Sadie?"

"I don't I swear," she said, speaking quickly.

He beamed down at her as if he were a benevolent god. "That's good, because I won't hesitate to punish you for being bad. What I like most about the machine is that it won't mark you up a bit, but it slowly turns you into a vegetable. You see, I really don't need you to think all that much to do your job."

She could only nod and blink back the tears.

"Would you like to see the machine?" Before she could say anything, he held up a finger. "The answer is yes by the way."

"Y-Yes, sir."

The machine was set in a corner of the truck on the first floor. To Sadie, it looked like an electric chair and it smelled of old urine and shit. She felt like throwing up.

Diamond Dave put a kind hand on her shoulder. "Just lube up, make the men happy and you'll never have to see it again."

Once more she said: "Yes, sir," which he seemed to appreciate.

"That's the right attitude," he said, loudly enough for everyone to hear. There were six women standing in the narrow hall of the first floor of the truck. A few others were, judging by the grunting and the over-the-top moaning, were working. "Why can't all of you have that attitude?" he asked of them. The women refused to look up or say anything besides: "Yes, sir."

"Hmm, that's a little better, I guess. Here you are, Sadie. This is going to be your home." He acted as if she had just won a prize. He smiled expansively as he showed her the stall. It was just large enough to fit a twin-sized mattress. Three feet above a shady-looking pillow was a cabinet bolted to the back wall.

"You'll put your stuff in here, when you get stuff that is. What size are you? A zero? A one? Here, take off your clothes. Let me see what I'm dealing with." She hesitated, causing him to snort. "Please. In case the diamonds didn't give it away, I'm gay and so are my men. It keeps everything on a business-like foundation."

The fact that he was gay shocked Sadie into speech. "If you're gay, how can you do this? How can you treat women like this?"

She could tell that the question had crossed into bad territory by the way he shot an eyebrow up. "Sweetie, are you really asking me how I can go about making a living in this horrible new world? Have you been living under a fucking rock? People do what they have to do, nowadays, and for you that means pleasing men and pleasing me."

Another: "Yes, sir," didn't have the same effect as the first two and she got the sinking feeling that it wouldn't work again. Diamond Dave was into punishments rather than into rewards. He was also into bondage and chained her iron collar to a ringbolt attached to the side of the wall.

"The River King has only stipulated that you're not to be *used* until we leave the environs of Cape Girardeau, which means you get the next couple of days off until we get to Cincinnati. And he also mentioned that if you escape before New York that I can kiss my balls goodbye. So don't bother asking about having any freedoms. You'll get the pot brought to you once every two hours. After Cincinnati, we'll see if you've earned any favors."

He turned to go, but she asked a question. "When will we be leaving?" As much as she didn't want to get on with this new life of hers, she didn't know if she could take hearing another of her friends being killed and she got the feeling that the screams would carry across the water.

"We leave when I say we leave," he answered, his eyes boring hard into her.

She dropped her head until he left and then she sat on her mattress and cried. At nine o'clock, Private Hill was skinned alive with the same leather whip that had killed countless others. Sadie could hear his screams as clear as day.

Chapter 37

Jillybean

As Private Hill was being killed, Jillybean sat under the pontoon wrapped in three sweaters, a heavy coat and a poncho. She wore gloves but that was mostly because of the intense heat of the welding torch in her hands. The weather had improved slightly. It was no longer raining and that made all the difference.

As she stared at the blank metal, her mind dwelt on creating a proper flow of water to the propellers. Simply burning holes in the metal, making it resemble a cheese grater, did not seem as though it was the optimum method.

Why not? Ipes asked. *Do you think it'll create drag? It can't be worse than the V itself.*

"That's what you think. The V planes the water away, while the holes will catch it. Hmmm, what do you think about wide slits both above and below the water line? Remember, we do have airflow to consider as well."

You're over-thinking this. We have three hundred miles to go. Just do enough to get us there before the sun comes up.

The necessity for speed decided Jillybean, who clunked down the faceplate, sparked her torch and began work on three horizontal slits per side. For her it was a piece of cake and she let her mind wander. A typical seven-year old might start thinking about dolls or tea sets or imagining herself as a princess, Jillybean began building a detailed layout of the River King's base in her mind.

She recreated the entire thing in a three-D image in her mind. And for her that was also a piece of cake. What wasn't, was guessing what had changed. Where was the new pontoon bridge? Where had the defenses been bolstered? Where had they been left the same? Had they changed the location of the prison? Had they kept it but added extra layers of security?

Unfortunately, she could imagine a great deal, in fact far more than the entire combined intellect of the River King and all his men. She imagined so much that it had her stomach in knots. The defenses that she could have created could not be overcome by the resources and the personnel—namely Neil—at her disposal.

She paused for a moment, flipped up her mask and stared at her work without really seeing it. "I'll need to know the true situation, preferably in real time. I will also need a distraction or two."

One thing was certain, she wasn't going to be able to ghost on and off the base as she had before. Thus the distractions. "Yes, Ipes, I'll need more than one. I'll need them coming and going. I'll need them running about not knowing where to turn. Which means I'm going to need more stuff."

Oh boy. I can already tell I'm not going to like this.

"You know, that's a mighty fine impersonation of Neil. See if you can do him fretting over…"

Neil suddenly stuck his head beneath the boat. "Did you call me? I thought I heard my name."

"No, I said 'meal.' I'm getting hungry, but I can eat on the boat, which is almost done by the way. Five minutes and then we can get going to St Louis."

"Oh boy," he said slowly, sounding just like Ipes had. "What's in St Louis? Nothing good, no doubt."

Ipes snorted and Jillybean knocked him with her elbow. "I think lots of stuff is in St Louis and lots of the stuff I need, and probably it's good stuff, too. Or it's good that we'll find the good stuff there. You know, as much as I like small town hardware stores, the big city is where you need to go to get cool, exotic stuff like drones."

Neil's one remaining eyebrow shot so high up it almost got lost in his hair. "Drones? I knew I wasn't going to like this. Where are we going to get drones in St Louis and why would we possibly need them?"

"For my plan, of course." That seemed so obvious she felt a little foolish even saying it.

"And what is your plan?"

She looked at him as if he were crazy, while Ipes rolled his eyes which Jillybean rightly interpreted as: *Can you believe this guy?* "I haven't thought of the plan, yet, but I'm pretty sure it's going to need drones. Drones is what means things without people in them but what you steer from far away."

"Right, I knew that. I thought you meant military style drones. You know the kind that carry bombs."

"Oh, mine will have bombs and cameras. That's why we have to go to St Louis. So, if you can get all our stuff on board, I'll finish here."

He left, muttering something but all she caught was the word "mule," which she didn't understand since the word didn't go with anything she had been saying. Ipes postulated that since Neil was old it meant that he was going senile and may have mistaken Ipes for a mule.

Or he was being insulting. You should tell him that going to St Louis wasn't my plan. My plan was to find someplace warm and dry and let the grown-ups work things out.

His plan was to be a chicken and it wasn't a bad plan as far as Jillybean was concerned. She was tired of saving people and tired of shooting guns and she was tired of bad guys. They were like a disease and she didn't want to be anywhere near them.

But she had Sadie to think about. And Captain Grey, too, but it was mostly the goth-girl, her apocalypse sister, that drove Jillybean on.

The little girl finished her welding and was about to set aside the equipment, thinking she wasn't going to need it anymore, when her eyes caught sight of a cement tube jutting from the bank of the river. Water gushed from it in torrents, and something clicked in her mind, but before she knew what it was, the river itself grabbed her attention.

A heavy fog had draped itself on its surface. She could barely see ten feet in front of her and down on the surface it was even worse. It gave her an idea which brought questions: *Is it possible to make fog?* Her next question was*: If so, how can I control it?*

A fog that thick would make getting on the base nothing but a matter of snipping some wires. But a fog could not be controlled—however fire could.

"Time to go," Neil said, breaking her concentration. She gave him a half-smile and then started to lug the welding equipment up. "Do you really need that stuff?" he asked.

"I think I just might. We'll also need to find some chemicals. Do you know where people keep potassium nitrate? I know they use it for rockets and fertilizer, but I don't know where any spaceships are and I never did see potassium nitrate on any farm."

Neil picked up the oxygen bottle and put it on the deck, saying, "Maybe you did and you didn't know what it looked like. I doubt I would be able to recognize potassium unless it was in a big barrel with the letter 'P' stenciled on it. I just know it's in bananas."

"Actually, it would have a 'K' on it, but don't ask me why, and I know what it looks like. I saw pictures of it in my chemistry book. It was called: *Chemistry- A Modern Molecular Study*. I know it makes a lot of smoke if you mix it with sugar and sodium bicarbonate, that's what means baking soda. We're going to need that, too."

"More stuff?" Neil said. "Then I guess we better get moving and hope this fog doesn't stretch the entire way to St Louis."

The fog was only a small bank and did not last for more than a mile, and very soon, they were driving the pontoon through the middle of St Louis. It was a dreary, scary and very dark place. Even the magnificent Gateway Arch was frightful— there were bodies dangling from it, hundreds of feet in the air.

Neither of them knew how the monsters could have got up there and neither hazarded a guess.

The pair went into the city dressed as zombies and lurching like zombies, and were soon surrounded by more zombies than they could count. Thankfully, Neil held it together.

"What's first?" he whispered when they were alone enough to talk.

Jillybean's brow crinkled as she looked around the dead city. "We have to find a Radio Shack and a chemical store." There wasn't either in sight, though she didn't really know what a "chemical store" actually looked like.

"You aren't going to find chemicals around here," Neil said, in a hiss. He was right. They were downtown where there were stadiums and museums and office buildings where grown-ups used to work, staring at computers all day.

"Follow me," Neil said and headed straight to the closest hotel…or what remained of it. The upper floors of it were just as black as night, and in spite being as cold as a tomb, the building reeked of smoke as though a fire was even then eating at its supports. It seemed like a dreadful possibility as the building swayed and groaned around them.

She followed him in, confused. "There aren't going to be chemicals here, neither." Though in a way, she was wrong. The fire that had burned months before had unleashed all sorts of chemicals, almost all of them hazardous. But he wasn't there for chemicals. He was there for a phone book.

"It's sort of a throwback, but for whatever reason, hotels always seemed to have phonebooks," he said, not only finding one behind the front desk, but also finding an entire stack of maps.

In no time, he discovered the locations of three Radio Shacks and six farm-related equipment companies, including a giant complex that was a stone's throw from what had once been Merchant's Bridge, but was now only a few concrete pillars rising up out of the river.

The Radio Shacks were spread out, so they were forced to stick the battery in a red Honda Civic that was parked close by and fill it part of the way with gas. It was annoying to have to do this, yet again, but in the end it saved them hours of walking time.

Well before midnight, they were back on the now laden down pontoon, streaking south at full speed. Because she knew she'd be busy, Jillybean had picked up a second spotlight. It lit the river and with her newly augmented V, Neil had no problem steering clear of obstacles in their way.

As the hours and miles raced past, Jillybean began work on a dozen projects at once, happy to have something to do instead of dwelling on the hidden memory of what had happened to the Colonel that sat inside her like a time bomb.

There were minor tasks that had to be completed, such as the re-charging of all sorts of batteries, and larger tasks such as preparing the drones which, according to the box, were Phantom 4, remote controlled quadcopters with a built in HD Camera RTF 4 Channel 2.4GHz 6-Gyro Headless System with a stated flight time of twenty-eight minutes.

The flight times were significantly altered when Jillybean attached the secondary payload to the drones: the inner workings of a claymore mine with remote controlled detonator.

Next, she went to work on the creation of her own fog bank. Starting with small amounts of her three ingredients, she huddled in the back of the boat with the wind blocked as best as possible with stacked boxes.

In the river warehouses that once belonged to a company called AMD, she was able to find hundreds of pounds of potassium nitrate. The place stank to high heaven because of it. The smell was so bad that her face twisted into a grimace as she scooped out a tablespoon's worth from the one barrel she had brought on board.

The baking soda was also easily found, though not in great amounts. Every house seemed to have at least one small box of the stuff. The simple sugar was simply not to be found in any amount. Luckily, the Budweiser brewery was three blocks from the river and in it they discovered vast amounts of one of the key ingredients of beer: malted barley, which was a fine sugar substitute. There were sacks and sacks of it, looking like dirty flour and smelling like vomit. The entire factory reeked of it—but it would work for her needs.

Onto a frying pan, she combined one tablespoon of the barley to the potassium and then added a third of a teaspoon of the baking soda. After giving it a quick stir, she lit it and then leapt back as it sparked into an uneven flame that jumped as if little volcanoes were hidden within it.

It also belched forth a fountain of smoke out of all proportion to the size of the fire.

"Is it supposed to burn like that?" Neil asked.

Clearly it wasn't. She tossed the flaming pile into the river and said: "That was just a first attempt." It took seven more tries to get the right mixture and when she did, the concoction only smoldered instead of bursting into flame and yet the smoke that came from it was the thickest yet.

The combination was five parts to three to one and when she tried it on a larger scale, the result was just as promising and the smoke output correspondingly larger. Next, she began working on the thermal fuses. This proved a challenge and she spent a dozen miles just sitting there racking her brains trying to figure out a way to take the charge from a battery and turn it into heat.

She had almost given up when she saw the bent butt of a cigarette sitting next to Neil's foot. Just like that she had the concept for her fuse. It started with a nine-volt battery, the inner coil from a car cigarette lighter, wire, electrician's tape and a remote controlled switch.

She tested the switch first, using a hand held radio that was set to the frequency of the switch. It sparked right away and when she leapt back, she noticed that Neil was slowing the boat and that the sky in the east was just beginning to take on a lighter hue.

"Are we there yet?" she asked, somewhat alarmed. She wasn't ready. The smoke bombs still had to be made, and the real bombs had to be modified as well, and she had to fashion flotation devices and...

"Yeah, basically. We just passed Indian Creek," he said. "Thank goodness there was a sign or I would have just kept plowing right down the river. We have to get out of sight before the sun comes up."

It was an easier than expected task. Two miles from Cape Girardeau, an arm of the Mississippi, only a hundred feet wide snaked inland. There was a sign here warning of "shallows" for the next three hundred yards.

The arm was heavily wooded on both banks, but on the eastern side there was a marsh into which Neil guided the pontoon. He found a spot where mossy willows acted as a screen, hiding them from casual observation.

Turning off the engine, he smiled at first and then looked around them in concern. He even glanced over the side of the boat, making a face. "This water stinks."

Ipes thought so too. *And you'll be wanting to get in it to look for a house to hole up in? Maybe you should leave me behind so I can guard the boat.*

"From the crocodiles?" Jillybean asked, slyly.

Crocodiles? Ipes also looked over the edge of the boat this time, shaking so badly his stripes began to blur. *Maybe you can leave me a gun or one of the bombs.*

"You'll be safe with me," she said and showed him a gallon-sized ziplock. He was still complaining about both going and not going when she zipped it up. When she saw that Neil was only looking at her in confusion, she said: "We need to go get a lay of the land—that's what Captain Grey always says. That's what means 'looking around.' We have to find out what, if anything has changed."

A guilty smile spread across his scarred and misshapen face. He was embarrassed that he had witnessed her talking to Ipes. "Right, I know. We'll go as monsters. It's just…never mind. Let's go."

After bagging a few items, including a pair of tasers, a set of binoculars, a change of clothes, and her pack, she slid into the frigid waters making a high noise in the back of her throat. Neil, holding a triple bagged drone, did the same thing, except his noise reached a higher note, almost a keening noise.

"If you had testicles, you'd understand," he said, his teeth chattering. She had her own cold parts, so she didn't understand in the least.

They crossed through the slag of the swamp, which rose only up to mid-chest on her but since the muck beneath the black water was like a cross between molasses and honey without the good smell, she did an ugly doggy-paddle.

Neil slogged until they reached that little arm of the river where the channel was too deep to walk. There were only a few dozen zombies here and they couldn't handle the water, so the pair swam across unharmed. Once on the other bank, they couldn't be so blasé about appearing human.

Jillybean changed clothes, while Neil looked out for zombies. Because he hadn't had the foresight to bring his own clothes, or perhaps because he knew he could go anywhere for a new and dry set, he waddled in a squishy way to the nearest house and emerged a few minutes later in a strange arrangement of women's clothing that were torn and tattered in lines that, to her were too obviously made by scissors. The zombies didn't notice and that was what counted.

"Don't laugh," he whispered as he made erratic walking motions toward Jillybean. "The guy who lived here must have been five hundred pounds. Everything was huge."

As the woman's outfit floated on him, she could only guess how big the man's outfit had been. As someone always on the receiving end, she, of all people, knew not to laugh or make fun. *At least it hid the drone*, she thought. It was strung up on his back under the layers of the cloth.

She only nodded, a slight motion of her head, before starting on the slow trek to Cape Girardeau. It wasn't far in the standards of the new undead world, just a couple of miles. A distance almost no one would have walked a year before unless it was for exercise.

For them it was nothing and they ground their way to the fenced perimeter. The base had tripled in size and now the original fence wasn't even in sight. The original had also been electrified but perhaps because it was so much longer now, it was just an ordinary, but very tall double fence.

Jillybean should have been in character, moaning and swaying—they were only a mile from the prison and the sun was above the tree tops. They had to be careful, however her eyes and her mind were somewhere else, picturing the city of Cape Girardeau in flat, map form.

Neil interrupted her imaginings by nudging her and jerking his head to the right; she followed as he led them around the partially enclosed city. There was little to see. The houses and businesses this close to the fence were clearly false fronts, designed to fool the zombies. No one lived anywhere close and the only sign of humanity were the partially drawn curtains beyond the fence where hidden eyes stared out.

Even Neil wasn't fooled. He lifted his one eyebrow and cocked his head again. They ambled slowly away. As much as they wished, they couldn't make the mistake of hurrying now, and so, with the expanded perimeter, it took them three hours to walk around the outer fence.

And although she had seen some promising spots to make an assault from, she hadn't seen any blatant holes in the defenses. She was rewinding everything she had seen in her mind when Neil said: "The base is really coming alive. Strange, how they're all moving towards one spot. Maybe they serve breakfast in one location."

They could see down a road that crowds of people were walking to the southern end of the base. "Maybe," Jillybean answered. "It would allow for mass rationing if needed. This is pretty lucky, either way. If everyone's indoors, it'll make flying the drone over the base less chancy."

The two moved away from the fence, crossed through a park and headed for the tallest building around: the *Rush Limbaugh Sr. Courthouse*. Neil stared at the name on the building and then grunted. "It's the little things that always take me back."

Jillybean didn't know what that meant and so Ipes told her: *Nostalgia. It's like remembering stuff, like Christmas or a fun time. Though I don't know why Mister Neil would feel it for a courthouse.*

"Maybe he went to jail and had ice cream with his dad or something," she suggested. Once inside where it was grey and depressing, she realized that she was probably mistaken. There weren't any ice cream stations or anything fun at all.

We'll make our own fun. Can I fly the copter first?

"Sorry, but it takes thumbs and all you have are hoofs. And asides, I thought of the drones and that's what means I get to fly it first."

Ipes groused about this, while Neil had no problem letting Jillybean run the copter, though he was very meticulous about reading the instructions, something Jillybean had only scanned.

They were just beginning to test the controls, which were slightly too big for Jillybean's small hands when a strange sound came to them. They both turned to look south. "What the heck?" Neil exclaimed. "Is that cheering? It sounds like a football game or something."

Jillybean, who thought that football had whistles and guys saying hut-hut, could only shrug. "Let's find out." She thumbed the up arrow on the controls and the drone lifted straight up. "How's the picture?"

Neil held a synched iPad in his hands. "Looks good. You can see everything and whoa, you can zoom in and out."

She glanced over at the screen; it looked just like a mini TV. "Cool. Zoom out so I can see us." She sent the drone higher while Neil zoomed out. In seconds, she could see herself, though it was only the top of her head since she was looking at the screen.

Next, she ran the drone to five hundred feet until it was almost too small to see. "Okay, let's see what that noise is all about." Using the screen to guide her, she propelled the drone south until she was over a huge crowd of people sitting in a circle of bleachers.

"Can you zoom in, Mister Neil? I can't see what that is in the middle." Seen from above, the cage looked like a simple square and even when he zoomed in to full magnitude she couldn't tell it was a cage except by the shadows of the bars.

"Move it to the left a little," Neil said, squinting down at the screen. "Everyone is looking at something just out of the view of…" He stopped, stunned by what came into view and they both stared in silence as the last of Grey's soldiers was stripped of his flesh and his humanity and eventually, with a whack of the axe, his life.

"Who was that?" Jillybean whispered. "That wasn't Mister Captain Grey, was it? That couldn't have been…"

"Shh! This thing has sound."

"…99! Wow! Who saw that coming?" It was the River King's voice, sounding amplified and slightly distorted. "And if that soldier could take 99, how many can the great captain take? We have saved the best for last. Let's bring him out so we can see him close up."

Captain Grey was marched out of the cage to stand in front of the crowd. Jeers rained down on him. The king let the crowd express its savagery until a rock was thrown.

"Stop that! We can't have fair betting if he's injured. If you want to see more blood, you'll have to wait until tonight. In exactly eleven hours and twenty-eight minutes, you'll get all the blood you can handle."

"The best for last," Neil said, tears in his eyes, his face slack. "They've killed her. They killed my Sadie."

"And they'll pay," Jillybean said. There were no tears in her eyes; the ice in her soul was back and colder than ever.

Chapter 38

Neil Martin

By all rights, Neil should have been petrified. He was minutes from pitting his weak body and Jillybean's mind against four thousand of the most horribly evil people he had ever known to save Captain Grey.

He should have been afraid, but he was too tired and too angry and too bitter to be afraid. In the last year and a half, since the start of the apocalypse, almost everything he cherished had been taken from him.

All that he had left was his friendship with Captain Grey and his odd relationship with Jillybean. He knew she wanted a mom and a dad, or just one of them if she couldn't have the full set. And they both knew he was a natural father-figure and yet, they would never be father and daughter.

Strangely enough, it was because she didn't really need a father. She was so amazingly self-sufficient that he felt useless around her. He didn't feel like a dad and he sure as heck didn't act like a dad.

A real father wouldn't have let her within a hundred miles of Cape Girardeau, and he certainly wouldn't have let her plan the most dangerous escape attempt in the history of escape attempts.

The only father-like action he'd taken so far was to not utter a word of complaint, not even when she had tasked him with the hardest, most risky part. He was going to infiltrate the base while she stayed further back in a command center of sorts.

As she explained it: "I would do it but I can't carry as much as you can."

He had barely been able to carry everything she wanted, especially as he was forced to dress and act like a "monster." As monsters didn't carry anything, Jillybean had fashioned a drag harness attached to a sleigh. At first, as he slowly made his way around the outer part of the city, the sleigh hadn't been much of an issue but as the miles heaped up, he found himself staggering, with sweat pouring off of him in buckets.

It wasn't entirely out of place for him as a "monster" to be dragging odd items. He had once seen a zombie with a fisherman's net strung about him that was filled with all sorts of refuse, including another zombie. And he had personally outfitted three captured zombies with ankle chains. The trio, wearing matching vests, were currently trapped in a garage two blocks from the fence line. Next door were another three zombies, and these also had vests, but no chains. They were Jillybean's monster allies. She had a few thousand more in a warehouse complex a mile away chasing phantom voices that she had recorded, looped and was broadcasting with just enough strength to be heard in a five-block radius.

Strangely, perhaps because of the closeness of the river, there hadn't been *enough* zombies for Jillybean's needs. She had fretted over this, biting her lower lip raw until Neil had said: "The river is full of them. Too bad we can't get them out of there."

To which she had responded: "That's a brilliant idea, Mister Neil, sir. We can get them from the river!" Neil didn't want to lose the label of being "brilliant" and so didn't ask how they were going to get slime covered zombies up a slime covered embankment.

Her solution was to extend twenty foot long, buoyed aluminum ladders into the river where the bank was lowest. A battery operated blinking traffic light set in a tree attracted the zombies who used the ladders to pull themselves to shore and up the bank. She then set up more blinking lights to entice them to the warehouse and just like that she had her army.

Having so many zombies around made everything a little more perilous, but just a little. Neil felt himself becoming more and more accustomed to being around the beasts once again and as he moved around the outside of the base, lugging the sleigh, none of the other zombies gave him a second look, especially as his strength diminished and his voice grew hoarse.

It was after dark by the time he reached his first position atop a hundred foot cell tower. Using heavy military binoculars, he had an excellent view of the bleachers where Grey was scheduled to die. On the off chance that Jillybean's timetable could be moved up, he scanned the cage, but it was empty. The captain was still in the prison and wouldn't be moved until the last minute.

And that meant the timing would have to be precise.

Although Neil's part of the plan was dangerous, it was also relatively simple, while Jillybean's was devilishly tricky and if the timing was off by even four or five minutes, Captain Grey would be halfway to being dead before they could save him which would make everything that followed a hundred times more difficult.

Jillybean had only the unknown span of time between when Grey was handcuffed to the pole and when the first lash struck to begin her *initial* distraction.

Because of the depth of the defenses, she had to arrange two different distractions simply to give Neil a fighting chance to slip onto the base without being seen and or killed.

"Just a chance," he said, keying the send button on the radio once. It was their prearranged signal that let Jillybean know he was ready. "Just a chance, that's all I need…and a cup of hot cocoa." It was cold on the tower and, since there was no real reason to be up there just yet, he decided to climb back to the earth where it was a touch warmer, but one look straight down had his hands locking tight and his heart in his throat.

He hated heights, and he hated how the tower swayed in the wind and he hated how his hands would go instantly moist, making the metal slip under his now frightened grip.

A state of panic had him, but only for a moment, only until, for the hundredth time, he pictured the unknown soldier having his skin flayed off of him. The burn from that overcame his fear, in fact it turned it to ash in his mouth and he went down the ladder, hand over hand, with a snarl on his lips.

Once at the bottom, he uncovered the goods on the sled: an M4 with a 4x60 DN463 Generation 3 Night Vision Riflescope with Illuminated Mil-Dot Reticle, a drone equipped with both a video camera and the insides of a claymore mine wrapped in cellophane with a radio transmitted detonator, a three-pound hand sledge, and a mask, snorkel and fins that went with the wetsuit he wore under his clothes.

Slinging the rifle, he snuck through the dark to get as close as possible to the fence line. He crept to within a block of the fence where, in the middle of someone's backyard, he set the drone in the dirt and then flicked it to the ready/receive setting. Next, he reached out with a shaking hand and armed the detonator on the mine.

He slithered back and could feel the sweat cool on his face. It's not that he didn't trust Jillybean, it was just hard to be around any bomb, particularly one put together by a seven-year-old girl with zero military training. It had his heart going.

It was still thrumming as he pulled the sled east to the river's edge where the zombies drifted by making a soulful moan. It was a haunting sound which covered the noise he made as he turned left, once more trying to get as close as he could to the fence.

This time he couldn't get as close. The River King had erected a guard tower where the fence hit the water. Neil brought the binoculars up and saw two dark figures in the tower, one with a lit cigarette in the corner of his mouth and the other leaning against the butt-end of a machine gun.

Next to the gun was a searchlight that was only a very quick click away from illuminating everything on the river.

The sight of it gave Neil the shivers. "Pull it together, Neil. They won't be able to see you." He hoped. Even with his new-found hatred burning in him, bolstering his courage, it was hard to see how Jillybean's plan was going to work. These were trained soldiers he was up against and he was nothing more than Neil Martin—a nice guy and an all-around little wimp.

Before the apocalypse his weapons of battle had been the calculator, the laptop and the dreaded spreadsheet and with them he'd been feared in a way. Now he was armed to the teeth and yet no one feared him.

"This isn't going to work," he said. "I'm going to die tonight." He paused as if to allow his body to respond—it did. His heart rate slowed and the jittery feeling in his stomach vanished. "I'm going to die, but I guess I don't seem to mind. Funny."

It almost seemed like a part of him was looking forward to death. He shrugged at the idea, left the sled and its contents in the grass, and made his way back to the tower where there was really nothing for him to do but wait.

A check of his watch showed that he would have almost an hour to sit around doing nothing. In this regard, Jillybean was luckier than he was. She still had things to do to occupy her time. In fact she had too many things to do. Neil had wanted to stick around to help, but she insisted that a time cushion for him to get into position was necessary, just in case.

She was all about the "just in case" of every little detail. It should have been a comfort to Neil, knowing that everything that could be controlled was being controlled. But it wasn't a comfort. Despite all her planning and devices and schemes, the only thing that was guaranteed was that he had a *chance* to get on the base. After that it was up to him to find Grey, kill his guards, kill anyone who got in their way and get off the base again with it crawling with the River King's men who were likely going to be as angry as bees.

"Nothing could be easier," he said and settled into a comfortable position with his back to the cell tower.

At thirty minutes of nine, the radio in Neil's hand clicked once, just a soft, very brief fuzz sound. If anyone else was listening to that particular channel, they probably didn't even notice the sound, and if they had heard it, they probably weren't all that concerned. Radios always made little noises.

Still, if they had heard it and were concerned, there was not much they could do about it. Scanners needed time to operate. They needed to be able to triangulate the signal—and Jillybean was already moving.

Actually, she had been on the move since seeing the death of the soldier. She had set a feverish pace that had exhausted Neil and now the little click of the radio told Neil that she was beginning to move her zombie army into position.

According to the plan, she would switch off the recorded human noises in the warehouse complex and then turn on the string of hooded lights that ran from the warehouse to the fence line opposite a small stretch of woods.

The lights could only be seen from one angle and, they hoped, the woods would keep the army from being noticed until it was too late.

Once the lights were going, Jillybean would race back to the river to release the "aqua-drones" as she called them. Using lifejackets, balloons and styrofoam attached to 2x4s capped with a sheet of steel, they had created eight mini-barges that were little more than small floating platforms. Each held enough of the potassium nitrate mix to blanket the thousand foot wide river in an impenetrable bank of smoke.

Although Jillybean called them drones, they had no steering device or motor. They relied on the gentle current of the river to move them into place. Of course, the little genius had taken into account the river's speed and so the platforms were staggered along the river every seventy-five feet so that there would be enough smoke to last throughout the length of the operation.

Since Jillybean was so small, Neil had earlier pushed the platforms into the water. All she had to do was arm the thermal fuses and cut the ropes, letting the drones free. After cutting loose the eighth one, she would run *back* to the homes near the fence line where the six "monster drones" waited in their garages.

All that running around made Neil's job seem easy. He stood, limboed a few cracks from his back and began climbing the cell tower. When he reached the top he worked the binoculars over the growing crowd filling the bleachers. The place was already a mad house that he could hear from his perch.

A few minutes later, under a heavy guard, Captain Grey was brought through the opening and into the arena by the executioner who dragged him forward by a chain that ran to Grey's handcuffed hands. He was followed by the River King, who received a huge wave of applause.

"Oh, crap! He's early," Neil said, checking his watch: it was twenty to nine. The zombie army would still be a quarter of a mile away and Jillybean would be just releasing her "monster drones" from the garages. It would take at least ten minutes to walk them to the fence, where she would have to chain them into position, while at the same time fooling both the zombies and the guards into believing she was also just a little zombie—in other words, she couldn't hurry no matter how much Grey needed her to.

They had captured the "monster drones" earlier in the day, singling out the smallest ones they could find. Jilly had used her red dot scope to attract them into a house where they were tased repeatedly until they couldn't even stand. Neil had rendered them mostly harmless by duct-taping oven mitts onto their hands and wrapping more of the tape around their mouths.

Still they could be dangerous if they suspected the little girl was more than she appeared.

A cheer went up from the crowd, causing Neil to blink. Grey had just been chained into position and now his clothes were being cut away—It was happening too soon!

Neil keyed the radio, sending out three long pulses that he was sure would cause Jillybean to panic. Once the last pulse was sent, he raced down the ladder as The River King began the opening ceremony in his spectacle of death.

"Ladies and gentlemen, I give you the ringleader!" The crowd howled in a frenzy, stamping their feet on the metal bleachers, making the air thrum. The River King went on, his amplified voice carrying for miles: "Yes, this is the moment we have all been waiting for since this fiend blew up our bridge. This is the moment we have our revenge!"

More cheering, which Neil assumed signaled the beginning of the blood lust that would grip the crowd. He was on the ground by then and hurrying for the river, hoping to God that Jillybean had fired the remote thermal fuses—and that they worked.

She had tested *one*, proclaimed it good, and went on to make the rest. If they didn't work, Neil would be forced to choose between making the attempt without them or going home empty handed. "And that's not going to happen."

He would make the attempt no matter what. It's what Grey would do for him.

"Please," he whispered as he pushed through the last of the foliage and saw the river…the wide open and very clear river.

Chapter 39

Neil Martin

Behind him, the River King proclaimed that the betting would end in five minutes. Neil, who had kicked off his shoes and was now struggling to get the first fin on his foot, checked his watch. That they were still early by five minutes could spell the difference between failure and success.

Another glance at the river showed him it was still flat and empty, save, that is, for the hundreds of zombies Neil would have to maneuver around.

"Come on Jillybean," he begged. The first flipper was on and there was no smoke. The same with the second. He wanted to call her using the radio, but he couldn't take the chance. What if she was surrounded by a hundred zombies? What if she was still too close to the fence line? What if she had already been caught?

The answer to that was the easiest: "I'll free her, too."

He left the binoculars on the shore. The M4 went on his back. The three thousand dollar scope and the ten dollar radio went into a baggy and that went into the small pack he wore on his back. There were different compartments in the pack and each was filled with bombs, detonators, and extra ammo.

It was a heavy pack and the three-pound sledge only made it more so. Unwanted buoyancy wasn't going to be a problem, but then again, neither was actually swimming. The fins would do their job at least for the hundred and twenty yards he'd have to traverse.

His point of entry onto the base was a rainwater drainage pipe that emptied into the Mississippi. It was well within sight of the guard tower, and was very likely barred in some fashion. Since they would have only minutes to complete the rescue, the bars would have to be blown off—thus the need for smoke to keep him from getting killed two seconds after the explosion.

But still no smoke as the River King cried: "It's time! We are going for a record here, folks. Let's see if our spy can endure a hundred and…"

Neil ducked beneath the water where everything was dark and murky. He blundered forward, gently kicking with his legs.

A hundred and twenty yards was not far, however the three mile an hour current running straight into him didn't help.

He kept his arms in, streamlining his body and pumped with his legs: up and down, over and over. After a few minutes, he poked his head up to get his bearings, hoping he hadn't accidentally turned to the east. Somehow, he was still on course and was halfway to the pipe and still the river was clear. In the background of the moans and his own heavy breathing, he heard the crowd cheering.

Again, he went down beneath the water with only his back and the snorkel showing, knocking against a zombie who had no idea what Neil was. It didn't stop to find out. Neil scooted away, huffing and puffing through the snorkel, his legs beginning to burn. He had to stop a second time and now his mask was fogged over and he couldn't tell which way was where.

When he lifted it up, however, he found that the mask was fine—it was the smoke obscuring his vision. It was finally creeping downriver! Behind him and to his left, he could hear the guards in the tower whispering to each other. They thought it was fog and it did have that gentle white appearance. But no fog Neil had ever seen grew so hugely thick so quickly.

Before he could duck down again, an alarm began to ring out, further up river. Perhaps one of the barges had been spotted through the smoke, or someone had caught the scent of it. There was no mistaking the smell for fog.

Neil didn't bother going under again. The smoke was all around him now and he had to push on to the pipe before someone turned on the searchlight and saw him…too late!

A harsh white light swept over him but didn't stop. Just as Jillybean had foreseen, the guards assumed that whatever attack was coming would come from the same direction as the smoke. The spotlight blazed straight into the white…uselessly. Just like with real fog, bright light was reflected and refracted, but did not penetrate it.

Seconds later, Neil was at the pipe and saw that there were indeed bars across it. Quickly he yanked off the fins and the mask, dug through the pack for a previously prepared C4 charge and pressed it into position on the top and bottom of two of the bars.

He then moved around to the other side of the pipe, prayed that the C4 wouldn't just blow the entire thing to smithereens and him with it, covered his ears and pressed the detonator.

The explosion sent a shockwave through him and it felt as though he was pushed and pulled in two different directions. He was still lying there in the mud next to the pipe when the gunner in the guard tower opened up with his M240.

He was firing blind, but still his aim was ridiculously on mark. Bullets smacked into the pipe, whining off its rounded cement surface. They withered the air above Neil's head, then slapped into the mud by his feet and danced across the water.

Guards all up and down the river were blasting into the fog as if they were being attacked by a marine regiment. Neil found himself pinned down, unable to move due to the volume of shooting. It was staggering in its ferocity.

He knew that eventually he would be struck either by a ricocheting bullet or through a lucky hit by one of the guards. And he was thinking about crawling towards the open end of the pipe when Jillybean unleashed the second distraction. The three vest-wearing zombies she had chained to the outer fence were each carrying thirty pounds of C4 a piece.

When Jillybean hit the detonator, the zombies evaporated in a great triple explosion: WHAM! WHAM! WHAM!

Seventy yards of fence went with them as well. The plan was to detonate the bombs just ahead of the zombie army. There was a second fence twenty yards further in that had probably been damaged by the first explosion and yet, in true Jillybean fashion, she wasn't going to take the chance.

Mixed in with the forefront of the zombie army were the three other "unchained" monster drones, each with a glow-stick tied into their hair. To monitor them, Jillybean had one of the flying drones up by then.

Neil foolishly glanced upward and of course saw only smoke. "Stupid," he muttered. The word sounded, in his concussed ears, as if he had spoken it into a tin can. He worked his jaw around hearing an odd clicking and it was then that he noticed that the firing around him had slacked off enough for him to try to crawl into the pipe.

The C4 had fractured the cement and had taken out three bars instead of two. Neil crawled through the debris in the three foot pipe, only remembering his flashlight after he was thirty feet into the tunnel.

He also remembered his radio. He stuck the wired ear-bud in and then yelled: "Jillybean! Jillybean! Are you there? I'm in the pipe."

"Cat, this is mouse. I copy that. Please use our code-names, okay? over."

"Oh, right. Sorry about that. When will you have eyes up? I'm worried…" Two tremendous but distant explosions puffed the air in and out of the pipe as if a giant was sucking on the end of it like it was a cigarette. "Jil…I mean Mouse. Was that you?"

There was a second of delay before she came on with a curt: "Yes." The way she said the one terse word, it was clear she wanted to add: *who else would it have been?* "I'll have eyes on your location in two mins. out."

That was Neil's cue to hurry. He had to get to the fourth manhole cover before her helicopter drone did. Because the drones had such a limited battery life, seconds counted. Neil huffed down the wet pipe going on his hands and knees as fast as he could, but still she beat him by about twenty seconds.

"It's clear! It's clear!" she cried through the radio. "But you better hurry. People are coming from the execution site on the run."

Neil redoubled his efforts, going as fast as he could and wishing he had thought about knee pads. He was cringing by the time he got to the fourth cover. He scrambled onto his side to get the hand-sledge out of the pack and when he did, he smashed it upwards with both hands. It made a sound like a lead gong as one end of the cover jumped up a tiny bit. Without hesitation, he struck it twice more, loosening it. With a deep breath, he gathered himself beneath the cover and thrust upwards.

It was ridiculously heavy, far more so than he had expected. With his frame of reference only what he had seen in movies, he was quite unprepared for the hundred and ten pounds that the cover weighed. Straining with all his might, he was able to move it halfway off before he gave up and scrambled out.

"Go to your right!" Jillybean's voice crackled through the earbud attached to the radio.

A secret agent with nerves of steel would have slid to the right without hesitation. Neil was just a normal, if not timid guy. His first impulse was to look at the radio in his left hand; his next was to glance upwards to see whether the drone was really there and not hovering over some random stranger. Only when Jillybean begged: "To your right, please," did he move, ducking behind a van parked on the side of the road.

A moment later, five armed men raced past; in the dark, none of them noticed the partially open manhole cover.

337

"My batteries are running down," Jillybean said. "I have another drone on the way, but it'll be a minute before I can link up with you. Just stay where you are."

"No. Find Grey and direct me to him. I'll be fine on my own."

She hesitated a moment before giving him an "A-firmative. There's gonna be a 'splosion up ahead. That's just me. I don't wanna waste a perfectly good bomb."

He had been hurrying in the direction of the outdoor arena, but now he slowed and once more glanced upwards, scanning the dark sky for a drone that was difficult to see in the bright light of day. His head was still up and his eyes straining when there came another explosion—this one just two blocks away. The light of it was a strobe that showed people going in every direction.

The thunder of the explosion rolled over the base, but it was quickly drowned out by screams that echoed up and down the streets. Neil found himself drawn to the site of the explosion. In the dark the blood looked black. The strewn bodies and parts of bodies were chilling the way they just lay there, looking extremely white as if they were made from fish belly and not flesh.

Some of the fleeing people stopped to help the crying wounded, but many others simply ran around the dark pools and the bodies and the mewling creatures crawling here and there.

Neil's first impulse was to help, but he forced himself away. He had to remind himself that these weren't just helpless civilians caught in the crossfire of war, these were his enemies. These were vile humans, who, up until three minutes before, had been cheering the torturous murder of his friend.

He ducked around the next block, hoping to skirt around the scene, and ran straight into a pair of men, both of whom had grim faces of chiseled shadow. One shone a light into Neil's eyes as the other demanded: "Who the hell are you?"

They were fierce and hard soldier-types and Neil had to wonder what he looked like to them in his shredded up and mud-soaked "monster" clothes; a bedraggled rat of a man, probably. Then he wondered what they were expecting from their enemies. If it were Neil under attack, his mind would immediately conjure up images of hardy, virile, special forces operatives, able to kill in a blink. Pretty much the opposite of Neil.

The only question: were the two men hampered by the same paradigm?

As the two men had drawn pistols, while Neil's weapon was still across his shoulders, he decided to gamble on human nature. In a blink, he changed his look from shocked surprise to cringing and miserable.

"There was a bomb!" he practically screamed as he pointed vaguely away. "There was a bomb and blood and people screaming. It was right there. It…it almost got me, I think. I was right there and then suddenly there was a flash and…"

"You look fine," one of the men growled, as the pair pushed past Neil. "Get to your battle station."

They bought it! Neil thought, relief sweeping him. In order to reinforce the paradigm, he whined: "What is it? Are we under attack? Are we under attack? Is that what all that shooting is?"

They didn't answer, they just ran off into the dark as another explosion thundered in the direction of where the zombie army was sweeping onto the base.

Neil turned in the opposite direction, heading south, dodging people running in the dark. He had gone only a few blocks when Jillybean came over the radio: "They're on the highway! They just passed Middle Street. Where are you?"

"Sprigg Street," Neil said and began running, pulling his M4 from his back. "How many are with him?"

"Thirteen."

Thirteen! He felt like screaming the word. This impulse was followed up by the very rational mental question: *How on earth am I going to take on thirteen trained soldiers?*

No answer came to him. His realistic mind couldn't even throw out the word: luck. If he lived through a minute of the coming fight, he'd count himself lucky. If he lived through two minutes, it would be a miracle. However, it would be downright impossible to actually be victorious against these odds. Even Captain Grey in his prime couldn't have done it.

The only person Neil thought had any chance was Jillybean and she was half a mile away…sort of.

"Okay, Cat, I have you on screen. Hang a right on Jefferson. There you go. If you hurry, you can catch them before they get to those buildings up ahead. They are on Ash and they'll pass you on the west."

Neil raced past stragglers and soldiers and men leading women on chains. He couldn't worry about them. The fact that they weren't hurrying to where two different "gun battles" were going on suggested that they were cowards. They would run when Neil started shooting.

After a hundred and thirty yard sprint, Neil was out of breath as he got to the buildings which had been the headquarters for a company called *Southeast Missouri Builders Supply Co*. There were three warehouses and a single story run of office suites. Neil slipped up to the largest of the warehouses; it was a rectangle that butted up against Ash Street.

A glance down the road showed a group heading his way. At first it was hard to tell who was who, but as they drew closer the tactical situation firmed up: two guards, armed with what looked like M16s, walked in front of the main group, preceding them by twenty yards; two more guards were in the back, just fifteen feet from the group; two were on the right side of the road and two were on the left.

In the middle was the River King, screaming into a two-way radio. Next to him was the executioner, leading a bleeding and dazed, looking Captain Grey by a chain, and two more men, both of whom openly carried pistols.

Neil ducked back into the shadows of the warehouse, dug out his fancy scope and fumbled it into place as the men hurried past. Trying to remember everything Grey had ever taught him, Neil thumbed his weapon to fire and peered into the scope seeing a line of red-lasered light stretching out to prick the guard on the furthest right—he was close to a doorway and if he didn't go down first, he'd just duck into it.

A breath went in and Neil held it, his finger on the trigger. Once again, a part of him knew he should have been pissing his pants in fear, but that part had pissed too many pants and the feeling had grown thin.

A pull of the trigger and the gun jumped in his hands. He was partially deafened by the sound as well as partially blinded by the sudden piercing white bloom in the scope, but that didn't stop him from shifting the M4 slightly to the left and firing three times, hoping that he was on target.

Normally, he would have ducked back behind the building where it was "safe," but when the odds were thirteen to one, there was no such thing as safe. Instead of ducking, he shifted the weapon even further left. This time, however, he waited for the scope to clear enough for him to fire.

It was a pause of only a second and a half, but in that time his enemies were falling all over themselves in an attempt to present less of a target. They also began shooting, but if they were shooting at Neil they weren't good shots. Neil had been shot at before and could tell that the whisper of the passing lead wasn't within five feet of him.

That second and a half of being exposed felt like five minutes, but finally the scope cleared enough to show him the two men on the left scrambling to get over a low fence. Neil fired and knew he hit the first man, however the scope blared white and he couldn't be certain where his next four shots went, but there was a cry, followed by an entire barrage that had Neil leaping back behind the corner of the building.

It was aluminum sided and the sound of the bullets smacking into the metal was like the loudest hail that Neil had ever heard. It almost drowned out Jillybean who was saying: "…circling around the building trying to get behind you."

For a moment, he felt the normal panic that he was used to, and he spun expecting to see a bad guy creeping around the far corner. But there was no one and there couldn't have been anyone. The building was too large for someone to try to "zip" around it in three seconds.

Neil ran for the far corner while behind him the guards were firing like mad, turning the edge of the warehouse he had just abandoned into Swiss cheese.

In seconds, he was at the corner. When he peeked around the edge, he saw nothing. The shadows here were too intense. Hoping that his own shadow was equally dark, Neil brought up the rifle and slid partially around the corner.

The guard showed up as a lighter shadow, greyish, with glowing eyes. He had his weapon up but he wasn't sighting along its iron sights. Neil could kill him easily—if only he could control his breathing. *He* wasn't afraid, but no one had told his body.

His breath was going in and out as if he had run a hundred yard dash, which he had not thirty seconds before. And his hands were shaking with excess adrenaline, making the sights jitter. He took a deep calming breath, and then another and then he said: "Fuck it," and fired until his gun clicked empty.

He turned on the spot to go back, but Jillybean said, "No, the other way. They're trying to leave. You have to cut them off."

That required more running. Neil took a wide path around the man he had shot at in the back of the building, keeping his gun pointed at the body, which moved only an arm, groping in the dark, perhaps for a lost weapon, perhaps trying to find the life leaking out of him.

Only when he was past, did Neil run for the end of the building, his pack *clinking* on his back, reminding him that there were extra magazines in the pack—and that he was empty. "Oh, jeeze," he whispered and dug out two magazines; one went into his gun, the other into his coat pocket for easy access.

When he got to the next corner of the building, Jillybean said: "Throw a grenade into the street, just make sure to lollypop it so it doesn't go over."

"A grenade? Give me a second."

"You don't have a grenade?" she hissed. "Neil, what are you doing? This is real serious." It was weird to be guilted by a seven-year-old and he found himself grinding his teeth as he fished about in the pack for a grenade. Before he could find one, Jillybean said. "I've got this. Don't get too close."

Knowing what sort of bombs she possessed, Neil dropped to the ground and covered his ears just as the night turned white then orange, then a Halloween color that was the stuff of nightmares.

"Go!" she cried into the radio, not realizing that his ears were ringing as if someone had stuck his head into a garbage can and then beat it with a baseball bat. She was right to tell him to move in. The River King's men had to be feeling it worse than Neil. They had to be thinking that the attacks were coming from every direction.

Neil dragged himself forward, the scope clear at his eye. Clear but jittering as he came up to the street. He almost didn't need it. There was a fire in the weeds on the side of the road that lit the street enough for Neil to see the bodies. There were three of them, mangled and ripped apart.

And the others were sprawled in a clump next to the side of the warehouse.

Who was who? Neil looked from shadowed body to shadowed body, uncertain what he was seeing. There was gore and guts and blood strewn like party streamers and the living were so drenched in it all that Neil couldn't tell friend from foe.

One of the wretched chum-covered beings fired a pistol at him. The man's pistol wavered uncertainly in his hand and his shots went high and wide. Still, Neil jumped back, using the building as cover.

"They're getting up," Jillybean said. "They're…they're… one just ran west. Now they're all going west."

Neil rushed around the side of the building, ran across the street, and paused at the fence. His hands were full: gun in one, grenade in the other. He began to shove the grenade away when someone started shooting at him from behind.

It was one of the guards he had thought he had killed. Neil dropped down into the gutter and fired blindly in the general direction of his attacker as more bullets came his way, passing uncomfortably close, flying inches over his head.

The two traded a few more shots before they each realized they were at an impasse. Twenty-five feet and a gentle hump in the road separated them, but since they were both in the gutters neither had a good angle and the bullets passed harmlessly by. Neil lifted his M4 to give him the required angle to shoot but before he could pull the trigger, a bullet smashed into the side of his gun.

The impact zinged through the metal so that it felt like an electric shock and the gun toppled out of his hands to thump him on the head. "Ow! Son of a bitch," Neil swore, feeling both anger and shame—he was sure this sort of thing never happened to Captain Grey.

"You missed me!" Neil cried and then rolled on his side, grabbed the grenade, pulled the pin and tossed it across the street. There was a moment where the night seemed strangely quiet and then there came another head-splitting explosion. It was so close that Neil felt as though he was lifted off the ground.

As debris rained down all around him, he shook his head. There was an echo inside of him that rumbled around his skull, making it difficult to think. Slowly, Neil got up on wobbly legs and glanced at the man who had been shooting at him, but couldn't see him through the pall of dust and smoke that hung in the air.

"Sorry," he muttered, and turned away to try to mount the fence. It was too much for him in his state and he started a slow jog towards the end of it.

"Cat, this is Mouse. They're on Archer Street, going slower now. It's two blocks over. One of them entered a building on the corner. I think he's hurt, but be careful."

"Roger that," he said and tried to pick up the pace, but he was feeling ragged and a little sick to his stomach. As he got to Archer, he stayed on the far side of the street where the trees hung heavily over the road, their canopies blocking the view from the building Jillybean had mentioned.

Unfortunately, it blocked her view as well. "Cat, I can't see you or them. You should be close." Neil tried to use the fancy scope on his rifle to pick out the River King and his men, however when he put it to his eye, it was straight black

"What the hell?" he whispered. The scope was broken. The bullet which struck his gun had kicked off of it and now glass rattled uselessly inside.

He bit back a curse and began slinking along. The dark beneath the trees was like velvet, hiding his enemies, and it was a moment before his eyes adjusted. By the time they did, he was in their midst.

The River King stood ten feet away, a guard at his side. To Neil's left was the executioner and another guard. The executioner was a giant of a man and at his feet was Captain Grey, the blood on him catching the starlight and shining slightly.

They saw Neil at about the same time as he saw them. Both the River King and the guard fired their guns in a brief burst. The sudden firing shocked Neil and he froze as the bullets sped past him, missing by inches. His shock turned into amazement that he was still alive and it was with shaking hands that he fired back.

Two bullets struck the guard who went down with a cry and one bullet missed the River King—and then Neil ran out of ammo.

He wasn't the only one. The River King's men had not been ready for a fire-fight and they had burned through their ammo. The king himself had a second magazine and as Neil fumbled in his pocket for his own ammo, the king calmly slapped his fresh magazine home.

"Stop," he growled, "or I will shoot you. I'll shoot you in the gut. You know, to keep you alive and in pain."

Neil stopped one hand in his pocket—the wrong pocket. This one held the radio. In his fumbling, he had pulled the wire from it and now it crackled: "Cat? What's going on? I saw flashes."

"That's that little bitch, isn't it?" the king snarled, coming closer. "And you're Neil-fucking-Martin. I should have known and I should have killed you a long time ago. Any last words?"

The pistol was pointed square into Neil's face and once more he was altogether without fear. He had fought his fight and he had fought well and the truth was, he wasn't at all afraid of dying.

Chapter 40

Captain Grey

Grey had walked into the outdoor arena spiritually and mentally drained. He had watched his entire squad brutally tortured to death; unlike Sadie, who had closed her eyes, he had forced himself to watch. He had led his men into the simple trap to begin with and he deserved to feel as much of their pain as he could take.

His own pain would be less than theirs. Not only had he not eaten or drunk anything in the last day and a half, he had also exercised past the point of exhaustion and to a level where his body could no longer produce a drop of sweat.

A man could go three days without water and although it had only been a day and a half, he was so dangerously dehydrated that he could hardly stand and he feared he wouldn't be able to make it to the arena.

He had to summon all of his energy just to make the walk— he was regretting his plan now. With an attack occurring on a scale that suggested there was at least a battalion of soldiers out there, Grey wished he was at full strength.

Not that he could do much with his hands cuffed in front of him. Still, as he was dragged through the streets he had looked for an opportunity to escape. Unfortunately, the executioner kept him on a leash like a dog. Seven feet of heavy chain kept him from getting away.

And perhaps more unfortunate was the discovery of who was behind the attack. "You brought Jillybean here?" Grey demanded before Neil could make his final statement. "What were you thinking? My life is not worth hers or yours."

"But what about Sadie's?" Neil snapped. "Both Jillybean and I loved her. I loved her like a *father*."

"Is that supposed to sting?" the River King asked. "Because it really doesn't. The truth is Neil, you were a horrible father. You turned her against me and worse, you turned her against reality. She was living in a dream world where everything was ice cream and cotton candy. But now she's getting some tough love. She's going to learn some valuable life lessons in New York."

"New York? Do you mean she's alive?"

Grey answered: "She went out as a slave with some eastbound traders this morning. You should have gone after her."

The River King grinned wickedly and cocked the pistol. "You really should have. You might have lived."

"Wait!" Neil cried. "What about my last words? They'll be short, I promise. Here goes: the street is wide open. Just drop down and head straight in. I'll tell you when to stop."

The king's eyes glittered with sudden fear. "What are you talking about?"

"Just that," Neil pointed as a small machine hummed down the street. Grey was taken aback to see it was a four-engine helicopter that, if not for the bomb hanging beneath it, looked like a toy. "Jillybean is controlling that and she has no problem releasing the bomb and killing all of us."

"It's true," her little voice said over the radio. Neil pulled the radio out as she went on. "You are evil, Mister River King, sir, and that's what means you should die if you don't let my friends go. And I think we all know I'll do it."

The River King was backing up from the machine, the gun now pointing at it instead of Neil. "Look. You can have them. They're nothing to me. Just call off the rest of the attack."

"Put down the gun," Jillybean ordered.

"But how do I know you'll keep your word..."

The River King had continued to back up and now he was fifteen feet away. "Hey, stop moving!" Neil ordered. The king did the opposite. He turned and ran, dashing across the street and into a house.

Jillybean's copter hesitated, not knowing what to do. "Get the River King!" Grey commanded. He knew that if the king got away there would be no escape for any of them.

The drone buzzed off toward the house with every eye following it—every eye but Captain Grey's. With Jillybean's bomb gone, Neil out of ammo and his owns hands cuffed, Grey saw that things could go from bad to worse if he didn't act in the next half-second.

He pivoted and snapped a roundhouse kick square into the executioner's throat, sending him reeling back. It hadn't been the fastest or strongest kick of his life, but it did the trick. Skinner dropped his axe and the chain, his hands going to his throat.

To Grey's left, Neil and the last guard were slower to react. They both watched Grey's first kick and then his second, a driving front kick that whooshed the air out of Skinner.

Then something must have clicked and the two charged each other. Neil was at a great disadvantage in size, speed, strength, skill, and training, and yet, he was full of holy, righteous anger and taking the M4 in his hands like a club, he swung it with all of his might. Grey wasn't surprised when he missed.

Neil spun in a circle, looking like a complete moron. Still, he was smarter than he looked and he didn't bother checking the spin he had thrown himself into and came around faster than the guard expected. Before he knew it the rifle was at him in a second wild swing. This time Neil connected and the guard let out a howl.

Grey didn't see where the blow landed. He was too busy with Skinner who was a giant of a man whom he guessed had to weigh over three hundred pounds. The front kick had felt as though he had kicked an elephant in the side and already the man was recovering. He lunged at Grey with both hands, each the size of dinner plates.

Regardless of his mass, had this been a fair fight, Grey would have won, easily. Perhaps because of his size, the giant was slow and lumbering, telegraphing his moves in advance. Grey dodged to the side, flailing with the chain to keep the man at bay.

He had to keep the metal flashing in the dim light. It was basically useless at rest. Skinner knew this too and he kept just out of reach, waiting for Grey to tire or make a mistake.

Grey tried his best to connect with the heavy chain but it was an imprecise weapon that required perfect timing. Five times he swung and five times he missed. In the breather before his next attempt, he glanced over at Neil and saw that the smallest man there was already down, with the guard on top.

"Son of a bitch!" Grey cursed and swung the seven-foot chain. This time he purposely made the swing so obvious that Skinner would have plenty of time to react.

He stepped back out of range and instead of following up the attack, Grey whipped the chain over his head in a blur and charged the oblivious guard who was busy pummeling Neil senseless.

As the guard was a stationary target, Grey couldn't miss and smacked the chain into his head, the end breaking the guard's cheek bone and ripping off a chunk of his face. Grey could only hope that was good enough because Skinner had rushed in as Grey tried to get the chain moving again.

The executioner wouldn't let him; he came on swinging monster haymakers, each as heavy as sledgehammers. One punch landed awkwardly in the dark, striking Grey on the side of the neck—he went sprawling from the force of the blow.

Right then would have been a perfect time for Skinner to leap on Grey and pound him into bloody chuck, however, the executioner had found his axe and he picked it up with a grin on his face. "I kilt all yo pussy soldiers and now I'm gonna kill you. You gonna whine and cry like them?"

Grey's strength had been sagging, but Skinner's vile words revived him enough to make one final push. He swung the chain at Skinner, and so useless had his previous attempts been, that he didn't care if the chain hit or not. The metal blur was only a distraction for his real attack, a second front kick, this one delivered with the entire weight of his two-hundred pounds behind it.

Skinner had been confident when he spoke, but he had also been winded. Fighting was an exhausting business and Grey knew if he could land a few more good kicks, and not die in the next thirty seconds, that Skinner would be reeling. The heavy axe would feel as though it weighed a hundred pounds instead of twenty-five.

The kick landed with a thud that almost jarred Grey's femur out of its socket. He stumbled while Skinner stepped back, folding inwards from the force of the blow. The axe came down where it was far less of a threat. Grey danced to his right, and then lunged in, not bothering to feint with the chain.

He went for Skinner's knee, hoping to get in a crippling shot but missing by the barest of margins and only managing to wobble the giant who swung his axe backhanded, driving Grey away.

Again, Grey went right. The axe was most effective moving from the right to the left in the natural swing of a right-handed person. He feinted twice with aborted lunges as Skinner's breath grew heavier and heavier. Grey also kept the chain going in slow circles, getting more and more of a feel for the weapon.

Each time the metal whirred by, Skinner leapt back. He was slowing, Grey noted and worse for the giant, he was reacting only when the chain passed his nose. His reactions had slowed by half a second and Grey took full advantage.

With the next pass of the chain. Grey stepped very close, betting his life that Skinner would again take a step back. Almost as though they were dancing, the pair move in sync with Grey a foot closer and instead of the chain passing harmlessly by, it whipped into Skinner's face smacking him across the bridge of the nose.

Blood splashed as Skinner cried out, flailing with the axe, one-handed while the other went to his suddenly gushing nose.

Grey went with another kick, stepping in, inches from the axe to land another ferocious blow to Skinner's wide open midsection. It folded the man square in half giving Grey a beautiful shot with the chain on the top of Skinner's head.

The horrible beast of a man collapsed at Grey's feet, the deadly executioner's axe dropping with a clang on the street. Grey picked it up. With his hands cuffed together, it was an awkward weapon and yet he felt the need to administer some much-needed revenge as well as a little poetic justice with it.

"You deserve far worse," Grey said and hefted the axe above his head.

It was then that the last guard ordered Grey to: "Put it down! Put it down nice and slow."

Neil had lost his fight. He laid on the ground groaning, bleeding as badly as Grey and Skinner were. The guard had a few scratches and a dangling arm from where Neil had hit it with the rifle, but he was more or less whole and he stood with Neil's M4 in his good hand, having slapped a fresh magazine into place.

Grey appraised the situation and saw that he had lost. He was twelve feet from the guard. He would need cheetah speed to close the distance before he was blown away. "You can kill me if you want, but Skinner dies."

"Okay, sure, but he's not the only one who can whip a man to death," the guard said, nodding to himself. "When I bring you two in, the king will probably let me do it. I can be the new *Skinner*."

"That would be a neat trick, seeing as you'll be dead." Grey pointed at Neil. "He's got a second grenade."

In a blink, the guard swiveled the gun to Neil, who only had the strength and the wit to roll over and was now blowing blood bubbles up at the sky. Even with the dark, it was clear that his hands were empty.

"He doesn't have a…" the guard said just as Grey threw the unwieldy axe. A movie version of Grey would have had him splitting the guard's head open, followed by the cheesy line: *Who axed you?*

The actual version saw him missing horribly. The heavily weighted end spun directly at the street and sparked off of it, seven feet from the guard! It clanged with a harsh, embarrassing sound and then whizzed past the guard, who was shocked and frightened at first, but then laughed as the axe handle hit Neil causing his moans to grow louder.

"That was pathetic…" the guard began to say but couldn't finish his sentence as Grey came flying at him. He hadn't expected a miracle with the axe. The best he had hoped for was a distraction and it had been lucky that Neil had been hit. It had given him that extra half-second that allowed Grey to close the distance.

He couldn't take the chance on a kick. He had to get close and stay close. If he gave the guard any room, he'd have the gun turned on him in a flash. Grey crumpled the man with a flying knee to the midsection. An inch higher and the guard would have had his diaphragm paralyzed. Still it was a heavy shot and in a fraction of a second, the two of them were down and grappling.

Despite of having his hands cuffed, Grey was easily the better fighter, able to use his legs to deadly effect even while he was flat on his back. For him it was the perfect position to put the guard in a simple jiu-jitsu move called the "triangle." It was a choke hold using the strength of the thighs to crush inward on an opponent's throat, and Grey's thighs had lost little muscle during his long convalescence.

In seconds, the guard was unconscious and seconds after that, he was dead. Grey did not extend mercy to a person who wanted to be the next "Skinner." Rolling the dead guard off of him, Grey went to the axe and hefted it. Somehow it felt even heavier as he advanced on the real Skinner who was still out cold. It took Grey two tries to separate the pumpkin-sized head from its beefy shoulders.

Exhausted, Grey crumpled down next to the body, but did not say a prayer. Skinner didn't deserve it and Grey didn't have the strength. He hadn't stopped bleeding since the whipping and now his head began to spin.

"Please don't pass out," he whispered as he dug in the folds of Skinner's odd wrappings. The huge man had the key to the cuffs somewhere on his person and yet, there was so much of him and the key was very small that Grey simply couldn't find it.

Giving up, he fell forward and rested his head on his arms which were propped up on Skinner's barrel of a chest. Blood came off of him in trickles and ran onto Skinner's corpse. He didn't care.

"Try this," Neil said, in a slurry whisper from behind him. Neil held a tiny silver key in his right hand. The hand swayed back and forth just as Neil did. He looked like he had been through hell and when a new explosion flashed in the night, he didn't even blink.

"Jillybean," he whispered and dropped the key. It tinkled on the ground and Grey searched for it with dull eyes as Neil went to find his radio. "Did you get him?" he asked.

Her voice, such a small thing that Grey pictured her as a four year old sitting at a school desk, whispering into a radio: "No, I was really, really close," she said. "I'm getting another drone."

Neil began shaking his head. "No. Forget the River King. We need you to guide us out of here. We're basically defenseless."

"But…what he did, Mister…sir," she answered, the radio cutting in and out. "He's real…evil. He has to die…Ipes thinks so."

For once, Grey had to agree with the stuffed toy. His heart felt black as he pictured the River King still alive, still king and still killing whoever he wanted. He had to die.

Neil added a different perspective. "Yes, but think about who would replace him—everyone here is evil. It'll be the same no matter who's in charge. And besides, Sadie is still alive. She has a day's head start and we can't rescue her if we're dead. Remember, Jillybean, life is more precious than death."

"I can have both," she said, curtly. "I have one more bomb."

Neil glanced over at Grey who had just managed to twist one of his hands around to get the key in the lock. He let the cuffs fall away saying: "Can we get off the base without her help?"

"No. I might pass as a blast victim, but we can't take the chance that someone will recognize you. Look." He pointed to where dozens of people were rushing about with flashlights. They were stopping everyone they ran into.

Seeing the lights, Grey felt his energy draining from him. He couldn't fight his way off base with one rifle, a handful of bullets, and a head that wouldn't stop spinning. "Yeah," was all he could say.

"Grey's on board, Jillybean. Your first priority is to guide us out of here. Do you copy?"

There was a long pause before she said, "I copy. I guess I won't be needing this bomb."

"Hold on," Neil said, "where do you plan on dropping..." The night went white once more and Grey squinted into the glare, enjoying the light that burned into his dark eyes. A grim smile played on his face as he watched the light bloom a second time, turning orange and then black.

"You got a fuel truck?" Neil asked.

"That's a-firmnative." There was a second explosion and then a third. "Oh, that...makes three of them...if they don't do... quick, they're going...Oh, too late." A fourth explosion thundered the night.

The light reached up to the stars and from where they stood they could see half the base; it was crawling with people, some running towards the fires, some running away.

To the east, the entire sky was filled, horizon to horizon with smoke. To the north, there was a battle raging. With all the explosions and the variety of weapons in use, Grey couldn't tell that it was a zombie on human battle. He figured that Neil and Jillybean hadn't come alone. And since he was the last person alive who needed rescuing, he felt he had to get off the base to keep their losses to a minimum.

"Let's go," Grey said. When he bent over to pick up the M4, his head spun and he almost fell over. Neil had to catch him and of course they did fall over then. Neil had blood trickling from both nostrils and one eye. There was blood in the cracks of his teeth.

"Sorry," he said and then struggled to stand. "It's...it's... Uh, Jillybean? Which way is the pipe? Jillybean? Jillybean? Where are you?"

It was a moment before she answered: "Turn around and go south and then take your first left. Stay close to the houses on the right. Okay, you're on Jefferson, so go left. Be careful. There's some people coming up the next block on Fredrick Street."

Grey hesitated and then went to the last guard. "Help me, will you?" He began tugging the man's clothes off. Grey was naked and the whip marks were painful and obvious. He couldn't walk around like that and expect to remain free. In a minute, he was dressed and stumbling along with Neil.

"Hide!" Jillybean suddenly said. "Go to your right."

The night was noisy with flames and gunshots and the two men didn't hear the guards coming around the corner. At Jillybean's warning, Grey pulled Neil down next to a jutting cement porch and watched six men hurry by. They were armed and pointed their guns at everything that moved and there was a lot moving, too much going on to pay attention to every shadow in the fire-lit night.

The group of six came on another group who had been coming up behind Grey and Neil, and before they knew it, the two groups were shooting at each other. It was mayhem. In fact, the entire base was in chaos with new fire-fights springing up everywhere.

"How many people did you bring with you?" Grey asked. "Wait! You didn't bring Deanna with you, did you? Because if you did, so help me…"

"No, it's just me and Jillybean. Speaking of which, where the hell is she?" While Neil attempted to raise Jillybean on the radio, Grey sat up slightly to stare in awe at the utter chaos caused by the mad genius of one little girl. It was amazing.

Finally, after a minute of repeating her name, Jillybean came on in a breathless whisper: "Just go around the house. There's no one back there. And I'd go through the next backyard if I was you guys."

"Roger that. Keep us posted." They went around the house and both men were nearly stymied by a six foot tall fence. Neil tried to mount it first, his feet scrambling against the wood without finding purchase. After ten seconds, he let go of the fence and stared at his hands which were crooked like an old woman's.

Grey didn't laugh at the sad display and nor did he try to climb the fence. It seemed too much for him just at the moment. Instead, he grabbed one of the planks and pulled with all his strength. When there was a slight gap, Neil got his fingers in and pulled as well. The board came off with a screech that was lost in the noise of all the shooting. They had to pull a second plank away before they could stumble through the backyard.

They were almost too far gone to care who was around them and they tramped through the next yard without looking left or right, both stumbling with exhaustion.

Jillybean was silent when they got to the next street. With the coast relatively clear, they crossed and made their way wearily through two more yards. Neil mentioned that they had to turn north, but Jillybean wouldn't answer the radio.

"She's doing a million things," Neil explained. "She probably getting the pontoon ready right now."

The little girl came on soon after: "Okay, I see you and you're not far. The drain pipe is up the block you are on and then halfway down the next. If you can keep cutting through the yards, that would be best."

Two more minutes, Grey thought. He had to hang on for two more minutes and the danger would be mostly behind them. Once in the pipe, they'd be fairly safe and then after a quick swim in zombie infested, frigid waters, he would be home free.

It was the longest two minutes of his life and by the time they made it across the street to the open manhole cover, Grey was barely keeping upright. "The water will wake me up," he said in a ghostly whisper that echoed down the pipe.

The two were now in the dark, crawling down the pipe. Grey left a trail of blood behind and his vision was fading in and out, and yet when he came to the river, which was still covered in smoke, he rejoiced and hugged Neil.

"Thanks for saving my life."

"It's not saved yet. Jillybean? I mean Mouse, this is Cat, come in. Mouse? Mouse? Do you copy?" She didn't answer. Neil had on thin diving shoes, over which he pulled on a pair of swim-fins. "Wait here. I'll go see if the pontoon is out on the river like it's supposed to be."

He came back five minutes later, pale and frightened. "There's no sign of the pontoon or Jillybean."

Chapter 41

Jillybean

The mission was not over. She had seen Neil and Captain
Grey drop down into the drainage pipe and, according to the
plan, she was supposed to cut the pontoon free, turn on the
electric motor and hum the boat through the clouds of smoke
until she was opposite of where the pipe jutted out.

But that would have left things incomplete.

This isn't what you and Mister Neil discussed, Ipes
reminded her again. How many times had he said this in the last
few minutes, Jillybean didn't know. She had stopped listening.
*Well, you should listen now. You are only thinking about revenge
and it's wrong.*

"No, it isn't. It's about being a necessity is what it is. Now
hush so I can think straight." She was trying to do too many
things at once. With a drone overhead helping her along, she was
picking her way through a convoluted fight between her monster
army and the River King's men, and at the same time she had a
drone following the River King, who was under the mistaken
illusion that he was safe. Lastly, she was just landing the drone
that had been keeping an eye on Neil and Grey.

It was mentally exhausting going back and forth from iPad
to iPad, while concentrating on the battle around her and trying
to get where she was supposed to be going.

Each time she switched views, she had to reorient herself.
And at one point, she suffered a slight panic attack when she saw
that the River King was no longer in view. "He can't be that far,"
she whispered, zooming out and moving the drone north,
looking for a lone man skulking along.

With a sigh of relief, she said: "There he is. You know what,
Ipes? Every hunter should have one of these."

See? Ipes hissed in her mind. *You said it yourself. You're
hunting him.* She hadn't actually said exactly that, but it had
been close. *Well, you were thinking it. You forget, I can hear
your thoughts…and I know what you're feeling.*

"Oh yeah," she said. "Feel this." What she was feeling right
then was the coldest rage imaginable, one that sent a shiver up
Ipes' back and twittered his ears.

So far on this adventure, she'd been able to coldly analyze
situations, weighing every pro and con and seeing the

ramifications of her actions down a hundred different tangents. It was this lack of emotion that had enabled her to focus on keeping her and Neil alive.

But now she was truly angry. She had seen a man whipped to death and knew he hadn't been the first. And she had found out that Sadie was going to be sold in the New York slave markets—by her own father!

Yes, he deserves to die, Ipes said, *but not this way. It's simply too dangerous. Let him go. After tonight, there might even be a revolt. Someone might do our dirty work for us.*

"This isn't dirty work. It's right and proper work if it means we can stop people like him. Maybe the next king of the river will think twice about being so bad. And asides, it's more dangerous to leave him alive. He's too slippery to be revolted. And asides that, he knows where we'll be going next."

To rescue Sadie?

"Of course. Mister Neil will definitely want to try and you know he couldn't rescue a cat from a tree without my help. If the River King lives, he'll try to stop us. It'll be hard enough to take on those trader trucks already."

But you have a plan, I suppose?

"A sorta one. They blow up like anything else even if they have steel on them. But you're putting the horse on top of the cart. There's still the River King and there's still getting away."

And there was still getting through the battlefield. Her initial three zombie drones had taken out more than seventy yards of the first fence. Both fences had come down and into the breach charged two thousand zombies.

The homes nearest to the fences had actually been fortified with sandbags and triple locked doors to help withstand attacks by either zombies or humans, but not both. Jillybean had monitored her three remaining monster drones and by chance, much like M&Ms randomly sorting themselves in a jar, they had split up, each heading to one of the houses where the king's men were frantically firing, taken by complete surprise by the horde.

Jillybean had exploded the drones one after another, taking out the homes and opening a wide hole in the base's defenses. There was no second line. The River King feared a large military and assumed that his people would step up in case of an emergency.

They were in no position to and soon there were zombies everywhere along the north side of the base. By the time

Jillybean decided to kill the River King, there was chaos. She went in as a little zombie, with her iPads hidden under her torn up coat. Every few feet she would kneel and gaze at the different feeds.

Ahead of her, the king's men couldn't decide whether to stay or fight, which resulted in pockets of fighters blasting away with everything they had, but also wide lanes where zombies were lurching along without resistance.

Jillybean followed them in and then detoured to intersect the king. He was alone. She watched him from above, seeing his fear. He ran from tree to tree and from car to car, frequently spinning around to stare back the way he had come or to gaze up at the sky hoping to see the drone that tracked him without mercy.

He should have spent more time looking ahead. Jillybean put herself in his path, hiding behind a tree that was wider than a dozen of her. She kept out of sight, watching the king on her screen and gently touching the .38 caliber pistol.

It was fully loaded and warm in her hand. The smell of it was heady strength. It gave a defenseless little girl the same power as a king. Without it she was a victim, with it…she was the executioner.

Jilly…Ipes said, a note of warning in her voice.

"What else do you call it? Murder? Because it's not. Murder is…"

I know what murder is. It's just that word, executioner. It's not you. Try to keep that in mind, ok? Do what you need to do and then be done.

"Nothing more," she agreed. "But I do have to face him, right? Unless you think it would be okay just to shoot him in the back?" It almost sounded as though she were asking permission.

She knew that confronting him was the right thing to do. It was the right thing only because it added a hint of legitimacy to his death—confronting him kept his death out of the category of murder, or so she hoped. Only time would tell. There was no way to know if tomorrow she would wake up with a new guilt-inspired personality haunting her. She hoped not.

On the screen, the king walked with a pistol in his hand. He couldn't decide where to point it. He swiveled it left, right, back and forth. The tree was big enough to hide a man behind and Jillybean was sure the gun would be pointed at it when he came by, so she watched the screen, stepping around the trunk as he passed. He did point the pistol at it, but only for a second and then his paranoia had him aiming at a parked car. The drone was directly above her and so she pressed the down button, letting it buzz to the ground where it landed with a gentle clack.

The king froze in place, the gun held out and pointing at the next car. Jilly's gun was centered on his back, ten feet away. "Don't move," she warned.

His right ear twitched and then his chin turned an inch to the left and she could picture his eyes canted as far over as they could go. She knew he was weighing factors in his mind. Could he turn fast enough? Would his aim be true? And more importantly, how good was Jillybean? Was she just a little girl who had gotten lucky one too many times, or was she really a genius when it came to death and destruction?

The proof of the latter was all around him and with his hand shaking, he slowly pointed the gun upwards. "Jillybean...I can keep you and your friends safe. I'm the only one who can. Are— are you listening? Don't shoot, okay? I'm turning around."

"Don't!" she snapped, her voice high and shrill as an angry bird's. The piercing voice didn't stop him, but the cocking .38 did, for a moment.

Both of his hands were trembling, badly. He couldn't stop himself from turning to look back at Jillybean, who was squatting behind her .38, making herself a tiny target. "Don't, please," he begged, looking for mercy...in the wrong place.

The little girl took a deep breath and, coming up out of her crouch said in soft voice as if reading from a list: "Mister River King, sir, you killed five soldiers by whipping them to death and they did nothing wrong. And you sold your daughter into slavery, which was really mean. And you did all that stuff from a few months ago when you put everyone in jail."

"Yes-yes, that stuff happened b-but it wasn't all m-me," he replied, his hands coming down.

"Get them up!" she hissed, threatening with the pistol.

"Why? You're going to shoot me anyway." His hands came down to just in front of his chest; the gun still pointing up. "This is crazy. Don't you realize why I sent Sadie to New York? To keep her alive. It was the only way to save her. And those poor men? Did you see the crowd? They were the ones who wanted them to die like that, not me. It was the judgment of the people."

The hands came down a little further. "Maybe if we could come to some sort of compromise, in which we work to end the barbarity, we could finally have peace. You have to believe me. I didn't want any of this to happen. Where is the profit in it?"

He had a slick delivery and a way of turning things around to make wrong seem like right and down seem like up. In a courtroom, his tactics most certainly would have worked, but Jillybean was still possessed with a tremendous anger.

"I saw you," she hissed. "I saw how you took pleasure in their deaths. I saw…"

"How do you know what you saw?" he cut in quietly, a strange and sudden concern for her etched into the lines on his face. "Sadie told me about you. She told me you are…unwell. That you are seeing things and hearing things that never happened. This-this is one of those times, Jillybean. You're suffering from a-a psychosis. It means you're not well in the mind."

Wait…what? Don't listen to him, Jillybean! Ipes cried. *He's lying. He did all that stuff and Sadie would never say you had a psychosis.*

Jillybean hesitated and the River King went on in a sad voice: "Look at you. You have a gun pointed at me. What sort of child carries a gun? It's not healthy, sweetie. Put it down before you do something you regret."

"I would never regret killing you," she answered, a snarl on her lip. "Even Ipes thinks I should."

"Is that Ipes the zebra? Since when do zebras talk? Since when do stuffed zebras talk? Come on Jillybean, you have to know that none of this is real. You've been living in a fantasy ever since your parents died. You do remember how they died, right?"

"Of course," she said with a touch of anxiety running through her. He was right that zebras didn't normally talk and he was right that she had been a little crazy before, but she was better now, she was almost sure of it…almost. "My daddy got scratched and got the monster fever and my mom stayed in bed and stopped eating and wasted away into being dead."

A look of pain washed over him. "No, I'm sorry, that's not what happened. Don't you remember the car crash? Your dad died right away, but your mom was in a coma. Do you know what a coma is?"

Her eyes were huge and her head began to sway back and forth on its own. "It's what means you go to sleep and you don't wake up."

"Exactly. And do you remember what happened to you?"

"I wasn't in a car accident," she said, but was suddenly unsure of herself, the ground beneath her feet no longer so firm. How did she know she hadn't been in an accident? When Eve had control of her mind, lots of stuff had happened that she hadn't known about until later. She had blanked on a whole block of last summer. And she had done something to the Colonel, but she didn't know what.

"You were in the accident and since then you've been living in a dream world...this dream world. You tell fantastic tales of adventures and zombies and narrow escapes. And sometimes you act out these fantasies and people get hurt. You don't want anyone to get hurt, do you?"

Confusion gripped her. "No, of course not. I never want people to get hurt, but they do and..."

Jillybean stop it, Ipes said, quickly, desperately. *He's just trying to trick you. He's messing with your head so you won't kill him.*

Jillybean fished out the zebra from the inner pocket of her monster coat and glanced down at it. "Was I in an accident?" she asked him. It was true there had been times when her head hurt for no reason. Was that from the accident? "Did that really happen or is this really happening?"

The River King shook his head sadly. "None of this is real. Not the zombies or the fires or the explosions. Those are just the trauma of your accident playing on your unconscious mind. You are actually in a hospital. Do you remember my name? It's Doctor Walcott. I've been doing my best to help you heal. Don't you want to be a normal girl again?"

Her heart leaped in her thin chest. There was nothing in the whole wide world she wanted more than that. "I do. I—I don't want any of this. But...but..."

"But it feels too real?" he asked with a smile turning up the edge of his goatee. "And at the same time, it doesn't feel real, right? That's part of your...your diagnosis. We've been trying to get you to let go of those things that aren't real, like Ipes. He's only a stuffed animal. He doesn't speak and he never has, but you knew that. It's why no one else can hear him."

He was right. No one else ever had. She glanced down at his black beady eyes and for once they seemed empty of life.

"Let's start with him," Doctor Walcott said in a kind voice. "Put him down and you'll see that he just sits there. He might be able to speak into your mind, but he can't move because…"

"Because he's not real," she said in a whisper. It hurt to say such a thing and it hurt deep inside to let go of him. It hurt too much it seemed, and instead of dropping him, she pulled him close. "But…but he's my friend."

Doctor Walcott nodded. "He has always been the hardest thing for you to let go of. Maybe we should build up to that. The road to recovery is made one step at a time. Let's have you let go of the gun, instead. It represents your anger. You are angry that all of this is happening to you. You need to let go of the anger."

"The gun's not real either?"

"No, of course not. How would you get a gun into a hospital? It's as imaginary as Ipes. Let it go. Put aside the world of make believe and just place it on the ground."

The gun had been aimed with a steady hand straight at Doctor Walcott during the entire conversation and for an imaginary gun it was getting heavy—which got her thinking: *couldn't she just imagine the gun away?* She tried to will it into nothingness, but it remained…and so did the undercurrent of anger in her. She had almost forgotten it.

Was that imaginary as well? "I feel angry. Am I angry because my parents died? Wouldn't that make me sad, instead?"

"We all deal with grief differently," he answered. "Now, put the gun down."

"Don't worry, Doctor, it won't hurt you, if it's imaginary." The gun might have been a figment of her imagination, but she was sure she saw fear pass across his face and for a moment he was the River King again, conniving and evil.

"It's for your sake that I want you to put the gun down," he said, "not mine. You're the one living in a horrible world where zombies walk the earth."

Her eyes narrowed and she said, slowly, carefully: "I call them monsters, because that's what they are. And you know what? That's twice now you've called them zombies. Whose fantasy world is this, yours or mine?"

His wise and caring smile faltered and he said: "Sorry, earlier you were calling them, I mean you were describing them as essentially…" He paused and smiled. Throughout their entire conversation, he had held his own pistol pointed upwards and suddenly in mid-sentence, he tried to turn the gun around, extend his arm, and fire.

Jillybean's reactions were honed by the constant danger she had been living with; she shot first, her bullet plowing into the right side of his chest where it tore a huge hole in his lungs before lodging in his spinal column.

A half-second later, he fired his own gun, missing wide and then he was falling as his legs gave out. His arms were oddly crimped in and as he was unable to catch himself, he landed hard with a thud. When he hit the road, his gun dropped from his now slack grip.

"I-I can't f-feel my legs," he said in a gasping, half-strangled voice as Jillybean came up, her pistol once more cocked. She could never fire it straight when it wasn't. She stepped on his pistol as one bloody hand groped for it.

She stood on the gun and it felt real enough, as did the smell of the spent powder and the ringing in her ears—and yet there were monsters lumbering slowly towards them. How were they possibly real?

"Aren't we in a hospital?" she asked, still trying to come to grips with reality.

"Fuck you," he hissed, breathing out bubbles of blood. *This* was her reality. There had been no car crash and no hospital. There were only lies, liars and monsters, and he was all three.

With two hands, she leveled the gun and fired. From three feet, she didn't miss. His body jumped as the bullet went into his face, just to the right of his nose, but he didn't die right away. He choked on blood and his feet drummed and he was still squirming when she left him, heading straight out the way she had come.

You did the right thing, Ipes said in what he supposed was a comforting voice. *He was a bad man who…*

"Not now, Ipes," she whispered, shutting him off. She needed to think, but she didn't want to. She needed to think about how easily she had been fooled by the River King. He had told her the baldest of lies and she had jumped at it.

Above her buzzed the last drone she had aloft, sending out signals to the iPad, but she didn't really need it. Monsters were now roaming freely across the base and all the king's men were hiding or shooting at each other. Jillybean left the base with weight on her shoulders, wishing with all her heart that the River King really had been Doctor Walcott.

Chapter 42

Neil Martin

"Something is definitely broken," Neil mumbled after caressing the left side of his face for the tenth time since they entered the pipe. It was either his cheek or his jaw or his temple. It was hard to tell which since the area in question was swollen to an alarming degree.

He cast a look at Grey for his opinion, but it looked as though the captain had passed out. His battered body was bleeding stripes through his stolen BDUs from the lashes he had endured before Neil and Jillybean had been able to get their plan moving.

Neil decided to let him rest for another minute before he got them moving again. There was an unspoken agreement between them: if Jillybean didn't call, they would go back for her. It would likely mean their deaths, but neither cared just then. Neil was exhausted and Grey was at a point well beyond the quaint notion of exhaustion.

Tired or not, Neil was just about to shake Grey awake when Jillybean spoke over the radio: "Cat, this is Mouse. I am inbound. ETA is three minutes, over."

Before he could answer, Grey cracked an eye and said: "Warn her that the smoke is lifting. It'll be a hot extraction."

"What does that…"

"Just tell her," Grey said in a gravelly voice, the closest thing he could come to his usual cranky growl.

"Fine, fine. Mouse be advised that our, uh, cover is not what it used to be. It's a bit thin which will make your approach somewhat warm."

There was a moment of silence from the radio and then her little voice piped: "Roger that. I will have two ropes ready. Out."

Grey grinned a smile that was only on his face long enough for him to say: "That's my girl." Neil opened his mouth to ask, but Grey waved him not to bother. "It means she won't be slowing down, so be prepared to grab on."

"She won't slow down?" Neil pictured being dragged in the wake for a mile before the rope slipped through his hands and he was left behind to fend for himself.

"Jillybean knows you, Neil. She knows what you're capable of, don't worry."

That was easy for Captain Grey to say. Even halfway to death, he was three times the man Neil was. He was already pushing out into the smoke-covered river and man the smoke was more than just thin, Neil thought as he flippered out. Closer in to shore, the smoke was iffy. Thirty yards further out it was little more than wisps drifting a few feet above the dark water.

There were zombies everywhere, splashing and moaning in great excitement. The battle had stirred them up but stuck in the river as they were, they could do nothing but splash about.

Neil, who was immune to a zombie's bite or scratch, swam ahead to clear the way. Zombies could float and flail, however, in general they were terrible swimmers and Neil was able to push a few out of the way so Grey could swim without interference.

"How far do we go?" Neil whispered. "What if she is way out…" Just then they heard a hum. It was close. Grey started swimming further out just as the pontoon slid out of the low smoke seeming huge and oddly majestic for such a normally unappealing boat.

Jillybean was in back, holding the steering handle of a fisherman's electric motor. When she saw Grey waving, she canted the handle and the ship gently turned in their direction. It was purring along slowly, maybe four miles an hour, and as it came abreast of them, the little girl threw coils of rope.

As the girl was so small the rope was little more than cord and couldn't have been more than a quarter inch in diameter. Grey grabbed one end and entwined it around his hand. Neil started pulling himself along the length of the cord, going hand over hand, hoping to get on deck before he froze to death or a zombie plowed into him and he accidentally let go of the rope.

He should have been worried about the gentle wind, which took that moment to shift slightly. There was a shout from shore followed by a clear voice asking: "Where?" In seconds only guns and the sudden roar of the pontoon's engine could be heard.

Through the remaining smoke, stabs of orange could be seen from the western bank of the river. Not everyone knew what they were shooting at, otherwise the pontoon would have been sunk in thirty seconds. Still enough bullets swept over and around Neil to cause him to duck down under the water where the sound of the shooting was muffled compared to the much closer and much more ominous noise of the engine's propellers digging through the water at full power, sounding as if it were headed right for him.

All Neil could think was: *Jillybean is going to run me over!* He popped out of the water only to get side-swiped by the long metal end of the shore-side pontoon runner. The props had been turned toward the bank and when Jillybean had started the engine it had gunned in that direction, right at Neil.

Jillybean realized her mistake and turned hard to port, sending a wall of foaming water over Neil, who began to choke on it. Drowning was a real fear, but it was distant third in his current fear rankings. The bullets skimming and skipping across the water were easily in the lead. Every gun on base seemed to be pointed at them and where the water wasn't white from the engine, it was white from the flying lead. He was going to die, turned to human mulch by a thousand bullets.

His second place fear of being left behind was coming true as the cord slithered through his wet hands with remarkable speed. Desperately, he tried to clamp down on it only to feel the rope burn through the flesh of his palms.

In four seconds, the pontoon was racing away and the end of the rope was yanked from his hands. He thought: *Now the smoke will clear completely and that'll be it. They'll gun me down…*

Before he could finish the thought, he was spun around and dragged backwards through the water by the collar of his coat. Grey had him, which was the good news. The bad news was that he was being choked by his own coat. He fought to get his fingers between the skin of his neck and the cutting edge of his zipper and prayed he wouldn't black out.

Dragged along, he had a horrifying view of a hundred guns ripping up the water all around them. "Jeeze!" he screamed in a strangled voice. The bullets were hitting so close they were kicking water into his eyes!

Thankfully, the misery of this lasted only a minute before they were at the first bend in the river and Jillybean immediately put the engine in neutral. Neil felt himself being pulled toward the boat and he started kicking with his flippered feet to help.

"You're alive," Grey said. It wasn't a question, it was more of a statement of surprise.

"Barely," Neil answered.

The pontoon was barely alive, as well. It listed heavily to the right where thirty bullet holes leaked water into the once airtight metal cylinder. The engine had also been struck and dark smoke wafted up from it.

Grey and Jillybean looked it over before shrugging at each other. The little girl then glanced at the holes in the side of the boat. "You two should try to move all the heavy stuff to this side of the boat or we'll sink. Well, I guess we're gonna sink no matter what, but I guess it'll be slower this way."

She didn't seem to care one way or the other and Neil thought she had a queer blank look on her face, making him wonder where she had been and what she'd been doing.

"Jillybean, are you okay? You don't look yourself."

"Does it matter what I look like? You're not a doctor and this isn't a hospital." Neil was at a loss to reply to this but she shrugged her remark away. "I'm fine, just a little tired of being me. It's usually not fun."

"You should try being a grown-up," Neil said and tried to give her his best possible smile, which had zero effect. "Probably because I look worse than a zombie, I bet," he mumbled.

Grey, who was also very zombie-ish in appearance, didn't comment. In fact, he didn't seem to have heard it. As Jillybean increased the throttle of the smoking engine, he picked up a few heavy crates of C4 and moved them to the high side of the boat.

After four such crates, he fell against the back of Jillybean's captain chair and passed out. Neil rushed over, but Jillybean stopped him. "No, you gotta right the boat first. I'll look at him, I guess."

To keep the boat headed in the right direction, she tied off the steering wheel with a piece of string, and then knelt down next to Grey. "Mister, Captain Grey, sir? Can you hear me?" He didn't budge, not even when she shook him and patted his cheek.

She put her delicate ear to his broad and bloody chest. When she sat back up, there was a frown on her face. Neil asked: "What is it?"

"His heart has tachi-cardia and that's what means it's going real fast, but it's not all that strong as it should be. Accordion to my books, he might be poisoned or gots a disease or he was shot and lost a lot of blood."

She looked him over, making a face as she touched the whip-marks that striped him. "Hmm, he looks bad, but he's not been shot and I don't think he bleeded enough to have tachi-cardia."

"So, what do you do?" Neil asked as he hefted another box. He could tell he was wasting his time. The boat was going to sink and probably within the next twenty minutes.

Jillybean was quiet for a while as she alternated between looking at the captain and the river ahead of them. Eventually, she said: "We treat the symptom I guess. That's what the book said. Mister Neil, can you get me the box of med stuff. It was in the front of the boat with a plus sign on it."

He fetched the box and offered to help, but she shooed him away, telling him: "I got this. You keep the boat on track and keep it from sinking."

He did what he could with the boxes, moving everything to the high side of the boat and steering on a river that was nearly half a mile wide in spots was not difficult. It afforded him plenty of time to watch Jillybean prepare an IV, something he had seen a number of times, but had never attempted.

Of course, neither had she, as far as he knew, and yet that didn't stop her from cracking the bag, running the lines and preparing the catheter. Grey normally had veins like rope, but now they were thin blue lines and were mostly hidden beneath the surface of his bloody flesh.

Jillybean tied off his arm above the elbow and let it hang lower than the rest of him. It took almost a minute before a vein began to plump up to the size of an earthworm. When it did, she slid the catheter in until there was a flash of blood at the top of it. She took out the needle portion, hooked up the tube and then ran the fluids into his arm, gently at first and then when she saw that the vein was holding, she went full bore.

In no time, the bag was empty and she put in a second. Midway through it, when the boat was riding very low in the water and the engine was spluttering badly, Captain Grey woke up. He took one look at the IV and said: "Good job, Jillybean. We'll make a doctor out of you yet."

"How do you know I didn't put it in you?" Neil demanded in faux but quiet outrage.

"The taping is her handiwork. It's exactly how I showed her in the past. Hey, do we have any Tylenol or morphine. I feel like three-day old crap."

Jillybean raised an eyebrow at the crudeness, although she didn't say anything. They had both medicines. Grey took morphine, which was an indication of the pain he was in and

Neil took five fat white pills of Tylenol. He was also in a lot of pain, but he wanted to be as clear-headed as he could be.

The motor conked out a minute later and they had to rely on the current and the little electric motor which wasn't very effective now that the weight of the pontoon was almost double with the water taken on.

"We don't need to go too much further," Jillybean said. "Do you remember Cairo? Oh wait, neither of you were with us for that part of the adventure. There's a town up ahead. It's got lots of cars and we can get one and…you know."

She fell silent, biting her lip.

Neil understood. They had succeeded in rescuing Captain Grey, but they weren't done yet. There was still more danger ahead and more killing. The thought was depressing, especially since they wouldn't be able to take a break.

The traders had a fourteen hour head start, which meant Neil would be driving again as soon as they found a car. He had been up already for the last fifty hours and was on the verge of falling asleep right there on deck as the river water began creeping over it.

"We better dock this thing, quick," he said. "Hey, do we have to take all this stuff with us?" He dreaded the idea of having to move it all once again. He would have to do it alone. Jillybean was too small to help and Grey was still listless—his last few days had to have been ten times worse than anything Neil had been through.

She gazed around. "I guess so, you never know what you'll need, right?"

"But you're the one with the plan. So, do we need all of this? It's kind of a pain to lug it around if we don't need it all."

"I don't have a plan," she said with surprising anger.

Neil put up his hands. "Hey, I'm sorry. It's just you always have a plan."

"Not this time and I don't want to think of one. Mister Neil, sir, I…I want to be normal." She said it as if it were a bad thing; something that she had been avoiding. "I want to be a normal, real girl."

Her pain was obvious and yet, Neil didn't know what to do. He had never been one for military plans and he couldn't turn to Grey; the morphine and his exhaustion had him nodding off. "Oh, Jillybean, we need you. Sadie needs you. You're the only one who can cook up a plan on the fly. I bet it would be a good one. You can be a normal girl once this is over, I promise."

"But it's never over. You guys made it to Estes where you promised it was safe, but it wasn't. Trouble followed you there and it will always follow you…unless you hide from it." Her voice dropped to a whisper: "You have to hide like a mouse until you're big enough to fight them."

"Jillybean, sweetheart, we don't have time for that. We…"

Her sudden glare stopped his lips. "Don't call me sweetheart. I-I don't like it. The River King called me that when he was trying to trick me into thinking I was crazy in the head."

"When did he try…wait, you went on the base, didn't you? That's why you were late. And you talked to the River King? And what happened?" She answered by setting her jaw and refusing to speak. He could guess easily enough. "You killed him? Well, I guess that's good, right? I would have done it. There's nothing to be ashamed of."

"I'm not ashamed. Why should I be ashamed? That's what means feeling bad and I don't feel bad. I feel tired. I just want to be done with all of this and I'm gonna be done with all of this."

"Of course. Don't worry, I'll, uh, I will figure it all out." Neil looked around at the sinking pontoon and what was left of their supplies. It wasn't much when he thought about the five armored mega-trucks they'd be facing.

The vehicles were battleships with wheels. Their armor could withstand everything up to .50 caliber machine guns. Even Jillybean's grenade launcher likely wouldn't make much of a dent in it. Their self-sealing tires were protected by hanging sheets of chain. They had gun ports front to back and each was topped by a revolving machine gun turret.

They had been built to withstand both zombie and human attacks and three people, no matter how smart or skilled, didn't stand a chance trying to take them on…unless one of the people was Jillybean and the other Captain Grey.

Neil was the one who didn't belong. He gazed at the remaining items: two-hundred rounds of ammo, a few grenades, thirty pounds of C4, but only two blasting caps, three helicopter drones, the single AT4 anti-tank rocket, and the nerve gas, the use of which was out of the question.

He supposed that the rocket, small as it was, would be able to take out one of the trucks. And *maybe* the drones would be able carry enough C4 to take out two others, but that would leave them facing a pair of armored dreadnoughts which had been built to repel attacks. Neil had no idea how to attack them without getting shredded into bloody bits.

"How about you rest while I go get us a vehicle?" he said, steering the pontoon to the nearest dock that jutted out over the river. He made sure to tie the sinking side of the boat fast to the dock to keep it from slipping under the black surface.

Jillybean watched him with dull, sleepy eyes and didn't say a word, which Neil took to mean he was tying up the boat correctly. Next, he hefted out the battery and a half gallon of gas and placed them on the dock.

"I'll be right…" he started to say, but the little girl was already asleep.

Chapter 43

Captain Grey

After a great deal of prodding, shaking, and calling his name, Neil managed to wake Captain Grey. The captain looked around without understanding. Jillybean stood on a dock, rubbing her eyes with one hand, while holding Ipes next to her chest with the other. She looked tiny and vulnerable.

Neil looked misshapen; one side of his face was swollen and purple. He said: "Come on. You're the one thing I can't carry."

It was only then that Grey realized the pontoon was empty save for a dark stain on the carpet. *Blood*, he thought, his mind unable to advance beyond the one word.

"Okay, yeah," Grey answered, and tried to sit up. He cried out and had to hold on to the back of a chair to keep from blacking out. His flesh felt as though it were on fire and it took everything he had not to cry out a second time as he pulled himself up and then climbed onto the dock.

"I'm getting too old for this shit," he said through gritted teeth as Neil helped to steady him.

Neil made a face that Grey assumed was supposed to be a smile. "At least you're still handsome," Neil said. "I don't know what more they can do to my face unless someone takes a cheese grater to it."

Grey tried to laugh only it hurt too much. Doing anything hurt and doing nothing hurt. He asked for and was given two more capsules of morphine before he crawled into the back seat of a dirty, metallic blue Chevy Suburban and laid down.

It hurt to lie down, it hurt to sit up, it hurt to do anything but sleep and he was soon out cold, leaving everything in Neil's hands. Jillybean had fallen asleep even before he had. Her eyes had been red, which made the dark circles under them stand out even more.

In spite of the pain, Grey slept for seven hours and woke with the sun blaring straight through the windshield. For a second, the view out the front was a little strange as it swept from forest to the tall grass in the median and then to the road again.

"You okay?" Grey asked, Neil.

"No," came the soft reply. Neil glanced back and Grey didn't think he had seen anyone so haggard looking in his life. "I keep falling asleep."

Grey, who felt immeasurably better, volunteered to drive. As he eased into the front seat, he asked: "Where are we?"

"We just got into Kentucky. The roads are crap, which is good. Those trucks will be going even slower…maybe we'll be able to catch up to them by this evening."

To do that meant they would have to drive like maniacs. It meant flooring it whenever possible, whenever the road opened up and the zombies were fewer in number. It meant taking obscene risks on the chance that the trucks were indeed heading straight to New York.

Sadie was doomed if they weren't. If the traders decided to go in any other direction, there would be no chance of catching them. There were just too many routes to the city. Grey would be forced to set up a very uncertain ambush in the city itself and that sort of firefight, even if they managed to win, would attract zombies by the tens of thousands as well as Yuri's men and they were no joke.

The rumor was that Yuri controlled every avenue into and out of the city. He could close every bridge with just a radio message—and then the hunt would be on.

Grey did not have the strength for that; none of them did, which meant they had to catch the traders that day or the next. "And then what?" Grey muttered. He had seen what they had to work with and it wasn't much. If he had more and better drones, he would be relatively certain he could execute a rescue, however the ones they had were little more than civilian toys.

They had a poor battery life, could only carry three pounds of explosives and had a max speed of only eighteen miles an hour. For these reasons, they were basically useless.

"Unless I can slow the trucks with the AT4," he mumbled. He pictured one scenario: they got ahead of the trucks and set up an ambush. Grey would take out the lead truck with the AT4. Jillybean and Neil would then fly the drones directly into the path of the following trucks. Direct hits on the driver's compartment would stop them.

"And then what?" The drivers had to have ambush protocols in place. They would likely flee and that meant a running battle against two armed and armored trucks. It was a battle they would lose.

"Okay…what if we ambush them where the road is narrow? Me and Neil take out the two lead trucks, while Jillybean takes out the last one. They'll be trapped…but they'll still have the advantage in numbers and weaponry. Damn!"

For the next two hours, he racked his brain as he drove at breakneck speeds, weaving in and out of thousands of zombies, stalled cars, downed trees, strange and inexplicable trash including shopping carts, three mattresses, a pile of lamps, and a washing machine.

"Where are we?" Jillybean asked, rubbing her eyes and gazing dully at the jumble of lamps that were piled in the middle of the road. "And what's that for?" Her hair was more than just fly-away at the moment. It looked like it had exploded off the top of her head.

"The lamps? I don't have a clue. But I do know we're in Kentucky, almost to Louisville. Once there we're going to have to flip a coin to decide which way to go. Northeast towards Cincinnati or a more direct approach straight east towards Lexington. I have a map up here and would love to hear what you think."

She didn't reply in any way he expected. "I'm hungry."

Grey was pleasantly surprised to find that he was too. The night before, along with three liters of IV fluids pumped into his veins, he had downed four bottles of water—and now he was hungry; he took this as a good sign.

Still, he wasn't himself. He had a military ambush to plan and so far, the culmination of each of his plans always ended with the three of them dead and Sadie still in captivity. There was a chance that no plan would work. After all, they had very limited resources and even more limited personnel.

But they did have Jillybean, only he was loathe to ask her for help. It wasn't right. She had helped, time and again, and she was always the main casualty.

"What's there to eat?" he asked.

She turned around and bent over the seat, her little bottom sticking up in the air. "Not much. Mister Neil brought enough food for a week. There's only a few cans of soup left. I know he's been saving them for me, but you can have some. And I have two cookies left, 'cept they gotted kinda smushed."

"Some soup would be nice. Too bad we can't stop to warm it up."

Jillybean was just climbing over the seat, going slowly so as not to disturb Neal, who was sleeping in the middle row as Grey said this. She paused and said: "Well…"

She wore a mischievous smile as she climbed into the first row. He liked the smile, on her it was completely natural. "Let's see what's in the glove compartment…okay, good." In a flash, she had a screwdriver twirling in the glove compartment and a minute after that, she pulled out a panel from inside.

"Just need a flashlight. Here we go." She stuck her head and one arm into the glove compartment for a moment before pulling out again. She grabbed a can of soup and said: "Try not to hit any bumps for a few seconds."

When she leaned back, she wore a wide grin. "There's all these black hoses that gets real hot. I wedged the can in between two of them. It should be ready in a few minutes."

"Thanks, hey, do you want to look at the map and see which way to go?"

Her grin slid down into a frown. "I guess it's just a map," she said and glanced at it and then shrugged. "It depends if any of them bridges are still up. If they have to detour all the way up to Madison, then they'll be going to Cincinnati. If not, then I don't know. Personally, I'd still go towards Cincinnati. The other way goes right through the apple mountains and they're awful twisty and slow."

"Appalachian Mountains," Grey said, absently gazing at the map. "64 is a pretty big highway, but I don't remember if it winds like some of those smaller ones. But there's also fog and snow to consider. Okay, I guess we'll go to Cincinnati, thanks."

She replied with a half-hearted: "You're welcome," making his eyes narrow. Before he could ask her what was wrong, she said: "You're going to ask me to help plan the attack on the trucks, but I don't want to. I want to be a normal seven-year-old girl."

"I can understand that, except you already are a normal seven-year-old girl. In fact, you're downright average."

"Huh?" she said wrinkling her nose in confusion. "I don't think so. I blowed things up and I killed people. Little girls don't do that."

"As far as I know, You're the only seven-year-old girl left, Jillybean and that means that not only are you average, mathematically speaking, you also set the bar for any girl thinking to turn seven. They will all look to you and your accomplishments and you've had many. You defeated the Azael. You saved the Valley. You saved your family from the River King, the weirdos down in New Eden and from Yuri in New York. You are an amazing seven-year-old."

She grinned a crooked grin, showing a single dimple, and then cocked a shoulder upwards. "I guess I did some stuff."

"You did. You saved me and I want to thank you for that from the bottom of my heart. And no, you don't have to plan an attack if you don't want to. Maybe you can listen to my plans and make some suggestions?"

"I guess," she answered, less than thrilled by the prospect. He explained his plans and they were met with a frozen smile. "They start off good, I guess."

He sighed: "But they don't end very well, I know. My problem is I always end up with two trucks and more men than we can handle. Even if I had..." He was about to say Wilson's name, but his death was too fresh in his mind. It was so fresh that every time he blinked all he saw was flesh and blood flying.

Grey cleared his throat and went on, "Even if I had a few more trained men, it wouldn't make a difference. I could take out the turrets, but they'd still rip us apart from their gun ports. They'd have over-lapping fields of fire. Do you remember what that is?"

She nodded unhappily. "That's when they can shoot you from different angles and there's no place to hide and you get shooted and die."

"Yeah, that's it and that's my problem. We have blasting caps and enough C4 to take out two of the trucks completely, but the AT4 isn't strong enough to take out an entire truck, not unless we get lucky."

"Ipes says we should be smart and not lucky. Luck comes and goes but smarts stays with us. Though sometimes I wish we could get lucky, too. Hey, how fast do those trucks drive?"

He shot her a look. "Why? You going to help me?"

"I can try." She started her preplanning phase by asking endless questions: *How fast do the trucks go? What would their spacing be like while on the road? How thick are the tires and the armor? How many men were in each? And, most importantly, how long would the gas in the 4Runner last?*

She figured it would make it to Cincinnati, but what then? Scrounging a full tank could take a day or two or even three. For that reason, they had to go through with whatever plan she came up with as soon as possible.

After the questions came the preplanning lunch of soup: nice and warm chicken and stars, which they shared equally. And then Jillybean stared out the window for so long that Grey had to ask: "How's it coming?"

She kept staring as she asked: "Do crazy people go to heaven? Ipes says they do, but he's not an expert. He's only a zebra."

"You will go to heaven for sure...why do you ask. If you don't think the plan will work, then we won't make the attempt."

"I say it's fifty-fifty and that's what means only okay odds. But the bad part is there won't be anywhere to hide. If we lose, we die."

Fifty-fifty was much better odds than any of his plans, but he didn't like the idea of the little girl being exposed to those sorts of odds. "Why don't you tell me what the plan is and we can go from there?"

"Well, first I need to know if you're afraid of heights like Mister Neil, cuz this plan goes outside the window if you are."

"Heights? Jillybean, you know those drones only carry so much weight and we don't have time to make life size ones and..." He stopped as he noted that she was looking at him as if he were crazy. "No, I'm not afraid of heights. Why? We're not going to attack the trucks from the air, are we?"

Her look turned to one of puzzlement. "Your question is confusing. If I say no, that'll mean that we *aren't* attacking from the air, right?" He nodded and she said: "Then my answer is yes, from the air is the only way."

Chapter 44

Jillybean

Of course, she knew drones couldn't carry a person—well she could make one that did, especially a person of her weight and weight was really the largest factor when it came to travel by air. But there was no time for that sort of thing. There had barely been time for their one stop to get rope and more cigarette lighters.

When Neil found out what the rope was for, he had choked —on air Jillybean supposed and then, ironically, he had said: "I need air."

Big, man-sized drones would have been nice, she thought, then again, a tank would have been even nicer. All that was wishful thinking and she cast it aside. She had to use what she had on hand, meaning the three remaining drones, which, with their limited speed and payload, would only be used as surveillance systems.

When the time came, they would give her vital information, the most important of which was the speed of the trucks and where in line the one with the sex slaves was. Both Captain Grey and Mister Neil said it would likely be in back, but she wasn't going to risk Sadie's and their lives on something that was only "likely."

The drones would also let her know the spacing of the trucks almost to the exact meter. With their bombs being so crude, ten feet could be the difference between a damaged truck and a dead truck, and they had to be dead.

Jillybean was almost overwhelmed with all the possibilities confronting her. Would the traders sense the trap and speed up? Or would they sense it and slow down? Would they sense it at all? When the road narrowed, would they draw closer, which was only natural, or would they fight that tendency and maintain their spacing? She worried over every little detail as she mixed her chemicals.

The idea of being out in the open where everyone could see her was worrisome, however the concept of over-lapping fields of fire scared her to no end. This was why she was making more smoke bombs, mixing in gasoline to speed up the reaction time.

She worried and fretted and time seemed to speed up. It was three in the afternoon when they caught up with the traders, spying them far down the road. For all of two seconds, the three of them were filled with relief that they had found Sadie—then the tension took hold and their smiles faded.

Jillybean's was the first to go as she discovered that her plan wasn't going to work. I-71 was four lanes of wide open land which was the worst-case in an ambush attempt. In fact it was straight up terrible.

"Go around them," she ordered, tersely, biting her lip. "Detour onto one of the smaller roads, we don't want to be seen."

Neil had woken and was driving at this point. He stayed well back until they reached an exit and then he sped forward, taking a frontage road that was hidden from the highway by a long run of trees.

It was a winding, bumpy, ill-kept road and at the speed Neil was driving it felt more like a roller-coaster which was not helping her stomach. She was nervous about the plan. Generally, she liked to make plans for *other* people to follow, while she hung back, only acting the part of heroine out of necessity.

This time she would be right in the thick of it, dodging bullets and probably shooting them as well. The idea made her queasy. *And that's what means you are not crazy*, Ipes told her, *Only a crazy person wouldn't be afraid of doing what you're planning. Did I mention I want to stay in the 4Runner?*

"You can't. We're not coming back for the 4Runner and you'd be left behind."

Ipes muttered: *I could catch up, later*, but Jillybean knew he didn't mean it. He was just scared. They all were, except for Captain Grey who was trying to finish the bombs as the truck bounced about.

After a few miles at this fearful pace, they took an on-ramp, rejoining the highway and raced ahead as fast as they dared. For miles, the highway remained wide open and all of them worried that the plan would have to be scrapped and a new, much more dangerous one put in its place.

But then they finally got lucky. The road suddenly seemed to end ahead of them. Neil slowed and crept up to where there was a huge chunk of the highway missing.

Long ago, someone had destroyed both spans of the road as it crossed the Little Miami River, turning it into the Little Miami Swamp. It was completely impassable. "Turn around!" Jillybean shouted at Neil as she ducked her head down at the map and ran her finger along the wobbly line that represented I-71.

She found it and traced it back to a point where two roads diverged away, one running roughly parallel to the north, the other to the south.

"Which way will they take?" she wondered aloud.

Grey leaned over the seat with his head canted so he could see the map. In no time, he said: "Take the south road, Highway 350. We have to assume they know that 71 is blocked here; if they took Route122, they would be backtracking a good ways."

Jillybean agreed, but on the safe side, she launched one of her three precious drones. "Bye, Bobby," she called to it as it whirred away. The heli-drone "Bobby" would be flying on a one-way mission since there would be no time to retrieve it.

Neil watched it until it went behind the trees. He then gazed down at the map and instead of turning around as Jillybean had ordered, he went off road, plowing down a fence and cutting straight south through a rutted field, saving them at least ten minutes. When he found Highway 350 he slowed, his eyes wide, his mouth stretched into a grimace as he looked both ways. "Does this look perfect to you guys?" His fear of the coming battle showing on his face.

"There's no turn off," Grey noted. "If we ambush them here, they may get trapped in place and that's a battle we can't win. We have to keep going."

Neil seemed relieved by the answer and he headed east on 350, speeding once more, sending leaves and trash skittering in their wake.

Seconds later Jillybean made a noise that was somewhere between a grunt and a yelp. "Oha! The drone has them. They're coming up on the exit and…they…they're turning south. They're coming this way!" She checked the map, measuring with her fingers. "We have a five mile head start. Is that enough time?"

"At thirty miles an hour, that's a ten minute lead," Grey said. "That's cutting it pretty close."

Neil understood what he had to do. He stamped on the gas and the 4Runner sprang forward, racing along the narrow and, thankfully, empty road. "Do we have everything ready?" he asked, not for a second taking his eyes off the asphalt speeding under his tires.

Grey stared around. "Thirty feet of knotted rope, two remote controlled mines, six smoke bombs each the size of an artillery round, a sledge hammer. All our weapons are locked and loaded, oh, and one AT4 anti-tank weapon."

He forgot about me, Ipes said, crossly. Jillybean hushed him. Her mind was going over every single detail of the plan. It would come down to timing, the speed of the vehicles and their spacing—in other words, things she couldn't control. Her stomach started to hurt.

"If everything is ready…" Neil paused and swallowed before finishing: "then ten minutes might be good enough. We just need to find the right spot."

Three miles went by and still they didn't find what they were looking for: a spot where the two-lane road was hemmed in by forest, basically they needed the forest to *overhang* the road. And they also needed a turn off very close to said overhang.

Time and again, they got one but not the other. Eventually, they had to settle on a spot just before the land opened up on fields of stunted and browned plants.

Jillybean, her heart going quick, said: "Right here. Stop the truck."

Grey was the first out. He jogged back down the road, staring up at the trees overhanging the road. "Right here. This is the only place where we can ambush them."

The little girl looked down at her iPad, which showed empty road; the trucks had out distanced her drone and so she sent up another. While she did that, Grey and Neil unloaded the 4Runner and then, as Grey mounted a tree with a length of rope rolled over one shoulder, Neil went to hide the truck in the forest.

"Well?" Neil asked when he got back. "Where do we put the first bomb?"

"I don't know, they're not in range yet. I don't have them on screen and it all depends where the slave truck is in relation to the rest." Every few seconds, Jillybean checked the screen, whispering: "Come on, come on." Finally, the drone's camera picked up the trucks chugging their way. "Which is the slave one?"

Neil squinted at the screen. "I can't tell from the front. The slave one usually has three Xs on it or some sort of picture of a woman…usually a naked woman."

Jillybean angled the heli-drone until she saw the Xs emblazoned in huge letters: "It's the third one, for all darn it."

The middle truck would be the hardest to cut out. If it followed the others too closely it could accidentally trap itself and attacking it like that would likely get them all killed.

She was suddenly frozen by indecision: should she abort the mission? Should she order them back into the 4Runner and hope there was an absolutely perfect spot up ahead? Or should she go through with it and pray?

"Where do I put the first bomb?" Neil asked, his voice straining at a higher than normal octave. He kept looking back and forth from Jillybean to the road west of them.

"And I need the first load," Grey called from above them. Climbing up into the tree where the branches were thin couldn't have been easy for the two hundred pound man.

"I-I just need a second," she said. They didn't have seconds to spare and every moment she dithered was a moment they would never get back, for good or for evil.

Ipes centered her. *So, it's third in line. So what? Nothing has really changed. You knew you weren't going to get them all and you knew it was going to be dangerous, so just roll with it.* Unlike Neil's voice, Ipes' was deeper, far more manly than his usual nasal tone.

"Okay...I will." She looked again at the screen showing the trucks chugging down the road. They were doing maybe twenty-five miles an hour and their intervals had shrunk. They weren't bumper to bumper. Jillybean thanked God for that, but there was maybe only thirty feet separating each.

It would mean trouble. "But that's okay, we have Captain Grey with us," she said. "And I'll have you, Mister Neil, sir. I need you to put the first mine across from that white trash bag and the next one will have to go across from the oak tree. Do you know which is the oak tree?"

She knew that when it came to woodland knowledge, he didn't know many facts and usually mixed up the ones he did have at his disposal. He surprised her. "I know what an oak looks like...the one with the reddish leaves, right?"

"Yes, now go." She spun on the spot and spied the rope Captain Grey was dangling from the overhead canopy. He had earlier knotted it to make it easier to climb, but she wasn't climbing. She snaked the loose end through the strap of the AT4 and then through the trigger guards of Grey's and Neil's M4s. She even hooked her own backpack and M79 on there as well.

It seemed like a heavy load to her, but Grey whisked it up as if it was nothing. A minute later the rope came down landing on her head as she was bent over the screen of her iPad. The trucks were leaving the drone far behind and were now small in the picture.

She could hear their rumbly engines as she looped the heavy sledge hammer into place and the satchel of tools and the plastic bag filled with the remotes for the detonators. Time was flying, not like sand in an hourglass but like a sandstorm in a desert.

A light wind was sweeping across the highway blowing yellow and red leaves along with it. It reminded her of a time long ago. She had read a Winnie the Pooh book that was all about a blustery day and this day was similar to that—except without the danger that was churning her guts and making her want to pee.

A pee had not been factored into her plans and now she wished it had been.

"You better hurry," Grey barked. "I can see the exhaust whenever they change gears."

"That can't be right," Jillybean said, but it was right. She could just see a puff of black at the tops of the trees getting carried away by the wind. The traders were early or traveling faster than she had reckoned…and the smoke bombs weren't even in place. Neil was still setting up the second bomb, so she ran to the smoke bombs—they were ultra smoke bombs. With the gasoline soaked in, they'd go right up. Yes, they would burn out quicker, but they weren't going to be needed for more than a minute.

If they were there after a minute, they would all be dead. The thought sent a shiver through her, but as it mixed with all the other shivers, she barely noticed.

The smoke bombs were not much to look at: a triple-layered ball of aluminum foil sitting in a brown bag. She grabbed two and bracketed the road just below where Captain Grey was trying to set the weapons in the tree branches to keep them from falling.

At first, she was glad for the wind as it swept leaves right on her and the bombs, burying them easily. However, when she ran to get the next two smoke bombs she saw that the wind had blown the leaves off again.

Leave them! Ipes ordered, again with that deep voice that was maddeningly familiar. *Concentrate on getting them in place. Worry about hiding them later.*

"There is no later!" she hissed, rushing to the next pair of brown bags and hurrying them across the road to set them in the tall grass at twenty foot intervals. As she armed the thermal detonators, she watched Neil struggling with the same issue she was having. He looked like a child trying to save his sandcastle from the ocean, clutching the leaves with both arms while a terrified look played on his face.

Jillybean had placed the "mines," a word she didn't quite understand, in garbage bags so they wouldn't look exactly like what they were: bombs. In her world, mines were things that people dug into the ground to find gems and jewels and gold; mines weren't bombs.

Whichever word they were called didn't matter as much as the fact that they seemed blatantly obvious lying in the middle of road. They had to be camouflaged but at the same time she wanted to scream at Neil to forget the bombs and get up into the tree. She didn't trust that Neil would be able to climb the tree in the time they had left. He had trouble with ladders and sometimes even stairs.

Again, she was struck with a decision that could get them killed if she chose wrong.

Trust your instincts, a voice in her head said. This wasn't Ipes. She just realized that the zebra was in a pocket of her backpack high up in the tree. This was a new voice, which meant, a new crazy.

I'm not new, Silly-Jilly. It's Daddy and I would never do anything to hurt you. Now, go with your gut. Listen to what's inside you.

The roar of engines from up the road grew louder. She didn't have a second to marvel or argue or question the new voice. She cried to Neil: "Leave them! Get up in the tree, please." He hesitated and she made a noise in her throat that sounded like a cat whining. It got him scrabbling at the tree, bark raining down into his face as he struggled against gravity.

A hard sound: *blatt!* had her turning west. Certain that she would see the trucks at the end of the road, aiming right for her, she froze, her legs straddling the yellow line, like a deer caught on the way to the watering hole.

The road was blessedly empty…for the moment. She ran for the last two smoke bombs. She should have been following Neil up into the tree, but her plan was gossamer thin, relying on luck as much as it did her native genius. She knew that anything including the last two smoke bombs could make the difference.

She put them in place on either side of where she hoped the fourth truck in line would stop and was just clicking the "go" button on the first bomb, when she heard her name being screamed. Her head didn't orient on the scream, which came from above her, what filled her with fear was being caught in the middle of the road without any camouflage or pretense. Her plans would be laid bare, pretty much naked to the world as the day she was born.

But the road was empty.

"They're right there!" Grey hollered. She ignored the scream and bent back toward the smoke bomb. It was needed. The fact was, just at that moment, the bomb was needed more than Jillybean was. She had made her plans and that would be pretty much her entire contribution. She wouldn't be much good in the coming fight. Likely, she would be only a detriment to the team. A fine example of which was getting caught out in the middle of the road like a silly fawn.

She scraped a handful of leaves over the bag that held the smoke bomb and did her best to bury it in the three seconds she had left, or the three seconds she thought she had left. The next *blatt* of the engines was so close it turned her stomach to ice. She was about to race for the tree that Neil was still struggling to climb when she saw the first of the trucks pull around the bend in the road, two hundred yards distant.

Just like the fawn, she feared she looked like, she froze, her Keds seemingly glued to the pavement. She froze and could easily imagine herself still standing there when that first massive truck plowed her into nothing but goo.

Run! her daddy screamed into her head.

She ran, angling for the tree, but then she saw the rope drop, its last knot touching the pavement, the rest going straight up. She didn't need Captain Grey's instructions. She ran and jumped on the rope, entwining her legs and gripping with all her might as she was hauled up as if she were a spider on a web.

Grey pulled her up until she dangled in front of his face. "Were you seen?" he asked.

"I don't know. Wait…" She pulled back a branch so she could see as the trucks came closer. "No. They woulda stopped if they saw me. They're still coming Mister Neil, sir, they're still coming. You gotta hurry."

His tree climbing skills were even worse than Jillybean feared. He was inching along the branch that snaked out over the road as if he were crawling across a tightrope a hundred feet over a river of lava. She turned from him and gave Captain Grey an arched eyebrow.

"Yeah," he whispered. "Hold this rope and this rifle, will you?" Very carefully, he slung the AT4 across his back. He then took the rifle from her and slung that as well. The satchel of tools went over one shoulder and he laid the sledgehammer across his knees.

Jillybean took up her backpack, hung her M79 grenade launcher across the top, cinched it down and put the pack on her back. When she looked up, she found Grey smiling at her.

"My little trooper," he said.

The trucks were close now and barreling along without pause. Neil, sweating and flushed, finally made it and hurriedly grabbed a rifle. "This is going to work," he said as though he was trying to convince himself. "We have the element of surprise."

And they have five armored trucks, fifty men, five .50 caliber machine guns and who knew what else, Jillybean didn't reply. There was no time and besides, what would be the point? They were going to do this come hell or high water and the little girl guessed it was going to be a whole lot of hell.

Captain Grey handed three detonators to Neil and two to Jillybean, keeping three for himself. "That," he said, pointing to the controller in her right hand and speaking quickly, "is for the second bomb. The nearer one. Wait one second after the truck goes over it and hit the button. Like this: one-one-thousand-go. Your other one and your three, Neil are for the smoke bombs. They'll take a few seconds to light so wait for my command to hit the button. They'll be going first."

"Got it," Neil said.

"A-firmative," Jillybean said.

The trucks were really loud now and Grey pulled back the branch slightly and took a deep breath. "Here we go. Be sharp and don't hesitate to kill. Okay, ready with the smoke bombs!"

Neil held up two of his detonators and Jillybean held up the one in her left hand. "Now!" Grey cried.

The buttons were clicked and, quicker than anyone thought, the smoke bombs puffed into life. A second later, one of the green trucks lumbered directly beneath them without slowing, and then came the next only this one began to brake with a heavy grinding noise.

Jillybean watched in horror as the second truck neared the bag with the bomb in it and stopped. Before she could ask what to do, Grey thumbed the controller for the first bomb and the effect was instantaneous. The lead truck seemed to disappear in a flash of orange only to partially reappear, it's tremendous hind end lifted off the ground, turning and twisting within the smoke and the flame.

The noise of the explosion was deafening. It swept over the three people in the tree like a blistering hurricane wind. Jillybean's ears rang so badly that she could barely hear Captain Grey shouting: "Blow it! Blow it, Jillybean!"

The first explosion, so close and so terrible, caused the little girl to cringe as she thumbed the controller. The second bomb, sixty feet nearer and without a huge truck absorbing most of the blast, seemed immense even compared to the first.

It blew in the windshield of the truck, flame-broiling the two men in the cab in a blink. The front two sets of wheels melted and the entire truck was turned sideways by the force of the explosion. It was so powerful that it reached out and seemed to grab the tree Jillybean and the others were perched in. The limbs washed back and forth alarmingly and as Neil tried to hold on, he dropped his M4.

With a clatter, it fell directly on top of the third truck whose wheels were locked and screeching. "Let's go!" Captain Grey cried and dropped the rope. He was flying down it even before the truck had fully stopped.

Although the plan was for Neil to go next, Jillybean was closer and she too went flying down the rope, landing just as the truck shuddered to a halt, spilling her backwards where she flailed for three seconds like a turtle before righting herself.

She was digging for her grenade launcher when Grey cried: "Back blast area clear!" Amazingly, he already had the AT4 perched at his shoulder and was aiming it square into the cab of the fourth truck in line. For a moment Jillybean marveled—her plan was working! Perhaps not in the exact manner she had envisioned, but it was close enough. The first two trucks were disabled, the fourth was a second from having its cab turned into a fireball and the three of them were currently standing on the third.

There was just one thing she had forgotten about the AT4: when it was fired, it shot a cone of flame out the back and there was almost no cover on the roof of the truck.

Chapter 45

Neil Martin

He heard the captain's cry, and for once, he put two and two together quicker than Jillybean. She had just stood up twenty feet directly behind the AT4.

"Wait!" he cried, as he reached for the girl. There was no *wait* in Captain Grey and likely, his ears rang almost to the point of being deaf, just as his own were. The warning Grey had given had come through muffled and dim.

Thankfully, Neil's fear of weapons such as the AT4, most guns and really, any bombs, even the smoke generating types, finally came in handy. He had been moving toward the one place of cover when he heard the warning and was shocked to see Jillybean just standing there.

Without another thought, he charged the girl and tackled her just as Grey fired the rocket. There was an almost instantaneous explosion and just as instantaneously, Neil was covered in a blanket of scalding air.

He hadn't gotten the brunt of it or he would have been literally cooked. Grey had the weapon canted so that the exhaust end was pointed slightly up and the deadly end of it was pointed at an angle down at the next truck. Still, the pain of it made him wonder if he'd had the hair singed off the top of his head.

"Oh, thanks, Mister Neil, sir. I forgot about that part of them rockets. I hope you're okay."

"I'm good," he answered, getting to his feet, noticing for the first time that the truck was now sitting in a sea of smoke—white smoke was rising on the sides and billowing black in front and behind.

While he was still marveling, Grey raced past, unslinging his M4. "Let's go!" He was talking to Neil. The plan from here was simple: he and Grey would kill the people in the cab of the truck, and then, while Neil drove them away, Grey would kill all of the guards in the truck and then, if needed, destroy any trucks following them.

This was where Jillybean's plan was rather weak. The idea that one man could take on seven or eight men in a cramped space was fantasy...unless that one man was Captain Grey. He hadn't even blinked at the idea of creeping down into the depths of the truck and killing whoever he had to.

Jillybean's job was to keep out of the way, if she could and, in a pinch, act as a distraction.

Neil knew she could take care of herself and so he ran to the front of the truck, just as it lurched to the right. The driver was taking the vehicle off road and there was precious little room to do so. The forest was close and the overhang of tree branches even closer.

Grey threw himself flat and Neil did as well, but he was nearer to the forest side of the vehicle and a branch snagged him. He found the truck sliding beneath him and, amazingly, the branch swept him right off the truck. With a cry, he fell and only his jacket getting caught on a bad welding joint kept him from dropping twenty to the ground, where he would have been left behind or run over.

In this instance, dangling by a torn jacket while getting raked by what felt like a hundred claws as more branches ripped against the side of the truck, was not an entirely bad thing.

Moments after going over the edge, a .50 caliber machine gun started firing and it wasn't the one on top of their truck. Someone in the fourth truck in line was blasting away, sending tracers inches over the top of the truck.

All Neil could think about was Jillybean and the fact she was exposed to the fire. Grey had been near the front of the truck where there was a drop down from the second floor roof to the roof of the cab. Neil was sure that he had jumped down to get to safety, but there was nowhere for Jillybean to hide.

As soon as the branches ceased trying to peel him from the side of the truck, he tried to scramble up, which for him was not easy. He got a hold of the roof easily enough, but he lacked the muscle to pull himself up with just his arms alone. Scraping and kicking at the side with his feet allowed him to get first an elbow up and then two.

Only then did he realize he was wrong about the lack of cover on the roof; he had forgotten about their own .50 caliber gun turret. It stood four feet tall which was plenty high enough for Jillybean who cowered behind it, waving for him to get down.

Where does she expect me to go? he wondered just as the tracers started whipping his way. He squinched down and scrunched up his face in fear of what he knew was coming, but he didn't give up his elbow rests because he was pretty sure that if he went back to dangling by his hands, he wouldn't be able to get back up again.

As he waited, either for a miracle to happen or, more than likely, a quick death, he saw Jillybean scamper around the turret and jump in!

"Jillybean!" he screamed. "Get out of there!" She didn't listen. She never listened. For a second, he considered calling out to Ipes, who could at least be reasoned with—in spite of his status as imaginary. Before he could say a thing, he saw her brace both of her cricket-legs and heave back with her entire strength on the charging handle of the gun.

A second later: *Bam! Bam! Bam!* Tracers started zipping back towards the fourth truck in line. She was so small that he couldn't see her behind the gun, but she was there, firing away, and missing as the tracers streaked by, just a few feet to the right.

Strangely, she wasn't correcting her aim and round after round went uselessly by. The other .50 caliber turned on Jillybean, hammering the turret. There was a scream from inside and the gun went silent.

Fearing the worst, Neil scrambled the rest of the way onto the roof. Once on his feet, he started running for the turret, only at that moment, the truck's driver stomped on the gas, surging faster. Once more, Neil was thrown. He turned half a dozen crazy summersaults and nearly rolled off the truck a second time, saving himself by flattening his body. From above, he looked somewhat like a panicked starfish.

"Jeeze!" he cried as huge .50 caliber rounds passed all around him. It almost seemed like they whispered words to him in a secret language as they winged by.

"Are you okay, Mister Neil?" Jillybean called out.

He had never felt less okay in his life. "I'm good. Stay down. I'll be right there."

"What about the plan?" she yelled. "You're supposed to be helping Captain Grey."

"I would if I could, but I'm getting shot at in case you haven't noticed!"

"I know, I'm sorry, but I'm too small to reach the pedals that control the turret. I can't aim and shoot at the same time. Hey, can you tell me when I'm lined up on the bad guys?"

For a long moment, he couldn't answer. The truck was turning from the road and heading out into the field, and it was all Neil could do to stay on the truck and not get thrown into the path of the flashing bullets. At one point, there was a steady river of bright orange passing so close to his cheek that he could feel the heat—he was pretty sure he screamed.

It felt as though he had been out in the open and exposed for ten minutes when it had really been less than one. Then suddenly, amazingly, the bullets stopped coming, they had made the turn and now they were in the comparative shelter of the trees.

Neil sat up, looking around like a person who had just had a tornado pass over him. He felt a giggle working its way up his throat, but Jillybean spoiled it by popping up from the torn up turret and yelling: "Go help Captain Grey!"

"Right," he said, mostly to himself, jumping to his feet. He was halfway to the front of the truck when, for the third time, he was sent flying. The truck, which was plowing ahead, had decelerated sharply.

Like a rag-doll, Neil went tumbling forward, fell off the front of the roof of the truck only to land on the roof of the cab. He almost fell off of that as well when the truck took a hard turn to the left. It seemed the smart thing to do was to spread himself out like a starfish once more, but he had to rethink this plan when there came a gunshot from in the cab and a hole appeared in the metal next to his head.

Perhaps thinking that lightning never struck twice in the same spot, Neil stared down into the hole to see a strange mash of arms and legs flailing about. Grey was fighting somebody! Neil crawled to the edge of the cab and looked over and yes, Grey was fighting a hugely fat slug of a man who looked to be trying to crush Grey with sheer bulk.

There was a second man but he was slumped in the footwell of the passenger side—he seemed to have drowned in a pool of his own blood.

Grey saw Neil and yelled: "Shoot him!"

It was only right at that moment that Neil realized he hadn't seen his M4 since he'd been up in the tree. "Uhhh," he said, "I think I dropped it."

"Damn it, Neil!" Grey shouted, shoving the fat man's hands to the side as there came another gunshot. A second hole appeared in the roof of the cab. Grey let go with one of his hands long enough to heave the steering wheel back to the right.

Instead of trying to grab the man's wrist again, he elbowed the man once, twice, three times in the temple.

The man seemed dazed and Grey was able to get some sort of fancy hold on his wrist and slowly bent it back so that the gun was pointed towards the passenger window when it fired a third time, blasting out the glass.

In the middle of the fight, Grey gasped: "We don't have a lot of time...the other truck is coming...you're going to have to get to Sadie...I'll take care of this guy and...see if I can outrun the other truck. Go."

"Uh, yeah, sure," Neil said. *How the hell am I supposed to do that?* he thought. *I don't have a freaking gun.*

But Jillybean probably did. There was never knowing what she had in that big bag of hers. In fact, as Neil wove his way unsteadily along the rocking roof of the truck, he saw the little girl pulling out the last of her drones. It was smaller than the others and she had named it "Petie."

"Do you have a gun I can borrow?" Neil asked, grabbing the side of the turret and holding on. It was the first steady grip he'd had since dropping from the tree, and he didn't want to give it up.

The revolving turret had taken a nasty beating. There were fat holes all through it, which begged the question: how had Jillybean survived? Possibly curled up at the bottom where there was a steel lip about five inches high that encased an odd porthole.

It was the way down into the bowels of the truck or, as they were about to find out, the way up. Jillybean was just setting down the drone when the handle of the portal began to turn.

She scrambled for her M79 grenade launcher, throwing it up to her shoulder just as the portal opened. Neil's eyes popped wide open, and he was about to scream: *Jillybean, no!* But he didn't. She knew perfectly well that a grenade shot from this distance would kill them all—she had to be using it just to scare the man coming up.

He was bald save for a fringe of hair horseshoeing his head. Where the hair had fallen out, he had long ago covered his flesh with tattoos. There were more tattoos covering the knuckles of his right hand. Neil could see them perfectly as he gripped a 9mm handgun.

There was no way he could have missed the grenade launcher or the little girl and it must have been her tiny size, the button nose, the sweet blue eyes that hid the sometimes murderous creature within that prompted him to ignore the grenade launcher and lift the gun.

This is it, Neil thought as he saw Jillybean's lips draw in and her eyes narrow. If he knew her at all, he knew she wasn't going to let that gun come all the way up and as she started to squeeze the trigger, he could do nothing but squinch his face in anticipation of the blast.

She pulled the trigger without hesitation, there came the usual odd, hollow *thump* sound as the grenade was shot out of the barrel and then a crack as it raced straight between the man's eyes. The grenade left a half-inch deep divot in the man's forehead and then bounced away—without exploding!

Neil couldn't believe their luck and was shaking from his near death experience. For some reason this seemed like a closer call than almost getting turned to goo by the .50 caliber.

"That was a freaking miracle!" he crowed.

For just a second, Jillybean looked at him as if he had gone bonkers. "What are you talking about?" she asked and then darted forward to grab the man's handgun before he slid down into the depths of the truck.

"The grenade," he explained. "It didn't go off. That has to be some sort of sign." So far, the plan had been a little sketchy with too many near misses. The grenade not going off had to be a propitious omen.

The little girl held out the pistol to Neil. "A sign? No, Mister Neil, there were instructions, on paper, you know, like in little writing. The bombs don't go off unless they travel thirty feet and he was only two feet away."

Suddenly deflated, Neil said: "Oh."

"I wouldn't have shotted it, if it woulda blowd up. That would have been silly." She clicked a few buttons on the drone and two on her iPad and asked: "Are you ready?"

"To go down there? I guess."

She then handed him a radio. "Just follow my instructions and…" She paused and looked back across the field to where the last truck was just pulling out of the great plumes of billowing smoke, looking like some sort of alien beast. "And hurry. Mister Captain Grey is not an expert at driving these things and I'm going to need you."

"Then let's go," he said, looking once at the pistol, checking to see if the safety was off. She turned on the heli-drone and set it hovering over the portal until she could see the picture from the mounted camera. "It's straight down and there's a guy to the right…"

The "guy" fired twice at the drone hitting it with his second shot. The device turned on its side and then flopped onto Neil's lap as more bullets whizzed up.

"Crap!" Neil hissed, leaning away from the portal. "Now what do we do?" He knew what he wasn't going to do: he wasn't going down into that portal for anything. And that included for Sadie. As much as he loved her, it would be quicker and less messy to just shoot himself in the head.

Besides, he had Jillybean. He could tell she was already thinking up a new plan. "Can you gimme me that?" She pointed at the drone and he handed it over without hesitation. In three quick moves, she broke the mounting for the camera. It was a small thing, the size and shape of a baseball.

With more bullets zipping up at them, she placed the camera at the edge of the portal and gazed at the iPad. "Okay, I have two bad guys at the bottom of the stairs and kinda to the right. Do you see them?" She showed him the screen. Mostly he saw shadows and flashes.

"Can you shoot them from here?"

He sat back. "What do you mean? Like using the camera as my aimer?" She nodded and he nodded back. It was worth a shot.

She pulled back the camera for a moment and whispered: "One, two, three, go," and placed it back at the edge. He saw the men clearer now: they stood out as grey figures against a darker background. They were crouched side by side, aiming their guns and when they fired, the screen bloomed white.

"Move," he hissed, and as she pulled the camera back, he stuck the gun in the portal and fired four times, using the ladder as his azimuth. His blind aim was spot on. There was a grunt and a cry. Someone fired from within, but none of the bullets came close to the portal. Neil tracked them across the roof.

These were the shots of a dying man. Jillybean stuck the camera into the opening again and the feed confirmed two more men were down on the deck. She spun the camera in both directions—there were two others bracketing the ladder but further back, neither would get too close.

She thought for a second and then completely flummoxed Neil by loading her M79 and firing it at the forest, forty feet to their right. The explosion was sharp and made Neil flinch. It also made the two men shy back.

"Not good enough," she said. Taking the grenade she had fired into the first trader, she whispered: "Yell, 'fire in the hole' and then I'll throw this down. It won't explode, so only hesitate a second before going down there. And take these with you." In her hand was a radio and the camera.

He took them, but all he really cared about was the grenade. "Are you sure it won't explode?"

"No," was all she said.

"Ah, Jeeze. Well, okay, here goes nothing. Fire in the hole!" She chucked the grenade down. There were what sounded like a hundred girlish screams and Neil waited only long enough to cringe his misshapen face before following the grenade down, going so fast that he was afraid he would lose his grip, which he did, however, the dead man with the huge dent in his head broke his fall.

It was dark and close in the truck. The main hall went twenty-five feet in both directions, with wooden stalls lining it. Most had curtains that were drawn, behind which female slaves hid. One curtain, ten feet away moved. A man with a gun peeked a frightened face out; he didn't see Neil sitting on the dead man's chest with his pistol aimed.

At ten feet, Neil was as deadly as anyone. He pulled the trigger, there was a flash and a bang and the man toppled, blood shooting out of his head. Fearing he would be shot from behind, Neil spun, but the second man was nowhere to be seen.

"I don't have anything you want!" the man screamed. "If you want the girls, just take 'em. I won't stop you."

"Where's the new girl?" Neil shouted back.

"Downstairs. Nobody has touched her, I promise. I won't stop you just don't come down here or I will shoot. Okay? Do we have a deal?"

Neil was about to answer when a hand touched his shoulder. He screamed and nearly shot Jillybean, but stopped himself just in time. She had zipped down the ladder in the two seconds he'd had his back turned. "I'll stand guard here," she said, peering down the hall. In one hand she had her .38 and in the other the iPad. Across her back were her pack and the M79. "We can figure out what to do with him when we're all safe and sound."

"Got it," Neil said. He plugged in his ear piece and put the radio in his pocket. He then grabbed extra magazines from the body he'd been sitting on. "We're almost through this," he whispered to himself. *Almost* meant who knew how many more enemies on the lower level?

"Go," she whispered back to him. "Keep the camera pointed and I'll be able to help you."

What the men on the bottom level of the truck were thinking was anyone's guess. They had to know they had been boarded, but there was no way they'd be able to guess that it was by only three people.

They were all huddled near the ladder at the back of the truck with their weapons aimed at it. Neil inched the camera down and panned it around.

"No good," Jillybean said into his ear. "Come back." He eased back, keeping his weapon trained down the hall. She held up a ball of tin foil that had a twisted bit of napkin sticking out of it. "Use this. You have a lighter, right?" After patting his pockets and shaking his head, she rolled her eyes, held out one of her own and said: "Please don't lose it, it's my last one."

"I can't promise anything." It was only half a joke. He hurried back to ladder and lit the foul-smelling smoke bomb. He waited long enough for it to ignite before squawking: "Ayah!" and throwing it down the ladder.

Bullets fired from below chased him back from the edge of the ladder. It took fifteen seconds for the smoke to cloud the back half of the truck. Holding his breath, he stuck the camera down and waited for Jillybean.

"There are four of them and they've moved back. The closer two are crouched in the hall."

"Do you think they'll be able to see me?"

She didn't hesitate: "No, get down there, quick. I thought I heard one of them getting weird about the smoke. They could do anything."

Neil took a deep breath and went down the ladder, holding onto the rungs this time. Now, he was down to it. He was in the lion's den. "Tell me when I'm aimed proper," he said, holding out both the gun and the camera at the same time.

"Now," she hissed. He fired twice and she practically yelled: "Hit!" With the sudden avalanche of gun fire from down the hall, he could barely hear her. He threw himself into one of the slave stalls, where a woman screamed and backed into the corner with her hands up.

"Hush," he said and stuck the camera out into the hall.

There was a pause and then Jillybean said: "Fire!"

"Sorry, I didn't have the gun out. How about now?"

She was quiet for a moment and then she said: "A little to the right. More...more...fire!" Two more shots and she hissed: "You got him. Oh, no...oh boy. Uh, Neil, start talking and don't stop."

"Start talking? What do you mean start talking? Is something wrong? Are you in trouble or am..." Three shots came from the second floor. They were heavy sounds, nothing like the thin crackle her .38 made.

"Jillybean? Jillybean?" he whispered.

The radio went fuzzy for a moment and then a man's voice came on. "Fuck you, dipshit. Your little friend is dead and you're never getting out of there alive. Even if I have to burn this bitch down."

Chapter 46

Jillybean

She heard him coming, or rather she heard the girls around him making scared noises as he checked each stall searching for the little girl. Jillybean had been too loud and the guard they had thought was out of the fight had heard her piping voice rise in excitement as she saw Neil actually winning the fight, something she had secretly doubted he would be able to accomplish.

The man was coming for Jillybean, but he was a chicken and he moved slowly. She could picture him squinting through the smoke, hiding behind his gun, trying to sneak up on a little girl.

Quick as a wink, Jillybean pulled off her back pack and her coat, pulled a thin filament of wire from the pack and went up the ladder to hang both the coat and the pack from the low ceiling. With the dark and the smoke, it looked *somewhat* like a person and she hoped that would be good enough.

She then left the radio on the floor with Neil hissing silly questions just as she knew he would. When the man jumped around the corner firing, he was partially blinded by the smoke and his own preconceived notions.

The bullets ripped down the pack and the jacket and he had enough humanity left in him not to touch what could have been a body lying next to the radio.

"Fuck you, dipshit," he whispered into the radio, wiping his eyes with the back of his hand. The brew that Jillybean had concocted was foul in the nostrils and worse on the eyes. "Your little friend is dead and you're never getting out of here alive. Even if I have to burn this bitch down"

The smoke must have given him an idea. It was the last one he would ever have.

Like a monkey, Jillybean had flown up the ladder, thinking that the man would want to go up for fresh air. When she heard his nasty words, she had leaned down through the portal, arm extended, the .38 already cocked.

She put a bullet in his head, right in the top, making a hole very much like a whale's blow hole. It began to spout blood. Three spurts and the man toppled over.

In a flash, she went down into the smoke to fetch the radio. "Cat, this is mouse. Stop pointing the camera at the floor!"

399

"Jilly…you…ay? …heard…shots." His voice cut in and out as the sharp crack of gunshots overrode all other sounds.

"I'm fine! Now listen, there's a man crawling towards you. He's twenty feet away on the other side of the hall. Are you aiming?" She couldn't see the front few inches of the barrel of his gun as she had the other times they had worked in conjunction.

"No, there…shooting…on. I'm pinned…can't get…"

It was a moment before she could decipher the fragmented sentence: he was pinned down by cover fire and couldn't expose himself enough to get off a shot.

The easy solution was to change positions. It sounded simple enough up on the roof of the mega-truck where the smoke was being blown behind them in a dense cloud and no one was shooting at her. Down in the murky depths of the truck where Neil probably couldn't see more than two feet in front of his face, it had to be a frightful thing to consider.

Neil wasn't the bravest of men—except when he had to be, and then he was a lion. She could hear his raspy breathing ramp up and then the view from the camera bounced around so much that she didn't know what she was seeing.

A second later, the view steadied and she saw the grey figures as Neil moved the camera from right to left: there was a small person huddled in a stall, then a quarter of a man visible at the end of the hall, his gun flaring white with every shot, and then there was the man on the floor, creeping forward.

He was ten feet closer, now. "Angle down," she said into the radio. "Stop! Fire for effect!" The screen flared white four times before the view jumped as Neil ducked back. Slowly, he brought the camera around the corner. The man on the floor was contorted in an odd position, but wasn't moving.

"Dead," she said, curtly. "Now the other one…oh my God!" Movement out of the corner of her eye caused her to glance away from the screen. The fifth truck had finally caught up. It loomed up out of the smoke, looking bigger than a house. The cab had its armor up and there were two men in the turret, one manning the .50 caliber machine gun, the other holding a shoulder-mounted rocket.

Jillybean leapt down into the smoke, just as Captain Grey swerved the truck to the right, trying to cut off his pursuers. She barely hung on and the iPad went flying and she could hear the glass crack plain as day.

"Oh no," she whispered, hurrying for it. Not only was the screen broken, the picture cut in and out. "It can still work if Neil…" The screen went completely blank.

A second later there was the *Bam! Bam! Bam!* of a .50 caliber. She dropped like a rock, expecting more shots but when no more came she suspected that the first three had been a warning.

"Cat! The other truck is here and the video feed is down. I'll be right there."

"What? No, don't come down here, it's too dangerous. I got this. Jillybean? Jillybean? Over?"

There was no time for arguing and Jillybean let him squawk as she ran for the rear ladder. She was down it and next to his elbow by the time he said: "Over?"

"Don't freak out," she said. He was crouched down and just the right height for her to speak into his ear, and yes, he freaked out. He almost leapt straight out of his skin; she only calmly stepped back.

"What are you doing here?" He was practically yelling. "I told you…"

She cut him off by slapping a hand over his mouth. The cold fury was back and for once Ipes wasn't butting in. "Cover me," she whispered. He started to resist and the whisper turned to a shocking growl: "Just do it."

Without waiting for a reply, she scurried low to the other side of the hall and then began to creep forward, making herself the tiniest of targets. Neil pulled himself together after a few seconds and started firing his weapon.

In no time, he ran out of ammo, and Jillybean paused as the last enemy left alive on the truck fired back. A frightful grin stretched across her face as the gun flared in orange blasts and the bullets slashed the smoke inches over her head. He was shooting wildly giving up his position and his range. If she wanted to, she could have taken the shot right there, but with Sadie somewhere close by, Jillybean wouldn't take the chance.

Neil began firing again and he must have been thinking the same thing. His shots were ridiculously high, one even hit the ceiling. As he shot, Jillybean crept closer, so close that when Neil paused and the trader leaned out to return fire, she was so close she could have reached out and touched him.

She did touch him with the barrel of the gun as she pulled the trigger. The bullet should have gone in one ear and out the other, but at that exact moment, the truck lurched hard and she didn't know where the bullet went, she only knew that the man was not dead.

His eyes were strangely wide as he turned toward Jillybean with his pistol sweeping in an arc just above her head. "I can't see," he said in a shocked voice. It was dim and with the smoke, everything was as hazy as could be, but he should have been able to see the little girl kneeling next to the edge of the next stall.

Jillybean raised her pistol and she knew that he was indeed blind when he didn't flinch as it came within a few inches of his face. There was no hesitancy in her as she pulled the trigger. Blind or not, the trader still held a gun, meaning he was still dangerous and he had yet to be held accountable for his crimes.

She found him guilty and the bullet settled accounts. She wished she could have been done with the killing, but the truck was swerving hard left and right and she could picture Grey frantically trying to keep the other truck directly behind them.

If they got around, they'd find Grey easy pickings since the armor designed to protect the driver was still down and couldn't be hauled up while he was busy driving. Jillybean would have to find a way to stop the other truck and quick.

"Neil!" she cried in her high, piping voice. "He's dead. Get the smoke bomb off the truck, quick. I gotta see what there is to see." This last she said quietly. Unless there were other weapons on board, they didn't stand a chance against the other truck. Both had nearly useless .50 caliber machine guns, but the other one had a rocket. If fired precisely, it could take out the front of the truck and leave the slaves still alive.

She was deep in thought when someone to her right asked: "Jillybean? Is that you?"

Startled, Jillybean glanced over and through the smoke she saw what looked like something out of a dream. Sadie sat against the side of the truck blinking back tears. She was so pale she looked dead and Jillybean was afraid that she was either seeing a ghost or her crazy mind was inventing the girl out of whole-cloth.

"Sadie? Are you real?" She wanted to go to her big sister, but she was afraid that she wouldn't be able to touch her, that her hand would pass right through.

Sadie grinned at the question. "Of course I am. You're the one who might not be real. How did you get here and how did you find me? And was that Neil who couldn't shoot straight?"

Jillybean couldn't answer. She was too overcome hearing her sister's voice and before she knew it, she broke down sobbing. Sadie stretched out as far as the chain around her neck would allow and pulled the little girl in close.

This was no ghost, no figment. She was as warm and wonderful as ever. "It's okay, it's going to be okay," Sadie said.

The goth-girl smelled of cheap perfume and cheap soap. She had been scrubbed clean and then doused with a sachet that reminded Jillybean of the old lady she had met in Oklahoma. It was a scent that only an uncultured, brute of a man would choose and it brought her back to her senses.

"It's not going to be okay," she said, pulling back. "Who has the keys to your lock?"

"A guy named Rick." Sadie pointed to the top of her own head and swirled her finger. "He's mostly bald except he's got hair around the fringes. He was…"

Jillybean held up a silencing hand as she pulled out her radio. "Cat, the keys to Sadie's lock is with the bald guy. You know the one I first shot with my grenade launcher."

"You have a grenade launcher?" Sadie asked, with a twinkle in her eyes. "Cool."

"It is kinda, I guess, but I wish it was a rocket launcher. There's still one more of them trucks out there and I don't have any of the good grenades left. I only have the anti-personnel ones and they aren't good against armor. Do you know if they have any good weapons on board this thing?"

There was a cross-breeze going through the truck and already, the heavy smoke was beginning to clear. A painted woman in a short skirt and heels spoke from across the hall: "No. This is the slave truck. They only have a few guns. Nothing that can hurt one of them trucks. If you were smart, New Girl, you would sit right back down and hope you don't get shot. Your friends don't stand a chance."

The rage in Jillybean flared—once more it was ice-cold and deadly. Her little pistol came up and she advanced on the woman. "I have blown up three of these trucks. I have only one left and I'm very, really tired of it all. If you were smart, you would tell me where they keep the weapons."

403

"Is she serious?" the woman asked, her eyes darting from the pistol to Sadie.

A grim laugh came from the teen. "This is her being calm. You saw what she did to Julio. If I was you, I'd tell her what she wants to know and I'd do it with a smile." Sadie had a wicked gleam in her eye and when she spoke she showed her teeth like a wolf might. She was angry. Jillybean could feel it coming off of her in waves.

And so could the woman in the short skirt. "Upstairs in the far back of the truck is where Rick's room was. He kept all of the weapons."

"I'll be back!" Jillybean cried and danced over the body of Julio and then was thrown against one of the stalls as Captain Grey heeled the truck far over to the left. The entire backside canted madly and Jillybean was helpless against the pull of gravity.

There came the *Bam! Bam! Bam!* of the enemy's .50 caliber and these weren't warning shots. The sound of the rounds smacking against the armor was terrifying and the women screamed. Jillybean didn't waste her breath; what was the point of screaming over a few bullets no matter how big?

What instilled a touch of fear into her was the crash that came seconds later. The left side of the truck hit something big enough to throw Jillybean from her feet. Luckily, at least for her, she landed on one of the sex slaves, who was soft as a pillow. The slave was also as weak as a milk-fed calf and had the air knocked out of her.

"Sorry," Jillybean said, over her shoulder as she raced for the ladder to the second floor. She had to wait a few seconds for Neil to fall from it as the truck whipped back and forth.

From the floor, Neil yelled: "Do something! Grey is ramming them to keep them off of us."

"Get Sadie!" Jillybean yelled back as she leapt onto the ladder and started climbing. "Don't trust the others. Not yet." She was on the second floor just as she finished her warning. Rick's room was not even three steps away and she burst in so quickly that she sent a dozen or so empty liquor bottles flying.

They had come rolling from under the bed and they went scurrying back again as the truck took another hard turn. Jillybean braced for another impact but instead Grey spun the wheel the other way and out came the bottles again.

She ignored them and opened up the steel locker at the foot of the bed. Inside were a few M4s, a couple of hunting rifles, some ammo and two grenades.

Disappointment froze her there and she was still staring half a minute later when Neil and Sadie came into the room. Jillybean held up the grenades. "This is it."

Neil grabbed them and said: "They could work. All we need is one good throw." He turned and headed for the ladder to the turret with the two girls following. When Sadie tried to mount the ladder, he stopped her. "Stay here. You are only to come up if something happens to me."

Jillybean thought that was silly. They had their own .50 caliber machine gun, Jillybean had her M79 and Neil had his two grenades. It made more sense to throw everything they had at the bad guys in one fell swoop.

"Come on," Jillybean said, showing Sadie the grenade launcher. They went up the ladder to find Neil crouching down in the turret, with his eyes barely edged up over the lip. The other truck was on a parallel course, thirty yards to their left and half a length back.

"Can you throw that far?" Jillybean asked.

He made a face and shrugged. "Maybe, I think. Here, move back." He took a deep breath, pulled the pin from the first grenade and heaved it in an arc at the truck. It bounced once, ten yards short and exploded harmlessly a few feet from the side of the truck.

Not even half a second later the enemy opened fire with the .50 caliber: *Bam! Bam! Bam!* Sadie flew down the ladder with Jillybean a step behind. Captain Grey, reacting to the sound, swerved right and went up a sharp embankment and once more everything was cockeyed. Jillybean hung by her hands, her feet dangling, her body twisting in response to gravity pulling her around.

She lost her grip and fell with a thud. Dazed, the little girl found herself lying on the corpse of Rick, staring up through the portal as glowing tracers raced by.

They were hypnotizing in a way and she watched them with more curiosity than fear, right up until Neil crawled to the portal and dove down, head first. He tried to grab the second rung and ended up doing a contorted, gravity-assisted cartwheel, and when he landed, somehow on his feet, he almost crushed her face.

"Oh, sorry," he said and then looked back up as the truck righted itself and the ride became so smooth it was like driving on glass. Neil stated the obvious: "We're on a road. Maybe if they get close enough…" He stopped and started patting his pockets and staring down around at the floor of the truck.

"What did you do?" Sadie asked, incredulously. "Did you lose the other grenade?"

He looked up at the portal. "I don't know, maybe. It's not here. You know what? It's probably right up there." He went up the ladder until his head stuck up into the daylight. When he glanced back down at them, it was with a guilty look on his beat up face.

"So, Jillybean are you any good with that grenade launcher? Because the other grenade must have rolled away."

"I think I can hit a truck." She was sure she could, however she didn't know if it would do any good. The grenades were small and lacked the punch needed to pierce armor.

Still, she had to try. Picking up the launcher, she went up the ladder and poked her head above the edge of the turret. They were on a two lane country road and where it headed and where it had come from she had no idea. What mattered was that she had perfect conditions to fire the gun.

Putting the launcher up to her shoulder, she rested the barrel on the turrets edge for support, aimed and fired. A shock of white light, orange sparks and grey smoke appeared square in the front of the truck, striking where the grill should have been if it hadn't been replaced with a slab of steel.

The steel had been dented and marred but otherwise remained intact. Jillybean gave it and the truck a hard look, studying it for any potential weaknesses. When the .50 caliber opened up again and more rounds started smacking into the turret, she went flat on her back, cracked the M79, popped out the casing of the spent round and stuck another in its place.

Neil poked his head up and remarked: "Sounds like you just pissed them off."

"Yeah, hold on." She rolled over and waited for a lull in the firing before standing, aiming and shooting the M79 in a span of a second and a half. Again, she scored a direct hit and again the truck rolled on.

"For all gal-darn it!" she griped, lying back down again. "These shooting grenades are too small. We need something with more power."

The turret was getting ripped up again and only the top few inches of Neil's head was visible. "I sent Sadie to scour the truck but I doubt she'll find anything."

Jillybean ran down the list of everything she knew about the truck and its contents. There was only one thing that stood out as a weapon and that was the truck itself. "I gotta see Captain Grey."

"But he's all the way in fron…" was all Neil could say before Jillybean monkeyed over the top of the turret and raced across the roof with the wind blasting into her face and tracer rounds whisking by from behind.

She was nimble and quick, her coltish legs speeding her to where the roof dropped down to the top of the cab. She turned and slid down the wall until her Keds were firmly planted.

"Mister Captain Grey, sir?" she asked, leaning precariously over the edge and gazing down at the soldier. He sat amid a pile of glass and the tangled limbs of two bodies.

"It's about time someone gave me a sit-rep," he cranked. "Is everyone okay?"

She climbed into the cab as easily as if she were playing on a jungle gym back in the old days. "Yeah, all 'cept the bad guys. They're all dead. Hey, do you happen to know how we can…"

Neil suddenly poked his head over the top of the cab; he was breathing in great gusts. In a display of over-caution, he climbed down into the cab and sat next to one of the bodies. On one hand, he acted like it wasn't there and on the other he acted as if it might come to life and grab him.

Jillybean, pretending not to notice, gave him a nod and a smile and continued, asking Grey: "Do you happen to know how to defeat that last truck? We tried shooting the little grenades and throwing the bigger ones, but nothing seems to be working."

"And there's nothing else in the truck except a few rifles," Neil added. "I suppose we could try to arm the slave-girls and… I don't know." He finished with a half-hearted shrug.

Grey made a growly sound in his throat as he thought this over. He then curled his lip and shook his head. Jillybean had to agree. The captive slaves were as weak-minded as they were weak physically.

"What about using the truck itself?" she asked. "Can you crash it into them somehow?"

Grey was quick to reply: "No. I've never driven a big-rig like this before and I've been lucky so far just keeping out of reach of them. If they quarter-panel me, we'll jack-knife for sure."

Jillybean looked at Neil, who shrugged again. Grey sighed and explained: "If they hit me on the back edge of the truck, it'll cause that side to slide outward."

"And then we crash, right?" Jillybean asked. It was a rhetorical question as she was easily able to imagine the competing forces acting on the different parts of the truck. And yet something wasn't adding up. "Do you think the other driver is better than you? You know, more experienced."

"Yes."

"That suggests you haven't been 'lucky' about being jack-knifed. It suggests that they would rather not destroy this truck and kill everyone in it." She went silent for a moment and then the simplest solution to their predicament struck her. "How much gas do we have? Can we just out distance them?"

Grey shook his head. "We have less than a quarter tank. Chances are that they have a similar amount and with a better driver they'll get better mileage."

They passed a sign *I-71 3 Miles*. The road would be wide open. It would be suicide to get on it—but suicide in what way? "The women are valuable to them. So how will they try to kill us but keep them alive?"

"By killing me," Grey said. "If they can get just a little ahead, they can shoot me easily and that will be that. But now that you're here, Neil we can raise the armor."

"Don't," Jillybean said. "They have a rocket like the one you had Mister, Captain Grey, sir. It's strong enough to blow up the entire front part of the cab." The image of what the AT4 had done to the fourth truck flashed into her mind: the initial blast and then the secondary explosion that went out the sides.

Grey was saying something about not wanting to get shot or blown up, but the little girl wasn't listening. She turned away, slid to the end of the bench, and cracked the heavy door that led to the outside world.

What she was looking for was under her feet protected by three inches of steel. "Go on to the highway and keep ahead of them until we're ready."

"Ready for what?" Grey asked.

Jillybean's one word answer: "Revenge." Everything she needed was on the truck. A missile would have been better than the idea she was entertaining, and so would a mine or even a drone, but she didn't have those things. She had one of man's earliest tools: fire. It was a clever tool: both liquid and gas. It could flow around armor and find the weak spots.

But they would have to get close to use it and they would have to have the element of surprise. She had five minutes to get her plan in place. "Let's go!" she barked at Neil as she mounted the roof of the cab with a quick swing of her legs. To get a hold of the second level she took a running jump and even then she barely got her fingers on the edge.

She struggled until Neil came up behind her and shoved her straight up, giving her a wedgie which she took the time to loosen before she ran for the turret, crying: "Sadie!"

The goth girl popped her head up. "Yeah?"

"I need a hose of some sort, two lighters and some fabric." She also needed her backpack. It was right where it had fallen after the guard had shot it. She wasted no time and dumped out the contents onto the floor next to the dead guard.

"What's the plan?" Neil asked as he came down the ladder, nearly slipping once more. Jillybean expected a snide comment out of Ipes concerning Neil's clumsiness and was prepared to remind Ipes that Neil only had eight fingers but the zebra remained on the floor with the other odds and ends, altogether silent.

"Fire in a bottle," she answered. "It's called something like *molly cocktail* which sounds like a drink, but these are gonna be ones you don't drink. We're gonna throw them."

Neil nodded however, as always, there was a question on his lips: "Where are we going to get the bot…"

She jumped up and opened the door to Rick's bedroom, where empty alcohol bottles were still rolling on the floor. She began stuffing them into her backpack. "Sadie!" she screamed, "I also need a broom and a white…never mind, just a broom."

Rick's pillowcase had been white at one point. Now, it was an ugly grey. Still it would work. "Take these to the Captain Grey. *Don't* break them," she warned.

Neil darted away with the backpack as Jillybean gazed around the room. Rick was a smoker and there was a lighter next to an ashtray on a nightstand. She grabbed it, the pillow case, and a sheet that was foul smelling and stiff.

"Sadie!"

"I can't find any hose!" she yelled back.

Jillybean gathered the pillow and the sheet and dragged them back into the hall. "Forget the hose." It was a ridiculous thing to say. How were they going to siphon the diesel from the tanks? "One thing at a time," the little girl whispered.

When Sadie ran up with the items she had been asked to gather, Jillybean explained the plan. "Start the fire now but keep out of sight." Jillybean was about to run off when Sadie grabbed her and squeezed ferociously without saying a word.

They had no time for words. Jillybean balled the old sheet, went up the ladder and then scampered to the front of the truck. The enemy truck was still behind them, but no one shot at her. She made it to the cab and immediately barked orders at Neil: "Use that sledge hammer and break open the dash. We need a hose."

Grey was just pulling onto the highway and he floored the vehicle as Neil began bashing at the dash. "They're two hundred yards back," Grey warned. Fifteen seconds later: "A hundred and fifty."

Jillybean was shredding the sheet with a knife while Neil was hammering as hard as he could and finally cracked his way into the engine compartment when Grey said: "Fifty yards," and began swerving back and forth.

There were three hoses within reach: one was scalding hot, the other was too short and the last ran up from the windshield wiper reserve tank. Jillybean reached as far as she could for the last and cut off seventeen inches of it.

"Hold me," she said to Neil and went to the door. The wind was sharp and cold, and the engine was a roar in her ears. With Neil grasping her by the collar of her pink shirt, she crawled out onto the armor covered gas tank.

It was designed with a hinged panel to give access to the gas cap, which was, thankfully within easy reach. After unscrewing it, she held out a hand. "Bottle."

The bottle came at the same time as the truck lurched hard to the left. Neil held tight as she went about siphoning the gas. The diesel tasted awful and her head spun from the fumes. The rocking of the truck as Grey fought to keep the other truck back didn't help, either.

After a minute, and three mostly filled bottles, she vomited onto the pavement rushing past. Neil hauled her back in. "I'll get the rest. Take these three to Sadie and stay back there. Captain

Grey and I can handle things up here. If you don't trust me, trust him."

"I trust you. We made it this far, right?" She grinned and just like Sadie had, he hugged her tight and then gave her a little push. She climbed onto the roof of the cab still smiling. "You know what, Ipes? Maybe it will be okay." When he didn't answer, she remembered that she had left him next to the dead trader.

"Poor guy. I bet he's ascared." She was the one that should have been ascared, Neil thought, moving with three bottles of diesel in her backpack. As before, he gave her a boost and she climbed to the second story of the rig while it lurched back and forth with ever increasing violence. It wasn't easy, but she persevered, going on her hands and knees until she was able to climb into the turret.

By then the enemy truck had its nose up against the back quarter panel of the truck. If the driver wanted to, he could have sent their truck jack-knifing all over the road.

"Quick," Jillybean said to Sadie, "wave the flag!" Whether Neil was ready or not, they had to begin the plan. There was no telling what was going through the enemy's mind.

They had no idea how many people were conducting the raid that cut out the slave truck. They had no idea how many had survived or what was going on inside. Jillybean had Sadie start a fire to put it into their minds that resistance was still occurring within.

The fire set the stage for the white flag.

From their perspective, locked away in their armored truck with only peepholes to see out of, Sadie would look like any other slave. They would see fear and desperation. The bombs were no longer being thrown and the .50 caliber had ceased firing. They would be cautious but optimistic. They would concentrate on the driver. They would go after Grey and he would be vulnerable as soon as they got ahead.

Sadie stuck the pillow case on the broom and raised it, canting it slightly so that it wouldn't blow away. It flapped in the breeze for a moment before she slowly raised up. "They're pointing the gun at me," she said, out of the corner of her mouth.

"Wave it harder," Jillybean answered. The little girl was crouched in the corner, stuffing strips of the blanket into the bottles and then turning them over briefly to soak the "wicks." The trucks were so close that metal ground on metal and a queer

411

vibration swept up from beneath her. And yet, Jillybean still wasn't afraid.

A wild fantasy suddenly struck her: this was a battleship and she was the ship's captain! If she radioed Grey and told him to slam on the brakes, he would. If she told Sadie to throw the first cocktail, she would do that, also. And Neil always did everything she asked.

Her command just then was: "Grey, this is Mouse. Give us more time."

As soon as the words left her mouth, the truck responded, heeling left and then breaking off to the right. In time, it bought them seconds only. In one other aspect, it helped a great deal.

"They're pointing the gun forward, now," Sadie said.

Jillybean resisted the urge to look. The trucks closed on each other once more and now Grey was forced into the far lane. The grinding of metal came again as the trucks jostled for position, but now there was a new metallic shriek as Grey was pushed against the guard rail.

"This is it, one way or the other," Jillybean said. She had the bottles ready and nestled in her backpack, a lighter in one hand, her thumb ready to flick it into life.

"Get ready, Neil," she said into the radio. "However many bottles you gots ready will have to be enough."

"I have three," he answered. "Well, two and a half." His queasiness evident in his voice.

Once more the silly fantasy gripped her and she said: "All it takes is one. Make it count." Had she heard that line in a movie or was she just making things up as she went along?

There were many holes in the turret and she stuck her eye to one and watched the enemy truck grind slowly up to "her ship" as she thought of the truck. The course of the battle was seconds from being wrest from her control and, frantically, she burned through the neurons of her mind trying to think of any tiny idea that would gain them a bit more of an advantage over their enemy.

"Give the word, Grey," Jillybean ordered, when nothing came. It was difficult to give up even the slightest control, but Grey, in the driver's seat, was in the best position to kick off the battle.

"Grey?" the captain asked, and she could hear the smile in his voice. "Since when do you call me, Grey?"

"Since now? Ha-ha," she said. "Sorry about that, Mister Captain Grey, sir."

"I was playing," he answered, and now his voice was hard as if his vocal cords had melded with steel. "Six seconds… five…"

Jillybean felt the fear of battle sweep her once more. Her hand shook as she flicked the lighter. The diesel's flame in her eyes was surprisingly bright. She always equated diesel with a darker, dirtier flame, perhaps because of the noxious smell.

But it was very bright and she leaned back from it lest her fly-away hair catch on fire. Sadie had her hand out and the hand was a rock! She was ready as Grey counted down. At "two" Jillybean handed the first cocktail to her and at one, Sadie threw it.

Her arm was strong and her aim was exact. The enemy turret was directly across from them, its gun pointed forward, the rocketeer standing behind it, ignoring them completely. They didn't see Sadie launch the flaming bottle at them in a shallow arc…too shallow of an arc.

It hit the turret and exploded like a *Fourth of July* firework. It was bright and shiny and loud, but the two men weren't hurt at all, the flames roared over metal, not flesh.

Sadie held out her hand, ready for the next. Jillybean slapped flaming bottle number two into her hand without hesitation and Sadie hurled it even as the gunner on the enemy truck started cranking his gun around to point straight at the teen who stood exposed and vulnerable.

She threw the bottle, knowing that if she missed she would be dead in a heartbeat. It flew straight and true. The gunner wore a shocked face, his eyes tracking the bottle as it spun in the air directly at him. He did nothing but stare in the two seconds the bottle floated across the twenty feet that separated them. By the time he reacted, the diesel-filled glass was breaking across his gun spraying liquid flame everywhere.

As the flames engulfed him, he screamed and went wild, turning this way and that, smashing into the sides of the turret and eventually falling through the portal and down into the truck.

The entire turret was in flames and the man with the AT4 threw it down and climbed out of the turret. Not knowing what else to do, he raised his hands as though he could surrender on the roof of a moving truck.

413

"Wait!" Jillybean commanded. Sadie had her hand out for the last bottle, but already the enemy truck was sliding back, its speed dropping. Fearless, Jillybean climbed to the top of the riddled turret and saw that Neil had come through.

An inferno roared over the front of the enemy truck. Although he hadn't scored a direct hit on the armored windshield, the engine compartment was engulfed in flame as the diesel ran down the cracks, setting fire to the interior.

There was a "chuff" sound from the engine, and a series of loud "bangs" followed by a screech of metal as the front of the truck swung parallel to them. Impatiently, Sadie snapped her fingers. She wanted the last cocktail and who was Jillybean to deny her?

The one time goth-girl stood like a hell-spawned Valkyrie with flame in her hand. She hurled it with all the vengeance in her soul, her face set in a hard mask of hatred.

She had her enemy dialed in and this throw hit the cab's armored "windshield." Screams erupted from within as the truck shuddered to a halt, flames sweeping over every inch of the cab. Seconds later the fuel tanks caught on fire and men began bailing out of the truck and running for their lives.

There was a shocked silence in the turret and then Neil asked: "Did we do it? Did we win?"

Jillybean, captain of the ship, stood to survey her battlefield. As a victory, it was as complete as she could ask. "Yes, we did," she answered.

Epilogue

Sadie's fingers on her throwing hand were the candles of a birthday cake. Each was alight. Each on fire. Each numb with the completeness of their victory. She held them up in front of her face and gazed for a moment, not quite connecting the flames on her fingers and the screams coming from the enemy truck.

They were two different things.

As an afterthought, she waved the fire into smoke, and then completely forgot the flames had ever been there as their truck chugged on, alone, unhindered, unmolested. She stood in the turret, her teeth set, her face grim and terribly stern for one so young. It was a long moment until she realized that the truck was chugging on to freedom, her freedom.

"I'm free?" she asked, staring around, not seeing anything but a blur of colors and not hearing anything but the *tha-dum* of the road beneath their wheels. She felt like someone had smacked her upside the head with a bat. Ten minutes before she had been sitting in her stall, leaking tears onto the chains that bound her and wondering if she could wrap them around her neck and choke herself to death.

Now, she was standing on the top of a dreadnaught, and she was young and free and she was SADIE! She was her own person once again. "Yes!" she cried, stamping her foot on the roof of the truck. "Fuck you! Fuck you! Fuck you!" She didn't know who she was screaming at it, but she didn't much care. She was alive and free.

She had been saved. Against all odds, she had been saved! She wanted to punch someone or something. She wanted to scream in joy! Sadie walked a circle around the turret, and found the thing to do was laugh. A great belly-laugh came up out of her. It was almost Santa-esque in its depth.

Jillybean seemed just as stunned as Sadie by the suddenness of their victory. "We won," Jillybean said, a strange smirk on her face. The smirk became a grin and then she, too was laughing, loud and shrill, a noise that wasn't completely sane.

When the laughter finally died down. Jillybean sighed and then blinked as she remembered: "Ipes! I have to tell him we won! If I know him, he's worried sick."

Sadie followed the little girl down the ladder as she chirped, happily: "We won Ipes. I had this cool plan. Remember the Witch? I used the…Ipes? Ipes?"

She had been rooting around in a jumble of stuff at the foot of the ladder but now she was frozen in place. In her hands was the stuffed zebra, only it was missing most of its stuffing. There was a fist-sized hole that went all the way through his round belly. His head hung back and his arms were outstretched and limp.

It had only been a toy. It had never really been alive and yet, just then it appeared truly dead. Jillybean whispered: "Ipes? Ipes? Ipes? Ipes?" As she repeated the name, she began to shake and twitch as though she were going into a convulsion.

Sadie grabbed the girl and turned her around. Jillybean's eyes were going in two different directions. "Aw, shit," Sadie said, aghast. She had never seen anything like this in her life. "Jillybean! Hey, Jillybean! Look at me. It's Sadie. There you go, look at me."

"Ipes is dead," Jillybean said, her voice hollow. Her eyes were back in sync, however they seemed to look beyond Sadie and into a bleak future.

"We can fix him," Sadie answered. "I-I can sew a bit. Maybe enough to get him back to the Valley. There's a woman... do you remember Valerie? She can sew him up as good as new."

Jillybean gently swayed her head back and forth. At first Sadie thought the rocking truck was causing the motion, then Jillybean said: "I'm not going back to the Valley. They hate me there. They-they think I'm c-crazy." Great tears ran down her cheeks and Sadie didn't think she had ever seen anything as sad in her life as those blue eyes.

"You're not crazy," Sadie insisted. "And I'll punch anyone who says so."

"I say so," Jillybean whispered. "Ipes was alive and—and that is crazy to say. I know it. I've always known it, and now he's dead. I can't hear him in my head anymore. I can't..." She broke down, falling to her knees and sobbing over the zebra.

Unbelievably, Sadie found herself crying over his "death" as well. "Please let me try to fix him."

Jillybean looked up and her face twisted, going from sad to angry in a blink. "No!" she cried. "Don't you get it? I want to be normal. I want to be a normal average girl and I c-can't w-w-with Ipes..." Sadness swept in again and mingled with the anger. She cried bitter tears.

She was still crying when Neil came down the ladder. "Is she okay?" he asked. "Was she injured?"

"No," Sadie answered, stepping back and marveling at the little girl as she always did whenever Jillybean showed her near super-human genius. "It's the opposite. She's finally healing."

While Sadie stayed with Jillybean, Neil and Grey freed the slave-women and to their utter astonishment, half of them were so afraid of the possibility of being recaptured and punished, that they begged to be allowed to go back with the remaining traders.

"Now, that's crazy," Sadie said to Jillybean. The little girl rewarded Sadie with half a smile.

The slaves weren't entirely crazy, however. There were huge bounties placed on their heads and hundreds of people were gunning for them as they turned back west to the Valley.

Their adventures were far from over. Still, Captain Grey was a fine leader and a brave man, and Neil was Neil. Sometimes he had the luck of the devil and when he didn't Sadie was always there to bail him out.

Jillybean remained quiet through most of these adventures, in fact, she barely spoke at all, and only once to herself. Three days after her rescue, Sadie overheard her say: "You're not daddy and I won't listen to anything you say." The little girl made sure to stay close to the ex-slaves after that. She liked to be around them and Sadie knew it was because they didn't see her as a freak and she did her best not to appear so smart around them.

On occasion, when her intelligence was needed, she still had a few tricks up her sleeves and a number of explosions left in her repertoire. Thanks to her ingenuity they were able to cross the Mississippi in an inflatable bounce-house and she wowed them with her bicycle-powered battery recharger. And she was generous to a fault. She led them to a gas station in the middle of Missouri where they pumped out almost ten thousand gallons of fuel. She only asked for a few hundred gallons.

"For Granny Annie," she explained. They found a tanker for the fuel and sped their way across southern Missouri and into Oklahoma to find the old woman. Jillybean planned to stay with her throughout the winter, and in spring she told them she was going to Scottsbluff, Nebraska.

Neil begged for her to come to the Valley with them, but she was adamant and when Sadie proclaimed that she would stay with Jillybean in Oklahoma, the little girl wouldn't hear of it. "You love Mister Neil and Mister, Captain Grey and they love you. The Valley is where you will be happy. You will not be happy babysitting me."

"But I'm your big sister."

"You'll also be a big sister to Miss Deanna's baby. She's gonna need you more than me. And we'll see each other again. I plan on visiting, and maybe, when I get bigger, I'll come live there one day. But I won't come as Jillybean. I don't think I can be her anymore."

"Then who will you be?"

Jillybean shrugged. "Maybe Jillian. That's who I was supposed to be when I got all grode up."

"You'll always be Jillybean to me," Neil said, with a smile and a tear that he quickly wiped away before Grey could see. "Jillybean is a good person and a sweet person, and I love her."

Grey reached out and touched the girl's hair, taming an errant strand. "I do too."

"Maybe if you don't want to be Jillybean," Sadie said, "you could be Jillybean Martin. That's an entirely new person with all the good parts of you and all the good parts of Mister Neil…if he'll adopt you?" She glanced at Neil, who scowled momentarily.

"That should not even be a question. Of course I'll adopt her." When Jillybean hesitated, he added: "I'll adopt you even if you don't come back to the Valley."

The little girl nodded, shyly. "Okay. Let's do that."

It was a bittersweet moment as it came just before they dropped Jillybean off with the old lady, and there were more tears. Neil cried openly, possibly because Captain Grey shed a few tears of his own. Sadie gave the little girl one last pinky swear and one last hug and said good bye to Jillybean. She then surprised Jillybean by suddenly sticking out a hand. "Hi, my name is Sadie. What's yours?"

The little girl grinned, happily, pumping the hand for all she was worth. "My name is Jillybean Martin. It is nice to meet you Sadie Walcott."

"It's not Sadie Walcott. It's Sadie Martin, now. I should have the same last name as my sister don't you think?"

Jillybean smiled through her tears and for a moment Sadie thought she had gotten through to the little girl and that she would come with them back to the Valley, but Jillybean only kissed her sister's hand and then let it go. "I'll see you later, Sis."

"Be good," Sadie answered, trying not to let her disappointment show. "And be smart. And come see us at least for your birthday. When is that again?"

She knew and Jillybean knew that she knew. "It's in May. I'm a May-flower, remember."

Sadie loved the innocence it took to say those words. The innocence was what made Jillybean perfect. "I'll never forget," she said, "As long as you stay a May-flower. Promise?"

Their fingers locked one last time. "I promise."

The End.

"The End" is another lie! The story continues in book number nine: **The Apocalypse Revenge** is now available:

For Jillybean, moments of utter happiness and pure sanity are as fleeting and wonderful as sun-showers at a July picnic. Her time with Granny Annie is one such moment, but as always it ends far too quickly and she is once more thrust back into a world of crushing loneliness and endless despair.

Setting out to find a family who will love her, she discovers an orphaned boy of her own age named Chris. He brings her a feeling of hope that she desperately needs because she also discovers a purpose, one fraught with danger and one that might end in the most horrifying death imaginable.

Having waded through an ocean of blood from New York to Colorado, Jillybean is haunted by the idea of revenge. How many fathers or mothers or loved ones has she struck down in her simple quest just to survive? Thousands upon thousands, in all probability. Perhaps more frightening is the question of how many enemies she has left alive and how many more she has created? And how many hundreds of them are consumed with the desire to take revenge on her?

When a terrifying weapon goes missing, the nightmare of revenge becomes a reality and Jillybean must throw herself into a quest to save the Estes Valley from utter destruction. There is just one problem: is the threat even real? Are there people actually roaming the valley at night killing in a terrifying manner? Or are all these enemies figments of her warped imagination?

As the death toll mounts, the people of the Valley begin to ask: Is Jillybean the nightmare? Is she the one doing the killing? And if so, who has the wits to match her genius and stand against her?

PS If you are interested in autographed copies of my books, souvenir posters of the covers, Apocalypse T-shirts and other awesome Swag, please visit my website at **https://www.petemeredith1.com**

Revenge should be ready by mid February so in the meantime—after you write your glowing review on Amazon(thanks BTW)—I really suggest you read: **The Apocalypse Crusade**.

In an apocalypse there is definitely a beginning where mistakes are made and the seeds of evil are allowed to sprout and take shape. However, an end is not so certain. Once an Apocalypse occurs not even death is certain. Sometimes death is only the beginning.

At first light that morning, Dr Lee steps into the Walton facility on the initial day of human trials; she can barely contain her excitement. The labs are brand spanking new and everything is sharp and clean. They've been built to her specifications and are, without a doubt, a scientist's dream. Yet even better than the gleaming instruments is the fact that Walton is where cancer is going to be cured once and for all. It's where Dr. Lee is going to become world famous…only she doesn't realize what she's going to be famous for.

By midnight of that first day, Walton is a place of fire, of blood and of death, a death that, like the Apocalypse, is seemingly never ending.

What readers say about The Apocalypse Crusade:

"DO NOT pick this up until you are ready to commit to an all-night sleep-defying read!"

"WAY OUT WICKED"

"…full of suspense and intrigue, love, both innocent and romantic, hate, both blinding and unnatural, non-stop action, and a very real gripping and palpable fear."

Fictional works by Peter Meredith:
A Perfect America
Infinite Reality: Daggerland Online Novel 1
Infinite Assassins: Daggerland Online Novel 2
Generation Z
Generation Z: The Queen of the Dead
Generation Z: The Queen of War
Generation Z: The Queen Unthroned
Generation Z: The Queen Enslaved
The Sacrificial Daughter
The Apocalypse Crusade War of the Undead: Day One
The Apocalypse Crusade War of the Undead: Day Two
The Apocalypse Crusade War of the Undead Day Three
The Apocalypse Crusade War of the Undead Day Four
The Horror of the Shade: Trilogy of the Void 1
An Illusion of Hell: Trilogy of the Void 2
Hell Blade: Trilogy of the Void 3
The Punished
Sprite
The Blood Lure The Hidden Land Novel 1
The King's Trap The Hidden Land Novel 2
To Ensnare a Queen The Hidden Land Novel 3
The Apocalypse: The Undead World Novel 1
The Apocalypse Survivors: The Undead World Novel 2
The Apocalypse Outcasts: The Undead World Novel 3
The Apocalypse Fugitives: The Undead World Novel 4
The Apocalypse Renegades: The Undead World Novel 5
The Apocalypse Exile: The Undead World Novel 6
The Apocalypse War: The Undead World Novel 7
The Apocalypse Executioner: The Undead World Novel 8
The Apocalypse Revenge: The Undead World Novel 9
The Apocalypse Sacrifice: The Undead World 10
The Edge of Hell: Gods of the Undead Book One
The Edge of Temptation: Gods of the Undead Book Two
The Witch: Jillybean in the Undead World
**Jillybean's First Adventure: An Undead World
Expansion**
Tales from the Butcher's Block

421